The Wrong Man

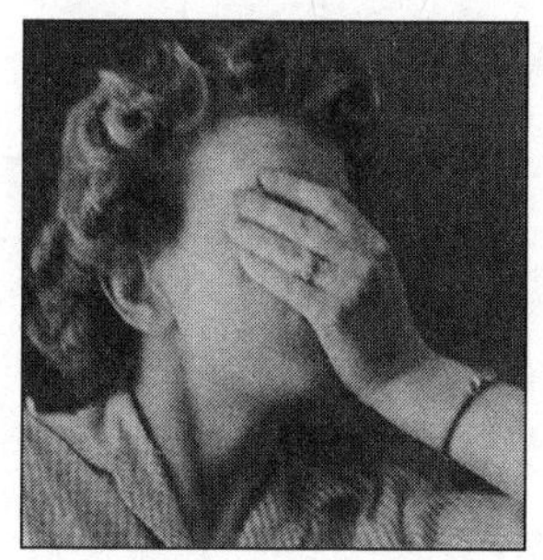

THE WRONG MAN

Laura Wilson

Felony & Mayhem Press • New York

All the characters and events portrayed in this work are fictitious.

THE WRONG MAN

A Felony & Mayhem mystery

PRINTING HISTORY
First UK edition (Quercus): 2010
Felony & Mayhem edition: 2014

ISBN: 978-1-937384-83-8

Manufactured in the United States of America

Printed on 100% recycled paper

Library of Congress Cataloging-in-Publication Data

Wilson, Laura, 1964-
[Capital Crime]
The wrong man / by Laura Wilson. -- Felony & Mayhem edition.
pages cm. -- (A Felony & Mayhem mystery)
"First UK edition (as A Capital Crime) (Quercus): 2010."
ISBN 978-1-937384-83-8
1. Great Britain. Metropolitan Police Office. Criminal Investigation Department--Fiction. 2. Police--England--London--Fiction. 3. Murder--Investigation--England--London--Fiction. 4. Trials (Murder)--England--London--Fiction. 5. Judicial error--England--London--Fiction. I. Title.
PR6073.I4716C37 2014
823'.914--dc23

2014034320

To George, with love

The icon above says you're holding a copy of a book in the Felony & Mayhem "Historical" category, which ranges from the ancient world up through the 1940s. If you enjoy this book, you may well like other "Historical" titles from Felony & Mayhem Press.

For more about these books, and other Felony & Mayhem titles, or to place an order, please visit our website at:

www.FelonyAndMayhem.com

Other "Historical" titles from

FELONY & MAYHEM

DAVID STUART DAVIES
Forests of the Night

ANTON GILL
City of the Horizon
City of Dreams
City of the Dead

KEITH HELLER
Man's Illegal Life

PETER LOVESEY
Bertie and the Seven Bodies
Bertie and the Crime of Passion

FIDELIS MORGAN
Unnatural Fire
The Rival Queens

KATE ROSS
Cut to the Quick
A Broken Vessel
Whom the Gods Love
The Devil in Music

CATHERINE SHAW
The Library Paradox
The Riddle of the River

LAURA WILSON
The Lover
The Innocent Spy
An Empty Death

The Wrong Man

1950

METROPOLITAN POLICE TELEGRAM
30-11-50

THE FOLLOWING TELEPHONE MESSAGE RECEIVED FROM POLICE, MERTHYR TYDFIL (TELE. 541). BEGINS:—

> A MAN NAMED JOHN WILFRED DAVIES HAS COME TO THIS STATION THIS AFTERNOON AND STATED THAT ON 7-11-50 AT 10, PARADISE STREET, W.C., HIS WIFE HAD A MISCARRIAGE AT THAT ADDRESS, AFTER SHE DRANK SOME LIQUID WHICH HE OBTAINED FROM A LORRY DRIVER SOME TIME PREVIOUS AT A CAFE IN IPSWICH. DURING THE NIGHT OF 8-11-50 BETWEEN 1AM AND 2AM HE DISPOSED OF HIS WIFES BODY DOWN A DRAIN OUTSIDE THE FRONT OF THAT ADDRESS. HE HANDED HIS 14 MONTH OLD CHILD TO A MAN NAMED

NORMAN BACKHOUSE AT THE SAME ADDRESS WHO STATED HE COULD HAVE THE CHILD TAKEN CARE OF. HE ALSO SOLD THE FURNITURE AND LEFT THE ADDRESS. WILL YOU PLEASE CAUSE ENQUIRIES TO BE MADE. A WRITTEN STATEMENT HAS BEEN TAKEN FROM DAVIES. ENDS.

FORWARDED FOR NECESSARY ACTIONS ON DIRECTIONS OF CH/SUPT

Detective Inspector Stratton closed the door of his superior's office. He stood for a moment, staring at the piece of paper, and then he looked out of the window, where the end-of-November morning sun was struggling, feebly, to shine through a sooty yellow blanket of smog that had turned the West End sky the colour of a dirty duster. Over four years after the war's end, sunshine seemed to be rationed, in line with pretty well everything else apart from the grime and drizzle through which the weary citizens moved, herd-like and damp-macintoshed, or shuffled, grumbling, in perpetual queues.

Stratton felt every day of his forty-four years, and then some: he'd had a cold since the middle of October, his chilblains were itching like buggery, and the last thing he wanted was a walk. If only he could lay hands on a pair of shoes that kept out the wet... He scanned the telegram again, shaking his head, and went to find Sergeant Ballard.

The sergeant was at the front desk, attempting to calm down an obviously drunk woman whose ravaged face, beneath the rouge, had an ominous greenish pallor, and who was missing the high heel of one shoe. Spit flew from her mouth as she berated motherly Policewoman Harris, who'd brought her in, the words spilling out loud but sloppy: 'Take your hands off me, you lesbian!'

'What's the problem?'

'It's Iris, sir,' said Ballard. 'She's been making a nuisance of herself again.' Despite the fact that his face was scratched and his dark suit was smudged with chalky powder where the woman had stumbled into him, he still managed to look as smart as paint. That, thought Stratton, was also how you could describe most of the local tarts, who were certainly better dressed than the rest of the female population— except for the odd one like Iris Manning, who was clinging on, by ragged fingernails, to the Soho beat she'd had since before the war. Iris was one of their regulars: drunk, disorderly, soliciting and, once, wounding another girl in a fight over a punter. Hearing Stratton's voice, she turned unsteadily, supporting herself on the desk, and tottered in his direction. Stratton, detecting the odour of decay and stale perfume, stepped smartly backwards.

'Inspector, you'll help me, won't you? I haven't done nothing. It's all a mistake. Won't you help me? I'll make it up to you.'

Shuddering inwardly at the idea of this ghoul—drunk at that—being let loose on his private parts, he said, 'That's very nice of you, Iris, and I appreciate it, but I'm afraid it's out of the question. You'll be much better off here.'

'But it's *her*,' Iris wailed, pointing a grubby, trembling finger at the policewoman. 'She's always had it in for me.'

'No, she hasn't.' Stratton exchanged glances with Miss Harris. 'She's got your best interests at heart. Now, you be a good girl and go quietly and I'm sure'—he grinned encouragingly—'that she'll make you a nice cup of tea.'

Behind her, Harris grimaced, and Stratton made an apologetic face at her. Iris Manning, still looking mutinous, allowed herself to be led away, limping.

'Thank you, sir,' said Ballard, as they left West End Central. 'That was getting nasty.'

'Poor old Iris.' Stratton peered through the fog for the police car that was to take them to Paradise Street. 'She's not been the same since the Yanks left.' It was too thick to see very far down the street, but they could hear the hiss and splash of tyres in the wet, a shouted curse, and a lot of coughing.

'Paradise Street's next to the goods yard off Euston Road,' he told the driver as they climbed in.

'On Mother Kelly's doorstep…' sang Ballard, *sotto voce*.

'That's Paradise *Row*,' said Stratton. He handed over the paper for Ballard to peer at.

'What's he doing in Wales, sir?'

'Dunno. Name's Davies, so he's Welsh, I suppose. Wife dies and he goes back home to Mum.'

'A drain, though…three weeks…' Ballard made a face.

'Look on the bright side—it's not the middle of summer. And it seems pretty straightforward—as long as we can find the baby, that is.'

'Seems a bit odd just handing the kid over like that, sir.'

'That's what I was thinking, but as long as it hasn't come to any harm, it should be plain sailing. We can fetch out the body, fetch Davies up from Wales, and have it sorted out by the end of the week.'

A fleet of lorries loaded with building materials—destined for the Festival of Britain site on the South Bank, Stratton guessed—was blocking Regent Street, so they went through Piccadilly Circus instead. Peering out of the window through the smoggy air, Stratton just managed to make out the oversized Bovril advert and the dramatic 'Export or Die' sign beneath it. Men in the unvarying civilian uniform of drab demob macs and trilby hats hurried along the pavements beside the car before being swallowed up by the fog, but occasionally Stratton caught a glimpse of something more colourful as a man pushing a grocer's barrow or a woman in a bright coat went past. The sootily looming Victorian buildings thinned out somewhat as they neared the Euston Road, broken up by bombsites untouched except, in the summer months, by swathes of purple rosebay willowherb.

They drove past shops selling second-hand clothes—a lot of grey stuff that looked suspiciously like demob suits, and war surplus in bundles of khaki and air-force blue; and rows of skinny, dilapidated three-storey houses with crumbling windowsills and walls that soaked up the damp like blotting paper. It was unusual enough to see a freshly repaired and painted building even in the fashionable parts of London; here, it would be a miracle, and Paradise Street seemed even more dingy than the rest. It was a cul-de-sac, ending in the back wall of the goods yard; a Victorian horror of blackened brick and rotting woodwork, one of the end houses shored up by a temporary plank buttress rising from a sea of mud that must once have been a garden. The terraced houses looked as if they had the plague, and the inhabitants, such as could be seen, didn't seem much better. The doors opened straight onto the street, and a grubby little girl of about six with scabs around her mouth, clad in a worn coat and a pixie hood and sitting on a front step, looked up as they passed. 'Sssh…' she admonished, one finger to her lips, then pointed to an equally filthy doll lying in her lap.

'Is your dolly asleep?' asked Stratton, bending down to her.

'No,' replied the child in a matter-of-fact tone. 'She's dead.'

Diana Calthrop stared out of her bedroom window and watched the hunched, elderly form of Reynolds, the gardener, making his slow progress down the weed-strewn gravel that surrounded the soggy, untended parterre. Looking past him to the woodlands and fields beyond, she thought, I shan't miss any of it—not the vast, dank garden or the enormous draughty mausoleum of a house.

Sighing, she turned to resume her packing. Despite several years of wartime practice making up parcels for the WVS, she was too sad and distracted to make a decent job of it—clothes were strewn across the double bed and hanging over the backs of chairs, and cosmetics and scent littered the dressing table. They hadn't had a maid since Ellen left in 1944, and asking Mrs Birkett, the irritable, arthritic cook who was the last remaining member of the indoor staff, to help her was out of the question. Besides, there wasn't really a great deal *to* pack—not much to show for fifteen years of marriage, when you came down to it. Not even a child. Five miscarriages had seen to that—and what was worse, she hadn't really minded. Emotionally, she'd felt only dull resignation, never the sharp grief of loss. The only thing I was bred to do, and I couldn't even manage that, she sneered at herself. One of the miscarriages hadn't even been her husband's child but the result of a wartime affair with a fellow agent while she was working at MI5. Guy had no idea of this, but her vengeful mother-in-law, Evie, who reigned supreme over both the house and her son, did, and had enjoyed making frequent, if mercifully oblique, references to it.

For the last few months, though, Evie—without bothering to hide the fact—had been grooming Diana's successor, the daughter of a local worthy. Round-faced, sweet-natured, and undoubtedly virginal, Genevieve Collier was younger, more malleable, and altogether less tarnished than herself. Guy seemed happy enough to go along with his mother's plans for his future, but then, Diana thought sourly, he always had, hadn't he?

A tentative knock produced the subject of her thoughts, standing uncomfortably in the open doorway and bearing a fistful of white hellebores. Diana stared at him, bewildered. She hadn't seen him since the previous day's stilted and painfully formal exchange when she'd finally announced the inevitable. In any case, it was a long time since they'd felt easy in each other's presence, and an even longer time since they'd entered each other's bedrooms without knocking. The war—Guy had spent almost three years as a prisoner in Malaya and returned rail-thin, plagued by nightmares and a silent, corrosive fury—and Evie, who somehow managed to be present even when she wasn't actually in the room with them, had seen to that.

'I thought'—the oak floorboards creaked as Guy advanced a couple of hesitant paces towards her—'that you might like these.'

Diana gaped at him, unsure if she wanted to laugh or cry. 'I haven't got anywhere to put them,' she said, gently. 'They'll die.'

'I thought…' Guy stared at the flowers in his hand as if he wasn't sure how they'd got there, and continued, lamely, 'I just wanted…' He shook his head. 'I don't know.'

'I *am* leaving, Guy,' said Diana. 'It's finished. We both know that.'

'Yes…'

'I was too young.'

'Yes…'

'The war...'

'Yes...'

'I'm sorry.'

'I'm sorry, too.'

It's hopeless, she thought. There's too much to say, and, at the same time, there's nothing at all. Guy crossed the room towards her, coming so close that, fearing he was about to embrace her, she flinched slightly. The movement was small and involuntary, but Guy was aware of it, his fingers fluttering against her upper arms for a second before he turned away to deposit the flowers in the wastepaper basket by her feet. For a moment, they both stared down at the pretty, discarded blooms, trying to pretend that it hadn't happened, and then Guy said, abruptly, 'I did love you, you know.'

'I loved you, too.' As she said it, Diana wondered if it had ever been true. When she looked back, she'd come to the conclusion that her marriage, at nineteen, six months an orphan and caught up, as she'd thought at the time, in a whirlwind of romance, had been entirely orchestrated by Evie.

'What will you do?' he asked.

'Oh, you know,' Diana tried to keep her tone light, 'there's lots of things I can do. I can type, and organise... I can even cook a little. I'm sure I can make myself useful to somebody.'

Guy nodded. 'You're different, now.'

Yes, thought Diana, I am: older, wiser, tougher and more practical. A small voice in the back of her mind warned her that the toughness and practicality remained to be tested—war-work was one thing, a peacetime job quite another.

'You are different too,' she said. 'It isn't surprising.'

'I suppose not.' Guy stared at her with a sort of miserable wonder. 'You're very beautiful, you know. I've always thought that.' He's trying to tell me I'll find another husband, Diana thought. Right at the moment she wasn't at all sure that she wanted one. 'I'm sorry I can't give you more money, but...' Mentally, Diana completed the sentence—*but Evie won't allow it.*

'It's all right, Guy,' she said. 'The first thing I'm going to do is go up to Gloucestershire and see what can be done with

Hambeyn House, now that the army's finally decided to relinquish it.'

'These big places…' said Guy doubtfully. He didn't need to complete that sentence, either, as both of them knew that Diana's childhood home was unlikely to fetch more than the small amount that a builder would pay for the raw materials. 'Well…' He glanced around the room. 'I can see you've got things to do, so I'll make myself scarce.'

'It might be best,' said Diana, glancing at her wristwatch. 'The taxi's due in half an hour.'

Guy acknowledged this with a nod but made no move to leave. After a few moments, looking more awkward than ever, he cleared his throat, said, 'Well…' again and held out his hand. Mechanically, she held out hers, and they shook for what felt like an age. Then the sheer absurdity of the gesture, coupled with the desire to make it clear that she was well aware of her mother-in-law's machinations, got the better of her, and looking Guy straight in the eye she said, 'I'm sure that you and Genevieve and Evie will be very happy.'

Blushing, he jerked his hand free of hers. 'Yes, well…' He swallowed. 'No hard feelings, I trust.'

'Not at all.'

Conscious that in this exchange at least she was the victor, Diana watched him squeak his way back across the room. He paused in the doorway and turned back, an almost beseeching expression on his face. 'You will say goodbye to Evie, won't you?' he asked.

Diana, who had asked herself several times in the past twenty-four hours if it were possible to slide away without saying anything to her mother-in-law, treated Guy to what she knew was her haughtiest expression. 'Of course.'

When he'd gone, closing the door behind him as gently and quietly as if someone had died, she thought, with a rush of confidence, I shall say goodbye to Evie, but I shall do it with my head held high. Suddenly, she found herself looking forward to the encounter, and with swift, sure movements, set about finishing her packing.

Number ten was at the end of Paradise Street, hard against the wall of the goods yard, with a manhole directly outside the downstairs bay window. At a nod from Stratton, Ballard squatted down and tried to lift the lid. After a few moments he looked up, shaking his head. 'Sorry, sir. Can't move it. It doesn't look as if it's been disturbed recently, does it?'

'Not really, no.' Stratton, kneeling beside him, put his fingers under the rim and heaved, but, try as they might, the two men couldn't budge the iron slab. 'It's no good,' said Stratton, finally, standing up and easing his back. 'He'd have to be Charles Atlas to get that up on his own.'

'Perhaps someone gave him a hand,' said Ballard, mopping his face.

'Mmm...' Sensing that he was being watched, Stratton turned towards number ten. The curtains were closed but a face was peering round them, a bald-pated, feeble-looking middle-aged man in a cardigan, blinking through pebble glasses. 'Him?' said Stratton derisively, jerking his head at the window.

The man made a curious sideways sucking motion with his

mouth and withdrew his head. 'He does look a bit of a maiden aunt, doesn't he?' said Ballard.

'We'd better have some help,' said Stratton. 'Take the car back to the station and get some reinforcements. Try and find someone with a bit of muscle, like Canning. And a crowbar.'

Ballard went off to telephone, leaving Stratton outside the house. A semicircle of neighbours, mainly putty-faced women and children, had gathered to stand at a discreet distance. The women, several of whom had their hair in curlers, wore cretonne overalls, and the children, snotty-nosed, concave-chested, and wearing an assortment of ill-fitting clothing and gumboots, trailed skipping ropes, sticks, and a broken tennis racket. The constant rumble of trains travelling along the line to Euston was counterpointed by an assortment of hollow, tubercular coughs and the thin, high wail of a baby, but no one spoke. Instead, they watched warily, ready to back away and scatter, reminding him of a herd of cows.

When Stratton turned back towards number ten he saw the man again, standing in front of the still-drawn curtains, this time with a cup and saucer held in a dainty manner, little finger slightly raised. Ballard's description of a maiden aunt was spot on, he thought. The man blinked at him for a moment, then withdrew.

Stratton wondered if that were Norman Backhouse, the man who'd taken Davies's baby into his care, and why he did not come out to see what was going on outside his home. Time enough for that later—the contents of the drain must come first. He squatted down once more to look at the manhole cover. Nobody was *that* strong, thought Stratton. Six foot three, broad-shouldered and a former boxer, he wasn't exactly a weakling, and neither, despite his slimmer physique, was Ballard. It would take at least three men, maybe four, to lift the thing. He lit a cigarette and wondered how many people lived in Paradise Street. They were little more than doll's houses, really—there couldn't be more than two rooms per storey, with one out the back on the ground floor—but he'd have bet that each building was inhabited by at least two families, plus the usual assortment of jobless ex-servicemen, part-time prostitutes, and forlorn elderly widows who eked out their meagre pensions in tea and bread and marge.

Ballard returned after ten minutes, followed by the towering, barrel-chested form of PC Canning, who was holding a crowbar, with old Arliss, the station's most incompetent policeman, grumbling along in the rear. Stratton issued instructions, but even with the four of them (not that Arliss did much more than complain about his back) it took a lot of grunting and heaving before they were able to move the cover aside sufficiently for Canning to shine his torch down the hole. When he looked up, he was shaking his head.

'What's up?' asked Stratton.

'See for yourself, sir.' Canning handed him the torch.

Stratton leant over the opening and looked. The shaft was empty. 'I don't believe there's ever been a body in there,' he said.

'There aren't any other drains nearby,' said Ballard.

Stratton turned to look down the road and found himself, instead, looking into a pair of round, pale-blue eyes, blinking rapidly behind thick glasses. 'Sorry, sir,' he said, stepping back smartly. 'Can I help you?'

The man, who Stratton now recognised as the chap who'd been watching them from inside the house, gave a soft cough. 'I think, Inspector,' he said in a voice so quiet that Stratton had to strain to hear it, 'that it might be more a question of how *I* can help *you*.'

'I see.' Wondering why he hadn't heard the man approach, Stratton looked down and saw that he was wearing plimsolls. Must have crept up behind us, he thought.

The man made the peculiar sideways movement with his mouth that he'd noticed before. Up close, it was accompanied by a small wet sucking noise. He looked, Stratton thought, like a bad ventriloquist. 'My name's Backhouse. I saw you through the window. Of course, I didn't want to obstruct you in the course of your duties—I know all about that because I was a special. In the recent war. Volunteered in nineteen thirty-nine and served for several years at West End Central. In fact…' he ducked his head, modestly, 'I had the honour to be commended on two occasions.' He stopped, clearly expecting a response. When none was forthcoming, he said, 'I wondered…are you looking for something?' During the course of this little speech, Backhouse's voice had risen in volume, so that by the end it was almost normal. He had the vestiges of a northern accent—Yorkshire, Stratton thought—eroded, like his own Devonian one had been, by years of contact with Cockneys, and spoke with exaggerated precision, taking great care with his consonants.

Stratton introduced himself, and then, drawing Backhouse to one side, said, 'Perhaps you can help us with some information about the Davieses.'

'They're not here now,' said Backhouse. 'They've left.'

'When was that?'

Backhouse considered this for a moment. 'The second week of November. I remember that because we had workmen here. The last time I saw them was the Tuesday of that week.'

'And you haven't seen them since?'

'Not Muriel—Mrs Davies, that is—or the baby. They went off then, you see, to stay with some friends in…Bristol, I think it was. That's what he told us.'

'Mr Davies told you that?'

'Yes, that's right. He said they were going for a holiday, and he was joining them later in the week. He told me he was going to find a job up there. Has something happened to them, Inspector?'

'That's what we're trying to find out.'

'Well, you'll not find them in the drain.' Backhouse spoke as if it were a perfectly normal place to look for someone, such as their home or the local pub.

'No,' agreed Stratton. 'Did Davies leave the baby with you at any time?'

Backhouse stared at him in surprise. When he spoke, it was

barely more than a whisper. 'No. My wife used to listen out for her from time to time if Muriel went out, but that was all.'

'So you didn't tell him you'd find someone to look after the baby?'

'Tell him…? I'm sorry, Inspector, I don't understand.'

'Mr Davies made a statement to the police in Wales, saying you told him you'd find someone to look after the baby.'

'Find someone? That's nonsense.' Backhouse cleared his throat and continued at normal pitch, 'He left some of her things with me, but that was all…but I don't understand. You said he'd made a statement?'

'Yes. He said he'd put his wife's body in the drain.'

'Oh, dear…' Backhouse shook his head. 'Well, I don't know anything about that. I'm sure we'd have noticed, if… There was nothing like that. He just gave me the things to look after. He'd sold the rest of his furniture, you see, before he left.'

'All of it?' asked Stratton, remembering the telegram.

'Yes. A man came for it a few days later.'

'Did Davies collect the baby's things?'

Backhouse shook his head. 'We've still got them. Would you like to see?'

'Yes, please.'

Stratton told the others to put the drain cover back in place and followed Backhouse inside number ten.

'Lucky I was here,' he said. 'I'd normally be at work, but I suffer with my back. It's so bad now I've had to have a certificate from the doctor.' Ignoring this, Stratton peered down the dim hallway. It was narrow, with a solitary gas bracket for lighting and a flight of stairs halfway back with a passage alongside which led to the back door and, adjacent to that, the door of what Stratton guessed must be Backhouse's kitchen. Glancing through a half-open door on the right, he caught sight of the corner of a table with a dark bobble-edged cloth on it and the edges of a couple of framed photographs. Faded sepia, he imagined, dead Victorians in all their dour glory. He was proved right about the kitchen when a plump, large-bosomed woman stepped out of it, tea towel in hand. Clad in a flowered cretonne overall, she had a placid, almost bovine expression. 'What is it, Norman?' Her accent was Yorkshire, too, but more pronounced.

'This is my wife,' explained Backhouse. 'It's the police, Edna. The ones who were looking down the drain.'

'Inspector Stratton,' added Stratton, by way of introduction.

'Is there something wrong with the drain?' Mrs Backhouse looked worried. 'Only we've not touched it.'

'There's nothing wrong with it, but I'd like to see the things that Mr Davies left with you for the baby.'

'Why? What's happened?'

'As I explained to Mr Backhouse,' said Stratton, feeling foolish, 'we aren't really sure at the moment.'

'Oh dear...' Mrs Backhouse put a hand over her mouth. 'They're in the kitchen. But they're not ours, so I don't know if—'

'Don't keep the inspector waiting, Edna,' said Backhouse. 'He's got to do his job.'

The Backhouses' kitchen was a cramped, cluttered room, no more than ten feet square, containing a gas stove, a range, a stone sink, shelves, a table and two chairs, and an odd-looking deckchair, its canvas replaced by a home-made sling of knotted ropes. Mrs Backhouse opened a wooden cupboard door in the back wall. 'It's all here,' she said. 'We haven't interfered with it.' Peering inside, Stratton saw an alcove stretching back about six feet which, by the looks of it, had once been used to store coal. Now, it held a pram, a baby's high chair, and two suitcases. Lifting the nearest case out, Stratton set it on the floor and, kneeling down, opened it. Inside was a grubby cot blanket, and underneath that, baby clothes.

'Do you recognise these?' he asked Mrs Backhouse, who was peering over his shoulder.

'Yes. That's one of Judy's frocks.'

Stratton took out his notebook. 'Judy's the baby's name, is it?'

'Yes.' Mrs Backhouse frowned. 'But I thought you knew… I mean, if you're looking for them.'

'We don't have much information,' said Stratton. 'We just want to make sure she's safe.'

Mrs Backhouse shook her head. 'Poor little thing…'

'If there's anything more we can do to help, Inspector,' said Backhouse, 'you've only to ask. As I said, I was with the police during the war, so I know—'

'If I might have the other case,' said Stratton, cutting him off. The way the man was toadying was downright creepy.

The second case contained a feeding bottle, napkins, and yet more baby clothes—a surprising amount, Stratton thought, for just one infant. Perhaps Backhouse thought so too, because he said, 'Davies's mother bought most of Judy's things. She's always done a lot for them, hasn't she, Edna?'

'Oh yes. She's very good to them.'

'Could Mrs Davies be looking after Judy?' asked Stratton.

'I suppose so,' said Mrs Backhouse. 'I don't know. Muriel didn't say anything to me.'

'She didn't even tell you they were going, did she, Edna?'

'No.'

'Edna was quite upset about it, her not saying goodbye. We've always tried to be good neighbours, Inspector. Always looked out for them. They're very young, you see.'

'Yes,' said Stratton, wondering why, if Mrs Davies was looking after Judy, she hadn't collected her things. Surely the baby couldn't have even *more* of them? And even if she had, Mrs Davies would certainly need the pram… He lifted up the baby's stuff to see what was at the bottom of the case and found what was clearly a woman's blouse and a cotton dress.

'Those are Muriel's,' said Mrs Backhouse. 'Summer things.'

That, at least, made sense, thought Stratton. She'd hardly need them at this time of year. 'Did Mr Davies say anything about picking these up or sending someone for them?'

'No,' said Backhouse. 'I assumed he was waiting until they were settled.'

'And he left when, exactly?'

'About a week after Muriel and the baby, wasn't it?'

Mrs Backhouse nodded.

'So that would be about a fortnight ago.'

'That's right. That's when he sold the furniture, and he'd given up his job. He came back about a week ago.'

'And he didn't say anything about taking these?' Stratton indicated the contents of the alcove.

Backhouse shook his head. 'The thing was, you see...' He tailed off, blinking rapidly.

'Yes?'

'I didn't think I ought to say anything...' Backhouse's voice had gone quiet again, 'but he told Edna that Muriel had walked out on him. Didn't he, dear?'

'Yes.' Mrs Backhouse looked awkward, and when she spoke, her voice, too, was hushed. 'I asked him how she was, and he said she was all right, but she'd left him.'

'In Bristol?'

'Well... I suppose it was. I don't know.'

Backhouse, who appeared to be staring at Muriel's clothes, made the strange sucking sound with his mouth again then cleared his throat and said, 'To be honest, Inspector, I can't say we were very surprised.'

'Oh? Why's that?'

'Well, they argued a lot, didn't they, dear?'

'Oh, yes.'

'A lot of shouting,' said Backhouse. 'Violence, sometimes. Muriel told my wife about it on several occasions. She told Edna she was afraid of him.' Mrs Backhouse nodded in confirmation of this. 'Not that we needed telling,' Backhouse continued. 'You could hear it quite clearly. So could the neighbours, I'm afraid. They were known around here for fighting.'

'Do you know what they fought about?'

'Debts, I think. It's hard for a young couple these days, and she wasn't very good with money, I'm afraid. And there was Davies's behaviour. He went off with a woman once. A friend of his wife's, too—she was stopping with them, you see, upstairs. I told them the tenancy agreement didn't allow it, but…' He shook his head. 'A dreadful business, shouting and screaming… Mrs Davies—his mother—came over to try and keep the peace, but the police were called in the end. Davies and the girl left, but he came back—the next day, I think it was. The girl had thrown him out, and he was in a terrible temper. Threatened to run her over in his van—he's a driver, you see, deliveries. He worked in the goods yard, just the other side of the wall here. You don't like to interfere, but…' He shook his head again. ' "I'll smash her up." That was what he said. "I'll smash her up." The whole thing was most regrettable.'

'When did it happen?'

'Sometime in August. There was a lot of rowing. I heard him threaten to throw Muriel out of the window on one occasion. And then there was the drinking. He was always in public houses. And I'm afraid he got a name as something of a liar. Telling stories. In fact, we've sometimes wondered if he isn't a bit mental.'

'I see.' Stratton rose, dusting his trouser legs.

'As I said,' concluded Backhouse, 'we weren't surprised when he said she'd left him.'

'Thank you,' said Stratton. 'You've been most helpful. Just one more thing—Mrs Davies's address. Do you know it?'

'It's nearby—twenty-two, Garton Road.'

As Stratton was taking his leave, Mrs Backhouse laid a hand on his arm. 'You will…' she began timidly and then, seeing her husband's frown, she stopped.

'Yes?' prompted Stratton.

'Just…you will tell us, won't you? About the baby, I mean. I—we—were very fond of her.'

The street was empty but for Ballard, who was waiting for him. 'Arliss says he remembers Backhouse being a special,' he said. 'I think I do, too.'

'Do you? I don't.'

'Well, you didn't really have much to do with them, sir. If he is the chap I remember, and I'm pretty sure he is, he was good, but a bit officious. Overdid it.'

'The power of the uniform, you mean?'

'Something like that, sir,' said Ballard wryly. 'And he was commended. Did you get much in there?'

'Well, there's no indication that any crime's been committed, but Davies did leave some baby things with the Backhouses, which tends to back up his story that Judy—that's the kid's name—was going to be looked after by somebody other than his wife. The Backhouses say they don't know anything about it. They also said that Davies and his wife rowed a lot and that he told them she'd upped and left him.'

'Odd that she didn't take the baby, sir, if that's the case.'

'That's what I thought. But she might be with Davies's mother, so we'd better go round there and see.'

'Righty-ho, sir.'

'I'll fill you in about the rest on the way. Backhouse said that Davies had a bit of a reputation for telling stories, so I suppose it's not impossible that this is one of them. Seems a bit drastic, though.'

Ballard raised his eyebrows and gave a silent whistle. 'You can say that again, sir.'

'I don't know what's going on.' Mrs Davies, neat and upright, with tight grey curls like steel wool, looked baffled. 'Muriel and Judy were supposed to be stopping with her father in Brighton, that's all I know about it.' Her voice was a Welsh sing-song, and as she spoke she rubbed her hands down the sides of her overalled hips. 'John told me, but I know that's not right because I wrote to Mr Binney—that's Muriel's father—and he says she's never been near the place. I've hardly slept since I had his telegram, I can tell you. I've no idea where Muriel is, or the baby—and she could write to me, even if John can't.'

'He can't write?'

Mrs Davies shook her head. 'Not much more than his signature. Missed a lot of school, you see—he was poorly when he was a boy, in and out of hospital. I can't understand why Muriel's not been in touch. I've always been good to her...' Seeing that her eyes were wet, Stratton hastily averted his own, looking around her neat, comfortable front room—the perfectly squared antimacassars, the symmetry of ornaments and photographs on the mantelpiece—while she collected herself. Her matronly dignity and obvious pride in her home reminded him of his mother-in-law, Nellie—dead now, like Jenny, his wife. He'd been deliberately circumspect about what he'd told Mrs Davies, with no mention of bodies put down drains, but it was obvious that she was already both desperately worried and very angry.

'I've done my best to help them both, but I'm at the end of my tether. Why would John say that Mr Backhouse had taken Judy off somewhere? It doesn't make any sense, and I don't know anything about these people John says are looking after her. I had a letter from my sister saying he's been stopping with them in Wales since the fourteenth. I wrote and told her she's welcome to him. It's like I told her, I've no idea where Muriel and Judy have gone to. If she's left him and taken the baby, nobody's told me about it. And I've had all sorts of people coming up here, saying John owes them money. I put my name down, guarantee for the furniture, and this is what I get… His name stinks round here, I can tell you, and I'm sick of his nonsense. I'm sorry, Inspector, but that's the truth.'

'When you say "nonsense", Mrs Davies,' said Stratton, 'what do you mean?'

'Making up stories—like this business about Mr Backhouse and the baby. He's always doing it. Telling people his father was an Italian count and he's going to have a Rolls-Royce and an aeroplane and heaven knows what else. All lies and boasting. You don't want to believe a word of it. Never had the education, see? We've done our best for him. And as for saying that about Judy, even if Muriel has gone off and left him…' Mrs Davies spread her hands in a gesture of hopelessness.

'When was the last time you saw Muriel, Mrs Davies?'

'A Saturday, it was. The beginning of November. We went shopping with John. I bought a little chair for Judy and a pram for the new baby.'

'Muriel is expecting, is she?'

'Yes, she is, so I don't know what she thinks she's playing at, going off like that.' Mouth pursed in condemnation, Mrs Davies shook her head.

'And she didn't say anything to you about getting rid of the baby?'

'Oh, no.' Mrs Davies looked shocked. 'Nothing like that. I really don't know what to say, Inspector. I'm ashamed of John, and that's the truth. I'd have looked after Judy if he and Muriel were having difficulties, he knows I would. It's been nothing but arguments between them for I don't know how long. John's got a temper on him all right, ever since he was a boy, but the fault's not all on his side, mind—Muriel's a nice girl, but she's terrible with the housekeeping. Always asking John for more… I'm not saying she was spending the money on new things for herself, but she never seemed to have enough. She's very young, of course, and not having had a mother so long I suppose she never had anyone to set an example. John should have been more patient with her. You don't like to speak ill of your own, but…'

'Poor woman,' said Stratton as, having secured a photograph of Muriel—pretty and delicate, with brown hair and doe eyes—they clattered down the stairs and into the street. 'Obviously at the end of her tether.'

'I don't blame her, sir. Sounds as if Davies isn't quite right in the head.'

'I don't know about that, but he certainly seems to have trouble telling the truth… We need to find that baby. I'll make another call to Merthyr Tydfil—perhaps they'll be able to shed a bit more light on the situation.'

'How's your nipper?' asked Stratton as the car took them back to West End Central. 'Still giving you sleepless nights?' Ballard, married two years before to Policewoman—now former-Policewoman—Gaines, had a six-month-old daughter.

The sergeant's face lit up. 'You should see her, sir. She's a smasher. And she's sleeping a lot better now.'

'Bet that's a relief,' said Stratton.

'You can say that again… How are yours, sir? Your boy'll be called up for National Service any day, won't he?'

Always a good working partnership, their relationship had, since Jenny's death at the hands of a madwoman, included regular enquiries about each other's families. Stratton, who had never before shared any information about his home life with a colleague, rather liked it—or some of it, anyway. He thought that Ballard did too, or at least pretended he did. At any rate, he always seemed to remember what Stratton told him about Monica and Pete.

'Went last week,' said Stratton. 'And Monica's just got herself a new job. At a film studio, of all things. Make-up and so forth—they're going to train her up a bit.'

'You don't sound very sure about it, sir.'

'Well… All those arty types… Mind you, she says I think the worst of everyone.'

'You've always said she was very sensible, sir.'

'She is. Takes after her mother.' That, he told himself, was no more than the truth. Every day, it seemed that something about Monica—her common sense, her kindness, even the way she laughed with her hand in front of her mouth—reminded him of Jenny. She looked like Jenny, too, the same curvaceous figure and creamy skin. The only thing that was different was her black hair, inherited from him. And, unlike Pete, he could talk about Monica, and think about her, without feeling guilty. The problem was his failure to engage with the boy—not that Pete ever seemed to want to be engaged with—or even, really, to 'get on' with him, in the six years since Jenny died.

Feeling that some of this might somehow have communicated itself to Ballard, he hastily changed the subject.

'Nothing?' echoed DC Williams, on the line from Merthyr Tydfil.

'Not a thing. And what's more,' added Stratton, 'it took four of us to lift the manhole cover.'

'Well, this one couldn't do much by himself. I'd say he's no more than five feet five inches high, and puny with it.'

'Obviously makes up in imagination for what he lacks in height, then.'

'Arglwydd Mawr...'

Stratton, taking this to be the Welsh equivalent of 'Good God', sympathised entirely with the man's heartfelt tone. There followed some further exasperated muttering, and then Williams said, 'Well, I'd better see what he's got to say for himself. The strange thing is, he was desperate to talk to me. Said he couldn't sleep and wanted to get it off his chest. Tell you the truth, I'm not sure he's all there... Seems a bit of a simpleton to me.'

Satisfied that there was nothing further he could do for the present, Stratton spent the next few hours writing up reports on, variously, a receiver who'd been found in possession of knocked-off goods ranging from whisky to tinned salmon; an inside job on a warehouse which had resulted in the theft of 20,000 pairs of nylons; and a disturbance at a Wardour Street club during which a Maltese pimp had been stabbed.

At five o'clock, Ballard put his head round the door of the office. 'Williams is on the line,' he said, 'from Wales. Says Davies has changed his story.'

Stratton hung up the telephone receiver. 'Well,' he said to Ballard, 'Miss Harris will take down the full statement, but now the gist is that Davies is claiming he lied to protect Backhouse. He says Backhouse volunteered to abort Muriel but it went wrong, and when he got back from work Backhouse told him she'd died. He says she was bleeding from the mouth when he saw her, which makes bugger-all sense. And he says Backhouse showed him some sort of medical book beforehand and said he'd had some training as a doctor so he knew how to get rid of the pregnancy…' Stratton paused to consult his notes. 'Says he helped Backhouse carry the body downstairs to the first-floor flat, which was empty, and Backhouse told him he was going to put the body in the drain, and that he'd take the baby to some people in Euston who'd look after her… Claims that Backhouse told him to sell all his furniture, get rid of Muriel's clothes to a rag dealer, and bugger off back home to the valleys, so that's what he did. Williams is going to have a word with the relatives he's been staying with—it's his aunt and her husband, a Mr and Mrs Howells—to see if they can shed any light on things. Williams is of the opinion—and I can't say I blame him—that Davies is off his head.'

'Sounds very much like it, sir.'

'Either that or he's buggering us about for some reason. Williams said when he first spoke to Davies and told him the body wasn't in the drain, Davies couldn't believe it. Kept insisting it must be because he'd put it there. Then he said he'd lied about the lorry driver in the café giving him the stuff for Muriel, and he wanted to make another statement. Not that this one sounds any more plausible... Oh, and Williams says he seems to be illiterate, apart from signing his name. Had to have his statement read back to him because he couldn't manage it himself.'

'His mother said that too, sir.'

'She did, didn't she? Perhaps Muriel's run off with another chap and it's sent Davies round the bend. Stranger things have happened, after all.'

'Then why not leave the baby with his mother, sir?'

'She'd have asked questions, wouldn't she? "Where's Muriel? Why isn't she here?" And if he didn't want to admit that she'd left him... Mind you, Williams also said that Davies wanted us to ask Backhouse the name of the people who'd taken Judy, so that doesn't really add up.' Stratton sighed. 'So, we still don't actually know if any crime's been committed, but we've got to find that child.'

'That seems about the size of it, sir. Back to Paradise Street, is it?'

There were only two lamps in Paradise Street, but faint yellow gaslight could be seen through the thin curtains hanging in the windows. All the children had gone indoors. Apart from the trains, any noise now was coming from the goods yard on the other side of the wall at the end. Revving and bawled instructions—'Go on, right hand down, straighten 'er up... Whoa!'—as the twelve-ton lorries were parked, and heavy thumps as goods—Stratton imagined rows of unidentifiable lumps shrouded in canvas—were loaded up for the night's run.

Backhouse poked his head round the door of number ten in the manner of a tortoise expecting attack. Seeing Stratton and Ballard he gave a weak cough and said, in a voice barely above a whisper, 'Inspector?'

'If we might come in for a moment, sir? This is my sergeant, Ballard.'

'Of course. Always glad to help.'

'We'd like to have a look at the Davies's flat, if you don't mind, and then we've got a few questions.'

Backhouse frowned. 'Well, I don't know… I don't mean to be obstructive, but there's the matter of—'

'It is rather urgent, Mr Backhouse,' said Stratton. 'I'm sure that, having served in the police force yourself, you'll understand that Judy's safety is paramount.'

As Stratton had hoped, this comradely appeal to Backhouse's vanity did the trick, and he stood back to let them enter. 'On this occasion, I don't suppose… It's the top floor. The flats aren't separated—no front doors—so you'll have no trouble.'

'Who lives on the first floor?' asked Stratton.

'Mr Gardiner. An elderly gentleman. He's in hospital at present—been there for the past two months.'

'Has the flat been empty during that time?'

'That's right. I shan't accompany you, Inspector.' He rubbed his back. 'I think I may have mentioned—I suffer with fibrositis.'

At least, thought Stratton, as they went up the stairs, what Davies had said about the first-floor flat being empty was true—the first thing, as far as he could see, that actually was. 'It's a bit bloody dark up here,' he said, as they got to the top landing. Seeing the shape of a gas bracket protruding from the wall, he pulled his matches out of his pocket and felt for the tap. He turned it, but there was no hiss of escaping gas. 'Looks like we'll have to put a shilling in the meter.'

He opened the door to the room at the front of the house. The curtains were open, and, even by the faint glow that reached them from the street lamp, they could see that the room was entirely empty. The back room was the kitchen. Stratton located the meter and dropped a coin in the slot, and Ballard put a match to the gas mantle. They saw a sink, an Ascot water heater, a gas stove, and a few shelves which were bare of everything except a couple of saucepans, a vase, and a clock. On the other side of the room was a fireplace. Whatever else had been in the room—table, chairs—had been removed. Dusty, battered wooden boards covered the floor, and a thin patterned paper, greyish, torn in places or sagging, lined the walls. It was darkened in the cooking area by spots of grease, but Stratton could see its original cream colour from a lighter rectangle over the mantelpiece, where a mirror or picture had been removed. The bottom half of the single sash window at the back was covered by a grimy net curtain. Raising it, Stratton made out the backs of the terrace beyond and was staring down into the garden below when Ballard said, 'There's a briefcase here, sir, and there's some newspaper cuttings on the mantelpiece.'

'Oh?' Stratton lowered the curtain.

Ballard opened the briefcase and rummaged inside. 'Just a few bits of paper in here. Looks as if it belongs to a Mr G. Parker...there's an address. Nicked, would you say?'

'Possibly. I can't imagine why a van driver would need a briefcase. We'll find out if it's been reported as stolen. What about the cuttings?'

'Four of them, all about Setty. You know, the torso murder last year.'

'Let's just hope we don't find bits of Mrs Davies all over the Essex marshes, then.'

'It's a bit odd, though, sir, when Williams said Davies is illiterate. Why would he keep cuttings if he couldn't read them?'

'Perhaps his wife was interested—or she read them to him. Any dates?'

'Can't see any, sir, but it happened in October, didn't it, and if Mrs Davies left here three weeks ago, that would be about the ninth of November—'

'So it's possible,' concluded Stratton. 'Mind you, if he was working as a van driver he must have been able to read labels and road signs and things, mustn't he?'

'Perhaps he can do individual words but not a whole lot together.'

'Perhaps.' Stratton sighed. 'Well, wherever his missus has got to, she's not here now.'

'And if she's not here…' Ballard continued his train of thought, 'then presumably she's not lying dead somewhere in this house, sir.'

'I should think the Backhouses would have noticed a body on the premises, wouldn't you? And he said they'd had builders here, too, remember? No, I think she's gone off somewhere. Let's just hope she's taken the baby with her.'

Mr and Mrs Backhouse were in the kitchen. Backhouse was sitting in the deckchair—Stratton saw Ballard's eyes widen slightly when he saw the knotted-rope sling—and beside him, curled up on a rag mat, was a black-and-white mongrel.

'Is it yours?' asked Stratton.

'Yes,' said Backhouse, looking fondly at the animal, which thumped its tail on the floor. 'Dora, her name is.'

'Friendly, is she?'

'Oh, yes.'

Stratton crouched down to pat the animal, which responded, delighted, by rolling over so that he could rub her belly.

'We were just about to have a little cup of tea. Would you like one?'

'No, thanks.' Stratton stood up and smiled at Mrs Backhouse, who was standing in front of the sink, twisting a tea towel in her hands and looking agitated. 'Just a couple of questions, and we'll leave you in peace. We found some newspaper cuttings about the torso murder. Do you know why they would be there?'

'He was interested in that sort of thing,' said Backhouse. 'He couldn't read much himself, but his wife used to read them to him, didn't she, Edna?' Before Mrs Backhouse could respond, he continued, 'You'll excuse me not getting up, but my back's been playing me up again. We're both very worried, Inspector. This whole thing is very regrettable—'

'The baby,' Mrs Backhouse interrupted, with a force that surprised Stratton. 'Have you found her?'

'Not yet,' said Stratton. 'But we're doing everything we can.'

'Edna's very upset,' said Backhouse. 'We both are.'

'Of course. Were you aware, Mrs Backhouse, that Muriel was pregnant?'

Again, Backhouse got in first. 'There was something—I wondered if I should have mentioned it this morning. Muriel did tell my wife that she was pregnant, and she wasn't happy about it. With only the two rooms, she couldn't see how they were going to manage, and she was worried about money. She told Edna she'd been using pills and syringes trying to give herself a miscarriage, didn't she, dear?'

Mrs Backhouse, looking more distressed than ever, made a noise that sounded as if a sob was locked in her throat, and nodded.

'We both told her to stop acting so silly,' said Backhouse. 'She was making herself a physical wreck.'

'When did she tell you this?' Stratton asked Mrs Backhouse.

'I think...a couple of days before she left...' She stopped and looked at her husband for confirmation.

'It's all right, dear... You can see how upset it's made her,' Backhouse reiterated. 'Muriel was in a bad way. She promised she wouldn't do anything silly, but I don't know—' He broke off, wincing, and bent forward to rub the small of his back.

'Did you suggest to Davies that you could help his wife to get rid of the baby, Mr Backhouse?'

Backhouse blinked several times before saying, 'I'm sorry, I don't understand what you mean.'

'Davies alleges that you showed him a medical book and said you could help his wife abort her pregnancy.'

'That's nonsense,' said Backhouse, firmly. 'He's making it up.' He pursed his lips then took off his glasses and began to polish them, slowly, with his handkerchief.

'Have you ever trained as a doctor?'

'No.'

'Did you tell Davies you'd trained as a doctor?'

'Certainly not. It's a lie.'

'Did you show him a medical book?'

'No, Inspector, I did not.'

'Do you have any medical books?' asked Stratton.

Backhouse thought for a moment, then said, 'I have a manual from the St John's Ambulance. I had it when I did first aid, during the war. I also,' he added, with a touch of pride, 'have two certificates. But I don't see…' Turning to Mrs Backhouse, he said, 'Would you have shown the book to Davies for some reason?'

Edna Backhouse shook her head in bewilderment. She was, thought Stratton, on the verge of tears.

'This is all made up,' said Backhouse. 'I don't know why he's saying these things.'

'I understand,' said Stratton soothingly. 'I'm sorry we had to disturb you, but that's everything—at least for the time being.'

'It's no trouble, Inspector.' Backhouse began to struggle out of the deckchair, but Stratton put up a restraining hand.

'Don't worry, we can see ourselves out.'

'Thank you, Inspector. If there's anything else, we're always glad to oblige.'

'Nice dog,' said Stratton, as they made their way back to the station. 'Didn't see her before. You certainly couldn't hide a body in there for three weeks without her knowing about it. Even if you buried it in the garden she'd have it up in no time.'

'Unless she's lost her sense of smell,' said Ballard. 'If that's possible.'

'Never heard of it,' said Stratton. 'What do you think of the Backhouses?'

'She seems a bit cowed by him, doesn't she?'

'Well, he certainly did the talking for both of them, but that's not unusual—not where we're concerned, anyway—and she's obviously pretty bothered about the whole thing, which is understandable. What a mess… I don't know about you, but last time I looked at a St John's Ambulance handbook, it didn't say anything about how to perform an abortion.'

'Another fairy story, sir.'

'Seems like it. Anyway, we need to know what the hell is going on, and I think it's high time we brought Davies to London. We can have him for that briefcase, if nothing else—I'd be willing to bet a hefty sum that it's been pinched. I'll speak to DCI Lamb when we get back.'

Ballard grimaced. 'Best of luck with that, sir.'

'Thanks,' said Stratton. 'I've a feeling I'm going to need it.'

CHAPTER 6

DCI Lamb let out a gusty sigh. Stratton was familiar with the man's repertoire of noises indicative of exasperation and forbearance and recognised this one as meaning that the person in front of him—in this case, himself—was arsing about, wasting time, and generally testing his superior's patience to the limit. Lamb, whose resemblance to George Formby seemed actually to be increasing as he grew older, took any deviation from by-the-book policing as a personal insult and had long regarded him, Stratton, as the chief culprit. In his lighter moments, Stratton had often wondered if what his superior would really like would be for him to arrest himself, lock himself in a cell, and beat himself up while he was at it.

'Let me get this clear,' said Lamb. 'You've no idea where this woman's body is—assuming that she is actually dead—and, more importantly, the baby's disappeared and you have no clue as to where she is, and everyone you've spoken to, including his own mother, thinks that Davies is off his head. Besides which, the chances of Backhouse and his wife failing to notice that they are sharing a house with a corpse are—to say the least—slender.'

'That's about the size of it, sir.'

'And Backhouse was a special constable, for God's sake! If he says Davies is off his rocker... Incidentally, Stratton, I hope you're treating him with a bit of respect.'

'Of course, sir.'

Lamb sighed again, looking more put-upon than ever. 'Nothing's ever straightforward with you, is it, Stratton?'

'With respect, sir—'

'Yes, yes, yes.' Lamb waved a hand in irritable dismissal. 'Let's just get this sorted out as soon as possible, shall we? You say that the briefcase has been reported as stolen, so get Davies up here for that.'

'Right away, sir.'

'Wait. On second thoughts, I'll send someone else to Merthyr Tydfil for Davies. You're to search the house, and for God's sake make sure you do it thoroughly.'

'Now, sir?'

'Yes, now!'

'It's going to be difficult in the garden, sir. In the dark.'

'Take a bloody torch, man. I want a full report on my desk before Davies is brought in.'

'Yes, sir.' Stratton tried to compose his features into a semblance of eager obedience.

'Don't stand there making faces—get over to Marlborough Street for the warrant.'

Going down the corridor to collect Ballard, Stratton relieved his feelings by singing 'When I'm Cleaning Windows' in a voice that he judged to be almost—but not quite—audible in his superior's office.

Having secured an emergency warrant from the magistrate's court, Stratton and Ballard made their way back to Paradise Street. By the time they reached number ten, it was after nine o'clock. 'Let's hope the poor sods aren't having an early night,' said Stratton grimly as they waited, stamping their feet in the cold, for the door to be answered.

When Backhouse answered the door he was dressed, as before, in a collarless shirt and trousers held up in the old-fashioned way with braces and a belt. He did the bad ventriloquist thing with his mouth, then took off his pebble glasses and polished them on a handkerchief, blinking myopically. Behind him, in the gloom of the hallway, stood Mrs Backhouse, who had taken off her overall to reveal a dark-green frock.

'Sorry to call back at this late hour, Mr Backhouse. We have a warrant to search the premises.'

Backhouse jammed his glasses back on his nose and stared at the two of them. 'Now?'

'I'm afraid so, sir.' Stratton produced the paper. 'May we come in? We're anxious to get this matter cleared up—as I'm sure you are.'

'It's all very unpleasant.' Backhouse grimaced and rubbed the small of his back with both hands. 'My wife's nerves...she was just about to take a sleeping pill and go off to bed.'

Behind him, Edna Backhouse nodded in tearful confirmation of this.

'We'll be as quick as we can, I assure you,' said Stratton soothingly.

They started at the top of the house, in the two rooms which had been the Davies's flat, then moved downstairs to Mr Gardiner's flat on the first floor. Sparsely furnished, it yielded nothing apart from the fact that its tenant had once worked on the railways and was a staunch supporter of the Conservative Party.

They returned down the narrow staircase and, watched in silence by Backhouse and Edna, they inspected first the ground-floor living room, which faced the street—utility furniture, a radiogram, a few books and a dejected-looking plant, as well as the framed first-aid certificates Backhouse had mentioned and a photograph of him, smiling proudly, in his police uniform—then the bedroom at the back, and finally, the kitchen. There was, as Stratton had predicted, nothing at all to suggest that Muriel Davies had ever been there, alive or otherwise. 'Now, if you don't mind,' said Stratton, turning to Backhouse, 'we'll need to see the garden. Is the back door unlocked?'

Backhouse looked puzzled. 'Yes, it's always unlocked, but there's only the lavatory and the washhouse out there, and there's no light. I can assure you—'

'I'm sorry,' said Stratton firmly, 'but we do have to look.' He pulled his torch from his overcoat pocket. 'If you'll keep the dog inside for the time being...'

The 'garden', which consisted of a yard and a muddy patch of lawn strewn with broken bricks and the corrugated-iron remains of an Anderson shelter, was no more than thirty feet by twelve. By the light of the torch, Stratton made out a lopsided washing-line post, the rusty shell of a dustbin, old newspapers, some gnawed bones that looked like chops, a lot of weeds, some dusty-looking bushes, and the sooty wall of the goods yard. On the top of it a cat, disturbed by the noise and light, fled with dainty tightrope-walker's steps into the darkness beyond.

Stratton checked the lavatory and, finding it empty, turned his attention to the fractionally larger washhouse beside it. 'These are used by all the tenants, are they?' he asked Backhouse, who was walking up and down the yard, rubbing his back and biting his lip as if in pain.

'That's right.'

'Bit stiff.' Stratton tried, and failed, to open the washhouse door.

'It gets jammed,' said Backhouse. Turning to his wife, who was standing on the threshold of the back door, shoulders hunched and arms crossed against the cold, he said, 'Fetch a knife, Edna.'

Edna Backhouse disappeared and returned a moment later with a kitchen knife which she inserted into the lock, and, after wiggling it for a few moments, managed to open the door. Shining his torch in, Stratton saw a room of about five feet square with an old copper covered by a plank of wood on which stood several tins of paint and varnish, presumably left behind by the builders Backhouse had mentioned. Next to it was a square stone sink with a single tap. A row of battered-looking planks of wood was propped up vertically in front of it.

'Those are from the hall,' said Backhouse. 'The builders gave them to me for firewood.'

Stratton nudged the plank a few inches and peered into the copper but saw nothing except dust. 'We don't use the washhouse any more,' Backhouse explained. 'Only for storing things and emptying slops…there's nothing more to see.'

Stratton pulled back one of the planks standing before the sink and shone his torch into the space behind. The beam illuminated what appeared to be a green-and-white-checked tablecloth, tied round with sash cord. He pulled a couple more of the planks away and saw that it was wrapped round a large parcel. Standing back, he motioned to Mrs Backhouse. 'Do you know what this is?' he asked. 'Is it your tablecloth?'

Edna Backhouse bent forward and peered at the bundle for a moment. Straightening up, she said, 'It's not one of mine. I've no idea what's in it.'

'Well, let's have it out.' Aided by Ballard, Stratton pulled the bundle—which was heavy—into the yard. 'You don't mind if we cut the cord?' he asked Mrs Backhouse.

Frowning, shaking her head, she said, 'No. I told you, it's not mine.'

Stratton took out his pocket knife and, his torch held steady between his teeth, cut the sash cord. As soon as it was loosened, one end of the green cloth raised itself up and, with jerky acceleration as of some ghastly mechanical toy, a pair of female feet and legs slid out onto the cement of the yard.

There was a sharp indrawn breath from Edna Backhouse, then silence, thick as a fog. After a long moment during which no one moved, spoke, or even seemed to breathe, Ballard's voice came from inside the washhouse. 'That's not all, sir. There's a baby.'

Diana's high heels echoed on the stone floor as she walked into the hall of Hambeyn House, startling a pair of wood pigeons so that they flapped upwards and away through the broken window at the top of the main staircase. The lower windows—those that had retained their glass—were opaque with dirt, and their decorative plasterwork surrounds were yellowing and crumbly like stale cake icing.

Shivering, she pulled the collar of her fur coat close around her neck and skirted the evidence of the birds' occupancy—by the look of things, there had been more than just two pigeons—to stand at the bottom of the staircase. The curved iron banister looked like the ribs of a dinosaur and, halfway up, a thin ray of winter sunlight illuminated an obscenity scrawled across the khaki-painted wall—left there, presumably, by a departing soldier. The words, Diana thought, were indicative of the fact that her childhood home, and what it symbolised, were obsolete in the new, post-war world.

Sitting in the train on the way up to Gloucestershire, the burst of confidence she'd felt on leaving Guy had ebbed away, and, in an attempt to lift her spirits, she'd convinced herself that somebody—a school, a nursing home, even an asylum—would want to buy the place. This hope had been all but demolished when the driver of the station taxi, hearing her destination, had looked aghast and said, 'You sure, miss?' Even so, she hadn't expected it to look quite so derelict. The house was a wreck, and she'd heard enough tales of woe from the owners of other properties requisitioned by the forces to know that whatever compensation she might be awarded would be too little to do much about it. Besides, it seemed to her that it was already too late.

It was hard to believe she'd ever lived here. The place was like an abandoned stage set for a play so long out of fashion that it was impossible to imagine how anyone could have enjoyed it. Not daring to go up the stairs, she recrossed the hall and walked down the corridor to the dining room, where she found more khaki and grey paint, loose—and in some places, missing—floorboards and heaps of rubbish in the once magnificent fireplaces. Gingerly, she made her way over to the windows and stood looking out over the terrace. Weeds had sprung up between the flagstones, and piles of cigarette ends in the bowls of the long-disused ornamental fountains had combined with rainwater to create a few inches of brownish nicotine soup. The lawn beyond was rutted with tyre tracks and the flowerbeds claimed by banks of nettles.

Hambeyn House was dead. Nothing—not repairs or fresh paint, even supposing these could be got, nor the joyful barking of dogs or even the laughter of children—could bring it back to life. At least, thought Diana, I don't feel sentimental about it. Being a lonely only child—her sole sibling, a boy, had not survived babyhood—with a distant father, an aloof mother, and a series of nannies with cold, perfunctory hands had seen to that. She dredged her memory for anything that would kindle a spark of feeling but nothing came. At least, she thought, turning away from the window, there are no death duties, because there's certainly no money to pay them. Her spendthrift father, who'd sold off parcel after parcel of land in his lifetime, had left her only a few thousand pounds, and as for what she'd get from Guy...

But I don't want to depend on anybody, she thought. For the first time in my life, I want to stand on my own two feet.

She would go to London. When she was dreaming of escape from Guy and Evie, that had always been her plan, but now, for the first time, she began to give it a practical form—impossible before, as Evie had a nasty habit of opening other people's letters 'by accident' and Diana knew, from bitter experience, just how vengeful her mother-in-law could be.

At least she'd had the good sense to ask the taxi to wait. She'd return to the station, collect her bags, and telephone to her friend Lally before she boarded the train. Lally, who'd been a fellow MI5 agent during the war and was now married to another old colleague, Jock Anderson, would surely let her stay while she found herself a job. Jock, who still worked for the Secret Service, might be able to help her with that. There was their former boss, too, Colonel Forbes-James—he might know of something. She'd find herself a small flat like the one she'd had in Tite Street during the war, and she'd make a brand new start.

'A well-nourished adult woman, five feet two inches in height, estimated weight seven and a half stone. The body has been tied up in a tablecloth. It is dressed in a blue woollen jacket, a spotted cotton blouse, and a black skirt. The skirt has been disarranged so that the lower parts are exposed. Knickers and stockings are absent…'

Dr McNally, the pathologist, looked like a clergyman—spare and ascetic in his white gown and rubber apron, with spectacles perched on his nose—and as he solemnly intoned the words, dictating to his secretary, Miss Lynn, he sounded like one, too. The Middlesex Hospital mortuary, to which both bodies had been removed, was a cold, low-ceilinged abattoir, its tiles and metal and porcelain surfaces gleaming in the harsh overhead light. It smelt of a mixture of decomposition and disinfectant. A tap dripped, and bronchitic coughing could be heard, intermittently, from somewhere in the basement corridor outside.

The pathologist turned to his assistant, a wizened little man called Higgs, who had been there for as long as Stratton could remember, working for McNally's predecessor, Dr Byrne, who had been murdered in 1944. 'You may begin removing the clothes.' To Stratton, he said, 'You'll be making a list, I trust.'

'That's correct.'

Ballard produced his notebook and pencil and wrote down each piece of clothing as it was removed. Finally naked, lying flat on the slab, neck resting on a wooden block and head tilted back on a white towel, the woman—confirmed as Muriel Davies by the Backhouses but not yet formally identified—looked as though she were snarling like a dog. The woman in the older Mrs Davies's photograph had been quite a looker, but now her upper lip was puffy and slightly drawn back from the teeth and there was a dark area—bruising and dried blood—around her nose and mouth. That, thought Stratton, explained the 'bleeding from the mouth' comment in Davies's second statement—the bastard had thumped her first. Her eyes were closed, and one was blackened. Stratton could see that her neck was bruised and that the body contours were beginning to disappear. There were maggots clustered on the mound of her left breast, as if suckling. Averting his eyes from this, Stratton noticed that her left hand was unadorned. 'You didn't remove her wedding ring, did you?' he asked Higgs.

The assistant shook his head. 'Never touch nothing till I'm told.'

'She *was* married, was she?' asked McNally.

'So we understand,' said Stratton. 'Perhaps she'd taken it off for some reason. Sorry to interrupt. Please...' He gestured at the pathologist to continue his work.

McNally had been dictating for some time, medical terminology, most of which Stratton didn't understand, letting it wash over him and deliberately keeping his eyes off the baby, who, lying on the slab next door to the mother, made a pathetically small shape under the white sheet. Ballard, he could see, was doing the same. Worse for him, thought Stratton, with a baby daughter himself. Something McNally said caught his attention. '...There are a series of abrasions three and a half inches long on the right side of the throat, varying from one and a quarter inches in width to three-eighths of an inch. On the left side of the back of the neck is another group of abrasions…'

'So she was strangled?' asked Stratton.

'It would appear so,' said McNally, 'but I can't be certain until I've finished. Would you like me to move to the child now and do the internal examinations later?'

'Please. If you don't mind.'

McNally finished his dictation, then motioned to Higgs to cover up the body. When the baby was unveiled, Stratton saw that its face was swollen and bluish. It was wearing a fancy knitted cardigan and a dress and had a large white handkerchief wrapped around its neck, but its legs and feet were bare. The sight of the tiny, wrinkled soles was almost more than Stratton could stand, and he turned away, blowing his nose.

'The body is of a well-nourished baby girl. Height is thirty-three and a half inches…' McNally held up his hand to indicate that Miss Lynn should stop writing. 'Start removing the clothes, please, Higgs.'

The procedure was repeated, with Ballard noting down the items. After taking off the top clothes, Higgs fumbled at something stuck inside the vest. 'Something in here, sir. Aha…here it is. One toy duck.' He held it up for Ballard and Stratton to see. It was a small, cheap thing, but, judging by its worn appearance, much loved. Stratton felt a lump rise in his throat.

'One…toy…duck,' repeated Ballard in a choked voice, writing in his notebook. Then he looked up, and Stratton saw that there were tears in his eyes. Clearing his throat, he said, 'If you could excuse me for a moment, sir…'

'Of course.' Stratton took the notebook and pencil. 'Get yourself some air.'

Ballard left the room in a rush and, after a moment's silence, Higgs continued, 'One white handkerchief.'

'One white handkerchief.' Stratton wrote it down and kept his eyes on the page, waiting for the next item. A sharply indrawn breath made him look up, and he saw that tied tightly round the baby's neck was a man's tie. 'Strangled,' he said.

'Certainly looks like it,' said McNally. 'Poor little thing.'

After a moment, Higgs said, 'Shall I carry on, sir?'

'Yes.'

'One vest.'

'One…vest.'

'One nappy.'

'One…nappy.'

'One nappy pin.'

'One…nappy…pin.'

'You all right, Mr Stratton?'

Unable to speak further, Stratton simply nodded.

'If you need some air…' Higgs continued.

Stratton swallowed. 'Yes. I'll be…outside.'

As he left the room, McNally was saying, 'Decomposition is most advanced in the upper part of the body…'

'Sorry about that, sir.' Ballard was in the yard, white-faced and leaning against the wall.

'No need to apologise. Cigarette?'

'Thank you.'

They smoked in silence for a moment before Stratton, feeling that he ought to say something, no matter how inadequate, said quietly, 'Terrible business.'

'Yes.' Ballard, staring down at his feet, shook his head. 'Just…'

'I know. Doesn't do to dwell on it.'

'Hard not to, sir.'

'Yes, it is.' Stratton allowed his hand to rest, momentarily, on the sergeant's shoulder. 'Never gets any easier, unfortunately.'

'Katy's got a little duck like that. Sleeps with it tucked in next to her… Duck and Teddy. She has to have those, or she can't settle.'

'Mine were the same at that age.'

'You can't help remembering, can you, sir?'

Stratton shook his head. 'Wouldn't be human if you didn't. The mother's about the same age as Monica.'

'Makes you sick.' Ballard shook his head again, then said, 'Someone's going to have to identify them formally.'

'Yes, they are. I suppose we'll have to ask Mrs Davies tomorrow. Poor woman.'

'How could he do it, sir?' Ballard burst out. 'Davies. How could he strangle his own daughter?'

'I don't know,' said Stratton. 'It's not as if we haven't had cases of people killing their own children before, but not like this. I suppose he must be off his head.'

'The bodies are in very good condition, considering the length of time,' said McNally later, as they sat in his office.

'Which was?'

'Approximately three weeks, I'd say.'

'For both of them?'

'Yes.'

'I certainly didn't notice a smell when we opened the wash-house,' said Stratton. 'Did you, Ballard?'

'No, sir. Nothing at all.'

'It would have been pretty cold,' said McNally, who'd been called to view the bodies *in situ*. 'Not refrigeration conditions but not too far off, otherwise the decomposition would be far more advanced. Incidentally, the woman was pregnant—a male foetus, about sixteen weeks along.'

Reminded instantly and vividly of Jenny, Stratton swallowed hard before he spoke. 'Any sign of interference?'

'No. A small amount of bruising to the…' McNally looked at his notes, 'posterior wall of the vagina, but that's not indicative. Just to clarify—you said that the woman has been provisionally identified as Muriel Davies, aged nineteen, and the child is…'

'Judy Davies. According to our information at the scene of discovery, she's fourteen months old.'

'That seems about right.' McNally wrote it down at the top of his notes. 'Both strangled by ligature—the tie, in the case of the infant.'

'And the mother?'

'Well, there was nothing on the body, so one can't be sure. A piece of cord, perhaps—'

'The sash cord used to tie up the blanket?'

'Possibly. Or a scarf or even a stocking. As I said, it's impossible to be certain. There's enough decomposition there to muddy the waters, I'm afraid. There's some bruising on the legs...' McNally looked at his notes once more, 'the inner aspect of the left thigh, four inches above the knee, and the inner aspect of the left calf directly below the knee, so it's possible she might have been held down—if someone had knelt on her legs, or something of that sort. And, as I'm sure you saw, there were blows to the face. She was only a slip of a thing, and as for the baby...' The pathologist shook his head in disgust.

Lally hadn't changed much in the last eight years, Diana thought. Tall, elegant, and blonde—people had often commented on the similarity in looks between the two of them—she was curled up in one corner of the brocade sofa, smoking a cigarette. The baby having been duly admired and removed to bed, and Jock not having arrived home from work ('some Ministry shindig, darling—frightfully important and bloody annoying because we've got people coming for dinner'), they had their first chance to talk. Since Diana had returned to Hampshire in forty-one, they'd communicated mainly by letter, with face-to-face contact restricted to social chit-chat at the occasional party when Diana came up (or rather, was permitted by her mother-in-law to come up) to London.

Lally and Jock Anderson had a large house in Albemarle Street, off Piccadilly. 'It's falling apart,' Lally wailed, as they sat drinking sherry. 'I know the furniture's lovely, but it's all bashed about, and with income tax at nine and six in the pound we can't afford to repair the place—and even if we *could* we'd probably never find anyone to do it. Jock says the roof's in such a state that it won't be long before we're putting out pails to catch the drips when it rains. But we'd love it if you'd stay. Just so long as you've brought your ration book—I'm utterly terrified of upsetting Mrs Robinson in case she decides to retire to her sister's at Bexhill. She's the only help we've got—well, apart from the nanny—and I still can't cook to save my life.'

'I've got it here.' Diana smiled and patted her handbag. Although Lally's flighty breeziness masked a very good brain and Diana would have been happy to bet that she was a lot more competent than she let on, it was clear that, after the excitement of the war, she hadn't settled well, even after five-odd years, into the duller routine of being a wife.

'Oh, good. Anyway, never mind all that. It's too boring for words. What about you? Are you and Guy... Is it still awful?'

'We're getting divorced, if that's what you mean.'

'Oh, darling... I did wonder when you asked if you could stay. Why on earth didn't you tell me?'

'I wanted to, but it was so difficult to telephone—I couldn't use the one in Guy's office, and Evie was so absolutely hawkish about the house telephone that I became quite neurotic about thinking she'd overhear... And she used to open my letters. The ridiculous thing was, I know that she wanted to see the back of me just as much as I wanted to leave, but if she'd thought I was planning it—you know, that it was my idea—she'd have... Well, I don't know what she'd have done but she'd certainly have made my life even more unpleasant than it was already. In the end, I managed to get Guy to agree to present it to her as a fait accompli, and he's agreed to let me divorce him, which means that he's got to go through the ghastly charade of being caught with a tart or a barmaid or something. I'm told it may take a while to arrange, but Guy's found someone else—or rather, Evie's found someone else for him, which amounts to the same thing. Local squire's daughter. She's young—about twenty-five—and completely awed by the pair of them. I'm sure they'll have lots of children, which is something I don't seem to be able to manage, but I don't envy her in the least. In fact, I'm quite grateful to her—she means I don't have to feel too guilty about it all. She doesn't know what she's getting herself into, poor thing.'

'With Evie, you mean?'

'Yes. Guy's as much under her thumb as ever. More, I think. I was absolutely astonished when he finally agreed with me about the divorce.'

'It sounds hellish. But he had a bad time, didn't he, being a prisoner? I don't suppose one ever really gets over that sort of thing.'

'He's never spoken about it, but I think it was pretty grim. One was always told not to ask, so I didn't. A lot of nightmares, and he'd never seem to want me to comfort him, or...or *anything*, really. He seemed almost to hate women—apart from his bloody mother, that is.'

'It must be hard, though, coming back from *that* and everyone expecting you to get on with things just the same as before.'

'Yes, but Guy *wants* things to be the same as before, and they're not. I've changed. He's changed. We've all changed—all except Evie.' Diana made a face. 'She's like a...I don't know, a monument or something. So sure of herself—as if she's determined not to change or allow anything to affect her views. Perhaps that's why Guy loves her so much. But I've thought for quite a while that perhaps we were always destined to fail, and it would have happened anyway, without the war.'

Lally sipped her drink and looked at Diana intently. 'You're not hoping to run into our old friend Claude Ventriss in London, are you?'

'No!' It came out too loud and vehement, and Diana was horribly aware that she was blushing. Claude—impossibly handsome, with velvet brown eyes—was the agent with whom she'd had the affair during the war.

'Really?' Lally sounded sceptical. 'Because if you are, you're in for a disappointment. The last Jock heard, he was in Palestine.'

'*Palestine?* What for?'

'Looking for another war, darling. That's what men like him *do*. He isn't marriage material.'

'I know that! Anyway, it's all in the past.'

Lally raised a warning finger. 'Just as long as it stays there. Claude can cast a very long shadow—believe me, I've seen it happen before. You're better off without him, Diana. Honestly. You're not the first woman to be stupid about Claude—'

'Don't I know it,' said Diana, ruefully.

'—and you won't be the last. But if you really must have someone to be stupid about, there's plenty of choice. *Everyone's* in London—Peter Calvert, Felix Hyde Thompson, Johnny—'

'I don't want anyone to be stupid about, Lally. I want a job. I thought I'd ask Colonel Forbes-James.'

Lally raised her eyebrows. 'I had the impression that you two parted company on…well, less than friendly terms.'

'Yes,' said Diana impatiently, 'but that was *ages* ago. Surely now it's all—'

'Don't be too sure, darling. F-J's wonderful, but he can certainly hold a grudge, and he's in a difficult position. After that business with Neville Apse…'

'Don't remind me. I was the one who found him, remember?' Diana shuddered, recalling Apse's body, suspended from the banisters of a fire escape by a pair of braces and hanging like a sack, with bulging eyes, mottled blue cheeks and a swollen, blackened tongue protruding obscenely from his mouth.

'F-J's got a great deal to lose,' said Lally.

'How do you know?' Diana had never discussed F-J's proclivities with anyone, apart from Inspector Stratton, and that was back in 1940.

'Jock mentioned something once that made me wonder.'

'But surely,' said Diana, 'it isn't *generally* known?'

'I think it is and it isn't, if you see what I mean. As Jock says, everyone knows everyone. And most of them,' Lally added pointedly, 'went to the same schools. The point is, Diana, that F-J might not be too pleased to see you.'

'Why? I'm no threat to him.'

'That isn't the point, and in any case, he probably won't see it like that.'

Remembering Claude's words when she'd told him about Apse—*That's the thing about buggers, darling. Blackmail. Very simple and very effective*—Diana said, 'But I'm not a…I don't know…a Russian spy, for goodness' sake.'

'Of course you're not, darling, but you might know—even if you don't know that you know—a man who is.'

'Claude, you mean?'

'I didn't, but I suppose it's possible. He's in Palestine, and Jock says the Soviets are giving the Israelis an awful lot of help.' Lally rolled her eyes. 'Trying to get them to join the club… Would you like another drink, darling? It's jolly good, isn't it? Jock knows a lovely wine merchant…' She made a dramatic finger-to-lips gesture.

'Thanks.' Diana held out her glass.

As Lally got up to refill it, she said, 'Can't remember if I told you, but he's written a book. Naval history—all very learned. I've been reading bits of it, but it's terribly hard going because his handwriting's impossible.'

'I can type it for him,' said Diana, eagerly. 'I had lots of practice in Hampshire. A woman from the village taught me properly so I could help Evie with the WVS and billeting and things.' Seeing Lally's raised eyebrows, she added, 'Oh, she was in her element with the chance to boss so many people around. Honestly, Lally, I'd be delighted to help Jock. It's so good of you to put me up at such short notice—it would be wonderful if I could do *something* in return.'

'I should think Jock would jump at it, but I don't suppose he'll be back for ages, so why don't—'

Hearing the sound of the front door, Lally stopped. 'That's odd. It can't be anyone else, but he told me—'

She stopped again as Jock Anderson walked into the room, an unhappy tension about him that was a world away from his usual urbane and cheerful self.

'Darling!' Lally sprang off the sofa. 'I thought you were out being grand.'

'Something came up,' he said with heavy irony, dumping his briefcase on the floor and sitting down in the space that Lally had vacated, head in hands. He rubbed his face for a moment, said, 'Christ!' and then, spotting the visitor, 'Evening, Diana. Didn't expect to see you here.'

'She's staying with us, darling.' Lally went to the tray. 'Have you had an awful day? You look as if you could do with a drink.'

'Thanks. Scotch.'

Sensing that she might be surplus to requirements, Diana said, 'Why don't I go and unpack or something?'

Jock put out a restraining hand. 'Thanks, but no need to be tactful. You might as well know. It's F-J.'

'We were just talking about him, weren't we, Lally? What's happened?'

Jock stared at her for a moment, as if he hadn't seen her properly before, and Diana noticed that the muscles in his jaw were clenched. 'He's dead.'

'Dead?' Diana echoed the word in disbelief. 'F-J?'

'I'm afraid so. The housekeeper found him this morning, at his flat in Dolphin Square. He'd hanged himself.'

'My God.' Lally handed Jock his drink, her face blank with shock. 'Why? Did he leave a note?'

Jock sighed, a long, uneven sound like a last exhalation. 'He didn't need to explain. He'd been arrested.'

'Arrested? When? For what?'

'Yesterday evening, for importuning.' Jock sounded weary and disgusted. 'In a public lavatory. Chap turned out to be a plain-clothes policeman.'

'I don't understand,' said Lally. 'What was F-J doing there in the first place?'

'Presumably,' said Diana, keeping her tone brisk to disguise her horror and embarrassment, 'he wanted to relieve himself.'

Jock shook his head. 'The place is known for that sort of thing, apparently.'

'But why go in there?' asked Diana, bewilderment giving place, with horrid clarity, to understanding. 'I mean, surely F-J doesn't—didn't—have to...well, you know... Go into public places like that.'

Jock sighed. 'It appears that was the attraction. Meeting a...a certain type of person. Excitement outside one's social circle. Like a married man who visits a prostitute, I suppose. Really, Diana,' he added irritably, 'I don't understand it any more than you do, but that's what happened.'

Diana thought of the night in Apse's flat during an air-raid when, hidden inside a cupboard, she'd overheard his conversation with the male tart he'd brought home, the unlikely coquettishness in his tone, and the rhythmic noises of their congress.

'F-J said he was a fool to think he could get away with it,' said Jock. 'Mind you, he said the policeman came up to him first, but the policeman said it was the other way round, and of course there's no doubt as to who would have been believed.'

'Do you mean,' said Diana, 'that there are policemen who specialise in that sort of thing? Trapping people?'

'Handsome young policemen,' said Jock. 'And this one,' he added, viciously, 'will doubtless be commended for behaving like a male prostitute. F-J gave a false name, but even if no one had recognised him, he wouldn't have been able to carry on working for the Service—too much of a risk. He was due in court this morning. God...' Shuddering, Jock took a large gulp of his drink. 'It was horrible, seeing him like that. Blank. As if he'd been stripped naked. He talked about it afterwards. How he put it was that men like him have two sets of friends. Two lives. He said he'd always been afraid that they'd collide and that he'd tried to leave it alone, but the loneliness...impulses—and sooner or later he'd always fall back into his former ways. He said that was a relief at first, not having to pretend all the time, but then the shame...'

'What about his wife?' asked Lally.

Jock shook his head and looked into his glass—now empty—then went to the drinks tray and poured himself a second Scotch. His back to them both, he said, 'I telephoned her. Someone had to tell her. It was...' Lally went to him and put a hand on his shoulder.

'I'm sure you were kind,' she said.

'She made it easy for me,' said Jock. 'When I'd told her how he'd died, she didn't ask me why he'd done it, or if he'd left a note, or anything.'

'Well, they did lead fairly separate lives, darling. Perhaps she knew about him.'

Gently, Jock pushed Lally's hand away and turned to face them. 'I don't know... If she did, she certainly didn't want to hear me say it. I can't blame her for that... F-J talked about her, too. He said that if things had been different, he would have told her what sort of man he was when he proposed, but he couldn't. He said, when he married her, he honestly thought he could begin again—wipe out the past.' Jock paused and looked directly at Diana, and a dull flush spread across his face. 'He told me he was...' he grimaced, '*in love* with Ventriss.'

'I know,' said Diana. 'I overheard them talking once.' She took a sip of her drink and lit a cigarette in order not to have to look at Jock, remembering how she'd stood outside the door of F-J's office and heard Claude taunting him. *Apse did it because he thought he could get away with it. After all, most of his friends do, don't they, Charles? At least I'm honest. I don't use women as camouflage... You made damn sure that Evie Calthrop got to know about Diana and me, didn't you, Charles? But I don't think you're in any position to preach morality, are you?* She remembered, too, the conversation she'd had later with lovely Inspector Stratton. He'd been so kind and understanding when she'd blurted out about Claude's hold over F-J and her suspicion that Apse's death was not, as officially recorded, a suicide...

'He said something about that—thinking they were alone and hearing the door of the flat close. He wondered if it was you.'

'Yes, it was.'

Although she was only about six feet away from Jock and Lally, the silence between them, as the implications of this sank in, felt like an immense void. She stared down at her shoes, knowing that she'd never be able to talk to them about it, even if it were allowed.

The chime of the hall clock made them all jump. 'Oh, Lord,' said Lally. 'We've got the Tremaines coming to dinner in half an hour. Does Davy know?' Davy Tremaine had been a colleague of Jock's since the war years.

'Yes.' Jock drained his glass and set it on the tray. 'Better go and dress, then.'

Sitting at the dressing table in her room, Diana brushed her hair mechanically. She could picture F-J quite clearly, as if it was his face reflected in the mirror and not her own—the round, dark eyes with their long lashes and the squashy button nose that gave him the slightly querulous charm of a pug. The first time she'd met him, she'd been tempted to pat him, despite his formidable intellect. She remembered his flat-cum-office in the monumental Art Deco grandeur of Dolphin Square, with its strange mixture of sturdy Edwardian brass-and-wood masculinity and the feminine delicacy of the *toile de Jouy* and petit point she'd assumed had come from the wife that no one ever saw. And that strange painting of the naked boy bather that had been a gift from Neville Apse... She thought of his desk, always—in contrast to his dapper appearance—so untidy and of how, after one of her first successes gathering information, he'd given her a jar of bath salts. That was when she'd trusted him. That was before his jealousy about her and Claude had led him to take steps to ensure that Evie got to hear of their affair and before he'd arranged, quite deliberately, that she be the one to find Apse's body. It had been his way of warning her—telling her that he knew she knew about him and she'd better keep her mouth shut, or...

Now, she found that she felt no anger towards him, only pity. All his precautions had come to nothing because, in the end, he'd betrayed himself. Setting down her hairbrush, Diana began powdering her face. Why on earth had he done it? Thinking of Claude, and the reckless way she'd behaved over him, she supposed she did understand, a little...

The Tremaines arrived and everyone acted, in an exhaustingly resolute and determined way, as if it were an entirely ordinary evening ('Our Mrs Robinson's such a treasure, she can conjure the most marvellous food out of thin air…'). Sitting over drinks, then dinner, trying to talk normally, was like being caught up in a bizarre nightmare. Jock and Davy discussed China and Mao Tse Tung. They even had an argument about it, but it seemed manufactured, a repetition of familiar positions without conviction or passion. Jean Tremaine and Lally nodded, asked occasional questions and looked interested, and no one said a word about F-J. Diana stared glassily at her plate, toying with her food—which was anything but marvellous, being the colour, texture and, probably, the taste of Thames mud—and, pleading tiredness from travelling, went up to bed as soon as she decently could.

Lying on her back, staring into the darkness, she thought that, in the end, F-J had lived up to the 'code' of behaviour that bound them all. Just like all those Romans he must have learnt about at school… She tried to imagine him as a boy, inkily cramming at his books, reading about senators ordered to commit suicide by emperors, doing the classical equivalent of the decent thing. We flatter ourselves that we've progressed so much, she thought, but we're just like they were: impaled, like butterflies are in display cases—not by belief in the system of things but by the *necessity* for that belief, whether we like it or not. Then, as now, it meant war and treachery and casualties, but it was immutable. We must think the same, say the same, *be* the same, and if, in any way, we find ourselves unable to conform, we must pretend. Hard on the heels of that idea came another: I've spent my life trying to conform and pretend, and I've failed. I don't want to try any more. I want to change.

It was well after one in the morning when Stratton and Ballard, accompanied by the piles of clothing removed from the bodies, returned to West End Central in a police car brought to the Middlesex for the purpose. The car nosed its way slowly through the acrid, sooty smog that swirled around it, reducing visibility to a few feet despite the street lamps and the headlights of occasional passing vehicles.

'Message for you from DCI Lamb, sir,' said Cudlipp, the desk sergeant, when they arrived. 'DI Grove and DS Porter went down to Merthyr Tydfil to collect Davies. They ought to be there now—they're awaiting your instructions, sir. Shall I place a call?'

'Yes, please.' Stratton blew his nose. It came out black. 'A real pea-souper out there,' he said, shoving the handkerchief back into his pocket. 'And if you could put these,' Stratton indicated the piles of clothing brought in by Ballard and the driver, 'in the Charge Room, and rustle up a spot of tea… We'll be in my office.'

'Right you are, sir. That their clothes, is it? Her and the nipper?'

'That's right.'

'This Davies sounds a right one.'

'You can say that again.'

'This came through, too. From Constable Williams in Wales, sir. Statements of a Mr and Mrs Howells.'

'Thanks.'

'Right.' Stratton put down the receiver. 'Grove and Porter will bring Davies back by the early train. They'll say nothing to him about finding the bodies—as far as he knows, it's still just the briefcase we want him for. The train gets into Paddington at ten past ten, so we'll need to organise a car to meet it. I'll go along. We'll need the formal identification first thing, and once we've interviewed Davies, which we'll do straight away, we need to get the Backhouses in to make separate statements. Then there's the workmen. Backhouse said they were at the house three weeks ago, which means they must have been around when Muriel and the baby were killed. We need to find out who they are and have a word with them, sharpish. Presumably the bodies weren't in the washhouse before they arrived, or they'd have spotted them—they seemed to have used the place for storing paint and whatnot. And we need to find out when they gave Backhouse those floorboards for firewood, assuming that's where they came from.'

'I was wondering why he hadn't used them, sir. After all, it's been pretty nippy recently.'

'Perhaps he was using up his coal,' said Stratton. 'The thing that's still puzzling me is the dog. I know that *we* couldn't smell anything, but you'd think it would have been scrabbling against the door and making no end of a fuss.'

'Perhaps they didn't let it into the garden, sir.'

'I didn't see any evidence of it—well, except for those bones, but they might have put them out there afterwards. Looked like they used the garden as a rubbish dump, didn't it?'

'It was in a bit of a state, sir.'

'Let's see what Davies's aunt and uncle have to say for themselves.' Stratton scanned the statements. 'Mrs Howells said that

Davies arrived unexpectedly on the fourteenth of November at six thirty in the morning. They hadn't seen him for three or four years, apparently. Said his employer's car had broken down in Cardiff and could he stay with them while it was being repaired... Left his suitcase at the station in Cardiff—Mr Howells said he saw a cloakroom ticket and that Davies told them Muriel and Judy were staying in Brighton until after Christmas... Left on the twenty-first and came back on the twenty-third with a suitcase. Told them Muriel was at their flat when he went back, but she walked out without a word and left him holding the baby...'

'Sounds like our boy all right, sir.'

'It certainly does. He told Mr and Mrs H. he'd given Judy to some people who'd look after her and paid them fifteen pounds to do it. When they asked why he hadn't taken her to his mother, he said it was because she was out working...hadn't thought to bring the baby to Wales with him, apparently...Seemed quite contented throughout his visit, went to the pub with his uncle, enjoyed himself...This is a bit odd...'

'What's that, sir?'

'Says Davies bought a present for Judy—a teddy bear.'

'To throw them off the scent, sir?'

'Doesn't sound like he's bright enough for that. I'd say it's more likely he was trying to pretend to himself he hadn't done it—that would fit with the statements he made, wouldn't it? Anyway... Mrs H. had written to Mrs Davies about him and got a letter back two days ago—which tallies with what she told us—telling her that Davies had sold his furniture and people were dunning her for cash. When Mrs H. confronted him about it, he said his mother was lying and the furniture was still in the flat. Very upset, apparently, couldn't finish his breakfast, and then he went to the police station. Well, it's all of a piece, isn't it?'

'Yes, sir. Beats me how he thought he could get away with it.'

'He probably didn't think at all... Just made it up as he went along. Right. We'll need a statement from Mrs Davies. She said she'd not seen him since the beginning of November, didn't she?

Now, I'd better get cracking on this report for DCI Lamb, but if you want to get some kip…'

'Don't think I could, sir. Honestly.'

'Well, ask Cudlipp to set up a couple of camp beds for later, anyway. And why don't you see if you can find us a drink? For medicinal purposes, of course. I'm sure there's a bottle knocking around.'

Left alone, Stratton started bashing out a report for Lamb on the typewriter with two fingers, concentrating like fury in an attempt to keep at bay the pathetic image of Muriel and little Judy lying side by side on their respective slabs. Ballard returned half an hour later, bearing a half-full bottle of brandy. 'All done, sir.' As he spoke, he produced a tea cup from each pocket. 'Shall I? Couldn't find any glasses, I'm afraid.'

'Why not?' Stratton took his fag out of his mouth and picked a shred of tobacco off his lower lip. 'I'm nearly finished.'

Ballard poured and pushed a cup across the desk towards him. Stratton swallowed and made a face. 'Filthy.' He held out the cup for more. 'Don't know about you, but I could have done with that a couple of hours ago.'

'Me too, sir.'

'Oh, *Christ*…Jenny was pregnant when she died. Not so far gone, but…They thought it would have been a boy.' It occurred to him then, for the first time, that Jenny might not have told him of the existence of the baby not only because she was afraid he'd be angry—they'd agreed to stop at two—but also because she'd been trying to get rid of it, as Muriel Davies had. That couldn't have been the case, could it? Jenny loved children, she'd been the best of mothers, she wouldn't…would she? But if she'd been afraid of giving birth with the doodlebugs, of the world she'd be bringing the child into…Stratton put his hands over his face. 'I just wish she'd told me,' he muttered thickly.

'I'm sorry, sir.'

Stratton jerked his head up. 'No, Ballard, *I'm* sorry. I shouldn't have mentioned it. I don't know why I did. But with something like this, it brings it back. You know, I've never told anyone—not even the children—only the lady who took them when they were evacuated. When Dr McNally said Muriel Davies definitely *was* pregnant, I felt as if I'd been punched. And Davies killed his wife...I'd give anything to have Jenny back, and the baby. Be five and a half years old, now, if he'd lived... Going off to school. Still...' Stratton rubbed a hand over his face. 'No use dwelling on it. Doesn't do a bloody bit of good.'

'I suppose not, sir, but it's rough, all the same. Drop more brandy?'

'Thank you. You'll have all that to come, your nipper learning to talk and walk and all the rest of it...'

'Unlike poor little Judy.'

'Yes...Too late. Best we can do is nail the bastard that killed her.'

'I'll drink to that, sir,' said Ballard, with fierce solemnity. 'I'll certainly drink to that.'

Davies was white-faced, haggard, and very small. Next to DI Grove, who was a large, avuncular type, he seemed like a pygmy, and the top of his head barely came up to Stratton's shoulder. The camel hair overcoat he wore looked too large, so that he looked like a boy in man's clothing. Grove had told Stratton on the telephone that Davies was twenty-four years old, but he looked younger. Constable Williams's description of him as 'puny' was spot on, thought Stratton, as the four men walked down the platform at Paddington Station towards the waiting car.

'All right, was he, on the way back?' Stratton asked DI Grove as DS Porter and the driver settled Davies in the back seat.

Grove removed the pipe he habitually chomped on and, wiping a hand over his droopy moustache, stained cinnamon with nicotine, said in his distinctive phlegmy rumble, 'Didn't talk much. Mind you, neither did we. I'm not sure the lad really understands what's going on. He's hardly the brightest—to be honest, I don't think he's all there. He asked if his mother'd got in touch with the people looking after his daughter.'

Stratton, aware of a slight ache behind his eyes—he and Ballard had polished off what was left in the bottle before they'd turned in—endeavoured to collect his thoughts.

'Well, he's not been told we've found the bodies, so perhaps he thinks it's a good idea to keep on with his story.'

'I suppose so. Oh, and he told us he didn't pinch the briefcase, but he didn't say who did.'

'I'm surprised he didn't say it was Backhouse. He seems to be blaming him for everything else.'

They rode to West End Central in silence, Stratton in front beside the driver and Davies, flanked by Grove and Porter, in the back.

Ballard met Stratton in the lobby. 'Mrs Davies has identified the bodies, sir, so there's no difficulty there. She's made a statement, too. There's not much new, although she did tell us that there's some insanity in the family. Her grandfather and an uncle died in asylums, and her father was violent.'

'I suppose it's not surprising. Grove and Porter are bringing Davies in now. Tell Cudlipp I want him taken straight through to the Charge Room. I'll be waiting.'

Once in the Charge Room, Stratton arranged the two piles of clothing on a desk so that the tablecloth and the sash cord were on top of Muriel's, and the tie—still tightly knotted, but slit at the back in order to remove it—on top of Judy's. Then he took his notebook out of his pocket and positioned himself beside the table. After a few minutes, the door opened and Davies appeared, escorted by Ballard and Porter. On seeing the clothing, Davies blinked several times, opened his mouth, then closed it again and looked at Stratton in bewilderment. Bang to rights, chum, thought Stratton. Bang to fucking rights.

Opening his notebook in case he needed a prompt, he said, 'At nine thirty p.m. yesterday I found the body of your wife, Muriel Davies, concealed behind timber in a washhouse at ten Paradise Street, also the body of your baby daughter Judy concealed in the same outbuilding, and this clothing was found on them. Later, I was at the Middlesex Hospital mortuary, when it was established that the cause of death was strangulation in both cases. I have reason to believe that you were responsible for their deaths.'

Davies stared at him, jaw hanging slack. Then he reached forward, picked up the tie, then dropped it back onto the pile of baby clothes. When he looked up, Stratton saw that his eyes were wet with tears. 'Yes,' he whispered, and then again, more loudly, 'Yes.'

'John Wilfred Davies, I am arresting you for the murder of your wife, Muriel Davies, and your daughter, Judy Davies. You are not obliged to say anything, but I must warn you that anything you do say will be taken down in writing and may be given in evidence against you.'

Stratton stared across the desk at the tiny man who sat beneath the naked light bulb in the interview room. There were deep troughs of exhaustion under his eyes. His coat removed, his over-large jacket stood proud of his shoulders as if there were a hanger still inside, and his grubby white shirt stood a quarter of an inch clear either side of the skinny column of his neck. Whatever else he looked like, Stratton thought, it wasn't a monster. 'Do you understand what I am saying to you?' he asked.

The man's prominent Adam's apple bobbed up and down as he swallowed, working saliva into his mouth. 'Yes.'

'Good. Please sign here.' Stratton pushed a pen and the paper with the caution statement across the scarred wooden table. Davies glanced at it, then looked up, bewildered.

'Sign?'

'Your name.' Stratton tapped the bottom of the paper. Davies picked up the pen awkwardly, as if he wasn't used to handling such an object, and turned it round in his fingers several times before writing his name in a series of cramped, upward-sloping loops.

'Thank you.' Stratton nodded to Ballard, who sat beside him, pen poised, and, turning back to Davies, said, 'Why did you strangle your wife and child, Mr Davies?'

'Why?' echoed Davies. Eyes narrowed, he peered intently round the room as if hoping to find an answer there.

'You killed them,' said Stratton, flatly. 'You've just told us that. Now we want to know why you did it.'

'I...' Davies didn't look directly at Stratton. His gaze hovered somewhere between the two policemen's shoulders. 'I done nothing wrong.' The Welsh melodiousness in his voice was discernable for the first time.

'Mr Davies.' Stratton's voice was deliberately loud. 'So far, you have given us a cock and bull story about putting your wife's body down a drain. You told us that your baby daughter was being looked after by people who turn out not to exist. You told your mother that your wife and child were in Brighton. You told your neighbours, the Backhouses, that they were in Bristol. Then you told us that Backhouse was responsible for your wife's death and that he told you he was going to put her body in the drain. Now you're telling us that you had nothing to do with any of it. It's been a tissue of lies from start to finish, hasn't it?'

'I done nothing,' repeated Davies, sullen now, like a schoolboy caught out in a falsehood.

'What you have certainly done—consistently, I grant you—is to tell lies. We know that you killed your wife and child. You've just told us that yourself. Now,' Stratton, resting his palms on the desk, pushed himself upwards and forwards across the table so that his face was barely six inches from Davies's, 'I suggest that you start telling the truth.'

Davies shrank in his chair, his white, creased brow beaded with sweat. 'But I didn't... I never...'

'Mr Davies.' Stratton leant backwards and folded his arms. 'You have no choice but to co-operate with us. If you don't…' He left the implied threat hanging in the air between them for a full thirty seconds, then uncrossed his arms and continued, in an eminently reasonable tone, 'Fortunately for you, we're patient men, and of course we have plenty of time. And I imagine,' he said in a kinder tone, 'that it will be quite a relief to get it off your chest. That's what you told the policeman in Wales, isn't it? You told him you couldn't sleep for worrying. If you tell us all about it, we can help you. If not…' Stratton sighed, sorrowfully, 'then—much as we'd like to help you—we can't.'

Davies cowered, seeming to collapse from within; hunched over in his chair he looked even smaller than before. Stratton could almost smell his fear, and with it the scent of victory. He leant forward, elbows on the table. 'Well?'

Once more, Davies's eyes darted about the room, frantic this time. Watching him twist uncertainly in his chair, Stratton thought, there's no escape, chum—just get on with it. *'Well?'* he barked.

'I'll tell you about it.' Eyes flitting from Stratton's face to Ballard's and back again, he was speaking fast, with terrified eagerness. 'It was the money, see? Muriel took the money off me, from my job, and she kept spending it, and she was always asking me for more, so I killed her.'

That's more like it, thought Stratton. Now we're getting somewhere. 'How did you kill her?' he asked.

'I strangled her, see?'

'With what?'

'What…?' Davies looked momentarily confused, then said, 'A rope, wasn't it?'

The way he said this gave Stratton the impression that it was something he'd learnt, or tried to learn, by heart and was now repeating. 'Was it?' he asked.

Davies screwed up his face, as if trying to remember something, and Stratton felt an odd and wholly unexpected twinge of uncertainty.

Davies's eyes half closed, so that his pupils were partly hidden beneath his eyelids, and Stratton had a sudden image of a lift stopped between two floors which, for some reason he was unable to pinpoint, increased his uncertain feeling. For Christ's sake, he told himself, the man's told so many lies that he's probably having trouble remembering the real version of events.

Davies's eyes popped open again, and, as if satisfied by some inner voice of confirmation, he said firmly, 'Yes. A rope.'

'Where did you get the rope?'

Davies stared at him as if this were not a question to which he could reasonably be expected to know the answer. 'I…I don't know. I think I had it off my van.'

'So you brought it in with you?'

'Yes.' He sounded more confident this time, and looked at Stratton expectantly.

Feeling that some sort of encouragement was due, Stratton said, 'Good… You brought it in with the intention of murdering your wife, did you?'

'I…' Davies's tentative smile of acknowledgement changed to a frown. 'No… No!' He was irritated now, his voice a peevish semitone higher. 'It was a row, see? Like I told you.'

'So why did you bring the rope up to your flat?'

'I… Well, I was tidying up, wasn't I? Tidying the van.'

'Tidying the van,' Stratton repeated in tones of disbelief. 'I see. And what did you do then—after you'd strangled her?'

'I took her down to the flat below.' The reply came quickly this time, without any doubt.

'Why?'

'Well… Because it was empty, see? Mr Gardiner was in hospital.'

'Then what?'

'I waited a bit and took her down to the washhouse when Mr and Mrs Backhouse were asleep.'

'And this was when?'

'The start of November.'

'Can you remember the date?' asked Stratton, leafing through his pocket diary.

'No.'

'The seventh?' asked Stratton, remembering Backhouse's words about the workmen. 'That was what you told the police at Merthyr Tydfil.'

'It must have been the seventh, then.'

'Fair enough. What did you do afterwards?'

Davies blinked in bewilderment. Thinking he hadn't understood the question, Stratton clarified it. 'I'm asking what you did after you'd taken the body downstairs.'

'Well, then… Then I went to sleep.'

'And when you woke up?'

'I fed my baby and went to work.'

'When did you strangle the baby?'

'Later. Two days. When I came home from my work I strangled her with my tie. I took her downstairs at night.'

'And you put her in the washhouse?'

'Yes, that's right.'

'Who was looking after the baby when you were at work?'

Davies looked indignant. 'I fed her all right. I done it when I come in.'

'Yes…' Wondering about this—surely any infant left alone and unfed for so long would have bawled its head off?—he said, 'Why did you kill her?'

Davies stared at him for a moment, his face a mask of stupid incomprehension, before tears came into his eyes and, closing them, he lowered his head, shaking it slowly from side to side. When he opened his eyes, his expression was one of utter defeat. His mouth worked for a moment, apparently trying—if his blank look was anything to go by—to frame words independently of his mind. Then he said, in a whisper, 'I don't know,' and, putting his head in his hands, began to sob.

At least, thought Stratton, he's got enough decency left to feel remorse. After a moment he said, 'I think we'll leave it there,' and nodded at Ballard, who finished writing and slid the statement towards him.

'Would you like to read it?' Stratton asked Davies, who looked up, wiping his eyes and nose on his sleeve.

'You read it to me,' he said, sniffing. 'I'm not very educated, see?'

'Very well.' Stratton picked up the paper. *'Muriel was incurring one debt after another and I could not stand it any longer, so I strangled her with a piece of rope...'*

Davies's blank look whilst listening to the statement caused Stratton to wonder how much he'd actually understood of the proceedings, but he concluded that it was because the words were not actually his, and, the language being rather more sophisticated than his own, he may not have understood it all. However, he felt satisfied that it was as good a summary of what Davies had said as any, and Davies seemed to feel the same way because he made no comment but picked up the pen once more and signed his name carefully in the place Ballard had indicated.

'Now,' said Stratton. 'Let's have a cup of tea, shall we? Smoke?' He fished his cigarettes out of his pocket and nudged the packet over to Davies. Ballard went to the door to request tea from the policeman standing outside. Reaching over to give Davies a light, Stratton said, 'That's better, isn't it?'

'Oh, yes.' Davies inhaled greedily. 'It's quite a relief, I can tell you.'

'Something's puzzling me.' Having left Davies in the interview room under the eye of PC Arliss, Stratton and Ballard were finishing their tea in the office.

'What's that, sir?'

'The Backhouses said that Muriel and the baby went away on the seventh of November—to Bristol, as they thought—when the workmen were in the house, didn't they?'

Ballard consulted his notebook. 'Yes, sir. And that Davies left about a week later.'

'Well, if the workmen were using the washhouse for storage, how was it that they didn't notice the bodies?'

'They were behind the floorboards, sir.'

'Nevertheless… And we need to find out when those floorboards were taken up, too.'

'The thing that's bothering me, sir, is the baby. If she was left alone for the best part of two days while Davies was at work, she must have howled a bit, and that's a small house…'

'Yes, I was thinking about that.'

'The Backhouses didn't hear anything—well, they thought she'd gone with the mother, didn't they? So if they had heard a baby crying you'd think they'd have gone to investigate.'

'Unless they thought it was coming from next door. I can't believe the walls are very thick.'

'That's true, sir.'

'Or the baby didn't make any noise. I suppose that's possible.' Ballard—the memory of interrupted nights evidently still fresh in his mind—looked dubious. 'And,' Stratton continued, 'I still can't understand about that bloody dog… Even if it's not allowed into the garden, the workmen must have left doors open, bringing things in and out, so why the hell didn't it start sniffing around?'

'Perhaps it did and nobody noticed, sir. Or Davies got the dates wrong. It was a few weeks ago, and it's hard to remember… And it's obvious he's not too bright.'

'You can say that again. I found myself feeling a bit sorry for the poor little sod, actually.'

Ballard nodded. 'So did I, sir. He seems so…well, harmless.'

'Probably is, when he's not strangling his family. Obviously lived in a bit of a fantasy world, and now it's all coming home to him.'

'He does seem to be having a job disentangling fact from fiction, sir.'

'Yes, I noticed that. And there's something else that's bothering me a bit—the way he didn't seem to know *why* he'd done things. Apart from strangling Muriel because of the row over money, I mean… He was pretty quick to agree with the things we put to him, but that business about the rope, and why he killed the baby… It was as if he genuinely didn't know what to answer.'

'Well, he's got a fair old temper, hasn't he? Even his mother said that. I can't imagine he thinks too much before he acts.'

'Loses his head, you mean. Actually, I don't suppose he thinks much *at all*, apart from making up stories.'

'That's his problem, sir—he's fine when he's making things up, but as to reality…'

'Yes,' said Stratton thoughtfully. 'That makes sense—in as much as anything does.' He read through the statement once more, looking for inconsistencies. 'The timing's the real bugger, with the baby alone for two days, but I'm sure we can sort it out when we interview the witnesses. Still...' he swilled down the rest of his tea and stood up, stretching, 'so far so good, eh? Come on, let's get back downstairs.'

They found Davies sitting quite still, head in hands. Arliss, standing behind him, hastily levered himself away from the wall and adopted what Stratton assumed was supposed to be an expression of observant obsequiousness, which merely succeeded in rendering him even more of an eyesore than usual.

Davies turned to look at him, and Stratton saw that he had been crying. He bent down and put an arm around Davies's thin shoulders. 'It's all right,' he said benevolently. 'You're doing well.'

Davies made noisy gulping sounds, then looked up at Stratton with eyes full of hope. You pathetic, inadequate little bastard, thought Stratton. He'd seen this look before—bloody awkward it was, too, when you were busy putting a noose round a man's neck and he started regarding you as some sort of saviour because you hadn't knocked him about... In his mind's eye, Stratton saw once more the tiny, crinkled-up soles of the baby's feet, heels resting on the cold mortuary slab, so utterly defenceless. The man was as guilty as hell, simple as that. And, Stratton reminded himself, he was doing his job, and if that meant getting murderers to regard him as a guardian angel, then so be it. Abruptly, he took his hand off Davies's shoulders, marched round the table, and took his seat.

'Now, let's start from the beginning.'

Davies wiped his nose with the back of his hand and blurted out, 'The money was the cause of it. I was working driving a van for Murchison's, off the Euston Road. Muriel kept asking for more money, so I borrowed twenty quid from the guv'nor. She had it off me, and I told the guv'nor to take it from my wages. She never told me who she owed the money to, see? Started a row whenever I asked about it. I borrowed off all different people to get more for her, but she never let up... We had a letter from the furniture people about money owing, and Muriel told me she never paid it. I went round there and gave them thirty bob, and then I told her she must pay every week what we owed…'

'That's the hire purchase?'

'Yes. Benfleet's, it is. After I done that I found she was behind with the rent, and that's when I blew up—she was wasting the money going to the pictures all the time, leaving the baby, and saying I never gave her enough. I wasn't going to stand for that.'

'When was this?'

'It was a Sunday. November, I think, early on. I had a row with her and then I went to the pub dinner time, and then the pictures. I come back about seven o'clock. I was listening to the wireless, but Muriel wouldn't stop about the money and the rent, and when we got up next morning she started arguing again. She told me she was going to Brighton with Judy, but she never, she was there when I come home from work. She said something about how she never went there because I'd have a good time while she was gone. I lost my temper and told her if she didn't pack it up I'd slap her face. She picked up a milk bottle—she was going to throw it at me—so I grabbed the bottle off her. I'd had enough of it, so I washed and went off to the pub.'

'Which pub?'

'The Horse and Groom in Great Portland Street. I stopped there till about ten o'clock, I think, and then I come home. Muriel started a row again, so I told her, "I'm going to bed." When I got up in the morning—'

'That was the Tuesday, was it? The seventh?'

'That's right. Well, I got up, and she never took no notice, so I went straight out to work. I come in at about six thirty, and she went at me again about the money, so then I lost my temper and hit her in the face.'

'How did you hit her?'

Davies's face clouded, and the familiar bewildered expression came back for a moment before he said truculently, 'I don't know. I just hit her, didn't I?'

'Did you punch her, or hit her with the flat of your hand?'

'My flat hand. I hit her, and she hit me back so I took this piece of rope I had from my van and strangled her with it.' Davies looked at Stratton expectantly, as if hoping for approval.

'What did you do then?'

Davies's face clouded once again. 'Then?'

'Yes. After you killed her.'

'I told you that,' said Davies irritably. 'Don't have to go into it again, do I?'

'Yes.' Stratton leant forward, arms on the table. 'We need the details.'

'Details?' echoed Davies. 'I just… I put her on the bed.'

'Was the rope still round her neck at that point?'

'I don't know. I think so. I covered her with the eiderdown, see. Then I carried her down the stairs to Mr Gardiner's flat, like I told you.'

'What time was that?'

'Half past ten, I think. Well, about that time.'

'And then?'

'I came back upstairs. Had to feed the baby, see? Then I put her to bed.'

'And?'

'Well, I had to wait, see? Till it was quiet. I sat in the kitchen and had a fag. I was waiting… Then I took her downstairs to the washhouse.'

'How?'

'I just told you,' said Davies impatiently. 'I took her downstairs, through the back door, and into the garden. I carried her.'

'You wrapped up the body first.'

'Wrapped it?'

'In a tablecloth, Mr Davies.'

Davies blinked and passed a hand across his face. 'Yes…'

'Was it your tablecloth?'

'I don't know.'

'Was it the one you saw in the Charge Room?'

'It must have been… I took her downstairs when it was quiet.'

'And you concealed her behind the boards in the washhouse?'

'Yes. Concealed her.'

'Under the sink?'

'Yes.'

Stratton and Ballard exchanged glances. Davies was tiring visibly, and his defeated air made Stratton feel that if he suggested that the man had put his wife's body in a hot air balloon, he'd agree to it in order to get them off his back. It wasn't unusual, and they'd both seen it before, many times. 'What did you do then?' he asked.

The strain of extreme effort on his face, Davies said, 'I locked the door.'

'Of the washhouse?'

'Yes, the washhouse. Then I went back upstairs. My baby was asleep then, so I went and laid on the bed until it was time to go to work. I made a feed of milk and cereal for Judy in the morning and gave it to her, then I changed her, and I went out to work. She was asleep when I come back. That was half past five.'

'So Judy was alone all day?'

'Yes. I fed her when I come in, and changed her. Then I sat with her in the kitchen. I had a cup of tea and a smoke. I made her another feed before I put her to bed, then I sat by the fire till I gone to bed. I don't know what time... Midnight, I think it was. I got up at six—'

'This was on Thursday?'

'Yes, it must have been. Thursday. I fed the baby and changed her and put her clothes on, then I had a cup of tea and went to work.'

'So the baby was on her own?'

'I didn't like it,' said Davies defensively, 'but I had to, see? I wrapped her up,' he added. 'I put her back in her cot.'

'And then?'

'I done my day's work, then I asked the guv'nor for money on my wages. He said what did I want it for, and I said to send to Muriel, so he asked me where she was and I said she'd gone to Bristol with the baby. He paid me the money but then he said he'd had enough of it—'

'Enough of what?'

'Me asking for money, he said. I was always asking before I done the work. He said I could come back tomorrow for my cards. I went home then. I didn't know what to do, see?'

Davies's face was creased, as if in pain, and Stratton could imagine the turmoil in his dull mind—caught like a rat in a trap, panicked and scrabbling for a way out—which had led to what surely must have been his next action. 'Was that when you strangled the baby?' he asked.

Davies blinked rapidly, holding back tears. 'Yes. With my tie. She was in the cot, so I left her there and I went into the kitchen. I made a cup of tea. I was waiting, like before. I took her downstairs later and put her in the washhouse.'

'What time was that?'

Davies looked at him with wet eyes. 'I don't know. It was later. Mr and Mrs Backhouse was asleep. I come back upstairs and lay down on my bed. Then I went to see a man to sell the furniture.'

'This was the next morning?'

'Yes, next morning. He come to my flat later and offered me forty quid for the lot.'

'What was his name?'

'Mr Lorrimer. Got a shop in Ingersoll Road, see? He asked me why did I want to sell it, and I told him I was going to Bristol. I said I had a job up there. He said the driver would come for it on Monday. They took all the furniture and lino, and he paid me for it then, and I put my things in my suitcase and went to Paddington for the train.'

'To Wales?'

Davies nodded. 'I went to Cardiff, then I found a lift to Merthyr Vale.'

'To your aunt?'

'Yes...' Davies slumped still further, pathetic and vanquished, his face, drained of colour, given a greenish cast by the harsh light of the naked bulb. 'Now you know all what happened,' he muttered.

At home in Tottenham, Stratton sat in his favourite armchair, slippers on his feet and the *Daily Express* in his lap and wished he didn't feel so tired. Not that he particularly wanted to read about the possible suspension of Marshall Aid to Europe, but he felt he had barely enough energy to drink his tea or have a smoke. Glancing at the cup and the ashtray on the small table beside him, he was reminded of Davies's litany of domesticity punctuated by violence—wife- and child-killing with breaks in between for tea and fags. Honestly, the whole thing was like a gruesome real-life rendition of a Punch and Judy show. 'That's the way to do it,' he murmured, opening his paper and shaking it into position in an attempt to convince himself that he did have the desire to read the bloody thing, otherwise why buy it in the first place?

'What's that, Dad?' Stratton looked over the paper to see Monica standing in the doorway and was struck, as he often was when he saw his daughter, by how attractive she was. It wasn't only her face and figure that made her lovely, he thought, but her animation and the way she presented herself. Now, she was carrying a slice of Victoria sponge on a plate. 'One of the girls brought a cake to the studio—it was her birthday—and I saved my piece for you.'

Stratton, touched beyond measure as he always was by her small acts of kindness—so like Jenny—said, 'Don't be silly. It's yours.'

'No, really…' Monica deposited the plate on the little table and flopped down on the sofa.

'Well, at least have half.'

'All right, then. You first.'

'Had a nice day?'

'Mmm… Busy. I spent most of it painting scratches.'

'Scratches? Don't they have a Works department for that sort of thing?'

Monica rolled her eyes in mock exasperation. 'No, Dad. It was a scene—two girls having a scrap. Hair-pulling, fingernails…a real cat-fight. One of them kept getting it wrong, so they had to do it again. Everyone says she's the producer's mistress and that's the only reason she's in it. I shouldn't be surprised if it's true, because she's rotten.' Before Stratton could register dismay that was only partly comical at such worldly sentiments so calmly uttered by his innocent child, Monica added, 'I did my first bruise, too. It was a jolly good one, if I do say so myself. Just here.' She tapped her left cheekbone.

'Pleased with it, were they?'

'Not half! Aren't you going to eat your cake?'

'All right, then.' Stratton picked up the plate. 'Bossyboots.'

'I'm not!'

'I know. I only said it to make you indignant.'

'I'm not indignant!'

'Yes, you are,' said Stratton.

'Ooh…' Monica pursed her lips and picked up a magazine from the sofa.

'Jolly good, this,' said Stratton, through a mouthful of cake. 'What's for supper?'

'Rabbit stew. At least, I think that's what it is. Auntie Lilian left it.'

'Ah.' Stratton raised his eyebrows. Lilian's cooking wasn't a patch on Doris's, but as her offerings were not only kindly meant but essential, he never complained. On the whole, he was grateful for the way in which his two sisters-in-law had taken over the domestic arrangements. His home might be shabby (wasn't everybody's, nowadays?), but, largely thanks to Lilian and Doris, it was comfortable and clean. Less appreciated were their efforts, in the past couple of years, to find him a wife. These had, so far, resulted in the unwanted attentions of a droopy but persistent widow, a fading but excruciatingly girlish spinster, and an ugly woman with a sniff whose husband, still listed as missing in action, had, in Stratton's view, simply buggered off sharpish while he had the chance. Worse than all these, however, were the advances of another local widow, mercifully unencouraged by either Doris or Lilian on the grounds that they found her common. Over-rouged, with hands like grappling hooks, she had taken the opportunity, at a party the previous Christmas, of manoeuvring him beneath a bunch of mistletoe and, to his appalled amazement, making a grab for his scrotum, causing him to jump backwards and upset a tray of tea. The memory of it still made his toes curl, and he had avoided her ever since.

He could see that Doris and Lilian meant well—and that having him off their hands would make their lives a lot easier—but he wished they wouldn't bother. He didn't want to get married again. The pricks of anger and resentment at the sight of other couples that he'd felt for several months after Jenny's death had given way to a numbness which still remained deep within him, so that it was impossible to contemplate that sort of intimacy with anyone else. He supposed that Doris might have a point when she said it was because he hadn't met the right person, but he wasn't at all sure whether there would ever be another 'right person' or even if he *wanted* there to be one.

'Dad?'

'Mmm? Oh… Sorry, love.' Stratton held out the remains of the cake, but Monica shook her head.

'Not that. I asked if you'd had a good day at work.'

'Oh. You know. Tiring.'

'It's just that I thought you must be doing something important because you didn't come back last night.'

'Too much to do...' Stratton hesitated, then said, 'New case. Chap killed his wife and child.'

'Oh, *Dad*!' Monica looked stricken. 'How horrible for you.' She put the magazine aside and stood up. 'It seems so...unfair... your having to do something like that.'

'It's the job, love.'

'I know, but...' Stratton knew what Monica was trying to say but was glad she seemed unable to articulate it. Instead, she looked at his now empty cup and said, 'Can I get you anything? More tea?'

'I'm fine. I suppose you might put the supper on...'

'All right.' Monica stood looking down at him, obviously trying to think of something to cheer him up. 'I think there might be some cocoa left. We could have it afterwards, if you like. And,' she added, 'why don't you finish the cake? Silly for me to have it—there's only a mouthful.'

Washing up after supper, Monica paid particular attention to her favourite plate, which was an old one, decorated in blue willow pattern. It wasn't just that she liked the colour and design, but she also thought of it as being friendly, somehow, unlike the cracked yellow one, which was definitely unfriendly—spiteful, almost. One of these days, she supposed, they'd be able to get some new china, and then everything would match and washing up wouldn't be the same at all. From childhood, she'd thought of everything in the house, from the largest items of furniture down to teaspoons and table mats, as having particular characters. It was a feeling—and not the only one, either—that, she strongly suspected, had persisted long after she ought to have grown out of it. If I were to tell anyone about these things, she thought, they'd say I was mad.

Having finished the drying up, she thought she ought to look in on Dad in the sitting room, just to see if he wanted anything, but he was fast asleep with the newspaper in his lap. He was obviously exhausted. Whatever he'd said about it just being his job, she still thought it was pretty unfair of them to give him a case where a man had killed his wife, after what had happened to Mum. It might have been five years ago, but all the same... She stood looking down at him for a moment, the sensation of fierce protectiveness welling inside her chest as it always did at such times, before going upstairs to her bedroom. A girl at the studio had lent her some fashion magazines to read—well, not read, exactly, because several of them were French, but look at—and she'd spent most of the day in happy expectation of a couple of hours by herself, immersed in a world of glamour and sophistication and colour. Not that there wasn't plenty of that at work—she still couldn't believe her luck in getting the job—but it certainly wasn't much in evidence elsewhere...

Flopping down on her bed, she opened the first magazine and began working her way through pages of long-necked beauties with perfectly arched eyebrows, high cheekbones, and expressions of serenely haughty composure, clad in gorgeous creations that, despite the ending of clothes rationing, you still couldn't buy in the shops even if you did have the money. Stroking the swathes of shining material that gleamed from the pages like soft jewels, she imagined the texture of the cloth beneath her fingertips. Her fingers moved, seemingly of their own accord, from a gorgeous drape of satin to the model's upper arm, and she found herself imagining how that might feel were she to be touching it. It was quite impossible, of course, that she could ever find herself, in real life, stroking the skin of such a loftily beautiful woman, but all the same...

Her hand strayed to her own breast, and she stared down at the photograph and then closed her eyes, imagining that the woman was touching her—and then the sound of a passing car recalled her, abruptly, to the present. She jumped, suddenly on fire with shame, and slapped the magazine shut. What was *wrong* with her? Other people didn't have thoughts like that. She stared down at the magazine's front cover where the model, chin raised, looked disdainfully away from her, as if in reproach. Whatever this feeling was, and its exact nature wasn't something she could bear to dwell on in any specific detail, she knew for certain that it wasn't—couldn't possibly be—shared by anyone else, anywhere. Perhaps she really *was* mad. All the girls she knew talked about boys and got soppy over the male film stars.

Her cousin Madeleine was always asking about the actors, what they were like and if they ever talked to her. She knew that Madeleine was disappointed by the lack of information and shared confidences, but, no matter how hard she tried, Monica could never think of anything interesting to say on the subject.

She used to think that her problem, like the silly business of believing that plates and cups had personalities, was to do with being young, and that, when she grew up, things would be straightforward. But she was grown up, wasn't she? She was twenty, with a proper job and everything, and the whole business of feelings seemed to be more complicated than ever.

She'd had boyfriends, for heaven's sake—well, one boyfriend anyway, last year. And it wasn't as if boys never asked her to come out with them, because they did, and fairly often. She didn't particularly mind the things they tried to do, all the kissing and stuff—the thing was that she didn't *feel* anything while they were doing it. It wasn't horrible or frightening or anything like that, it just wasn't... well, it wasn't anything at all, really. Other girls, judging from their conversation, seemed actually to like it—or they said they did. She'd tried to persuade herself that she enjoyed it, too, but she didn't. Not unless she was thinking of something else, anyway. Once or twice with Leonard she'd got quite passionate, but that was because she was imagining he was Lucy, the farmer's daughter she'd been friendly with when she was evacuated in Suffolk. When he'd put his hand on her breast she'd imagined it was Lucy's hand and things had got quite interesting for a bit, until Leonard had started talking to her and she couldn't pretend any more.

Taking the magazines off the bed so that they wouldn't get creased, she lay down on her back with her hands behind her head and stared up at the damp patch—also friendly, because it was crescent-shaped, like a smile—on the ceiling. Her future, in so far as she imagined it, had always involved—ideally—sharing a flat with another girl. And carrying on working at the studio, of course, either in Make-up or designing frocks—or perhaps even making special props, assuming they let women do that. It would be lovely if she could share a flat with Lucy, or someone like her… She'd liked being with Lucy so much—well, that was normal, because everyone enjoyed being with their friends, otherwise they wouldn't *be* friends with them in the first place—but the peculiar hot feeling she'd had inside, the sort of pleasant mild ache that she'd thought, aged fifteen, must be the effect of too much sun, was, in retrospect, disturbing. It wasn't until Madeleine had mentioned something similar, in connection with a boyfriend, that she'd realised that it was actually *bad*. Not bad like, say, Hitler, or even bad like her cousin Johnny, who'd stolen things and got involved with the wrong sort of people, but definitely wrong and not normal at all. At work, surrounded by half-dressed actresses in Make-up, so casual about their nakedness, she kept her eyes averted for fear that one of them might spot her staring. And supposing she were to betray, somehow, what was going through her mind, nobody would ever speak to her again and she would lose her job… She might even end up in a mental asylum.

Even thinking about it like this was dangerous; it made her feel all morbid and just…not *right*. She'd put the whole thing out of her mind, and she wouldn't look at the magazines any more. She sat up, swung her legs over the side of the bed and looked at her watch: twenty to ten. She'd promised Dad some cocoa, hadn't she?

But she must do something else first—something ordinary, to put a barrier between her thoughts and going downstairs. If ever Dad, the person she loved and admired more than anyone else in the world, got to know about her problem… No, it was unthinkable. She'd rather be dead.

She must pretend to be normal, even if she wasn't. Perhaps, if she pretended for long enough, the strange feelings would go away, like the constant and terrible grief she'd felt when her mother had died. No one need ever know she'd been 'different'. Glancing round her room, she spotted an old jigsaw. That would do. Grabbing the box, she upended the pieces onto the rug and, kneeling down, began feverishly assembling the picture of a fallow deer in a woodland clearing.

The following morning, Stratton spent half an hour with Lamb, who, having been away from the station the previous day, needed to be put in the picture before Davies was taken to the magistrates' court at Marlborough Street. 'This is more like it,' said the DCI, when Stratton had taken him through Davies's statements. He wasn't quite rubbing his hands together, but Stratton thought he wasn't far off it. 'The thing's open and shut. Get your case straight, and for God's sake try not to complicate matters in your usual fashion, and we'll be home and dry. Bring Mr and Mrs Backhouse in here as soon as you can. I'll ask Grove and Porter to help you with interviews to speed things up. I must say, this man Davies sounds a thoroughly nasty piece of work.'

'As a matter of fact, sir,' said Stratton, 'I thought he was rather pathetic.'

'Yes, well...as long as you don't let him fool you. Unusual for you, Stratton,'—here, Lamb gave a disconcertingly roguish leer—'it's generally the women who pull the wool over your eyes, isn't it?' Stratton tried not to wince as one side of his superior's face screwed itself up in a wink. 'I know you've always been rather susceptible to the ladies...' This patronising attempt to be chummy, never before seen, was far worse than Lamb's normally irritable demeanour. Stratton managed to excuse himself before any more gruesome bonhomie came his way and, once in the corridor, shook himself like a dog after a swim to rid himself of what felt like an all-over coating of embarrassment before returning to his office.

Sitting beside Stratton in the back of the car en route to the magistrates' court, Davies looked smaller than ever. Silent and hunched inside his overcoat, he stared straight ahead for most of the short journey and then, just as the car rounded the corner into Marlborough Street, he turned to Stratton and said, urgently, 'There's something I forgot to tell you.'

Automatically, Stratton began to caution him, but Davies, plucking at his sleeve, cut him off: 'No, I meant to tell you before, and I want to get it off my chest. I took Muriel's wedding ring and I sold it.'

Staring into his eyes, Stratton saw the same hope of approval one might see on the face of a child and, to his surprise, felt pity for the inadequate little man. He said encouragingly, 'It's good that you told me. Was that after you killed her?'

Davies blinked at him for a moment, then nodded. 'After. I got six shillings for it from a jeweller in Merthyr Tydfil.'

'Do you remember the name?'

'No.' Davies looked crestfallen. 'It was some shop… I feel bad about it, Mr Stratton. I shouldn't have taken it off her.'

The car stopped and the driver walked round to open the back door nearest the kerb. They scrambled out, Stratton first and Davies, handcuffed to him, close behind. 'Here we are,' said Stratton.

Davies looked up at him. 'Are you going to stay with me?'

'For the time being,' said Stratton. Seeing some flecks of dandruff on Davies's shoulders, he batted them away with his free hand. 'Come on. It's just a few questions this morning.'

'Questions? But I've told you—'

'Nothing like that. Just your name and occ—your job. That sort of thing. Just remember to speak up when you're asked.'

Davies looked at him again, the boy eager to please. 'Yes,' he said. 'Thank you, Mr Stratton.'

The hearing was over in minutes. Davies was remanded, given a legal-aid certificate, then led away to be taken to Pentonville. The last glimpse of him Stratton had was a strained white face, as Davies twisted round to look back at him between the solid, dark-blue shoulders of two burly policemen. Whatever Lamb said, he thought, 'pathetic' was the right word for Davies. He'd dealt with people of low intelligence before—plenty of them, including a couple of murderers—but he'd rarely felt moved by them and certainly not by anyone who'd killed a child. Davies obviously hadn't understood the consequences of his actions. How anyone could think that if you strangled a baby it might still live was beyond him, and yet Davies's remarks to Grove on the journey from Wales showed that it was exactly what he *had* thought. What a sad little family, Stratton thought, and trudged back to West End Central to continue the process of putting a noose around Davies's neck.

CHAPTER 18

Sergeant Ballard and Mr Backhouse were waiting for Stratton in the lobby, Backhouse standing up very straight and staring about him with an air of self-important concern. 'Of course we came at once, Mr Stratton,' he said. 'We want to help in any way we can. Edna—Mrs Backhouse—well, she can't sleep with the worry of it.'

'Where is she?' asked Stratton.

'In the interview room with DI Grove and DS Porter,' said Ballard, drawing him aside. 'They've taken her to identify the clothes, sir. We thought it made more sense—women tend to notice more what other women wear.'

'We'll need to ask Backhouse about the tie, though. Davies said it was his, but we ought to make sure. Right, then,' Stratton turned to Backhouse. 'Let's go through to my office, shall we?'

'You've been most helpful already, Mr Backhouse,' said Stratton as they pulled up chairs around his desk. Backhouse glanced about him with, Stratton thought, some satisfaction, clearly pleased to be taken to Stratton's own office and not some anonymous interview room. He'd seemed thoroughly at home as they'd walked down the corridor, joking that, despite the circumstances, it was nice to be 'back in the old place'. 'Well,' he said, 'anything I can do to help you with this…' he pursed his lips prissily as he deliberated over his choice of word, '*regrettable* matter.'

Stratton thought that, as understatements went, 'regrettable' was masterly, and wondered why he couldn't feel any kinship with the man, even though he was a former special. 'Now,' he said, 'you've given us quite a bit of information already, but we need to make sure of the specific details. When was the last time you saw Muriel and Judy Davies?'

The answer came fluently, with no hesitation. 'I saw Muriel on the Tuesday—that would be the seventh—she was going out to empty some slops. The last time I saw the baby was Monday.'

'The day before?'

'That's correct,' he said, smartly. Then, wetting his lips with the tip of his tongue and making the strange sideways sucking motion with his mouth, he continued, 'I did remember, after we spoke before, that Edna and I heard some odd noises on the Tuesday night.'

'What time was this?'

'Around midnight, I should think. There was a bump that woke us up. I did wonder if it wasn't the Davieses arguing again, and I thought I might go upstairs—I've had to do that before, on a number of occasions, to ask them to keep the noise down, for the neighbours—but my wife said she thought it sounded like someone moving furniture.'

'And that was definitely the night of the seventh?'

'Oh, yes. I remember that because I'd been to the doctor, and I always go on a Tuesday. For my fibrositis. I've had to take rather a lot of time off work recently. I'm afraid to say I've been rather troubled by diarrhoea, as well…' Here Stratton, trying not to grimace at the mental picture this created, stole a glance at Ballard, but his head was firmly down and he was writing busily with the air of one giving total attention to his work. 'The doctor had given me a compound,' Backhouse continued, 'which I took so as not to have to get up during the night and wake Edna.'

'Of course,' said Stratton, hastily. 'What is your occupation, Mr Backhouse?'

'Ledger clerk. For the British Road Services.' This was said more quietly than before, and Stratton had to strain to hear it. The whispering and the finicky precision of the voice were beginning to get on his nerves.

'Would you mind speaking up a bit, Mr Backhouse?'

Again, the tongue moistened the lips. After more sucking and swallowing, Backhouse said, 'I'm sorry. I have a quiet voice. It's from being gassed during the war. It affected the larynx.' He put his hand up and fiddled with the knot of his tie as if to illustrate this.

'The last war?' asked Stratton, incredulously.

'In nineteen seventeen. I lost my voice entirely for a couple of years, and I'm afraid it still affects me from time to time.'

'That's a pity,' said Stratton, sorry for the man but not liking him any more than before. 'Did you see Davies on the seventh?'

'That was when he told us that Muriel had taken the baby to Bristol for a holiday. It was about seven o'clock, I think.'

'In the evening?'

'That's right. He said he was going down later to visit them.'

'And when did Davies leave?'

'On the thirteenth, after the van came for the furniture. We'd seen him on the Thursday, too, the ninth, in the evening, and he told me he'd left his job. "Packed it in," he said. He told me he'd asked for his cards back, and he was going to see about a job in Bristol. I saw him again on Friday the tenth—I remember telling him to be careful because of the flooring being up in the hall.'

'That's what the workmen were doing? Replacing the boards?'

'Yes. Some of them were quite rotten. They did some repairs in the washhouse, too, and the toilet.'

'So they would have had no reason to go upstairs?'

'Oh, no. There was nothing to do up there.'

'Did Davies say anything else to you on the Friday?'

'Yes, he told me he was selling his furniture. He said he wouldn't be able to take it with him to Bristol.'

'Did you see him again before he left?'

'On the Monday,' said Backhouse promptly. 'He said that the man had given him sixty pounds for the furniture. He had a suitcase with him, and he said he was going to Bristol.'

Interesting, thought Stratton, that Davies had told him he'd got forty pounds for the furniture. He was obviously unable to resist telling lies, even about something as pointless as that. 'Did you see Davies after that?' he asked.

'Yes, I did.' Backhouse's voice had descended once more to a whisper. 'Nine or ten days after, I think. He said that Muriel had left him and taken the baby, and he couldn't find a job. He said he'd been travelling about a lot and he'd just come from Wales. I told him he should go back there and try and get himself some work. When I said he should find a place to stay and use the sixty pounds from the furniture to tide him over he told me he'd spent most of it.'

'Did he say how?'

'Travelling, he said. I took it to mean that he'd been going to public houses, and visiting...' Backhouse fingered his tie again, ran his tongue round his mouth and added, in an even quieter voice, so that Stratton had almost to read his moist lips, '*prostitutes*.' He shook his head with an air of pious disgust.

'Did he tell you that?' asked Stratton.

Backhouse screwed his mouth to the side once more and said, 'Not exactly, but it was of a piece with his previous behaviour. I told him he was being foolish, and he left soon after. I did wonder if he'd gone to see Shirley Morgan. That's the friend of Muriel's I told you about. She lives nearby.'

'That's not very likely, is it, if he'd threatened to...what was it you said? "Run her over in his van"?'

'Well...she did come back to the house, you see. On the Monday, I think.'

'Which Monday?'

'The sixth. I told her to clear off, because it would only upset Muriel, and there'd been quite enough rowing as it was. My wife and I live very quietly, Inspector. My health is poor, and Edna suffers with her nerves. We didn't like all the upset.'

'So she didn't see Muriel?'

'Not as far as I know. She'd been up and knocked on the door, and I heard her calling out, but Muriel evidently wasn't answering.'

'Was Muriel there at the time?'

'I don't know. I think so.'

'Did you hear the baby at all during that week?'

'Not that I can remember. Edna used to listen for her, if Muriel was going out, but we thought they were in Bristol.'

'But you didn't know that then, did you? You said the last time you'd seen Muriel and the baby was on the seventh and that Davies told you a few days later that they'd gone away.'

'Yes...' Backhouse dropped his voice again. 'That's right. But we didn't hear anything, so we thought all was well and Muriel was up there with her.'

'So—and I apologise for asking this again, Mr Backhouse, but we need to include it in your statement—you did not, at any time, tell Davies that you could help his wife to get rid of a baby?'

Backhouse blinked and licked his lips. 'No, I did not.'

'Davies said you'd showed him a medical book and said you could help his wife abort her pregnancy.'

'That's nonsense,' said Backhouse firmly. 'He's making it up.'

'Did you ever tell Davies you'd trained as a doctor?'

'Certainly not. It's not true.'

'Did you show him a medical book?'

'No, Inspector, I did not. As I told you, the only medical book I have is a St John's Ambulance manual.' Backhouse shifted in his chair. 'Would you mind if I stood up for a moment? If I sit too long, it's a strain on my back.'

'Of course,' said Stratton. 'Please...'

Grimacing, and with great care, Backhouse stood up slowly and rubbed the small of his back. 'I suppose that Muriel might have spotted the book and told him about it… I really don't know, Inspector, but that's all nonsense.'

'He told the police in Wales that you helped him to carry the body.'

'Inspector…' Backhouse rubbed his back once more, 'that is ridiculous. My fibrositis has been so bad that I have to get on my hands and knees to pick something up from the floor. I certainly couldn't lift anyone.' He shook his head slowly. 'I don't understand why John is saying these things about me.'

'It must be upsetting for you,' said Stratton. 'Did you visit the washhouse during the week of the sixth of November?'

Backhouse blinked for a moment, then shook his head. 'I don't believe so. I wasn't at all well…'

'But you would have visited the washhouse at some time in the following week?'

'Oh, yes. I remember that, because I went to get some wood to light the fire, and I noticed the timber stacked in front of the sink. That was on the Monday—the thirteenth.'

'What time was that? Do you remember?'

'Early in the day. About half past seven in the morning, I think.'

'I see. And did you notice your dog paying particular attention to the washhouse at any time? Nosing around, scrabbling at the door, anything like that?'

'No, nothing like that. But then, Inspector, I was in bed a lot of the time, because of my back.'

'I see. Just one more thing, Mr Backhouse, and then you're free to go. Sergeant Ballard, would you mind fetching the exhibit?'

Ballard was back in under a minute, bearing a tray on which lay the tie that had been found around the baby's neck. Twisted, it looked like a flat red-and-black-striped snake. All three men eyed it as if it might begin to writhe at any moment.

'Do you recognise this?' asked Stratton.

Backhouse's tongue popped out once more to moisten his lips, which it did with a slow turgidity that repulsed Stratton who noticed, out of the corner of his eye, that Ballard had averted his face from the man.

'That isn't mine,' said Backhouse, finally.

'Do you know who it belongs to?'

Backhouse cleared his throat. 'I'm not certain, but I think I've seen John wearing a tie very like that one.'

'Fair enough.' Stratton stood up. 'Thank you, Mr Backhouse. You've been most helpful.'

'I'm sure he means well,' Stratton said to Ballard when he'd returned from seeing Backhouse out, 'and he *is* very helpful, but he makes my flesh crawl.'

'Me too, sir. DI Grove says he'll be along in a minute. They've finished—Mrs Backhouse was waiting in the lobby.'

'Right. Whatever we think of Backhouse, it looks like an open and shut case.'

'That'll please DCI Lamb, sir.'

'Let's hope so.' Stratton rolled his eyes, then sprang up to open the door as a heavy tread, which could belong to nobody except DI Grove, echoed in the corridor. Grove paused on the threshold, chewing his empty pipe thoughtfully.

'Mrs Backhouse identified Muriel Davies's clothes,' he said, plonking himself heavily on the nearest chair. 'She recognised the baby's cardigan, too, and the little frock. Nice woman—very distressed about the kid. Said that although they'd never been blessed, she'd looked after little Judy a lot and thought of her as almost like her own.' Clamping his teeth angrily round the pipe and grimacing so that they showed up to the roots, he added, 'When I think of what that bastard did...' Leaning forward for emphasis, he chomped the pipe into the corner of his mouth and continued, 'My girl came round to see us last night, with my little granddaughter. God, I'd like to get hold of that murdering little shit for five minutes...'

Grove was a kindly man who, despite years in the police force, rarely said a sharp thing about anyone, but now his rage seemed to reverberate around the walls of the little room, unchecked and raw. Stratton saw his own anger and incomprehension reflected in Grove's eyes and saw, also, from Ballard's face, that he felt exactly the same way.

Grove cleared his throat and opened his notebook. 'Mrs Backhouse said she saw Judy on Monday the sixth—looked after her when Muriel went out. That was the last day she saw either of them. Shirley Morgan came to the house on the same day. Backhouse told her to clear off, apparently. And...she said they've got a medical book—St John's Ambulance—but when I asked her about Backhouse training to be a doctor, she said Davies was making it up.'

'He seems to have done a lot of that,' said Stratton.

Grove nodded, chewing his pipe. 'Said she knew Mrs Davies was pregnant but that she and her husband were moral people and wouldn't help anyone to get rid of a baby... Seemed quite genuine. Said they didn't know of any childless couple who wanted a baby in Euston or anywhere else... She saw Davies on the seventh, in the evening, and he told her that Muriel and the baby had gone to Bristol. Said she was surprised because Muriel hadn't said anything about it to her. Davies told her that Muriel hadn't told his mother, either... Also said she heard a bump in the night of Tuesday the seventh of November. Sounded like furniture being moved about. She saw Davies at about quarter to seven on the evening of the ninth when he came downstairs and told Backhouse he'd given up his job... Then she saw him a few times on the Friday when he came in and out, because he wasn't working then... Didn't see him at all after that. She said she'd been in and out of the washhouse since the seventh of November, as usual, getting water to rinse the slop-pail... There were some bits of wood in there, stacked in front of the sink...'

Stratton nodded. 'That tallies with what Davies said about concealing the body. Backhouse said he'd noticed planks stacked in front of the sink on the thirteenth—the same ones, presumably.'

'She said she didn't notice anything out of the ordinary,' Grove continued. 'No smell or anything out of place. There's not much more, really...they were married in nineteen twenty, in May...they've lived in Paradise Street since thirty-eight...came to London in twenty-three...Halifax before that...she was away for a while during the war, stopping with relatives in Sheffield, and came back in forty-four...never had any trouble...'

'A model citizen, in fact,' said Stratton. 'I mean, you've seen the man. Anyway, the accounts seem to fit, so it's just the workmen and the tradesmen and the Morgan woman and then we're home and dry.'

'So,' said Stratton, when Grove had gone, 'we'll need to see the men from the building firm. The name's in Backhouse's statement somewhere, isn't it?'

Ballard scanned the document. 'Kendall's, sir. Premises in Drummond Street, off the Hampstead Road. There's Mr Kendall, and the plasterer's name's Walker, according to this, and the chippie—if you can believe it—is called Carpenter.'

'Sounds like Happy Families,' said Stratton, scribbling in his notebook.

Ballard grimaced. 'We wouldn't be doing this if it were, sir.'

'Quite,' said Stratton, hastily. 'Take PC Canning and round them up, tell them exactly why we want them, and don't take no for an answer. Get hold of the time sheets for the job while you're at it. Then we've got the bloke from the hire-purchase place, Benfleet's, and the chap who bought the furniture...'

'Lorrimer, sir,' said Ballard. 'They're both on the telephone. I have the numbers here.'

'Good...and there's Davies's boss at Murchison's van company and that woman Backhouse was talking about—Muriel Davies's friend.'

'Shirley Morgan.' Ballard found the relevant page in the statement. 'Says here "she lives nearby".'

'I'll do that. Shouldn't be too hard to find out where she is. And I'd better get someone to speak to the owner of that briefcase, too, although I can't imagine he's got anything to do with it.'

'That's a Mr Parker. Address in Everton Buildings. I think that's somewhere off the Hampstead Road, too, sir.'

'In that case, maybe you can kill two birds with one stone. Canning can escort Kendall's lot back here, and you see if you can get Parker to come and identify the thing. And,' he added, getting heavily to his feet, 'while you're doing that, I'll go and tell DCI Lamb what we've been up to.'

Twenty minutes later, Stratton unlaced his shoes and spent several minutes rubbing his feet violently against each other to ease his itchy chilblains—Lamb ('for God's sake make sure it's watertight') seemed to have had a bad effect on them. Somewhat relieved, he lit a cigarette and picked up the telephone. In short order, he spoke to Mr Benfleet from the hire-purchase outfit and to the furniture dealer, Lorrimer, requesting their presence at the station, then ascertained Shirley Morgan's address and packed an unwilling Arliss off to fetch her. He'd just spoken to Davies's former employer, Murchison, when PC Canning put his head round the door and summoned him to the lobby, where he found Kendall, Walker, and the carpenter called Carpenter sitting in a depressed-looking row.

Stratton and PC Canning started with Kendall, a lugubrious man with a soggy roll-up glued to his lower lip. 'I don't like this,' he said, unhappily. 'Don't like it at all. It's nothing to do with any of my men. Been working for me for years, they have, and we've never had nothing like it.'

'I'm sure you haven't,' said Stratton. 'But we need to clarify a few things. When did you begin the work at Paradise Street?'

'We started the job on the Tuesday—that was the seventh of November. We'd have gone in on the Monday'—here, the fag drooped disconsolately—'but the weather was bad. I give your bobby'—Kendall nodded righteously at Canning—'the time sheets for Walker—'

'That's the plasterer?'

'That's right. There's time sheets for Walker and Carpenter there.'

PC Canning produced a sheaf of time sheets from his tunic, and Stratton peered at the scrawl, trying to make sense of it. 'It says here…' he indicated Walker's first sheet, dated 7 November, ' "taking material to job"…and he was working there until Friday the tenth. Where would this material have been stored?'

'In the washhouse. Same as Carpenter, for his tools, only he come later.'

This, thought Stratton, was going to be more difficult than he'd imagined—Davies had told them he'd put Muriel's body in the washhouse on the night of the seventh, and there was the Backhouses' description of the noises in the night… 'So Walker would have been in and out of the washhouse from Tuesday until Friday?'

'Yes. Well, he had to, see?'

'You're absolutely sure about this, are you?'

'Well,' said Kendall, with exaggerated reasonableness, 'he would, wouldn't he, if that's where he was storing things? Mind you, I wasn't there so much, only in the beginning and when we cleared out the tools and that on the Friday.'

'And you didn't notice anything unusual about the washhouse during that time?'

'Can't say I did.' Kendall scratched his chin with a thumb and forefinger stained cinnamon by nicotine. 'And I don't reckon Walker did neither, or he'd have told me.'

'Did you see any wood in there—planks?'

Kendall shifted the limp dog-end ruminatively from side to side. 'Can't say I did.'

Stratton sighed. 'I see. Did you see this woman at any time?' He pushed the photograph of Muriel Davies across the table.

'Is that the girl who was killed?'

'Yes.'

'Poor lass.' He shook his head. 'Nice-looking, too… I didn't see her. I'd remember if I had.'

'Fair enough,' said Stratton. 'Now, let's look at Carpenter's time sheets, shall we?' As Stratton read the scribbled notes his heart sank: Lamb wasn't going to like this one little bit. 'They say Carpenter pulled up the rotten joists and flooring in the ground-floor passage on the Thursday afternoon and the Friday and laid new flooring on the Saturday. He fitted the new skirting on Monday the thirteenth, and then he'd finished the job, had he?'

'That's right.'

'So you're saying there wouldn't have been any timber stacked in the washhouse until Friday the tenth?'

'No. There wasn't nothing to put there, was there?'

'What about the stuff taken up on the Thursday?'

'Well, he had to loosen it first, see, so he'd have done that then… Even if he'd started taking it up, I doubt there'd have been much to move.'

'What about the new flooring?'

'I picked that up myself, on the Friday, and he collected it on the Saturday, before he started.'

'Mr Kendall,' said Stratton, 'as I'm sure you understand, it's very important that we get a clear picture of what happened.' Here, he looked hard at Kendall, who waggled the remains of his roll-up solemnly in response. 'These time sheets,' Stratton indicated the grubby pages, 'would you say that they give an accurate picture of what happened and when?'

'Well…' Kendall pinched the fag end out of his mouth, and gave a deep sigh. 'It was a contract job, see, so what's on the sheets is a bit… Well, put it this way, what it is, I have to make sure that the work's done in the time allowed.'

'So you wouldn't check them?'

'I'd have a look, but unless the bloke's put down that he's at another site where he shouldn't be, or he's doing a job that's not in the contract…then I'd have to have a word, because that's a mistake, see? I mean, the time sheets aren't really a timetable for the job, as such.'

At least, thought Stratton, that gives us a bit of room for manoeuvre. Nevertheless, after Canning had escorted Kendall from the room, he shook his head gloomily. Lamb was going to go berserk, even with dodgy time sheets. It was more likely, he thought, that Davies had muddled up the dates, but that said... Stratton pulled the telegram towards him to check—the date of the seventh was the one thing he'd been consistent about right from the beginning. Backhouse had said the seventh was the last time he'd seen Muriel, so perhaps it was possible that Davies had killed Muriel later on the same day, as he'd said, and brought her downstairs on the evening of the tenth. Or that there'd been two lots of wood...but in that case, surely Kendall would have noticed? He'd have to ask Carpenter.

Stratton leafed through his notebook. Backhouse had said Davies had left 'about a week' after the seventh, and Davies himself said he'd gone to Wales on the Monday, which was the thirteenth, and that he'd put the baby's body in the washhouse on the night of the ninth... 'Balls!' Stratton flipped his pencil across the desk. Providing the timings were right and that Carpenter had put the timber in the washhouse on the tenth, as Kendall said, it might still fit... It might even explain the noises in the night, if Davies had moved his wife's body down one flight of stairs into Gardiner's flat instead of right down to the ground floor. But if that was the case, why not say so? A mixture of confusion, fear, and wanting to please might muddy the waters, he supposed, especially with someone as feeble-minded as Davies clearly was—and with such difficulty telling the difference between fiction and reality.

PC Canning put his head round the door. 'Next one, sir?'

'Yes. Let's have Walker.'

The plasterer was an elderly man with a red face, a thin white moustache which reminded Stratton of a milk mark on a baby's upper lip, and a defensive air. His account tallied with Kendall's in every respect, until Stratton pushed the photograph of Muriel under his nose. 'Did you see this woman at any time?'

'Is that the one who...?' Walker tailed off, shaking his head, as Stratton nodded. 'And her kiddie, too. Terrible business. I did see a woman on the Tuesday, going out. Never saw the face, so I don't know.'

'Did she have a baby with her?'

Walker shook his head. 'I just saw her go out the front door, that's all.'

'And it wasn't Mrs Backhouse.'

Again, Walker shook his head. 'No. I saw Mrs Backhouse several times, and this woman was younger. Quite a bit younger, I'd say.'

'Can you describe her?'

'Well, I didn't pay much attention…'

'Fat? Thin?'

'I suppose…about sort of medium-sized really. A woman.'

'How old?'

'Youngish, I'd say. Hard to tell.'

'Do you remember what time?'

'In the daytime. I mean, it was light…but morning or afternoon, I couldn't say.'

Walker's statement taken, Stratton told PC Canning to fetch Carpenter, who was a solid chap, heavy and square. He gave the impression of immovability—he wouldn't go out of his way to swat a fly, but neither would he step out of the way of a charging bull. Hoping fervently that this was just his appearance and not his character, Stratton fixed him with a basilisk stare, thinking, you're my last hope, you fucker. Don't let me down.

CHAPTER 20

'Lamb'll have my guts for garters,' said Stratton, gloomily, when Carpenter left half an hour later.

'It's not all bad news, sir,' said Ballard. 'The Brighton police have telephoned a statement from Muriel's father, Mr Binney.'

'Oh? What's the gist of that?'

Ballard scanned the sheet in his hand. 'Says Muriel told him she wanted a divorce and asked if she could take Judy and go and live with him... She told him Davies never gave her any money and spent most of his free time in the pub.'

'Useful, I suppose, but it doesn't help us sort out this mess with the timing. That was like trying to dig a hole in cement with your fingers.'

Carpenter hadn't seen Muriel, and he'd been adamant that he'd left the pulled-up boards on the stairs on the Thursday and Friday evenings and only put them in the washhouse on the Monday, and, when shown a photograph of the boards *in situ*, he'd been equally positive that they were the ones taken up from the passage.

'If the boards were in the passage all weekend, it's odd that no one else mentioned it, sir,' said Ballard.

'Bloody odd. Apart from anything else, it's a nuisance. Of course, the only person it would have really affected is Davies, especially if he was taking a body, or—if he's got the dates for Muriel wrong—two bodies, downstairs...'

'Or maybe Backhouse moved some of them into the wash-house over the weekend—but then, of course, he'd have seen what was in there.'

'And the furniture bloke, sir. Lorrimer. He'd have noticed wood on the stairs, wouldn't he?'

'That's true. Except he only valued the stuff, didn't he? He didn't actually take anything away till the Monday, according to Davies.'

'Well, we'll have to see what he's got to say for himself. But the Backhouses must have seen the planks on the stairs, mustn't they? And they didn't mention it.'

'Well, we didn't ask them, but all the same...' Stratton passed his hands over his face.

'Of course, the workmen don't have to be called to give evidence, sir.'

'I suppose not. Let's see if we can get something sensible out of the Morgan woman, at any rate.'

Shirley Morgan was a lumpy girl in her late teens with a poor complexion and an air of cheerful incompetence which Stratton found surprising, given the circumstances. Charitably, he decided that it must be because disengagement and inanity were her response to everything and she was simply incapable of behaving in a different manner. 'Funny,' she said, brightly, 'I thought it was the Tuesday I went round there.'

'The seventh of November?'

'Was it? I don't know. I'm no good at remembering things. It might have been the Monday, for all I know. It's a while ago, isn't it? I can barely think what I was doing yesterday...' Here, apparently involuntarily, she gave a grating, shrieky laugh. 'Mr Backhouse was very funny with me.'

'In what way?'

'Well...' She leant forward conspiratorially. 'He said I shouldn't come round again because my clothes were so nice,' she smoothed her skirt complacently, 'they made Muriel jealous. I mean, what a thing to say!' She shrieked again.

Stratton winced. 'Where was this?'

'Where?' Another shriek. 'Oh, I see what you mean! Yes. On the landing. I'd gone up to knock on the door of Muriel's kitchen, you see... Oh, no, wait, that was afterwards...or was it before? I'm all confused—I told you I couldn't remember things. Oh, dear, I'm not being much help, am I?'

Stratton felt like slapping her. 'It's important that you remember, Miss Morgan. Please try to keep calm.'

'Oh!' The single syllable came out on a high, squealing note. It sounded like the rending of metal.

'This is a murder enquiry,' he said, in his most soothing voice, adding, mentally, 'you silly bitch.'

'Oh, I know...of course...oh, dear...I don't know what to say.'

'When did Mr Backhouse tell you not to come round?'

'Because of my clothes, you mean?'

'Yes. Was that before or after the sixth or seventh of November?'

Shirley Morgan thought for a moment. It looked like quite a strain. 'Before,' she said, finally. 'About a month, I think. I remember now...there'd been some trouble, you see. I'd stopped there for a few nights, and John—that's Muriel's husband—didn't like it, because we were in the bed and he had to sleep in the kitchen. He didn't like that at all.'

I don't blame him, thought Stratton. Half-deafening a bloke with that laugh and then turfing him out of his own bed...

'Muriel wanted me to stay because John was going to work somewhere foreign. Something to do with aeroplanes, I think he said. It turned out to be one of his stories... The second night I was there they had a row. John hit Muriel, so she got hold of the bread-knife. He said he'd push her out of the window. I've heard him say things like that before to Muriel—"I'll do you in," that sort of thing... Well, it got very nasty. Mr Backhouse came up, and he told me to leave.'

'You left with Davies, didn't you?'

'No, he came after me. He was always giving me the eye. That was after Mr Backhouse said those things about my clothes. He shut the door in my face and told me not to come back, and then a minute later John came out and suggested we go somewhere together. Well…' She gave Stratton a meaningful look. 'I didn't know what to do—I didn't have anywhere to go, so we walked around… Miserable, it was. Cold. I said I was going to get lodgings, but I didn't want him coming with me. He was Muriel's husband,' she added, as if this might not have occurred to Stratton. 'John said to pretend we were married, but I said what if we were found out, so then we had a row about it and he got nasty again…'

For Christ's sake, thought Stratton, wondering if—given the trouble she was having with a sequence of fairly drastic and important events—it would actually have registered if Davies had beaten the living daylights out of her. 'What happened then?' he asked.

'Like I said, we walked around and sat on benches. I found some lodgings. That was the next day… I suppose he must have gone home, because I didn't see him again. I went to see Muriel because she's my friend, and she was feeling poorly, with the baby coming.'

'You knew she was pregnant.'

'Yes.' Shirley's dull eyes registered surprise. 'She told me.'

'Did she tell you she was trying to get rid of the baby?'

'Get rid of it?' Surprise was replaced by incomprehension. 'Why would she tell me that?'

Good question, thought Stratton. You'd be a fat lot of use. Poor Muriel, surrounded by idiots. 'What happened,' he asked, 'when you went back to see her?'

'Well, I didn't see her, did I? I knocked on the door, but there was no answer. I thought she must be in there, so I said if she didn't want to see me, she'd only got to say so.'

'Why did you think she was in there?'

'I don't know. I just thought she would be, I suppose. I tried the kitchen door, but it wouldn't open.'

'Did you hear anything?'

Shirley shook her head. 'No. I just had a feeling she was, because when I tried the door, it wasn't as if it was locked—'

'Are you sure about that?'

'Yes, because it gave a bit. I thought that was because she was pushing against it to stop me opening it.'

'Leaning on the other side, you mean?'

'Yes. That's when I said if she didn't want to talk to me, she should just say, and I'd go. I was quite upset about it, because we were friends.'

Except that you'd just gone off with her husband, thought Stratton. 'Did you see anyone in the house?'

Shirley shook her head, then said, 'No, but I think Mr Backhouse was there, because I heard something when I went downstairs.'

'Why *Mr* Backhouse in particular?'

'Because it was a very quiet noise. I couldn't really tell where it was coming from. I suppose it could have been Muriel, if she was there, but I thought it was him because he's always creeping about in those plimsolls of his.'

'Frankly,' said Stratton, when Shirley Morgan had been shown out by PC Canning, 'that young woman struck me as pretty half-witted, so I think we'd better take Backhouse's word for it that she visited on the Monday and not the Tuesday. Of course, it could have been her that Walker saw, but Muriel was still alive then, and she could have popped out for something, couldn't she? And Backhouse saw her on the seventh as well, so that seems more likely.'

PC Canning appeared at the door. 'DI Grove is talking to Mr Benfleet now, sir, and Mr Lorrimer's here. Shall I bring him in?'

Lorrimer, a small man who looked as if he'd been kept under the stairs for a number of years, wore a flat grey cap that gave him the appearance of a mushroom and had a palm so damp you could have grown mustard-and-cress on it without much difficulty. 'Davies come into my shop on Friday the tenth.

Said he wanted to sell his furniture because he'd got a job abroad, so I said I'd come and have a look later and give him a price for it. I offered him forty pounds for the lot, and I sent my boy round Monday to collect it and give him the money.'

'When you went to look at the furniture, did you see any wood on the staircase? Floorboards?'

'Yes, there was something. A few boards, I think. In a pile. Wasn't much room to get past. I remember thinking my boy'd have a bit of a job if they weren't moved.'

'And how did Davies seem to you?'

'Well, I don't know the bloke, so that's a bit difficult. He seemed like he was in a bit of a hurry, but he'd told me he'd got this work abroad so I thought he wanted things sorting out, you know... He wanted me to take all the stuff except the baby's things. Said the bloke downstairs was keeping them for him until he'd fixed up a place for them to live.'

'Did you see the baby?'

Lorrimer shook his head. 'Didn't see no one except him.'

'More lies,' said Stratton, after Lorrimer had gone. 'That tale about working abroad.'

'And about the money, sir,' said Ballard. 'He told Backhouse he'd got sixty pounds for the furniture.'

'Yes, I remember that... It's odd that he didn't include the baby's things. I mean, he sold his wife's wedding ring, didn't he? He doesn't strike me as the type to see the consequences of his actions.'

'You mean looking suspicious, sir?'

'Yes. Mind you, I suppose he had to have something to tell Backhouse, and asking him to keep the baby's things would have put him off the scent, at least.'

'That must be it, sir. It's the only thing that makes sense. Pity about the wood on the stairs.'

'Yes...he said a few boards—perhaps some of them had already been put in the washhouse.'

'Not a long passage though, is it, sir? I mean, you'd only need a few.'

DI Grove's pipe-bowl appeared round the door, followed, in short order, by the rest of him. 'Here you are,' he said, proffering a piece of paper. 'Benfleet's statement. Davies sold the furniture on before it was paid for. Said they were behind on payments—forty-eight pounds, he owes—and Benfleet's had been dunning the mother for the money.'

'Yes,' said Stratton. 'She said something of the sort to us.'

Grove grunted. 'I saw Murchison, as well, from the van company, and one of the drivers who was a pal of his. Murchison said Davies was always asking for advances on his wages, and when he wouldn't give him any more Davies told him to stuff the job because he had a better one lined up. That was on Thursday the ninth of November. Murchison paid him off, and that was that. Said he wasn't sorry to see him go because he'd been mucking things up—he'd had people complaining the orders weren't delivered. The other bloke—McAllister, his name is—said that Davies was always complaining about his wife spending too much money and he'd told him that he wished he'd never married her.'

Ballard, who'd been scanning through Backhouse's statement, looked up and said, 'That all fits, sir.'

'That's a relief,' said Stratton. 'Now I suppose I'd better go and report all this to DCI Lamb.'

Grove grimaced. 'Best of British luck,' he murmured, as Stratton left the office.

'I thought I told you,' said DCI Lamb, stabbing his forefinger on his desk for emphasis, 'to make sure it was watertight.'

'Yes, sir. But, as I've explained, there's a discrepancy between when Davies says the bodies were put in the washhouse and when the workmen say the floorboards were put there. If they weren't stacked in front of the bodies, it would have been obvious that something was there, even if it just looked like a bundle of stuff wrapped in a tablecloth. That washhouse is tiny, sir, and those workmen were in and out all the time for their tools. We can't just ignore it, sir.'

'You're sure about this, are you?'

'Yes, sir. All three statements—Kendall, Walker, and Carpenter. Walker swept out the washhouse on the morning of Wednesday the eighth when, according to Davies, Muriel's body was in there, and he says he saw nothing at all. And Carpenter says he left the pulled-up boards from the hall on the stairs on the Thursday and Friday and only put them into the washhouse on the Monday—'

'Get them back in here, Stratton. I'll see them myself. Not Carpenter, just the foreman and the plasterer—they'll do.'

'But Carpenter's the one who moved the—'

'Stratton!' This time, it wasn't a forefinger but a fist that pounded Lamb's desk. Realising that the offer of any more elaboration would be met with an apoplectic response, Stratton decided that his best bet was to say as little as possible and let his superior get it out of his system.

'Look,' said Lamb, making an obvious effort to restrain himself and adopt a reasonable tone. 'Your man's confessed, hasn't he?'

'Yes, sir.'

'Well then. There's no point in overcomplicating matters. What we need to do—what you should be doing—is make sure that there aren't any weak links in the chain of evidence.'

'Yes, sir.'

'And—as I believe I've already reminded you—Mr Backhouse was a Special Constable. You couldn't have a better witness if you'd invented him, man. His word's going to weigh more than some dullard of a workman—and you've just told me that even the foreman admits that what's on the time sheets is poppycock.'

'He didn't quite say that, sir.'

'As near as, dammit! For God's sake, man, stop wasting my time! Just get out of here and fetch those witnesses. You'll be present, but I don't want you sticking your oar in unless I tell you. And I'll need all the statements you've taken on my desk as soon as you can.'

'Yes, sir.'

Having delivered the statements, Stratton sat down at his own desk and closed his eyes. Feeling Jenny's presence so strongly that she seemed almost to be physically there beside him, he kept his eyes shut so as not to dispel the illusion. 'Stay with me for a moment, love,' he murmured. 'It's going to be a very long day.'

Despite his resentment at Lamb's mental armour-plating against any new, unfamiliar idea, Stratton knew that his superior was right. It *wasn't* going to be anyone else: in cases of domestic murder, spouses or lovers were, invariably, responsible. Besides which, there were no other suspects, just a problem with consistency. Lamb's words about Backhouse—*You couldn't have a better witness if you'd invented him*—echoed in his mind. He thought of Shirley Morgan's shudder of disgust when she'd talked about Backhouse padding around in his plimsolls and giving her the willies. Half-witted she might be but Stratton, remembering the first time he'd met Backhouse—the way the man had sidled up behind him, the soft cough, the quiet precision of the speech, the blinking eyes behind the thick glasses, the general creepiness—knew exactly how she felt. Perhaps they ought to look into Mr Backhouse. After all, if something seemed too good to be true, then it probably was. He'd ask Ballard to check Backhouse's background. It was pretty unlikely, Stratton thought, that he would turn up anything, but it was best to be on the safe side, especially with Lamb on the warpath.

At half past seven the next morning, Stratton and Ballard stood side by side in the Gents' at West End Central, staring bleary-eyed into the mirror and wearily scraping razors across their chins. By the end of Lamb's interviews, first with Kendall and then with Walker, Stratton had been almost as desperate to get out of the room as the witnesses themselves. For a total of five hours, Lamb had first made the workmen wait, then alternately threatened and cajoled, thumping the table and shoving mortuary photographs of Muriel and the baby under their noses, until, in the end, he'd got what he wanted. Although Stratton had witnessed Lamb in action often enough—and he was bloody good, you had to give him that—and he had used similar methods himself on numerous occasions, he'd felt increasingly uneasy, despite the fact that both the Backhouses had, independently of each other, given statements that the wood had been stacked in the washhouse during the week. What really bothered him was that he couldn't put his finger on quite *why* he felt so uneasy.

Lamb had backtracked, gone in circles, insisted, and generally muddied the waters until the workmen began to question their recollections of events. Stratton had seen the uncertainty in their eyes—reality, as they saw it, assuming different shapes until, finally, it became unrecognisable. Their statements now suggested that there may have been planks of wood and dead bodies in the washhouse but they'd somehow failed to notice them; even, in the case of Walker, when sweeping the place—not, of course, that workmen were ever very good at cleaning up after themselves…

With Carpenter out of the picture altogether, the timings were certainly looking more solid, but nevertheless… And as for Lamb telling Walker that they had ten witnesses who'd seen planks in the washhouse during the week… 'Talk about entering the realms of fantasy,' he muttered.

'We seem to have been there from the beginning, sir,' said Ballard, rubbing his chin. 'What with Davies's first statements from Wales, I mean.'

'That's true. Mind you, Davies wouldn't recognise the truth if it bashed him on the nose. If it wasn't for the Backhouses saying they heard bumps in the night of the seventh, I'd think he'd got the dates wrong.'

'He's been consistent about the seventh throughout, though, sir—it's practically the only thing that's been the same in all the statements: that she died sometime on that day.'

'Well, the business with the bumps couldn't have just been a case of Edna Backhouse backing up what her husband said, because she told Grove about it when she made her statement. She said the wood was in the washhouse before the workmen did, too, and of course she was up and about the place—Backhouse said he'd spent a lot of time in bed for his back, remember? Mind you, it's still a bit of a mess, what with the muddle over days and the baby being left alone all that time and not crying…not to mention the dog. I don't know what to think.'

Ballard looked surprised. 'We *have* got a case, sir.'

'Oh, yes…' Stratton rolled his eyes. 'We've got one of those all right.'

The sergeant's surprise turned to incredulity. 'Do you mean, sir, that you think Davies *isn't* guilty?'

'Course he is,' said Stratton. 'I just wish it were a bit clearer, that's all. Have you got any hot water?'

Ballard shook his head. 'Tepid, sir.'

'So's this.' Stratton leant on the edge of the basin. He did feel bloody tired, but it wasn't just that. The inconsistencies nagged at him, as did the thought that Davies might well hang as a result of partial evidence. The other capital cases he'd worked on had been, on the face of it, a lot more complicated than this one, but there was just something... 'You know,' he said, 'Monica brought back a book from the library a few months ago. Abstract paintings—Cubism and what-have-you. All the pictures had names telling you what they were—*Still Life With a Newspaper* or something—and I could see that was what they were supposed to be, but not how they fitted together, or why anyone would want to paint them like that in the first place. This whole business is a bit like that. Mind you, I don't know anything about art and paintings, and they were in black and white...' And, he thought, no one got hanged at the end of it.

As he'd said this, Stratton had been staring at the porcelain tiles, but, looking up, he saw the worried expression on the sergeant's face. Hardly surprising, thought Stratton, with him talking a lot of bollocks like that. 'Sorry, Ballard. You must think I'm going off my head, too.'

'No, sir, but are you sure you're all right?'

'Fine. I'm tired, that's what it is. Those bloody camp beds... You'd get a better night's sleep on a park bench.' He unplugged the basin. Watching the scummy grey water gurgle away, he thought, I must be even more tired than I feel.

His job was to uphold the law, not to question it. That was the reason—well, one of them, anyway—that he'd joined the police force in the first place. It's the best justice system there is, he told himself, and then reflected that he didn't actually know that because, without knowledge of other places, he wasn't in a position to make comparisons. He adjusted the towel on its roller and turned back to Ballard, who was still regarding him with some concern. 'Do you think,' he asked, 'that British justice is the best there is?'

Ballard raised his eyebrows. 'That's a pretty big question, sir. I don't really know. I don't suppose any system in the world is perfect—ours isn't—but it's reckoned to be the best by people who know about these things.'

'Wiser heads than ours, you mean.'

'Well, yes, I suppose so.'

'Just as well there are some wiser heads, then. Wiser than mine, anyway. Tell you what, let's see if we can get some breakfast, shall we? Round the corner—I don't know about you, but I could do with getting out of here for a bit. Oh, and it's on me.'

Fortified by a cooked breakfast and several cups of strong tea, he felt much better, and things improved still more when the sun began to come out as they returned to the station, where he took a telephone call from Dr Sutherland, the Principal Medical Officer at Pentonville. Stratton, who'd had previous dealings with Sutherland, pictured him in his office—a man with suspiciously luxuriant hair and the square, determined jaw of the sort of film actor who stands about radiating quiet strength before performing heroic and morally impeccable acts. 'You'll be glad to know that Davies is fit to plead,' said Sutherland. 'We went through the family history, personal history and so on...He spoke quite freely. Told me he'd killed his wife on the seventh, and the infant on the ninth, and put the bodies in a washhouse at the back of the property.'

'He said that, did he?' Stratton was surprised. Sutherland's job was to make sure that Davies was fit to plead and stand trial, not to take confessions.

'Yes. I didn't question him about it—in fact, I warned him I'd have to report it, but he carried on...' Sutherland paused, and Stratton wondered if he was radiating a spot of quiet strength at the fixtures and fittings. 'Davies said it distressed him to think about it, but he seemed more shocked than distressed to me. Understandable in the circumstances, I think. He seemed worn out, which again is understandable. Low intelligence quotient—sixty-eight, and I'd estimate a mental age of about twelve to thirteen years.'

'Is that all?'

'I'd say so. That seems to be largely an educational defect and not an innate one—he missed a lot of schooling because of an infected foot—but it's an inadequate personality, psychopathic in the sense of wanting his own way, acting without thought, and a clear lack of understanding about the consequences of his actions, coupled, of course, with an absence of reasoning power. However, there are no insane impulses or delusions, and observations made on the ward suggest that he's reasonably cheerful and talkative, gets along with others and so on. I'll put it all in the report, anyway.'

'Do you think,' asked Stratton, 'that he was telling the truth?'

Another pause—for a bit more radiating, presumably—and then the doctor said, 'Yes. I believe he was. He did show some emotion talking about his daughter. I had the impression he loved her very much.'

IQ 68, Stratton scribbled in his notebook. *Mental Age 12-13 years.* That meant that if Davies were found guilty, they'd be hanging someone who was, in all but years, a child. He tried to remember what Monica and Pete were like when they were twelve or thirteen and found it surprisingly difficult. That was probably, he thought dully, because they'd been evacuated and he hadn't seen much of them. Maybe that was why he and Pete never seemed to hit it off—they'd missed some vital stage that could never be got back…

Grove appeared and rumbled over to his desk followed closely by Ballard with a cup of tea and a sheaf of notes, both of which he deposited under Stratton's nose. 'Thought you might need this, sir.'

'Oh? Why? And what's that lot?'

'Backhouse's record, sir. Turns out he's not the golden boy we took him for.'

'That's all we need. What's he done?'

'Well, in nineteen twenty-one he was sentenced to three concurrent terms of three months for stealing postal orders, and in nineteen twenty-nine he assaulted a prostitute. He was living with her, apparently, in Battersea, and—'

'Hold on. What about Mrs Backhouse? He'd been married a few years by then, hadn't he?'

Raising his head from the paperwork, Grove said, 'She was away. Up north, staying with relatives, and he was down here. She was away during the war, as well.'

Stratton flicked through his notes. 'Assaulted the woman with a cricket bat—must have been pretty bad, because he got six months' hard labour.'

'You're sure it's the same bloke?' asked Grove.

'Afraid so, sir,' said Ballard. 'He told the court he was just practising his strokes. You know, the sort of thing that could happen to anyone.'

'I'll bet Dennis Compton does it all the time.' Remembering Backhouse's smug gentility, Stratton added, 'Dishonesty *and* violence—what a pious little hypocrite.'

'There's more sir. In nineteen thirty-three he stole a car. From a Roman Catholic priest, of all people.'

Stratton groaned. 'Tell me you're joking.'

'Sorry, sir. He got three months for it, but the good news is, he's been straight ever since. Wife came back to him after—maybe that had something to do with it.'

'Sounds like it, doesn't it? Why the hell didn't they find out about this when he applied to be a special?'

'I suppose they didn't check, sir, and he wasn't going to tell them, was he? And what with everything else going on, I suppose it got overlooked.'

Stratton groaned again, louder. 'Bloody hell! It would have only taken one telephone call… I'll have to tell Lamb about this—it was this station, so I shouldn't be at all surprised if he somehow comes to the conclusion that I'm personally responsible for not checking. Type it all up, could you?'

'Yes, sir.' Ballard scooped up the papers and left.

Stratton could easily imagine Backhouse going to a prostitute—the usual dreary story of the reserved, cautious man, seeking to gratify a timid itch for amorous adventure, guilty in anticipation, remembering halfway through the fumbled act all the dire, lurid warnings he'd ever heard about chancres and insanity, and becoming impotent and creeping apologetically away... All that he could see happening, but *living* with—and therefore, presumably, *off*—a prostitute? And *hitting* her? That was an entirely different kettle of fish...

'Grove?'

The older policeman looked up and, with a deft movement of his jaw, transferred his—currently unlit—pipe from one side of his mouth to the other. 'Mmmph?'

'You don't think it's possible that Davies didn't do it, do you? Just,' Stratton added quickly, seeing Grove's normally placid features take on an exasperated cast, 'for the sake of argument, I mean...'

Grove took his pipe out of his mouth, then peered at it and poked the bowl with his finger before applying a match. 'You're thinking about Backhouse walloping that tart, aren't you?' he asked, between puffs.

'Yes...'

'Bit of a turn-up, I grant you. Not the sort of thing you'd expect.'

'Not really, no.'

Squinting at Stratton through a dense cloud of smoke, Grove said, 'Surprised me, too. But when all's said and done, it was over twenty years ago, and he's been as good as gold for the last...what? seventeen-odd years. No reason for him to start murdering people, is there?'

'I suppose not, but I was just thinking…'

'I can guess what you're thinking. You can't help liking Davies—or at least feeling sorry for him, in spite of what he's done—and you don't like Backhouse.'

'Something like that, yes.'

'I found myself liking him, too. Davies, I mean—when we were bringing him back. Same as the kids we get in here sometimes, the delinquents. You know they're villains all right, but you can't help feeling sorry for the little sods. And from what I've seen of Backhouse, well… I don't know if you remember him from when he was a special, but I had a few dealings with him, and he was a proper little Hitler, I can tell you. Uniform went straight to his head.'

'I don't remember him, but Ballard said something similar.'

'Well, he's right. I shouldn't be at all surprised if he'd taken a few favours off a few of the girls, but nothing more—'

'Well, apart from bashing one of them senseless.'

'Yes—years ago. But it doesn't mean he'd suddenly strangle his neighbour's wife for no reason at all. He's a nasty piece of work, but he's not a murderer. You've got your case: Davies is bang to rights and what's more, he's confessed. Apart from anything else, you start suggesting that to Lamb—'

'I wasn't going to,' said Stratton hastily.

'Good. Because if you did, he'd have your head on a plate, and you know it. And he may be an irascible old…you know… but in this case, he'd be right. You take it from me, mate. I've seen it all.'

'You're right, of course.' Stratton sighed. Grove *was* right. Not only that, but he was as sensible a copper as you could hope to find. It was him, looking at things cock-eyed—he was as bad as those blokes who'd painted the pictures in Monica's book. There *was* no reason for Backhouse to have killed either Muriel or the baby, whereas *Davies*… In any case, Backhouse having a record wasn't a disaster. Far from it. As Grove had pointed out, the man had been as good as gold for years, and any half-decent barrister would have no trouble at all in presenting their best witness as a man who'd learnt from his mistakes and was now firmly on the straight and narrow.

Grove was right about Lamb, too. For all his faults, the man had done a bloody good job, and people who lived in glass houses...because he wasn't exactly a saint when it came to coercing witnesses, and neither was Grove or any other copper he knew, come to that. If you found a weak link in the chain of evidence, you replaced it with a stronger one—that was how things were done. Davies was guilty of a hideous, unforgivable crime, and if the witnesses weren't perfect, so be it. They were, Stratton thought, good *enough*, and that was what mattered.

Nineteenth-century Baker Street was rotting in the damp December air—much, Diana thought, like its real, twentieth-century counterpart. At the end of the row of quaint but peeling shopfronts stood a guillotine and, beside it, a weather-beaten pile of canoes which were leaning against what surely couldn't be—no, actually was—a baby Sphinx. To the right stood a grey platform topped with a funnel-like structure which Diana guessed was the upper part of a submarine.

Her guide was a young man with a chalk-white face haloed by orange curls which, combined with a skewed, upstanding collar and expansive gestures, made her think of a painting she'd once seen of Queen Elizabeth rallying the troops at Tilbury. 'We do try to economise,' he said, 'but we can't reuse everything, and there isn't room to store it all in the Scene Dock. The backlot's over there by the river,' he added, flinging out an arm so near Diana's nose that she flinched involuntarily. 'That's for exterior stuff. We had two hundred Zulus camped out there last week—not real ones, black sailors from Cardiff. Mayhem! We've got fifteen stages—they're so big you can't miss them. The workshops,' Queen Elizabeth, whose name was really Alex

McPherson, gestured again, this time at a row of boxy, flat-roofed buildings across a concrete causeway, 'are there—carpentry and so on—and the Cutting Rooms, where film is edited—you'll see that later—and then there's the Dressing Rooms and the Art Department and Viewing Theatre and what-have-you over to the right. The producers have offices in the old house, that-a-way,' he spun round and waved a hand at a Victorian mansion, bits of which were visible behind a row of trees, 'and the bar is there, as well.' Alex raised his eyebrows. '*Most* important, as you'll soon find out. The restaurant is in there, too. That's for the units, of course. Extras and clerical staff and groundsmen and people like that eat in the big canteen,' he spun round again, and jerked out a thumb, 'down there.'

While he was talking, several girls in pink tulle hurried past, shivering, followed by a boy carrying an elaborate Regency wig on a stand, and another in overalls, hauling on the leash of a goat, which kept craning its neck to try and eat the wig, sending little puffs of powder into the air each time its nose brushed the horsehair curls. Bringing up the rear was a ludicrously handsome man in tails, his hair held in place by kirby grips. Seeing Diana's slack jaw and following her gaze, Alex said, 'Oh, those won't be in the shot. It's just so it stays in place.'

'And the goat?'

'Background. They're shooting a Victorian melodrama on C Stage. Humble farmer's daughter, lusty young squire—doomed love affair, with picturesque haystacks and beasts of the field dotted about the place. You know the sort of thing... Actually,' Alex lowered his voice, 'it's been rather awful because Robert Monckton—that's the leading man—has got this absolute horror of watching women eat. God knows why, but it's holding everything up because there's all this stuff with Jessica Miles biting into apples and things. You know, ripeness and bountiful nature and all the rest of it... So poor old Jessica is nibbling away, take after take, and he's meant to be looming over her, all dark and brooding, but instead he looks as if he's going to throw up at any moment. They had to do separate reaction shots in the end.'

'Oh dear,' said Diana.

'Not really,' said Alex. 'They're supposed to be madly in love, but they can't stand the sight of each other and it doesn't half show. Anyway, come and see the costumes.'

Rounding a corner and ducking under a precarious-looking balustrade complete with a swathe of artificial ivy, they entered a warehouse the size of an aircraft hangar where, suspended from a hundred rails, Nazi uniforms cosied up to crinolines and poke bonnets and yokels' smocks were crushed against angels' wings and sailor suits. 'Extraordinary, isn't it?' said Alex. 'Well, that's really the end of the outside tour. I'd better show you the stages.'

'If it's not too much trouble,' said Diana. She was feeling rather giddy—there was so much to absorb, and most of her attention seemed to be taken up in keeping out of the way of Alex's flailing arms.

'Not at all.' Alex raked a hand through the orange curls so that they sprang up even higher. 'Follow me. You've got to get to know your way around if you're going to work for Mr Carleton. You're jolly lucky, you know. Most people get thrown in at the deep end, but I was told to take special care of you.'

The job with Mr Carleton, a film director at Ashwood Studios, was Jock Anderson's idea. She, Jock, and Lally had been amongst the few who'd attended F-J's funeral the week before. It had been an unconvivial affair, the hymn-singing faltering and the mourners avoiding each other's eyes. The whole thing was conducted at a forced, slightly desperate pace, as if everyone present feared that the thin ice of distant politeness might give way between them at any moment. Mrs Forbes-James was absent, and after the service the congregation dispersed hastily, in the guilty manner of conspirators.

At dinner afterwards, Jock, who'd been impressed by the speed and efficiency with which she'd typed his manuscript, had told her that he'd arranged a meeting for her with an old acquaintance, Julian Vernon, who was head of Ashwood Studios. Diana had liked Mr Vernon but had left with only the vaguest idea of what she might be expected to do as assistant to Mr Carleton, whom she had not yet met, and Alex, who was Mr Vernon's assistant, hadn't enlightened her. 'Supposing Mr Carleton doesn't like me?' she'd said to Lally after the meeting. 'And what if I can't do whatever it is I'm meant to do?' Lally'd just laughed and told her she'd pick it up, adding that it was probably just fetching cups of coffee and looking decorative.

Diana's apprehension about being up to the job—whatever it turned out to be—took an instant and vertiginous hike when they entered the enormous studio where she'd be working. Inside, beyond a painfully brightly lit area which appeared to be where the action was about to take place, everything was dark and shadowy, but the entire building echoed with the din of a dozen men in brown overalls who were manhandling pieces of heavy ornate furniture, laying cables, getting in each other's way, and shouting almost continually. Thirty feet above her head were more shouting men, some perched precariously on rails angling giant lamps, while others lowered a vast, glittering chandelier into place. Still other men fussed over two enormous cameras on tracks, and groups of people in old-fashioned clothes stood in the shadows, patiently, like cattle. 'Extras,' murmured Alex, propelling her forwards. 'Another Victorian melodrama, I'm afraid. We've had rather a run of them recently, and they're very tiresome. Lots of nonsense about historical accuracy when all they really want is grand clothes and a lot of flouncing about.'

Diana laughed. 'What's it called?'

'*Trial at Midnight*. I ask you!' Alex rolled his eyes. 'It's about a bloke who's trying to drive his wife mad so he can get his hands on her money. That's him, there.' He flapped a hand at an exhausted-looking individual in a frock coat who was slumped in a chair at the side of the set being fussed over by a make-up girl in a white smock. He appeared to take no notice of her at all, but sat listlessly, arms hanging down. His face, shiny with greasepaint, looked like a drying death mask with the eyes like two black marbles pressed into wet plaster.

'He looks ill.'

'He is. His doctor forced him to go on the wagon a few months ago, and it doesn't suit him.'

The young make-up girl, apparently flustered by the direction of their gaze, looked up, dropping her sponge as she did so. 'Then why is he doing it?' asked Diana, turning away slightly to spare the girl's embarrassment.

'No choice,' said Alex. 'Not if he wants to stay alive, anyway. Although,' he added sardonically, 'I'd say that's debatable at the moment.'

Shocked by his flippancy but trying not to show it, Diana said, 'I meant, why is he doing the film?'

'Last chance saloon. Five other actors turned it down because they're sick and tired of moustache-twirling parts, and he's turned down so many things himself that the studio threatened not to renew his contract. They won't anyway, but…' Alex shrugged.

'Poor man.'

'Poor man who's wasting everyone's time and the studio's money. It's a pity, because he used to be good.'

'Who is he?'

'Anthony Renwick.'

'*Really?* But he's…'

'I know. Taller, slimmer, better-looking… Mind you, it's always odd the first time you see film actors in the flesh, whatever shape they're in. One's so used to seeing bits of them vastly enlarged on screens that one imagines they must actually be the size of hills or something. Anyway, mighty fallen and all that. It'd be a mercy to give him a drink, really—might improve his performance, at any rate.'

'Excuse me, miss.' Diana turned to see an electrician behind her with a lamp on wheels.

She stepped smartly backwards, tripped over a length of cable, and would have fallen if Alex hadn't rescued her.

'Don't worry, happens all the time.' He took her arm. 'We should get back a bit,' he murmured. 'They're about to go. That's the second assistant director, marshalling the extras.' Diana saw a group of women in ball gowns being herded across the floor by a slight, nervous-looking individual. 'Oh,' added Alex, *sotto voce*, 'and that's Mr Carleton, sitting under the camera. I'll introduce you when they break for lunch.'

Following his gaze, Diana saw the profile of a dark-haired man in a grubby open-necked shirt, sleeves rolled up, elbows on knees, staring intently in front of him. At his side was a thin woman in a plain black frock, her expression permanently fixed at surprise by the high arches of her pencilled brows. 'Who's that?' she whispered.

'Marita Neill. She's the continuity girl. Makes sure all the shots match up and nobody's wearing a wristwatch and so forth. You need eyes in the back of your head, and she's the best in the business. Been here for *ever*.'

Diana jumped as a hugely amplified voice boomed, 'Quiet, please!' A sudden silence, so tense that it was almost palpable, filled the studio.

'That's the first assistant director,' Alex muttered in her ear. 'You'll meet him later.'

'Scene Five, Take One,' said the voice. Mr Carleton and the continuity girl moved away from the camera as the dapper boy dashed forward, snapped his board in front of the camera, and beat a hasty retreat.

Mr Carleton, hands on knees and leaning so far forward that Diana felt he might topple over at any moment, shouted, 'Action!'

There was a buzz of conversation from the extras, and Anthony Renwick, side by side with another frock-coated man, strolled through them towards the camera, which retreated before them on its tracks. Renwick's face lacked animation, even when he began to speak, and he was gripping a champagne glass with a white-knuckled immobility that looked actually painful.

The exchange of dialogue completed, leaden on Renwick's part, with desperate over-compensation in both energy and emphasis by his companion, Mr Carleton shouted, 'Cut!'

'Not so much acting as an endurance test,' Alex muttered into the wave of noise which enveloped them as suddenly as had the silence before. Glancing at his watch, he said, 'Quarter to one. I'd say we've got at least an hour before there's any hope of lunch, so you might as well see round the rest of the place.'

They returned just in time for the final take. To Diana's eyes, it seemed no different to the first, but Mr Carleton said, 'Print that one—it won't get any better. Reserve, take three.'

As Renwick walked off the set, his head sunk between his shoulders like a tortoise retreating into its shell, Alex murmured, 'Better than yesterday, at any rate. He had to slap Anne Chalmers—she's the leading lady, by the way. Took the *entire* afternoon, and she got very fed up. At one point she asked him if he was actually awake.'

They waited while Mr Carleton had a complicated exchange with the continuity girl about playing time and footage. Close to, he seemed to radiate waves of energy, like heat, and when he stood up she saw that he was tall, thin, and scruffier than she'd expected. Also younger—thirty-five or -six, perhaps—but anyway, not much older than she was. His face, aquiline, with the beginnings of cragginess, was screwed up in concentration, and the words seemed to rush from his mouth, falling over each other as if he couldn't quite keep pace with his thoughts. Dismissing the continuity girl, he stared into space for a moment, rubbing the back of his neck, apparently oblivious to their presence until Alex coughed, making him shy like a nervous horse.

'Mr Carleton, this is Mrs Calthrop,' said Alex.

Mr Carleton raised his head and looked at Diana. Staring into his muddy-brown eyes, she experienced a physical jolt inside that made her catch her breath.

'She's come to work for you,' prompted Alex.

'Oh…yes. Yes, of course. That's…yes…'

Diana was aware of opening her mouth, but could think of nothing to say and closed it again. Her brain seemed to have stalled like an engine refusing to fire up. It was a moment before she realised that Mr Carleton was holding out his hand and then, after staring at it for what seemed like a full minute—*what was wrong with her?*—she took it and felt a tingle shoot up her arm like a small electric shock. 'James Carleton. Pleased to meet you.'

'Yes… Diana Calthrop.'

'Well, Mrs Calthrop—'

'Diana, please.'

Mr Carleton raised his eyebrows fractionally, and to her horror, Diana felt herself beginning to blush. Why was she behaving like a schoolgirl? Not only would she not be up to the job, whatever it turned out to be, but she was making a fool of herself. Why him, she thought desperately. Why now? Perhaps she should just excuse herself and leave before she did something really stupid… 'I feel,' she began, 'that I'm here under rather false pretences. Mr Vernon only gave me a job as a favour to a friend, so if you don't want—'

Mr Carleton held up his hand. 'But I *do* want,' he said, seriously. 'I want very much. If you'll come with me, I'll tell you what I want over lunch.'

'Thank you. It's very kind—'

'No it isn't.' He put his head on one side and stared at her, intently. 'Welcome, *Diana*, to the place where nothing is real.'

'I trust you, Inspector. I don't trust the others, see? But I trust you.' Davies's words echoed in Stratton's mind as he brushed earth off the parsnips he'd just dug up and laid them down on a sheet of newspaper. It was Saturday afternoon and he'd been at his allotment for over four hours, harvesting carrots and potatoes, preparing earth, tidying up, and then pottering about and making work, even though it was getting too dark to do anything really useful. Although he'd told himself it was because he ought to make the most of his severely limited free time—and it was entirely true that, in the past week, he'd barely been home except to snatch some sleep—he was deliberately stretching things out until darkness fell at teatime because he wanted to be on his own and outside. There were still times when being in a Jenny-less house felt like solitary confinement. And although working on the allotment was a great improvement on sitting in an armchair and staring at the empty one opposite, the fresh air hadn't blown the thoughts of Davies out of his mind in the way that he'd hoped.

Especially those last few words of his. They'd been uttered in the car, on the return journey from the committal. Staring down at the parsnips—feeble things, not a patch on last year's crop—he shook his head. Grove was absolutely right—he must not let his emotions get in the way of his work. Davies might have a mental age of twelve, but he'd killed his wife and child and been judged fit to stand trial, and that was all there was to it. Hanging him wouldn't bring back Muriel or the baby, but justice would be served. And if he, Stratton, wasn't doing his job to the best of his ability, he might as well give it up and go and be a market gardener or something. Not that he'd be much good at that on the present showing, he thought, fingering one of the pathetic-looking parsnips.

He thought back to the chats he'd had with Davies in the car to and from the committal hearing, of the slight, childish form beside him, hunched inside the overcoat. 'I want to tell Mam what I done, but I can't do it, Mr Stratton.'

'You should tell her the truth. Tell your family and your legal advisors. It's the best way.' Davies had reminded him of Pete when he was younger and caught out over a falsehood or a broken window—right down to the mumbled responses, the chin glued to the chest, and the sharp tang of boy sweat. Then the excuses, 'I was married too young, see? Never had any money, that was my trouble. I could have made a bit of money if I hadn't married, then I'd have managed all right, see?' Then he'd talked about what he'd done on occasions when he did have money—football matches and going to the dogs, this with improbable boasts about the quantity and frequency of his winnings, followed by equally improbable—and inappropriate—boasts about his sexual conquests. Stratton could easily imagine him saying these things in a pub and engaging in banter with other men—he'd be able to hold his own in that company or with his fellow van drivers at work. He had been cheerful and talkative, as Dr Sutherland had said, even to the extent of eliciting from Stratton that he supported Tottenham Hotspur and teasing him about their recent poor performance. His under-developed mind, Stratton thought, did not allow him to dwell on his predicament for long. When they'd parted, Davies had shaken his hand and asked when they'd meet again. Stratton remembered the little man's face falling in dismay as he'd explained that it would be on opposite sides of the Court and how Davies had gripped his hand once more and said that he was sorry...

'Dad! There you are!' Stratton looked up to see Monica standing over him in the near-darkness. 'Are you all right?'

'Oh... Yes, love.'

'You were all hunched over, snapping parsnips in half and talking to yourself.'

'Was I?'

Monica knelt down next to him and pointed at a heap of broken vegetables. 'It doesn't matter—Auntie Doris will only cut them up anyway. Are you going to come back now? It's gone six.'

'I lost track of time.'

'*Are* you all right, Dad? *Really?*'

'I'm sorry, love. Just feeling a bit blue, that's all. Nothing to worry about.'

'I thought I'd better come and fetch you. It's way past teatime.'

'I didn't mean to put you out.'

'You didn't. Anyway, I wanted to tell you—I met someone you know.'

'Did you? Where?'

'Yesterday, at work.'

'Work?' echoed Stratton, trying to imagine what on earth anyone he knew could possibly be doing on a film set.

'Yesterday. Her name's Mrs Calthrop.'

Thank God she can't see my face properly, thought Stratton. 'Diana Calthrop?' he asked, in what he hoped was a neutral tone. He hadn't thought about Diana—well, not much, anyway—for a long time. Not consciously, at least. He'd dreamt about her quite a few times in the years since they'd met and now, in Monica's presence, the sudden and excruciatingly detailed memory of those dreams made him hot and uncomfortable.

'That's right. She said to give you her regards.'

'What was she doing at the studio?'

'She's just started there. She's working on Mr Carleton's picture, same as me. She asked if I was any relation to you.'

'I don't understand. How did she know who you were?'

'She said she'd heard someone calling my name.'

Stratton couldn't remember ever telling Diana about his family, but he supposed that he must have done. Either that or, Diana's world being what it was—everyone knowing, or knowing *of*, everyone else—she'd simply made an assumption. 'But why is she there?' he asked. 'She lives in Hampshire, and she's married. She's got a family.'

'I don't know, Dad. I could hardly ask, could I? It would have been rude. It was jolly strange as it was. She said she'd met you in the war and asked how you were. Then she said it was only her third day so she was still finding her feet.' Rising, Monica tugged at Stratton's elbow. 'Come on, Dad. Your supper'll be all dried up.'

They walked in silence for some minutes, Stratton cradling his package of vegetables, his mind a whirl of questions. What was Diana doing working at a film studio? Perhaps her husband had died—or she'd left him...but in that case, what about the children? Colonel Forbes-James had definitely said she was starting a family. Perhaps her child was Ventriss's after all, and she'd run away with him. Not married him, though, or she wouldn't still be called Mrs Calthrop. Besides, he thought sourly, Claude Ventriss wasn't the marrying kind, baby or no. She'd had a war job, but that, for her class, was simply doing one's bit with well-bred courage and county phlegm and all the rest of it—a normal, peacetime job, with connotations of *having* to earn one's living, was an entirely different kettle of fish. There were a dozen questions he wanted to ask Monica: how did she look, what did they talk about, did she seem happy, was she wearing a wedding ring... But he couldn't. Not without her getting the wrong impression—an impression as absurd as it was unthinkable. Because it *was* unthinkable. He was just a copper, and Diana was...was... Well, she was *Diana*. She belonged to a different world—not his, and not Monica's, either. But then, what was she doing working at a film studio?

'She's nice, isn't she?' said Monica, as they turned the corner into Lansdowne Road. 'I mean, terribly posh and cut-glass and everything, but she's not stand-offish at all. How on earth did you meet her, Dad? I didn't like to ask in case it was something awful.'

Stratton hesitated. 'Well...she wasn't a suspect, if that's what you mean.'

'Can't you talk about it?'

'Not really, love. Not allowed to.'

'Oh.' Monica sounded disappointed. 'Oh, well...'

Stratton decided to change the subject before he said something he'd regret. 'Aren't you going out tonight?'

'No. I was going to the pictures with Madeleine, but we said we'd help Auntie Doris with the mending instead. I thought I'd keep you company—I haven't had supper yet—and go round later.'

That's nice of you,' said Stratton, pushing open the gate of number twenty-seven, 'but you shouldn't have waited. What's Auntie Doris left for supper?'

'Cheese pie and tomatoes.'

Stratton had tried growing tomatoes for the first time in the summer. The experiment had gone well—a bit too well, in fact, because they'd ended up with a glut, and, having been bottled by Doris, they appeared with monotonous regularity. Stratton stabbed the largest one with a fork, causing a gout of warmish liquid to spurt across the plate. He realised that he couldn't actually remember the last home-cooked meal—breakfast included—that hadn't involved the bloody things. Shoving the deflated tomato to the side of the plate so that it wouldn't turn the cheese pie, which he rather liked, into a soggy mess, he wondered what Diana was doing. Eating, perhaps? Stratton glanced up at the kitchen clock. Half past six. Too early. She'd be having drinks somewhere, or getting dressed up to go out to a party, or even—

'Dad? I said, I've left it on the mantelpiece.' Monica's raised voice shattered a wholly inappropriate image of Diana clad in nothing but camiknickers.

'Left what?' he asked.

'Honestly! Pete's letter, of course.'

'Oh. When did that come?'

Monica rolled her eyes. 'This morning. I just told you.'

'Sorry, love. What's the news?'

'Only that he's fed up and so's everyone else, and the sergeant can't even be bothered to sound properly fierce when they do their bayonet drill, whatever that is.'

'Charging at straw-filled sacks and stabbing them and bawling a lot, like this.' Stratton lowered his knife and fork, thrust his head forward, and emitted a blood-curdling yell.

'Blimey, Dad. You'll give yourself indigestion, doing that.'

'Your Uncle Reg used to do it up at the football ground with the Home Guard. It wasn't a pretty sight.' Stratton winced—not entirely theatrically—at the memory of his brother-in-law, pop-eyed and bulging in khaki, wheezing as he launched himself at a stuffed sack hanging from a gibbet.

'I can't imagine Uncle Reg charging at anything.' Monica giggled.

'Don't try, or you'll be the one with indigestion. What else did Pete say?'

'Just that when they're not doing the charging, they're doing silly things like polishing belt brasses on the insides and that he's skinned his palms trying to get round the assault course… That's it, really—except that he's coming home for Christmas.'

'That's good, anyway.' Stratton pushed his plate away. 'I'm sorry, love, but I don't feel very hungry.'

'It's the tomatoes, isn't it?'

' 'Fraid so.'

Monica put her knife and fork together. 'I'm not that hungry, either. I won't tell Auntie Doris if you don't. Can I have a cig? I've run out.'

'If you make me a cup of tea before you go.' Stratton stood up. 'I'm going next door to have a look at Pete's letter.'

After a cursory glance at the letter, which said no more than Monica had reported, Stratton sat down in his armchair to read the paper. In the five minutes before his tea arrived, he managed to concentrate fairly well on a piece about whether all the money spent on the Festival of Britain wouldn't be better put towards rehoming people, but as soon as he heard the front door close he let the paper fall and, leaning back, closed his eyes and allowed the image of Diana back into his mind. After a few moments of this, an obscure feeling—he mentally skirted the word 'guilt'—that despite being alone he really ought to give the appearance of doing something else, made him get up and turn on the wireless. Returning to his chair, he settled back and let his thoughts take him where they would.

Clutching her notes to her chest, Diana stared down at her shoes. She'd been told that they were days behind schedule, and Anthony Renwick had spent the morning—it was now quarter past eleven—stumbling through take after take, disorientated and constantly forgetting his lines, until nobody could bear to look at him. Now, the unit were avoiding each other's eyes, too, ashamed at being part of a disaster. Only Carleton kept on staring at Renwick with pinpoint concentration, as if he were trying to force a performance from the actor by sheer willpower.

'Action!'

Diana glanced up in time to see a look of consternation momentarily animate Renwick's otherwise immobile features. A second later, he let out a long, wailing fart.

'Cut! Cut!' Carleton jumped up and strode towards him. 'For Christ's sake, Tony…'

The crescendo of laughter—a release of tension, if not actual merriment—stopped abruptly when Renwick burst into noisy, gulping tears. Carleton put an arm round his shoulders—'Break, everybody! Ten minutes!'—and escorted him outside, motioning Diana to follow. She'd been working at Ashwood for two weeks now, and while she felt she'd never be on top of the myriad jobs involved in assisting Marita Neill, the continuity girl—it turned out that Mr Carleton had a perfectly good secretary already—she was at least beginning to understand how things worked. And when she wasn't worrying about missing something or getting it wrong, which was still quite a lot of the time, she was enjoying herself a great deal. The other good thing was that, although his attraction was undeniable, she was managing not to be openly stupid about Mr Carleton (as Lally—who'd guessed immediately, much to her chagrin, from the way she spoke about him—had put it).

Anthony Renwick stood in the feeble winter sunlight, shoulders heaving, with Carleton wiping his nose for him as if he were a baby. As Diana approached, Carleton broke away and took her by the arm. He seemed so supercharged with tension that it was like being inside an electric force field. 'Get him a drink.'

'But he's not supposed to—'

'For Christ's sake, Diana, *look at him*!'

'You'll kill him. His doctor—'

'His doctor hasn't got the studio breathing down his neck. Just go across to the bar and get him a bloody drink,' Carleton hissed. 'You can get one for me, too, while you're at it.'

Seeing that it was useless to argue, Diana said, 'What would you like?'

'Anything! Just make sure it's strong.'

Renwick, who'd been staring into the middle distance somewhere over Diana's left shoulder during this exchange, suddenly said, with more firmness and clarity than he'd managed all week, 'Brandy. I want brandy.'

'There you are,' said Carleton. 'He wants brandy, and I'll have the same. Now go!'

Dismissing her, he returned to Renwick and steered him back towards the studio. 'Come on, Tony,' she heard him say. 'Pull yourself together. You'll be all right now.'

As she walked down the causeway, Diana felt very doubtful that Renwick would ever be 'all right'. Certainly, judging from the way in which Mr Vernon had harangued Carleton the previous evening—she and Marita had been in Carleton's office when he took the telephone call, and his feelings, if not his actual words, had been excruciatingly obvious—Renwick wouldn't be working for Ashwood again. Whether Carleton himself would, having told Mr Vernon in no uncertain terms that he hadn't wanted Renwick in the first place, also seemed open to question.

As she entered the old house, Diana was nearly knocked off her feet by a young lad with an armful of paperchains and a grin so wide that it threatened to meet itself at the back of his head. There were people up ladders tacking coloured streamers to the gallery and the whole place had an atmosphere of bustling, anticipatory festivity.

The restaurant, in contrast, was deserted except for a few waitresses laying tables and the old barman who, on seeing Diana, raised his eyebrows so high that they all but disappeared beneath his toupee. 'You're on G Stage, aren't you, miss? I thought it couldn't last.'

'It's just the one,' said Diana, defensively, taken aback by the man's familiarity and instant summing-up of the situation. 'Well, just the two, anyway. Brandy.'

The barman picked up two balloons and looked pointedly from the one in his left hand to the one in his right. 'For Mr Carleton, is it?'

'Mr Renwick,' said Diana, assuming that he must know about the actor's problem.

'*Both* of them?'

'Well, no. The other one's for Mr Carleton.' Diana wondered why she was explaining this—after all, what business was it of his?

'Is it indeed?' The barman's tone was arch, but he turned away too quickly for Diana to read his expression, busying himself with the optics. 'Can't say I'm surprised.' He turned and slid a tray across the polished surface. 'Would you like a siphon?'

'Yes, please,' said Diana, briskly.

'Right you are.'

'Thank you.'

As Diana picked up the tray and turned to leave, the barman said, 'I'll see you later, miss.'

'Naturally,' said Diana, with hauteur. 'I shall return the tray.'

'Of course, miss.' To her astonishment, the barman closed one eye in a deliberate, conspiratorial wink.

She returned to G Stage to find Carleton and Renwick huddled at the side of the building, smoking in silence. Ignoring the soda, Carleton picked both balloons off the tray and held one up to Renwick, whose eyes followed it with a precision of focus Diana hadn't seen from him before. If he were a dog, she thought, he'd be slobbering. 'There you are,' said Carleton. 'Just what the doctor didn't order.'

As they clinked their glasses, Diana saw a look pass between them, a strange mix of solemnity and devilment, as of a secret shared. Obviously, Carleton had supplied Renwick with illicit drinks before. But surely, she thought, he can't really believe that everyone inside hasn't guessed what Renwick's doing out here? And even if they don't, they're bound to smell it the moment the two of them walk back in.

Renwick drank greedily and returned the glass to the tray with a flourish. 'Bless you, my child,' he said, giving her a mock bow.

'That,' said Carleton, tossing back the remains of his own brandy, 'should get us through till lunch, at any rate.'

Two hours and three scenes later, Diana was forced to admit that the brandy—and the second helpings she'd fetched an hour later, to the unconcealed amusement of the barman—had done the trick. Renwick was a changed man and the alteration infused the unit with new energy. As he seemed almost to blaze before her, Diana felt herself lit up by the presence and the vitality that had made him a star. Now everyone was looking at him. He didn't draw your attention so much as actually drag it to him, so that you barely noticed any of the other actors. But we're watching him die, she thought, remembering what Alex had told her about the doctor's warning. If he carries on with it, then he really *will* die. And she'd got him the brandy, hadn't she? And, she thought ruefully, she would again if Carleton requested it. She not only needed the job, especially as Hambeyn House was still on the market and she was looking for a flat—despite their protests to the contrary, she felt she'd imposed herself on Jock and Lally for quite long enough—but she loved working at the studio.

Only obeying orders, she mocked herself, that's what I'm doing. Would Renwick, she wondered, have cracked if Carleton hadn't suggested the brandy? He could have refused it, of course, if he'd had the mental strength, but anyone could see how weak he was.

As if he could read her thoughts, Carleton beckoned her over during a pause for set-dressing and said, 'There's no option, Diana. It's him or the picture.'

When they finally broke for lunch and Carleton and Renwick strolled off towards the restaurant, arms round one another's shoulders, Diana, too disturbed to be hungry, decided to take herself off for a walk. It was a desire to be elsewhere, rather than a conscious decision, that led her in the direction of Make-up, where, peering through a half-open door, she caught sight of Monica Stratton. Kneeling on the floor beside a supine and almost naked actress who was unconcernedly smoking a cigarette, the policeman's daughter was occupied in painting a delicate lacework of what was obviously meant to be blood across the young woman's legs.

'We've got company,' said the actress, raising her head fractionally from its cushion. 'Can I get up now?'

'No, you've got to dry...Oh!' Monica half-turned and, catching sight of Diana, blushed.

Hoping the girl hadn't thought she was eavesdropping—she certainly hadn't overheard anything—Diana felt uncomfortable. 'I didn't mean to disturb you,' she said lamely.

'Can I help you?' asked Monica, getting to her feet.

Diana, having only talked to her briefly on the previous occasion they'd met, now had the chance for a proper look at her. Despite the severe hairstyle and unbecoming overall, her fresh complexion and bright-green eyes made the languid sophisticate who sprawled before them on the floor in her *maquillage* and silk underwear seem tawdry and stale.

'I was just getting a breath of air,' she said. 'Wandering about, really.'

'Oh…' Monica, too, seemed at a loss for what to say. 'Well, it's a nice day, for a change.'

'I am sorry if I disturbed you.'

'Oh, no. I wouldn't mind some fresh air myself. We're starting again in ten minutes, and I've missed lunch, so…'

'Do you fancy a quick walk?' Honestly, thought Diana, anyone would think they were a boy and a girl at their first dance, tongue-tied by proximity and etiquette.

Monica looked down at her paint brush. 'I'll have to wash this first, or it'll get hard.'

'What about me?' asked the actress.

'You'll have to stay put till we start again,' said Monica. 'I'll finish you off on set. It's all right, I'll put a notice on the door so no one'll come in. It's for a Donald Colgate picture,' she explained to Diana. 'I'm not supposed to be doing it, but one of the girls is off with chickenpox.'

'I'm just the legs,' added the actress. 'Still, at least I'll be able to tell everyone I've been killed by Donald Colgate. It's practically a rite of passage.'

'Is it?'

'Oh, yes,' said Monica placidly, from the basin, 'he's always playing men who murder their wives—they get him if they can't have James Mason.'

She put on her coat and scarf, and the two of them wandered down the causeway. Despite Monica's remark, it wasn't a 'nice day'. It wasn't raining, but above them dark clouds were beginning to conjoin so that the sky resembled an ominously heavy grey eiderdown. Turning her collar up, Monica said, 'I told Dad about meeting you.'

'Oh…' Diana, gratified by this—she'd thought the girl might have forgotten—asked, 'What did he say?'

'He remembered you.' Another grin, quick this time. 'Very well, I think—although he didn't say that.'

Diana, wondering what to make of this, said, 'He was very kind to me.'

'That sounds like Dad.' The girl stared at Diana for a moment, then blurted, 'I'm worried about him,' and stopped abruptly, looking alarmed.

Surprised, Diana said, 'Why?'

Monica looked as if she wished she hadn't said anything. 'It's probably nothing, but he's gone sort of quiet. Gone into himself.'

'Perhaps he's worried about something…a case.'

Monica nodded. 'I know he is,' she said, more enthusiastically this time. 'It's a man who killed his wife, and it's horrible for Dad because of Mum.' Before Diana could say anything, she added, 'Mum was killed, you see.'

'During the war?'

'Yes, but it wasn't a bomb. It was a woman that Mum and my Auntie Doris were looking after when she was bombed out, and she went sort of mad and attacked Mum…stabbed her. It happened while I was evacuated. Dad feels guilty because he thinks he should have saved her, but he wasn't there in time. He's never told me that, but I know he does. I've known for ages. And I know he keeps on remembering what happened, and it's this case, making it all worse… He misses her like mad. We all do, but… I'm sorry, I don't really know why I'm telling you this. I don't normally talk about it.' Monica huddled into her coat, and Diana had the impression that she was battening down the hatches.

'I'm not surprised.' Seeing Monica's stricken face, she hurried on, 'I just meant it must be very hard for you, that's all. But you can tell me, if you like.' She smiled encouragingly. 'I'm quite good at listening.'

Monica considered, biting her lip, then said, 'I didn't really think about it until recently—or I suppose I didn't notice—but it's as if his life has sort of stopped. His memory, I mean. Sometimes he tells me things, stuff from the past… It's always me he tells, never Pete—that's my brother—because he won't talk about Mum at all, and anyway he's not at home any more… But when Dad says things, it's always stuff from when Mum was here.'

'Perhaps he thinks those are the things you want to hear about.'

'Yes, I do, but… The years between then and now are like a big…*nothing*, as if there's only what happened today, or yesterday, and then before that it was nineteen forty-four, before Mum died. I mean, I don't want him to forget about her, but I think he should start living properly, not just going to work and his allotment and reading the paper as if he's just pretending, because that's how it seems. Auntie Doris and Auntie Lilian think he should get married again.'

'What do you think?'

'I don't know. I don't think I'd mind if it was someone nice, but I don't see why he should have to if he doesn't want to. Look, I really am sorry for telling you. It's just that I really can't talk about it with Pete, or Auntie Doris, or my cousin Madeleine, and you're…you're…'

'I'm…?' Diana prompted.

'You're so…*different*, I suppose—sorry, I hope that doesn't sound rude or anything.' Monica paused for a moment, frowning at Diana, then added, 'Was your husband killed in the war?'

'No,' said Diana. 'Why do you ask?'

'Well…' The colour in Monica's cheeks intensified.

'Go on. I shan't be offended.'

'Working here, for one thing. And it was what came into my mind when I first saw you—that you'd had a loss. I mean,' she said, 'I suppose it could have been anything,' Monica gave an awkward little laugh, 'but it seemed as if you'd lost something important.'

Although taken aback—Monica was clearly as observant as her father—Diana found that she didn't in the least mind the girl's frankness and found herself willing to repay one confidence with another. 'I did lose my husband in the war—just not in the way you thought. We're divorcing.'

Monica's blush was now a vivid scarlet. 'I really didn't mean to pry, Mrs Calthrop. I'm terribly sorry.'

'I'm not,' said Diana. 'I left him. Not,' she added hastily, 'that I'd like it generally known.'

'No. No, of course not. I shan't tell anyone.' She put her hand on her chest and said, 'Not a soul—cross my heart.' The childishness was deliberate, put-on, but the sincerity was real enough.

'Thank you. And please...tell your father how very, very sorry I am.'

A few minutes later, Monica set off back to her drying actress, mimicking 'At least I'll be able to tell everyone I've been killed by Donald Colgate!' with surprising accuracy, and leaving Diana to contemplate the sheer magnitude of grief, in all its forms, in everything that the girl hadn't said. A sudden image made her wince and blink as if avoiding something real: the picture of a prim, rigid little woman, lace handkerchief dangling from one sleeve of her cardigan, who said, 'I beg your pardon,' and set about gouging at Monica's cowering mother with a pair of sewing shears. Ridiculous, she thought. She had no idea what Mrs Stratton was like, or the woman who'd killed her. She had, in fact, no idea about Stratton's home life at all, except that it must now be lonely and, judging by what Monica had said, haunted by the spectres of guilt and regret as well as his murdered wife. Poor, poor man... She hoped he'd got somebody he could talk to—if he wanted, that was, because men very often didn't. He'd been so understanding—a good friend to her, when she'd needed one. It would be nice, she thought, if she could do the same for him—comfort, perhaps, or just listen. But I shall probably never see him again, she thought sadly—after all, she wasn't likely to meet him socially, was she?

Diana found Marita in the restaurant, huddled with Alex McPherson in the corner. The tables around them were deserted, but across the room, in the middle of an appreciative coterie of studio staff and partially costumed actors, was Anthony Renwick, declaiming, brandy balloon held aloft. 'Don't mind me,' said Alex. 'I'm on a spying mission for Mr Vernon. Management needs to keep tabs on the Means of Production, and I shall have to report that one of the Means has dined not wisely, but a bit too well. And,' he added, glancing at his watch, 'we'll have the unions on our backs if this sort of thing keeps happening.'

'Mr Renwick was wonderful this morning,' said Diana.

'So I gather,' said Alex wryly. 'Let's just hope he gets a few more takes under his belt before he falls over. Coffee?'

'Thanks.'

'Have this,' said Marita, pushing a full cup towards her. 'I haven't touched it, and I need to get back.'

When she'd gone, Alex said, 'So… Mr Carleton is making quite a pet of you, according to Marita. Taking you under his wing, so to speak.'

'He's been very…kind,' said Diana carefully, realising, as she said it, that these were the exact words she'd just used to Monica about Inspector Stratton.

'So I understand.'

This seemed so pointed that Diana found herself saying, 'Marita hasn't taken against me, has she? She certainly hasn't said—'

Alex held up one hand like a traffic policeman. 'Marita,' he said, 'never "takes against" anyone. She may look like a human exclamation mark, but she's as tender as a lamb. Except where the interests of the studio are concerned, and frankly, my darling, it's not you that's likely to incapacitate the Means of Production. In fact,' he raised an eyebrow, 'you may have quite the opposite effect, so—'

Whatever else he'd been going to say was lost in a bellow of laughter from the other side of the dining room. This seemed to signal the end of Renwick's performance, because a moment later people began to leave. Alex glanced at his wristwatch and stood up. 'The triumph of hope over experience,' he murmured. 'Well, he can't say we didn't warn him.'

'Mr Renwick, you mean?'

'Mr Vernon. Sorry, Diana, got to dash.' He loped off, waving his arms at someone at the far end of the room.

As she gulped the remains of her coffee, Diana wondered what on earth Alex had been talking about. Still, he'd seemed to have implied that she was an asset to the picture and not the reverse, which was obviously a good thing. Anyway, it couldn't have been all that important, or he'd have stayed and elaborated...

Diana looked up as a shadow fell across the table. Mr Carleton was standing beside her. 'My rudeness this morning was unforgivable,' he said. 'I've come to apologise.'

Jolted by this, Diana said, 'Really, there's no need.'

'Yes, there is. There's every need. In fact, I was wondering if you'd like to have dinner with me... By way of apology, of course.' His expression, as he looked down at her, was solemn, but there was a light in his eyes that made her heart jump inside her chest.

'Well, then,' she said, in a deliberately measured tone. 'By way of accepting your apology, I accept your invitation.'

'Does tomorrow suit?'

'It does.'

'Wonderful. I'll take you to one of my favourite haunts.' He tapped the face of his wristwatch. 'Drink up, then. We start in five minutes. Oh, and talking of drinking...' He pulled a silver hip flask out of his pocket. 'Would you mind asking the barman to fill this up? I fear that neither Mr Renwick nor I will last the distance without it.'

Reg, who was carolling away fit to bust in ill-fitting suit and bulging knitted maroon waistcoat, had his back to the fire and his arms around the restive shoulders of Monica and her cousin Madeleine. It was extraordinary, thought Stratton, how his brother-in-law managed to look as if he, personally, had orchestrated all the Christmas festivities. In fact, it was Doris and Lilian who had, between them, managed to obtain everything from turkey to tangerines, and then knocked themselves out in Doris's steaming, fragrant kitchen to produce a feast. Monica and Madeleine had livened up the place with holly, ivy, and berries, provided along with the vegetables by Stratton, and Donald had fashioned ingenious decorations from newspaper and coloured inks. All Reg had done was fiddle with the wireless and give unnecessary advice to the people doing the actual work, accompanied by infuriating jabs of his pipe.

Still, there was nothing like being warm and full of grub, with a bottle of beer at your elbow, new leather slippers (from Lilian and Reg) on your feet, and two new jazz records (from Doris and Donald) to listen to later, for putting you in a forgiving mood, and he had to admit that Reg ('Joy-ful all ye nay-shons ri-ise') did have a very nice baritone. Don wasn't bad, either—he'd been in a church choir as a kid—and even Pete, who was on leave from Catterick for forty-eight hours, could sing a bit. He, on the other hand, couldn't hold a tune in a bucket and, not wishing to give anyone a chance to comment on this, kept his mouth shut on such occasions. He thought of all the previous Christmases he'd had to miss when Jenny was alive—and now here he was, and she wasn't. The nipper would have been getting old enough to appreciate it now, too, and they could have filled the stocking together and crept into the bedroom, Jenny shushing and giggling as Stratton put his hand on her bottom on the way upstairs and then pretended to drop things, just as he had when Monica and Pete were little…

The whole family hadn't been together for a while, and looking round the room, Stratton noticed that the older members were definitely showing signs of age. Don's sandy hair was pepper-and-salt now, but at least, unlike Reg, who admittedly had several years on both of them, he'd still got quite a lot on top—although not as much, Stratton thought with more satisfaction than he'd have cared to admit, as he himself had. And his hair was still, except for a few bits near the temples, almost entirely its original black. He was pretty much the same shape that he'd always been, too, whereas Reg and Don seemed to be growing fatter and skinnier at equal rates and Lilian and Doris appeared to be following their husbands' examples. He supposed they couldn't help it. Jenny, he was sure, would have kept her figure, which had, in any case, been better than either of her sisters'. But she never had the chance to grow old, he thought, so I'll never know…

Wrenching his mind away from the subject, he found himself wondering what Davies was doing in Pentonville. Last time he'd been there at Christmas, the eye-catching jollity of a big painted sign—Merry Christmas To All!—suspended over the counter in the reception had struck him as gruesome in the extreme. He knew that the food rations in prison became smaller in the weeks before Christmas as the cooks saved up for a big, rich blow-out, but that was all. Christmas in prison, he thought, must be much the same as Christmas was for him nowadays: a milestone. In his case, it was a measure of time passing since Jenny died; for a prisoner, it would be a measure of how near (or far away) was the release date or, in Davies's case, the trial. Remembering what Sutherland, the prison doctor, had said, Stratton doubted that Davies was much aware of this. Like an animal not knowing that it was destined for the abattoir... It was, he supposed, a symptom of the unease that he still felt about the whole thing that it continued to nag at him, even at a time like this.

'Dad?' Stratton jumped. The singing had ended and Monica was bending over him. 'Nodded off,' he lied. 'Sorry, love.' Seeing the lavish-looking box of chocolates in her hand, he added, 'Where did those come from?'

'A present.'

'Got a boyfriend, Monica?' Pete looked up from poking the fire. 'Took your time about it, didn't you?'

'No, but Madeleine has—as you very well know,' said Monica, speaking with exaggerated patience. 'He gave them to her.'

'You want to get yourself a boyfriend, too.' Pete put the poker back on the stand, then getting to his feet, added with studied casualness, 'Or perhaps you don't.'

Seeing Monica's face flush, and feeling that if anyone was going to interrogate *his* daughter about having admirers it would be *him*, and in private if at all, Stratton said, 'Leave her alone, Pete. It's none of your business.' Monica shot him a look of gratitude. She'd had a boyfriend some time back, Stratton remembered, but he didn't think it had lasted very long. He had no idea why it had ended—Monica hadn't been forthcoming and he hadn't wanted to pry—but as far as he could recall, she hadn't seemed particularly upset by it. Or maybe she had been, because that was evidently what Pete was alluding to.

He stopped listening and considered his son. Pete was, he thought, already bigger, stronger, and fitter-looking than when he'd left. Unlike Monica, who'd been straight up and down like a boy until she was at least sixteen, Pete had looked adult early on and, compared to him, other National Servicemen Stratton had seen seemed puny and not fully formed. Pete's build was just like his own, although he was—Stratton felt a flicker of surprise that he'd never really noticed this before—considerably better-looking; handsome, in fact, with thick, conker-brown hair and pale skin that was just like Jenny's. He was cruder than before, though, with an undercurrent of belligerence that showed itself in an abruptness of manner, a tendency—as just now, with Monica—to talk out of turn, and the generally rough way he moved about the place. The latter, of course, could be because he was still growing—Stratton had painful memories of his own clumsiness at seventeen and eighteen. The crudeness, he supposed, was hardly surprising, as he must be billeted with a lot of young chaps wanking and boasting about girls, with all the talk ritualised into mocking, joking, and one-upmanship as they probed for one another's weaknesses. It was all too easy to imagine the fetid atmosphere of the barracks, farts and arse-scratching and sweaty armpits and meaningless obscenities... He suddenly realised that he had no idea whether or not Pete was still a virgin. Not that he particularly wanted this information, but it was another indication of the boy moving even further away from him, and more especially because he himself had never served in the forces. He wondered if Pete might hold this omission against him. Donald hadn't fought, either. Only Reg, the family buffoon, had; the trenches in the Great War and then—if you could count it, which Stratton supposed you had to—the Home Guard.

Later, when the women went to prepare a supper of ham and salad and the men were left alone, the conversation turned—or rather, Reg turned it—to army life. After they'd listened to a lot of guff, so familiar that Stratton knew the phrases off by heart, about shaping an efficient fighting force and a fine body of men and all the rest of it, Donald asked, in a suspiciously neutral tone, 'So what do you think, Pete, about the *modern* army?'

'It's all right, I suppose, except there's no bloody privacy, unless you're asleep. And even then the bloke next to me keeps having nightmares and shouting. The sergeant told him he was going to be shot for some breach of regulations and the stupid berk actually believed him—he's a bit simple, you see. The sergeant even had him dictating a last letter to his mum, and he was bawling his eyes out.' To Stratton's horror, Pete laughed. 'It's about the only fun we've had. If you're not exhausted, you're bored stupid. We do all these war exercises—outside for hours, freezing your arse off, and then they tap you on the shoulder and tell you you're dead. Still, as long as I don't get shipped out to Korea…'

Reg, his voice quivering under the weight of betrayed courage and despairing patriotism, said, 'Don't you want to fight for your country—'

'It wouldn't be for my country,' said Pete, mildly. 'I wouldn't mind getting stuck in, if I thought there was something to fight *for*.'

'You'd be fighting against Communism,' said Reg.

Pete shrugged.

'You won't get very far with that attitude. What about the Selection Board?'

'Selection Board? I'm not *officer* material, Uncle Reg. That's for the public school types. They only let blokes like me make up the numbers in wartime.' Pete wasn't aware of it, but this was so entirely the reason that Reg had been made a captain in the Home Guard that Stratton almost choked trying to turn a laugh into a cough. 'Look,' Pete continued, 'I don't mind the drill and all that, and most of the chaps are OK, but they never let you think for yourself.'

Stratton was about to point out that this was pretty much true of any job when Reg declared in a professorial tone, 'I think that you haven't understood the fundamental aim of a fighting force. A good soldier must accept rules and regulations. Discipline'—here, the pipe stem did its stuff—'is vital on a battlefield.'

Stratton felt that this was a bit rich coming from someone whose son, turned down for active service during the war on health grounds, had such a lack of regard for rules and regulations that he'd narrowly avoided Borstal. Johnny having left straight after their meal, Stratton thought of mentioning him, but was prevented by a warning grimace from Donald. It wouldn't be fair—Lilian had been very upset by her son's abrupt departure. In any case, Stratton thought sourly as Reg carried on pontificating, he knew perfectly well what Johnny was doing: working for a very dodgy car dealer in Warren Street. Having had to deal in an official capacity with his nephew before, he frequently and fervently hoped that next time Johnny got into trouble, some other poor sod would get there first.

He had resisted the temptation to say anything but was fairly sure that Pete, who was beginning to look irritated, might not. Seeing that this could be the beginning of a row—Pete calling Reg a warmonger and Reg calling him a Communist—Stratton decided it was high time he left the room.

He could do with a breath of fresh air. He went down the passage and let himself out of the back door. It was bloody cold—although, thought Stratton, it wasn't a patch on the winter of forty-six, when the pipes froze again and again and your breath was visible even inside the house and no matter how many clothes you wore, in bed or out of it, you never seemed to get warm. Peering into the almost darkness, he could make out the shapes of Donald's apple and plum trees at the bottom of the garden. He stamped his feet a few times, trying to keep warm. He didn't want to go back inside with the others—at least, until there was a good chance of any row having blown over. He'd had enough of Reg anyway, and, if he was honest, he wasn't really sure what to say to Pete.

This was partly, he supposed guiltily, because—aside from what he could glean by observing—he actually had very little idea about the sort of man his son was becoming. A callous one, judging by what he'd said to Monica and his reaction to the poor simple sod who'd been so tormented by the sergeant—or maybe that was the effect of the army, with its brutal ideas about toughening people up. But either way, at that precise moment, he wasn't even sure he *liked* his son very much.

He found himself wondering about the boy's taciturn reaction to Jenny's death—he'd assumed it was grief and that the lad had simply found the subject too painful to talk about. Stratton had been six when his own mother had died, but that was expected—tuberculosis—and he couldn't remember ever discussing it with his father or his brothers. He'd assumed that, even though the circumstances were entirely different, Pete must have had similar feelings to his own about losing his mother, but now he wondered if that were the case. Perhaps Pete simply hadn't cared all that much. Or perhaps Jenny's death had begun an inexorable hardening process within him.

Jenny'd once told him that she'd like Pete to have an office job, although he couldn't remember if she'd said what sort. Maybe she'd meant an accountant or something like that—something that involved wearing a suit, anyway. The other thing she'd said, which he *did* remember clearly, was that she didn't mind what the children ended up doing as long as they were happy. Pete's papers had come through soon after he'd left school, where he'd done surprisingly well, especially in science and mathematics. Perhaps some sort of conversation about his future was in order—although of course any future would have to be postponed until he'd done his National Service—but Stratton felt that this would need, if not actual preparation, then certainly a bit of thought.

Had he, after all, been so different to Pete at eighteen? He pictured himself, slimmer and fresher faced, marching down the endless corridors of the police-training school—shiny green and cream paint—and remembered the smell of disinfectant, sometimes so strong that it seemed to permeate the food. The army was probably quite like that, he thought. Unlike Pete, the training school was the first time he'd been away from home, and for a long time he'd missed his family and the sights, smells, and sounds of the Devon farm where he'd spent his childhood. Somehow, he doubted that Pete had been very homesick. After all, he'd been evacuated, and he seemed too self-contained, too assured...

Perhaps Pete's confidence was a bluff, too. Stratton had never tried very hard to find out. The truth was that he'd been afraid of being rebuffed and was still afraid. Jenny wouldn't have been. He suddenly remembered their honeymoon, walking hand in hand across sand dunes covered in scrubby grass and rabbit holes, and the hotel—the first time either had stayed in one—their awkwardness in the big, echoing dining room with its stiff napery and even stiffer waiters, and their giggly relief afterwards, finding themselves alone in the bedroom. How her beautiful green eyes had shone as she turned her face up to his for a kiss...

Hearing a tapping noise, he swung round and, seeing the same eyes looking out at him from behind the glass panel in the back door, he thought, for a split second, that—

'Dad! Tea's ready!' Monica opened the door. 'What are you doing out here? You'll catch your death.'

To his absolute horror, Stratton felt tears pricking at his eyelids, and he turned away from her, squeezing his eyes shut. For God's sake, he told himself, get a grip. Monica stepped out and put a hand on his sleeve. 'Were you thinking about Mum again?' she asked.

'Yes, love. Stupid, really...'

'No, it's not. It's normal.'

Stratton put his arm round her, and they stood for a moment in silence. Then she said, 'I meant to tell you before, but I forgot.'

'What's that?'

'About Mrs Calthrop. I bumped into her again—well, she was walking past the Make-up Department... Anyway, we had a chat. I was telling her about Mum, and she was ever so nice, and then—'

'Do you often tell people about Mum?'

'No, but… I don't know why I told her, really.' Monica sounded embarrassed. 'Anyway, she told me that she and her husband are…well, they're divorcing. I wasn't being nosy or anything, but she just said it, and… It was an odd conversation all round, really.'

'Must have been,' said Stratton. 'I suppose that's why she's working at the studio.'

He wasn't sure that he wanted to continue this conversation. Hearing about Diana Calthrop, especially from Monica, made him distinctly uncomfortable. An image of Diana as he'd first seen her came into his mind: the slender, glacial beauty, the gorgeous long legs, the expensive perfume…she'd exuded an air of exclusivity so strong that she might as well have had a label attached to her reading 'Not for the likes of you…' Although, of course, that was quite out of the question, him being married, and—

Oh, to hell with it. 'Let's go in,' he said. 'No sense in both of us freezing.'

'Mrs Garland'll be here in a minute,' said Monica, as she bent down to bolt the back door behind them. To stop me running away, Stratton thought, with an inward shudder. Mrs Garland was the latest in the line of war widows who were very much, according to his sisters-in-law, *for* the likes of him, and was obviously about to be paraded before him as a potential wife. Unnervingly small, with kittenish blue eyes, her main tactic was, he remembered, to get him to talk about his work and pretend to be fascinated while he did so. It was a sort of game, he supposed, but not one that he felt like playing, especially with Doris and Lilian monitoring every word. He had hoped—obviously foolishly—that on Christmas Day he'd be safe from that sort of thing.

Monica straightened up. 'Auntie Doris invited her for tea. Don't look like that, Dad. She's quite nice, really.'

'I'm sure she's delightful,' said Stratton, who wasn't sure of any such thing. 'It's the *reason* your aunt invited her that I'm not so keen on.' Talk about going from the sublime to the ridiculous, he thought.

'You should look on the bright side, Dad.' Monica giggled. 'It could be Miss Trew.'

'Oh, very funny.' Miss Trew was a tough old bird with iron hair and a kippered face who'd been in charge of the local Girl Guides for as long as anyone could remember. 'Come on then, let's get it over with…'

CHAPTER 26

Monica rubbed her hands vigorously, trying to dry them on the thin towel that hung on the back of the scullery door. The fabric had barely any nap left to absorb moisture. All the towels in the house were like that. Unlike hard things, she didn't categorise them as good or bad, friendly or unfriendly—they were simply worn out. The previous week, she'd gone into the dressing room of a visiting American star who must have brought her own towels because they were thicker and fleecier than any she'd ever seen. She'd been sent in there to fetch something, but she'd lingered, touching them and marvelling at how luxurious they were—much more so than the ones they used in Make-up, which were scarcely better than the ones at home.

She stepped back quickly as the door was shoved open. Dad had gone straight up to bed when they'd returned from Auntie Doris's, and she'd thought Pete had done the same—or hoped he had. It was late—almost eleven—but she wasn't tired enough to go to bed. She just wanted to be by herself for a while. She certainly didn't want to talk to Pete after he'd embarrassed her this afternoon, talking about boyfriends in front of everyone, but here he was, lounging in the doorway. 'Got a cig, Monica? I've run out.'

'In my bag. Wait a minute.'

Pete followed her into the kitchen. 'Fancy making us a cup of tea?' he asked when he'd lit up.

'At this hour?' said Monica, even though she'd been thinking about making some tea for herself.

'Why not?' Pete plonked himself down at the kitchen table. 'I'm not ready for bed yet.'

'Oh, all right.'

'What about that Mrs Garland?' said Pete, when she came back from filling the kettle. 'Ooh, Mr Stratton...' He launched into a cruel but accurate impersonation. 'Your work must be *so* interesting... Do tell me *all* about it. Honestly, I'm surprised she didn't jump into his lap.'

'Oh, stop it.' Monica lit the gas. It had been an uncomfortable evening, with Mrs Garland being embarrassingly skittish and Dad, who'd obviously hated every minute of it, almost painfully polite.

'Mind you,' said Pete, 'he could do a lot worse. She's not a bad-looking woman...for her age, I mean.'

'He's not interested,' said Monica. 'In case you hadn't noticed, he still misses Mum.'

'Oh, yes,' said Pete, narrowing his eyes. '*Mum*. Now there's a subject...'

Knowing what was coming—the few conversations she and Pete had had about their mother since her death had ended in rows—and determined not to be goaded, Monica said, 'Not now, Pete. I know what you think, but you're wrong. It wasn't Dad's fault.'

'Of course not,' said Pete, sarcastically. 'She was murdered by a lunatic with him standing two feet away, but let's not blame him.'

'I'm not going to argue about it.' Monica turned her back on him and began taking the tea things out of the cupboard.

Pete blew smoke at her. 'You're a real daddy's girl, aren't you? You think the sun shines out of him.'

'Pete, I'm not—'

'That why you don't have a boyfriend, is it? Can't find anyone as good as your precious Daddy?'

'Stop it!' Close to tears, and furious not only with him, but with herself for letting him upset her, Monica dumped two cups on the table. 'Why do you always have to be so horrible? You can't even start a conversation without turning it into a fight or insinuating something—like you did this afternoon.'

'This afternoon?' Pete asked, pretending innocence. 'I don't know what you're talking about.'

'You know damn well what I'm talking about.'

Pete shook his head. 'You're imagining things. Or,' he regarded her shrewdly, head on one side, 'you've got a guilty conscience.'

'Oh, rubbish!' Monica whirled round and threw the saucers down on the table so that they spun and clattered.

'Steady the buffs.' Pete put a hand out to still the wobbling china. 'Well, it must be one or the other,' he added, 'because as I said, I've got absolutely no idea what you mean.'

'You know exactly what I mean—that stuff about boyfriends.' The moment the words were out of her mouth, Monica knew she shouldn't have said it. Pete was nodding, a smug expression on his face, as if she'd blurted out something incriminatingly significant.

'What did you think I was *insinuating*?' he asked, folding his arms. 'Because that was the word you used.'

'Nothing! Stop it!' she raged at him, furious at having fallen into his trap. 'Just…stop bullying me!'

'You'd better stop shouting or you'll wake Dad,' said Pete, in tones of exaggerated reasonableness. 'And I wasn't bullying, I was asking a question, so…?'

'I don't want to discuss it,' said Monica. 'You were being horrible this afternoon, and you're doing the same thing now.'

'Oh, come on, Monica,' said Pete, in a wheedling tone. 'It was a joke. I wasn't suggesting anything.'

'Weren't you? It certainly sounded like it.'

'What could I have been suggesting?' The tone of mock innocence was back again.

'I told you, I don't want to discuss it.' The kettle was boiling. Monica grabbed the cloth and went over to the stove to take it off the gas. At the same moment, Pete stood up and then, just as she'd begun to lift the kettle, took hold of her arm so that she jerked and a few drops of hot water splashed on her hand.

'Ouch!' She let go of the kettle and shook her sore fingers. 'What the hell do you think you're doing?'

'Trying to make you answer the question. Be fair, Monica. You can't keep telling me that I've *insinuated* things and *suggested* things and then not say what they are.'

Monica suddenly felt as if she couldn't breathe. 'But you know bloody well what they are!' she burst out. 'You were suggesting I wasn't normal and you said it right in front of everybody and—'

'They wouldn't have understood,' said Pete, dismissively. 'And anyway,' he said, 'it *was* a joke. I wasn't really suggesting that you were…you know…one of *them*. Here, give me that,' he took the cloth from her, 'and I'll make the tea. You sit down.'

Monica sat down. Watching Pete as he made the tea, she wondered if he had meant it as a joke. If it really was a joke, then why had he just done all that business pretending he didn't understand what she was talking about? She knew why he was making the tea—because he knew he'd gone too far and upset her, and he was trying to make up for it. Or perhaps he was doing it because he'd got what he wanted—even though she hadn't actually admitted anything…or not in so many words, anyway. With a sinking heart, she thought, he's being nice *now*, but he'll never leave the subject alone—sly digs, little comments that couldn't be understood by anyone else… She should never have said anything. Of course, he might have carried on doing it anyway, but now that he knew she knew what he was getting at, he'd be impossible.

She'd only found out what 'one of *them*' meant a couple of weeks ago, when Anne, her best friend in the Make-up Department, had referred to a woman who worked in the Ashwood administration block in that way. Monica knew the woman in question, though not her name; she stood out because she was mannish, with cropped hair and a deep, fruity voice, and stomped about in severely tailored suits and brogues. When she'd asked Anne what it meant, Anne had giggled and said, 'You know, one of Nature's mistakes. A woman who wants to be a man.' When Monica asked, 'How do you mean?' Anne said that she was more attracted to other women than she was to men. She'd heard people laughing about the woman behind her back, or speaking about her in pitying tones or worse, contempt.

Monica had been thinking about the woman on and off ever since. I'm not like her, she kept telling herself. I'm not like her because I don't want to be a man. In fact, she couldn't think of anything she wanted less. Men did get more opportunities to do things, but if she'd been a boy she'd have had to do National Service, and she didn't fancy that at all. Imagine having to spend all your time with a lot of blokes like Pete! It wasn't that she disliked men—after all, Dad was a man, and she loved him, and so was Uncle Donald, and he was lovely, and...

She didn't want to end up like the woman at work, with everyone laughing behind her back. But they would if she carried on making a fool of herself as she had with Mrs Calthrop. Since that awful afternoon when she'd blurted out all of that stuff about Dad and being worried about him and Mum dying, Monica had avoided her. It was impossible not to think about her, though: she was so unbelievably beautiful, just like the women in the magazines. Being anywhere near her made Monica feel breathless. When she was actually with her, she felt that she couldn't even have told anyone her name, let alone anything else, and then she'd suddenly found herself jabbering about her family. She glanced at Pete, who was taking his time stirring the pot, and realised how odd it was that, despite the embarrassment and the rest of it, it was far easier to talk about Mum to Mrs Calthrop, a virtual stranger, than it was to talk to her own brother. She wished she didn't blush so easily, though—that was a dead give-away.

Taking her tea upstairs—she'd had more than enough of Pete for one day—she decided, as she very often did nowadays, that it would be all right to think about Mrs Calthrop for, say, five minutes before she went to sleep. She'd fallen into the habit of asking herself permission to do this, which she usually granted, but only for short periods—and only *thinking*, nothing more—as otherwise it was almost impossible to wrench her mind onto a different subject. She felt an agonising sense of guilt about doing it at home, because Dad was clearly keen on Mrs Calthrop himself, and the thought of him somehow picking up on her imaginings was horrifying. And with Pete here as well, it felt even less safe than usual, but tonight, she felt, she deserved it. In any case, Monica reasoned, Dad was bound to be asleep by now, and Pete would soon follow, so it would be—sort of—like being alone in the house.

Even if she did, by and large, manage to avoid Mrs Calthrop at the studio in the sense of staying out of her way, it had become impossible in the last week to avoid the subject of her. Speculation about her and Mr Carleton was rife, and there was a different rumour every day—almost as many as the rumours about how Mr Carleton had fallen off the waggon. It was a shame, Monica thought, because everyone said he was the best director working at Ashwood. She supposed Mrs Calthrop must be aware of it. If Mr Carleton was in love with her, Monica thought, and she with him, that would be enough to make anyone stop drinking, wouldn't it? Not that other people in the studio thought so. There's so much, she thought as she cleaned her teeth, that I don't understand.

In spite of her anxiety about seeing Mrs Calthrop, she was half-hoping she'd be working on Mr Carleton's next picture. This was partly because it would be fun and partly—well, mainly—because Mrs Calthrop would be on the set.

Monica took off her clothes, put on her nightdress, and got into bed. Closing her eyes, she indulged—for twelve minutes, rather than the allotted five—in a fantasy of telling Mrs Calthrop about Mr Carleton's drinking, and Mrs Calthrop thanking her and looking into her eyes and pressing her hand in gratitude... And then, feeling—temporarily at least—a great deal happier, she fell asleep.

1951

'You're going to marry me, darling,' said James Carleton. 'The moment you're free.'

Diana laughed. 'Are you sure you haven't had too much champagne?' It was the beginning of February, and they were walking through the Green Park mist after celebrating her imminent move into her own, albeit rented, flat by lunching at the Ritz so lavishly ('Always be extravagant when you're in funds, darling—you never know when the chance'll come again') that it was almost possible to believe that rationing had ceased to exist.

'There's no such thing as too much champagne,' said James solemnly. 'Left hand, please. And close your eyes.' Still thinking that he was joking, Diana did so and, presenting her hand, felt something being slid onto her third finger. 'You can look now.'

Whatever she'd expected, it certainly wasn't a ring with diamonds and sapphires twinkling in an art-deco setting. It was old-fashioned, but so lovely that it almost took her breath away. In the two months since their first dinner together, they'd seen a great deal of each other—most evenings as well as every day at the studio—and James, as Diana had admitted to a sceptical Lally, had swept her off her feet. She'd never met a man who *knew* so much: films, the theatre, classical music, poetry, philosophy, mathematics, jazz… His knowledge and zest for life made her giddy. He'd opened new worlds to her—things she'd never thought about or barely knew existed—and she listened, rapt, to his explanations, devoured the books he recommended and listened to the records, bombarding him with questions afterwards. 'I'm not intelligent enough for you,' she'd told him, and he'd replied, 'Yes you are, you just don't know it yet.' And it was true that she'd felt her senses heightened, not only by falling in love, but by all this new information, as if she could suddenly see and hear things that weren't apparent to other people. Lally, despite her initial caution, had taken to him immediately when they'd met at Christmas, and so, Diana thought, had Jock, although he hadn't said as much. But then, as Lally'd pointed out, you could hardly expect him to gush, and the nature of his work did tend to make you suspicious about people, even when there was no need to be.

Unlike Claude Ventriss, James was devoid of cynicism, and, also unlike Claude, he hadn't yet attempted to get her into bed. Part of Diana was glad about this, but another part was rather offended. Remembering Guy's hands-off behaviour during their courtship, she worried that it might not bode well for the future. 'Are you serious about this?' she asked.

'Don't you like the ring?' James's tone had an uncertainty she'd never heard before. 'It belonged to my mother but we can get it reset, if you don't like—'

'It's not the ring, darling. That's perfect—beautiful… It's…' Diana looked down at her hand and then back at James. 'It's just that you…you… Oh, I'm being stupid again.'

'Of course I'm serious, Diana. I love you. Don't you love me?'

'Yes…'

'Then say it.' James made his hands into a loudspeaker and said, 'Cue lights… Turn over…and… Action!'

Squaring her shoulders, Diana looked him straight in the eye and said, 'I love you, James Carleton.'

'Very good. Almost believable, in fact.'

Confused, Diana said, 'But I do—'

Laying a finger on her lips, James said, 'That was a *joke*, darling. People make them from time to time. I believe you.'

'Oh.' Diana took a step back, not quite sure whether she wanted to laugh or cry.

'Then why didn't you think…' James stopped and regarded her, head on one side. 'Ah *ha*! You're worried because I haven't pounced on you. That's it, isn't it?'

'No!' It came out too shrill, too vehement. 'That wasn't what I—'

'Oh yes, it was.' James's hand closed around her wrist, and she was aware of the pressure of his thumb against her racing pulse. 'VSITPQ as the debs used to say. You remember… Yes, you do, you're blushing. "Very safe in taxis, probably queer",' he declared in the clipped tones of Noel Coward. 'Well, I'm not.' His hand moved up her arm, pushing back the sleeves of her fur coat and dress so that his thumb was now massaging the soft flesh of her inner arm, hard enough to hurt. Diana stood and let him do it. There was nothing particularly intimate about an arm, and James's face wore a casual expression, as if completely unaffected by what he was doing. How can he be? she thought. It was one of the most sexual things she had ever experienced, and the sensation was so intense that she was aware of nothing else but a fierce erotic warmth that seemed to overtake her entire body.

It stopped abruptly when he removed his hand in a single movement so sudden that he almost tore the material of her dress, then grabbed her round the waist and pulled her towards him, whispering, 'I'll take you behind that tree and ravish you right now if you want me to prove it.'

Diana gasped, and, flustered, tried to right herself, pushing him away. 'That won't be necessary,' she said, primly. 'My mother always told me that once the season's over, ravishing should take place indoors or not at all.'

'That's better! Come here…' Gathering her to him once more, James ran his thumb down her cheek as if he was sculpting her, then, in a swift movement, tilted up her chin. 'I'll settle for a kiss.'

It lasted a long time. At the end of it, Diana felt as though they were already lovers.

'I'd better not wear this ring, you know,' she said later, when they were strolling towards Hyde Park Corner. 'I'm not yet divorced.'

'I've never cared much how things look, but you're right. You can wear it in private. We mustn't spoil your reputation.'

'I don't think I've got one to spoil,' said Diana, ruefully. 'Not any more.'

'You did the right thing, you know,' said James. 'You'd have gone mad with frustration and boredom stuck out in the country. Anyway, I need you, and now I've got you I'm certainly not going to let you go.' He stared around him. 'Extraordinary, isn't it, the way that history is crumbling into dust before our eyes. Mutability...the way bombed-out places'—he pointed at the hulk of a huge wrecked building in the distance, its harsh outlines rising, softened, out of the mist—'look like the ruins of ancient castles from a distance, especially in this light. We could be in a fairytale.'

'Until we get close to it and see the nettles and the rubbish and the stray cats,' said Diana.

'That's no way for a princess to talk. Especially in one of my fairytales.'

'Well, what happens next in your tale, then?'

'Well, the princess is so beautiful that everyone is madly in love with her, down to the castle's lowliest scullion and kitchen-maid—'

'Rubbish!'

'Stop interrupting. In any case, it's perfectly true. Even that little make-up girl. I've seen how she looks at you.'

'What little make-up girl?'

'The one you're always sneaking off to chat to. In fact, I've been wondering whether I shouldn't be starting to get jealous...'

'You mean Monica Stratton?' asked Diana, incredulously.

'Never heard of a schoolgirl crush, my dear?'

'I didn't go to school. That's why I don't know anything.'

'I wouldn't say that.' James leant over and kissed her cheek, squeezing her bottom at the same time. 'Well, not quite… Anyway, where was I?'

'Everyone's in love with this wretched princess.'

'Oh, yes. Well, the prince—that's me, in case you're wondering—being possessed of infinite sagacity as well as the courage of a lion, a countenance like the sun, and a…oh, you know, all that other stuff that princes have… Anyway, he leads the princess to a nice little place where an aged crone peps them up with the elixir of life.'

'But we've only just had lunch.'

'The tragedy of this particular prince, my darling, is that he was born several drinks behind the rest of the world and is doomed to spend his life catching up… And we've got to celebrate. This is the beginning of a real adventure, my darling.' His eyes were shining, his excitement almost palpable. 'And apart from anything else, it's bloody cold out here. Come on!' He began to run across the grass, tugging her behind him.

Much later, alone in the taxi on the way back to Jock and Lally's, she closed her eyes and rested her head against the back of the seat. Flushed, tipsy, and languorous, with a delightful tingly pain between her thighs, she felt as though she actually had been making love all afternoon. When she arrived at Albemarle Street, a disapproving Mrs Robinson was waiting for her with a note from Lally. 'Mr and Mrs Anderson were waiting,' she said, and Diana remembered, with a guilty pang, that she'd agreed to accompany the two of them to a performance of choral music at St James's Church in Piccadilly with a reception afterwards.

Despite the housekeeper's ill-concealed censoriousness, Lally's note was breezy.

Waited for you as long as we could—you're obviously gadding about somewhere with gorgeous Mr Carleton (don't blame you at all—much more fun!). Hope you enjoyed yourselves. Jock brought back a letter for you from F-J. He found it when he was going through the last of F-J's papers and thought you ought to have it. It's on yr bed—I thought you'd prefer to read it in private. See you as soon as we can get away, L.

Diana carried the cup of tea, grudgingly produced by Mrs Robinson, up to her room. Picking up the letter, she sank into the armchair without bothering to remove her gloves or coat and sat turning the envelope over in her hands. It was neither addressed nor sealed, so clearly someone—Jock, perhaps—had already read its contents. Given the nature of F-J's work and the manner of his death, she decided, that was inevitable.

The juxtaposition of these thoughts with the events of the afternoon made her feel uneasy, guilty about her new-found happiness, and she couldn't help wondering if it would last. Had F-J ever thought he could be happy, she wondered, or had he merely hoped to escape detection?

The letter inside the envelope was scrawled so that the words were ugly tangles, hard to decipher, with minimal punctuation, degenerating into a list of sentences down the page. Diana wondered if F-J had been drunk when he wrote it. Perhaps, she thought, it was just some notes towards a letter he'd been planning to send her, but had never got round to finishing. Anyway, why did it matter? It meant he'd thought of her, didn't it?

Dear Diana,
I owe you an apology. I am sorry not to be able to deliver it in person.
I deeply regret my behaviour over Neville Apse. I hope that you can now forgive me.

He must have known what he was going to do when he wrote it, Diana thought—he'd never have set those words down on paper otherwise. 'I do forgive you, F-J,' she murmured. 'Of course I do.' From her cocoon of happiness, she could have forgiven anything.

That slate is clean at least.
Perhaps the only one, who knows?
I hope you will be happy.
Remember what I said about Ventriss. You are the natural prey of an unscrupulous man (as I was)
If in trouble, you might contact Edward Stratton
I am sure you remember him. He is a good man

It wasn't signed, but at the bottom of the page there was an address—somewhere in north-east London, with a street name Diana couldn't read, but which she supposed must be where Inspector Stratton lived. F-J's trying to provide me with a guardian angel, she thought. The fact that she didn't now need one made it, somehow, all the more touching. Perhaps F-J had guessed how unhappy she was in Hampshire and had thought that Stratton might be able to save her from Claude Ventriss at some unspecified future time... Diana glanced at the letter again. *The natural prey of an unscrupulous man.* The words leapt at her as if they were written in crimson ink. But James wasn't unscrupulous, so she had nothing to fear. A tiny flare of alarm, like some misshapen thing glimpsed out of the corner of the eye and not quite recognised, flickered in her mind, then died. Regretfully, she tugged James's ring off her finger and bent down to put it into her handbag. Nothing must be said before the divorce, not even to Lally. The gesture made her remember how she'd taken her wedding ring off in the war years, working for F-J. Even in the depths of his despair, about to take his own life, he had thought of her...

'You were a good man too, F-J,' she said aloud. 'You were, and you didn't deserve this.'

Later, lying wakeful in bed, she found herself clutching at the sides of the mattress as if the room were about to start shifting around her. Everything seemed to be mutating so much that really, there was no reason for the furniture—the very house—not to move as well. All the old values, the ones she'd grown up with, must be re-examined, weighed in the balance. Never, she thought, had life seemed so precious and so fragile.

CHAPTER 28

From the witness box, Stratton looked down at the sea of wigs in the Old Bailey's Number One Court. The greyish-white curls reminded him, as they always did, of cauliflowers with the leaves cut off, and they seemed incongruous, bobbing about amidst the wood and leather of the heavy, dark furniture and the rolls of paper tied up with pink tape. He looked round at the jury, upright and self-consciously solemn in their box, at the press in the well of the court, and then up at the gallery, which was packed with the usual array of ghouls. They all looked the same, somehow, with dull hair and dun-coloured faces, leaning down, mouths agape, as if they had all been cut out of the same piece of damp wool. So far, February had been very cold and very wet, and periodically the ghouls broke the silences with salvos of bronchitic coughing, so that Stratton imagined a thickening cloud of germs hanging in the air above the lawyers and clerks.

He looked across at the judge, Lord Justice Spencer, seated on his elaborate throne. He was an ascetic-looking man who reminded Stratton of newspaper pictures he'd seen of Sir Stafford Cripps. He wore half-moon spectacles and, staring at Davies over the top of them, he could have served as a symbol for the unwavering and pitiless scrutiny of the law.

Some criminals Stratton had seen in the dock seemed to have a sense of their celebrity, a consciousness that they were the focus of attention. Davies wasn't one of them. Standing in the pen that was easily large enough to hold ten or even twelve people, he seemed smaller and more insignificant than ever. Tidy, in a clean shirt, with hair so neat and shiny that it might have been creosoted, he stood quite still, eyes down, while behind him the seated guard doodled with a slightly open mouth and the absorbed air of a child with a crayon in its fist. For Davies, it was the difference between life and death; for the guard, it was the rather dull means of putting food on the table, regardless of the impressive surroundings.

And they were impressive—everything about the Old Bailey was meant to intimidate, from the high ceilings and the paintings of varnished darkness on the walls to the unassailable might of the law in all its pomp and ceremony. Stratton had given evidence at the Old Bailey a fair few times in his career but still found it unnerving enough to get an actual sensation of discomfort in his scrotum; what it must be doing to Davies was anybody's guess...

August Ronstadt, for the Crown, was a man with the sort of fine-grained portliness that looked as though it came from beef and good wine, whose appearance exactly matched his rich, plump voice. He strode about the court—no mere walking for him—and, even though he was on their side, Stratton's instinctive dislike of all lawyers, but especially ones like this, made him wonder sourly if the man ever merely ate, drank, or farted, either. Not for him such ordinary animal functions—he would devour, imbibe, and blast like a celestial trumpet afterwards. Although Stratton had put hundreds of dullards in the dock and witnessed equal numbers of barristers smashing their evidence to pieces, the immense gulf between Ronstadt and Davies—in stature, intellect, opportunity, entitlement, and every other possible thing—impressed him as never before.

The Crown had decided to proceed on the indictment charging Davies with Judy's murder rather than his wife's. It was easy to see why, although there had been a sticky half hour's wait earlier on while counsel argued whether evidence about the death of Muriel was admissible. Hearing that it was, Stratton uttered one of the most heartfelt Thank Christ's of his whole career, and hearing that none of the workmen would be called and that Davies would be the only witness for the defence had made him feel even better.

Of course, if Lord Justice Spencer had deemed the evidence inadmissible, the Crown could simply have gone ahead with the indictment for Muriel's killing, but it was much more likely to be plain sailing this way round—as, so far, it had proved. Dr McNally, the pathologist, Backhouse, Edna Backhouse, Mrs Howells, and the Welsh policeman, Williams, had so far been called for the prosecution, and August Ronstadt had done a splendid job. The judge had helped, too. As Ballard had remarked, *sotto voce*, 'Well, he's on our side.' Despite the business of Backhouse's previous convictions, Ronstadt, with a surprising amount of assistance from the judge, had done a very good job of painting the chief witness as a reformed character, a hero of the Great War, and a man struggling valiantly against ill health. Lord Justice Spencer had even asked him if he'd prefer to give his evidence sitting down, and when the time came for the defence lawyer, Humphrey Shillingworth (less richly plump than Ronstadt but, in Stratton's opinion, well on the way there) to suggest that Backhouse had had something to do with the baby's death, it looked like simple bullying. Shillingworth himself clearly found the task distasteful. His unease had been evident when he'd questioned Backhouse; he'd hedged the allegations round with semi-apologies to a degree that Stratton couldn't remember ever having heard before. After all, given what they did for a living, expecting sincerity from barristers was as unreasonable as expecting genuine passion from prostitutes. It was appearance that counted, which was why Shillingworth's obvious lack of appetite for his work had made an impression on him, and, Stratton thought, the jury.

Given that there was no medical evidence whatsoever to back up Davies's cock and bull story about Backhouse killing Muriel in the performance of an unsuccessful abortion—not to mention a single reason why Backhouse should want to kill the baby—Stratton was surprised that nobody had tried to talk the little man out of issuing instructions that would be bound to fail, but he could see that they had bugger-all else to go on.

The questions from Ronstadt were a piece of cake. After a brief pause, filled with a lot more coughing and wheezing from the gallery, Shillingworth stood up and started taking Stratton through the statements Davies had made at West End Central with a lot of questions about the timings and who'd said what to whom and when. Stratton could see the point of these—Shillingworth was trying to find out if they'd put words into Davies's mouth about the circumstances in which the bodies were found. This had given him a couple of sleepless nights before the trial started, but when it came to the point, it was all pretty straightforward, and he hadn't needed to check his notebook once. This wasn't something he liked doing, because it called up the image of the comedy plod, shuffling and thumb-licking, and the bloody lawyers were quite condescending enough already, thanks very much, without all that.

After that, Shillingworth started on the timber used to hide the bodies from view. 'He told us he'd concealed his wife's body behind timber in the washhouse, sir.'

'He said that, did he?' asked Shillingworth. ' "Concealed behind timber"?'

'Yes, sir.' The moment he'd spoken he realised that he wasn't actually sure that Davies had used those words—in fact, he had a distinct memory of saying them himself when he'd cautioned the man—but Shillingworth moved on to another question, and it was too late to go back. Not that he wanted to go back, of course, and besides, Davies had known about the timber because of the workmen, hadn't he, so… Trying to clarify it all in his mind, Stratton failed to hear Shillingworth's next question and had to ask for it to be repeated. Bloody well *concentrate*, he told himself. Just get through the next ten minutes without landing on your arse, and we're laughing.

After a break for lunch, during which Stratton and Ballard, who'd followed him into the witness box, toyed with two pieces of very dead plaice, they sat together at the back of the court. They'd found, on checking their notebooks, that Stratton *had* mentioned the timber in the caution, but, Ballard having agreed with him that Davies knew about the timber because he knew about the workmen, he'd felt reassured. In any case, the moment had passed, and it was only one tiny thing... Something in the back of his mind told him that that wasn't the only incidence where they'd put words into Davies's mouth, but it had been so bloody hard to untangle the truth from all the lies the man had told. And he'd confessed, hadn't he? So why did he, Stratton, feel the need to justify his actions? Why did it bother him? Irritable with himself, he put the thoughts from his mind and concentrated on Davies, who was giving evidence.

Shillingworth was taking Davies through the statements he'd given in Wales, his allegations about Backhouse, and the stuff about selling his furniture. Standing alone in the dock, clutching the rail with white knuckles, Davies looked more insignificant than ever, as if struggling against the onslaught of some remorseless force of nature against which he was powerless. This, thought Stratton, was entirely true, even if the bloke was supposed to be acting for him. As for when Ronstadt got to his feet… Stratton scribbled 'What do you think?' in his notebook, tore out the page, and pushed it towards Ballard. After a moment, the answer came back. 'Hasn't got a prayer.'

'What happened when you got to West End Central police station?' asked Shillingworth.

'Inspector Stratton told me my wife and baby were dead, sir.'

'Did he say where?'

'Yes, sir. At number ten Paradise Street in the washhouse, and he said he thought I'd done it.'

'Did he say how it appeared they died?'

'Yes, sir, by strangulation.'

'Did he say with what?'

Puffy-eyed and squinting with concentration, Davies said, 'With a rope, sir, and my daughter had been strangled with a tie.'

'Did I say she'd been strangled with a tie?' whispered Stratton to Ballard.

The sergeant looked through his notebook. 'No, sir, but the tie was in the Charge Room with the rest of the stuff.'

'Was anything shown to you at that time?' said Shillingworth.

'Yes, sir. The clothing of my wife and daughter.'

'Before Inspector Stratton told you, had you any idea that anything had happened to your daughter?'

'No, sir. No idea at all.'

Stratton and Ballard exchanged glances, and Ballard grimaced and rolled his eyes. Taking this line, Stratton supposed, was a bit like the business of accusing Backhouse. Shillingworth was bound to take Davies's instructions, even if they were ridiculous.

'Did he tell you,' continued Shillingworth, 'when he said the bodies had been found in the washhouse, whether they had been concealed or not?'

'He told me they had been concealed by timber.'

Stratton and Ballard exchanged glances again.

'When Inspector Stratton said he had reason to believe that you were responsible for the deaths of your wife and daughter, what did you say?' asked Shillingworth.

'I said, "Yes".'

'Why?'

'Well, when I found out about my daughter being dead, I was upset. I didn't care what happened to me then.'

'Was there any other reason why you said "Yes" as well as the fact that you gave up everything when you heard that your daughter was dead?'

'Yes, sir. I was frightened at the time.'

'Why were you frightened?'

'I thought that if I did not make a statement the police would take me downstairs and start knocking me about.'

'Did you then make this statement saying that your wife was incurring one debt after another: "I could not stand it any longer so I strangled her with a piece of rope"?'

'Yes, sir.'

'And later that you had strangled the baby on the Thursday evening with your tie?'

'Yes, sir.'

'Is it your tie which is Exhibit Three in this case?'

'No, sir.'

'Had you ever seen the tie before you were shown it by the Inspector?'

'No, sir.'

'That's nonsense, sir,' murmured Ballard to Stratton. 'He told us at least twice that he'd strangled the baby with it.'

Stratton nodded and would have dismissed the matter, but something occurred to him. 'Did we ever ask him to identify the tie?' he whispered.

Ballard shook his head. 'Not after he'd seen it in the Charge Room. He picked it up, remember? But then he's a great one for changing his mind... Anyway,' he added, after a moment's thought, 'Backhouse identified it for us, didn't he?'

'That's true enough.' But, thought Stratton, Davies had never been able to explain to them *why* he killed the baby, had he? Oh, pull yourself together, he told himself—it wasn't as if it could have been anyone else, and you're a policeman, not a bloody trick cyclist. Rubbing his face, he suddenly realised quite how much he wanted the trial to be over and done.

'Is it true that your wife was incurring debts?' asked Shillingworth.

'Yes, sir.'

'But untrue that you strangled her?'

'Yes, sir.'

'Why, if you had not committed these murders, did you say that you had?'

'I was upset. I don't think I knew what I was saying. I was afraid that the police would take me downstairs.'

'Is that why you told a lie to them?'

'Yes, sir. I was upset pretty bad. I had been believing my daughter was still alive.'

Davies was doing surprisingly well, thought Stratton. In fact, his part in these exchanges was so prompt and fluent that it must surely have been rehearsed many times. All the same, he couldn't help thinking it was a bit daft of Shillingworth to try and let Davies have it both ways—it was one thing if the man hadn't known what he was saying because he was upset, but quite another if he had deliberately confessed because he'd been scared. Which, Stratton thought, he had been—after all, he'd been caught, hadn't he?

'Trying to have his cake and eat it,' whispered Ballard, confirming his thoughts. In the hiatus that followed when Shillingworth had concluded and the prosecution was readying itself, Ballard added, 'Ronstadt's going to make mincemeat of him.'

Stratton looked round the courtroom and, after a moment, picked out the neat, upright form of Davies's mother from the rows of people in the gallery. What must she be thinking? Her baby granddaughter was dead and her son was a murderer twice over—three times, if you counted the baby Muriel had on the way. For a moment, the elderly woman's pinched little face became Jenny's, and Stratton, blinking rapidly, looked away.

The Backhouses were sitting together on the other side, a solid, respectable unit of two. Edna Backhouse, in a dark coat with a matching hat firmly planted on her head, had her lips pursed and her hands primly folded over the capacious bag in her lap. Backhouse, next to her, bent over to polish his glasses, the light reflecting off his domed, bald head. Stratton hadn't warmed to the man, and he certainly thought he was laying it on with a trowel about his various ailments, but the sort of ordeal the poor sod had been through in court was something you wouldn't wish on your worst enemy, never mind the fact that he and his wife were having to live in a house where murder had been committed.

Feeling that he was staring, he lowered his gaze. In the dock, the author of all the misery looked smaller and more pitiful than ever.

'Is it true,' began Ronstadt, 'that on five different occasions at different places and to different persons you have confessed to the murder of your wife and to the murder of your child?'

Stratton raised his eyebrows at Ballard. He couldn't see how he'd arrived at *five* different occasions and thought that Shillingworth must be straight on his feet, but there was no objection.

'Well…' Davies hesitated, a baffled look on his face. Finally, he said, 'I have confessed it, sir, but it isn't true.'

'But you did confess five times?'

Again, Stratton looked towards Shillingworth, but he remained in his seat.

Davies looked completely lost. Stratton could well imagine how lost—caught up in the vast tangle of the lies he'd told, he was trying to work out how to answer, and, of course, he wouldn't have been able to rehearse any of this.

After some hesitation and in the voice of one giving up on an insurmountable challenge, Davies said simply, 'Yes, sir. I was upset.'

'Are you saying,' Ronstadt asked, in tones that rang with disbelief, 'that on each of these occasions you were upset?'

'Not all of them,' said Davies, who now appeared to have taken the five occasions as gospel, 'but the last one I was.'

'If you were not upset on all of the five, why did you confess to wilful murder, unless it was true?'

Davies blinked rapidly several times, then said, 'Well, I knew my wife was dead, but I didn't know my daughter was dead.'

Ballard murmured, 'Still sticking to it, then. Surprised he can remember, after all he's said.'

'You say you didn't know your daughter was dead,' said Ronstadt. 'What had that got to do with it?'

'It had a lot to do with it.' Davies sounded petulant.

'We're on our way…' Ballard murmured.

'Is that a reason for pleading guilty to murder, that you are upset because your daughter is dead by someone else's hand?'

'Yes.'

'Is it?' It wasn't only Ronstadt's voice that was heavy with disbelief now, but the very air in the courtroom, as if all those present had somehow exhaled their thoughts.

'Do you think that's possible?' Stratton asked Ballard out of the corner of his mouth.

Ballard, looking at him as if he'd suddenly grown an extra head, gave a firm shake of his own. 'Sir, he's making it up as he goes along. Look at him—he hasn't got a clue what he's saying.'

That was certainly true. Davies, in the dock, looked as if he barely knew where he was, let alone anything else. 'Yes,' he repeated, after a long pause.

'I see,' said Ronstadt, making it clear that he didn't, at all. 'Let's just look at those occasions. You voluntarily went, did you not, to the police on November the thirtieth after having had read to you a letter from your mother to your aunt?'

'That's right.'

'It was because in the letter your previous lies were exposed that you decided to go to the police, was it?'

'It was not because of the lies,' said Davies, suddenly truculent. 'I was getting worried about my daughter.'

Ronstadt raised an elegant eyebrow. 'Are you seriously telling the jury that you went to the police and confessed to murder because you were worried about the whereabouts of your daughter?'

At this, Shillingworth did get to his feet. 'With respect,' he said, 'there was no confession of murder. He said, "I have disposed of my wife. I have put her down the drain."'

'It sounds very like murder,' said the judge, dismissively.

'Blimey, sir,' whispered Ballard, in the short silence that followed. 'That's going a bit far.'

'Blimey indeed,' murmured Stratton. Despite the niggling worries, things were going better than he could possibly have imagined. Lamb, he thought, was going to be delighted.

'I will amend my question,' said Ronstadt, with an exaggerated air of patience. 'Because you are upset about your daughter, who so far as you know is perfectly well, you go to the police and confess to the disposition of your dead wife's body. Is that right?'

After a moment, during which Stratton wondered if Davies knew what 'disposition' meant, he said, 'Yes, sir.'

Might as well give him a spade and tell him to dig his own grave, thought Stratton, scanning the jury members' faces and seeing expressions that ran the gamut from incredulity to revulsion.

'I see,' said Ronstadt. 'So that is your defence, that you confessed to the murder of your wife and child because you were upset… And therefore you make an allegation through your counsel against a perfectly innocent man that he caused the murder.'

Again, Shillingworth got to his feet. Save your breath, chum, thought Stratton. You're on a hiding to nothing with this one. 'Is that the proper way of asking the question, with the greatest respect? "You make an allegation against a perfectly innocent man" can only be a statement based on the assumption that his witness is innocent and mine is not. My friend has no right to make a statement describing Mr Backhouse as "a perfectly innocent man".'

The judge looked perplexed. 'Why not?'

'Well, it can only be done for the purpose of prejudice.'

'I crave leave,' said Ronstadt, in a voice that dripped with irony, 'not to have to believe that everything the accused says is true.'

'Bloody hell,' muttered Ballard.

There followed some to-ing and fro-ing over statements, during which Davies appeared to get into a complete muddle about which one was being discussed. By the end of it, the picture of a man whose past was rapidly and remorselessly catching up with him was clearer than ever. 'So,' concluded Ronstadt, 'you are saying that, out of the four statements you made, three of them were lies, and only the second statement from Wales—the one in which you accuse Mr Backhouse—is true?'

'Yes.' Davies sounded surer now.

'So, would it not be right to say that you are a person who is prepared to lie or tell the truth at your convenience?'

'Why should I tell lies?' Davies burst out angrily. His eyes were bright with panic, and for a moment Stratton had the impression of some tiny, furtive animal, flushed into the open and then cornered, twisting frantically this way and that to escape its captors. Stratton glanced at Ballard and guessed from the flinty, set expression on his face that the sergeant was thinking exactly what he was: Shame you didn't consider that before you murdered a woman and a helpless baby. He felt no sympathy now, just the excited anticipation of watching a fellow hunter using all his skills and training to go smoothly for the kill. The rest of the court felt it too; where there had been disbelief, there was now a different undercurrent—almost a thrill, as, necks craning and mouths agape, people leaned forward as if straining to catch Ronstadt's next words.

'After you made the first statement at the police station in London—that's Exhibit Eight, which is the short statement of confession—you told the police, "It is a great relief to get it off my chest." That's correct, isn't it?'

Stratton raised a questioning eyebrow at Ballard, who tapped his notebook by way of confirmation.

'Yes.'

'So it was a relief to you to tell the truth at last to the police, which was a confession of murder?'

Davies looked puzzled. 'It wasn't the truth,' he said at last. 'It was a lot of lies.'

'You are telling us that it was a relief to tell a lot of lies?'

'I was upset,' said Davies, doggedly.

'Do answer the question,' said the judge, testily. 'Was it a relief to you to tell a lot more lies?'

'I…' Davies paused, mouth agape. 'No,' he said, 'it wasn't a relief.'

'Now,' said Ronstadt, 'you've told us that the second of your statements, in which you accuse Mr Backhouse, is true. Is that right?'

'Yes, sir.'

'You've said that Mr Backhouse commits an abortion on your wife so that she dies of it, and that knowing that he is responsible for her death, he organises the disposition of her body and the removal of your child to some other place? Is that right?'

'Yes.'

'And then he comes along here and commits perjury against you? Is that what you are saying?'

'Yes, sir.'

'I see. Let's look a little further at what I suggest is your habit of lying to suit your convenience. You lied to the Backhouses, didn't you, about your wife being away?'

'I lied to Mrs Backhouse, yes.'

'You lied to Mrs Backhouse. And you lied to your aunt down in Wales, didn't you?'

'Yes, sir.'

'You then told half a dozen separate, distinct, and deliberate lies to the police, inventing any story that came into your head, didn't you?'

'Not any story, sir,' said Davies, desperately. It didn't really matter now, thought Stratton, what he said. Ronstadt's hammering home of the words 'lied' and 'lies' were so effective and so final that they might as well have been nails in the little man's coffin.

'Well, you began by lying about putting your wife's body down the drain. That wasn't true, was it?'

'No, it wasn't true.'

'You lied about helping Mr Backhouse carry your wife's body downstairs, didn't you?'

'No, I didn't. That was true.'

'Do you not realise from what you have heard today,' said Ronstadt, with the air of patient, even compassionate, explanation, 'that he was physically incapable of doing that or even of carrying the baby?'

'I still say I helped him carry my wife's body,' said Davies stubbornly.

Ronstadt sighed audibly. The sound managed to convey a dozen things unspoken—regret, sorrow, dismay at such a blatant show of mendacity… Despite his antipathy to the man, Stratton was impressed. There was no coughing now, no stirring or rustling, just a taut silence.

'I suggest,' said Ronstadt, 'that that is another lie. You lied to your employer, didn't you?'

'Yes.'

'Another lie. You lied to Mrs Backhouse, your aunt, the police, and your boss.'

'Yes. I did it because Mr Backhouse told me to.'

'Mr *Backhouse* told you to lie to all these people?'

'He said that if anyone asked about my wife and daughter, I should say they'd gone on holiday.'

'I see.' Ronstadt half-turned from Davies and then, swivelling back on the balls of his feet with the dexterity of a matador about to administer the *coup de grâce* in a bullring, said, 'And now you are alleging that Mr Backhouse is the murderer in this case? Perhaps you can suggest *why* he should have strangled your wife?'

Davies opened his mouth, then closed it again. Unblinking, Ronstadt stared at him, waiting, a predator about to spring.

'Well,' he said uncertainly, 'he was home all day.'

'I asked you,' said Ronstadt, 'if you can suggest *why* he should have strangled her?'

Davies looked dazed and appeared to shrink a little more, as if squashed by the air itself. The silence seemed to be quivering with electricity, and Stratton felt the blood pounding in his ears. As if in slow motion, Davies bent, then raised, his head, then looked around the court as if he might find an answer there. When he finally answered, it was in the thick voice of a man waking from a dream. 'No,' he said, 'I can't.'

'Well,' said Ronstadt, in tones of the utmost reasonableness, 'perhaps you can suggest why he should have strangled your daughter.'

Davies shook his head, defeated. 'No,' he said.

With elaborate courtesy, Ronstadt said, 'Thank you, Mr Davies,' and, striding across the courtroom, resumed his seat. As he did so an audible exhalation, like a sigh, went round the court, and, the tension evaporating, people began to shift about and murmur to one another.

Shillingworth rose. 'My lord,' he said, wearily, 'that is the case for the defence.'

'I think that must be the shortest closing speech from a prosecuting counsel I've ever heard,' said Stratton, when they emerged at the end of the day.

'Caught Shillingworth on the hop, didn't it?' said Ballard. 'He looked as if he wasn't expecting to have to do anything till tomorrow.'

'Yes, he did. Mind you, it's not going to make any difference—not unless the judge changes his mind overnight. I've got to get back to the station—DCI Lamb'll be waiting with bated breath, I shouldn't wonder, but why don't you cut off home?'

'I'd like to, sir, if it's all right. See the nipper before she goes to sleep.'

'Don't blame you.' For want of a more intimate gesture, Stratton clapped Ballard on the back. 'Off you go, then. Give my best to your missus, won't you?'

'Course, sir. And...you know...' Ballard's grin became lopsided in the effort to hide his embarrassment, 'thanks.'

CHAPTER 31

Listening to the judge's summing-up the following day, Davies, dead-eyed, looked more like some sort of grotesque, outsized man-doll than a human being. Stratton wondered how much of the arcane language he understood. Behind him, the warder had stopped doodling and was alert, head on one side, rather in the manner of an attentive dog. Looking about him, Stratton thought that he was the only one whose focus had sharpened—compared to the previous afternoon the atmosphere in the court was calm, the silence no longer twanging with anticipation. No cut and thrust here—this was a formality, and it was going pretty much as they'd expected—Mr Justice Spencer, bless his ermine socks, was restating the case for the prosecution with as much, if not more, righteous ire, than Ronstadt. After insisting to the jury in no uncertain terms that Davies had 'lied and lied and lied', he told them, almost as an afterthought, that of course they had to make up their own minds about whether he was telling the truth. Stratton, scanning their twelve faces, decided that they'd done that already.

'It's in the bag,' he said, as the jury, armed with copies of Davies's statements, filed out of the court.

'Seems so, sir,' said Ballard.

'I almost felt sorry for him…' Stratton said. Now it was almost over, it was much easier to dismiss the nagging, unfocused worries that had been bedevilling him. They were, he told himself, a consequence of trying to do a good job, and nothing worse than anything he'd experienced with other cases. 'Talk about a poisoned chalice,' he added.

'We didn't need to worry about the stuff we never got straight, after all.'

'Can't dot all the i's and cross all the t's every time,' said Stratton, easily. 'Always one or two little mysteries. Still,' he added, 'the judge did everything but tell them to convict him.'

'He convicted himself, sir. The jury won't have believed him any more than we did.'

When, after only forty more minutes, they were told that the jury were about to return, Stratton knew they'd been right about the conviction. As he followed Ballard into the courtroom, he tried to stabilise himself, mentally, against the conflicting rush of emotions that he remembered all too clearly from the handful of capital cases he'd worked on. There was something horribly primitive about the soaring sense of triumph that overcame him, but it was, at least, undermined by his shame for feeling it and blunted by his pity and sorrow for Davies's victims—who were, after all, going to be given some form of revenge. Not, of course, that it would do them any good, but all the same… Still, Stratton supposed, feeling those things was better than being indifferent, because that would mean one didn't care.

'Members of the jury,' intoned Mr Justice-Spencer, 'are you agreed upon your verdict?'

The foreman, a dapper individual who looked as if he might work in a gents' outfitters, stood up. 'We are.'

'Do you find the prisoner, John Wilfred Davies, guilty or not guilty of the murder of Judy Davies?'

There was a second's silence, and Stratton felt a tightness grip his chest, as if a collective intake of breath had robbed the air of oxygen, and then the foreman said, 'Guilty.'

A hastily stifled cry came from the gallery. Davies's mother, thought Stratton. In the dock, Davies, who'd been standing with his head bowed, jerked like a marionette being twitched into life on invisible strings, his face as taut as a mask.

'You find him guilty and that is the verdict of you all?'

'It is.'

'John Wilfred Davies, you stand convicted of murder. Have you anything to say why the court shall not give you judgement of death according to the law?'

Davies's expression did not change, but his voice quavered as he said, 'No, sir.'

An usher, as sombre and reverent as if he were serving at an altar, laid the black square on Mr Justice Spencer's head and, backing slowly away, returned to his seat. Get on with it, for God's sake, thought Stratton. He'd seen this before, a couple of times, and it never got any better. There was something terrible about the way that the ceremony of it all, the pauses, the sheer theatricality, cloaked desire for retribution and the sheer barbarism of putting a man to death, no matter how much he deserved it. Turning it into a spectacle like this was sickening, and the repulsed fascination he felt about it disgusted him.

Straightening his back, the judge turned to the dock and spoke. 'John Wilfred Davies, the jury have found you guilty of wilful murder and the sentence of the court upon you is that you be taken from this place to a lawful prison, and thence to a place of execution, and there to suffer death by hanging, and that your body be buried within the precincts of the prison in which you shall have been last confined before your execution, and may the Lord have mercy upon your soul.'

Stratton saw Davies take a deep breath, as though preparing for a dive, and close his eyes. Startled by a sudden, harsh sob from the other side of the court, he turned to look and saw that Backhouse, head in hands, was weeping.

Emerging into the street, Stratton and Ballard were distracted from their conversation by shouts just ahead of them. Moving quickly to the site of the disturbance, they heard a female voice: 'Murderer! You've killed my son!'

It was Mrs Davies. No longer small and neat, she was shrill and vengeful, eyes popping and fists clenched in rage, and yelling at the top of her voice with a hatred so palpable that everyone close was backing out of range. She was screaming at Backhouse who, vacant with shock, was staring at her. Just as Stratton and Ballard reached the pair of them, Edna Backhouse, goaded from her habitual meekness, sprang in front of her husband and, handbag clutched in front of her like a shield, shouted into the other woman's face, 'Don't you dare say that! He's a good man!'

As Ballard moved forward to take Mrs Davies's arm and lead her away, Backhouse caught sight of Stratton and registering through pink-rimmed eyes who he was looking at, gave the discreet, complacent smile of one firmly reestablished on the moral high ground.

Doris gazed at the dish of meagre-looking chops. 'Tuppence off the meat ration—again,' she said wistfully. 'I do wish they'd end it.'

'Plenty of greens, anyway,' said Donald, nodding approvingly at the khaki-coloured mound of spring cabbage, which was all that Stratton's allotment was capable of producing in such a relentlessly wet April as this one.

'Nature's policemen, those,' said Reg, helping himself. 'Shouldn't eat too much meat, anyway. Bungs you up.'

In order to forestall any enquiry as to the state of everyone's bowels—Reg, who'd recently taken to studying the 'Home Doctor' book and now fancied himself an expert, was quite capable of it and he could see the fear in Lilian's eyes—Stratton turned to Doris and said, 'You decided to go to the Festival, then, when it opens?'

Before she could reply, Donald said, 'The whole thing's irresponsible, if you ask me. Eleven million pounds on a bloody carnival—'

'Don!' Doris glared at him.

'Sorry, love, but that's what it is. Eleven million quid on that when there's people still need homes to live in—the government must want their heads seeing to.'

Stratton, who'd momentarily forgotten Don's feelings about the Festival of Britain in his attempt to steer Reg away from bowel movements, said mildly, 'Well, now we've got the thing, it might make a nice day out for the girls. I know Monica's keen, aren't you, love?'

Monica, her mouth full, nodded enthusiastically. Swallowing, she said, 'Madeleine wants to go, too.'

'Waste of money, if you ask me,' grumbled Don.

'Ted didn't ask you, he asked me,' said Doris. 'And I want to go, too. I'd say we could all do with a day out.'

'Well, I shall certainly be attending,' said Reg, making it sound as if the aldermen of London were going to turn out *en masse* to greet him. 'I think it's a very good thing all round—"a tonic to the nation" as it's been said.'

'Opium for the nation, more like it,' muttered Don.

'Well I, for one, will be very interested to see these new scientific developments they've been talking about. It's important to keep abreast of these things.'

After a brief pause, during which Doris looked daggers at Don and Stratton kept his eyes firmly on his plate so as not to have to look at him at all, Monica said, 'What about you, Dad? Can you come?'

'I'll do my best.' Stratton grinned at her. At least he got on with one of his children, he thought—Pete, taciturn and sullen throughout most of his Christmas visit, had hardly written since. 'If you're sure you want your old dad tagging along, that is...' Monica made a face at him. 'Now things have calmed down a bit at work, I should think—'

'Oh, Dad, I nearly forgot... Was this your man?' Monica produced a folded sheet of newspaper from her pocket and passed it across the table to Stratton.

'Reading *The Times* now, are we?' asked Reg. 'Very clever.'

'Somebody had it at the studio, and I asked if I could take the cutting.' Stratton unfolded the sheet and saw:

MURDERER HANGED

John Wilfred Davies, 25, lorry driver, of Paradise Street, Euston, London W.C., was executed yesterday at Pentonville for the murder of Judy, his 14-month-old daughter, on November 10, 1950. Davies was sentenced to death at the Central Criminal Court on February 13.

'Yes,' he said, 'that was him.' He'd known it was going to happen, but since he'd heard that Davies's appeal had failed, he'd been trying not to think about it and especially not about Davies's mother. It was all too easy to imagine the woman's pitiful hope of a reprieve and how she must have felt when that had failed as the inexorable days, and then the minutes, ticked away towards the bag on the head, the yank on the lever, the sudden drop… He pushed away the remains of his lunch.

'Aren't you going to finish that?' asked Reg, leaning forward, fork poised to spear the remaining bits of meat.

Stratton shook his head. 'Help yourself.'

'Let's have a look at the cutting,' said Don. 'Nasty… Looks like he got what he deserved.' The piece of newspaper was handed around until, to Stratton's relief, Doris announced that hanging wasn't a suitable subject for the dinner table and removed it.

'I'm sorry, Dad,' said Monica, as they walked up to the allotment together after lunch. He hadn't been looking for company, but she'd volunteered to help him carry some flowerpots.

'What for, love?'

'That cutting about your murderer. I was trying to change the subject because I thought Uncle Reg and Uncle Don were going to have a row. I didn't mean to upset you.'

'You didn't, love.'

'Dad, I could see your face.'

'Yes. I suppose…'

'But he did do it, Dad, didn't he?'

'Oh, yes. He did it.'

'Why? Who would kill a baby?'

'We never got to the bottom of that. Davies was a pretty simple creature—it's hard to understand how these people's minds work.'

'Well, I think it's vile. He must have been horrible.'

But he wasn't, thought Stratton. In many ways, he was rather likeable. 'Let's talk about something else, love, shall we? What are you up to at work?'

'I started work on a new picture this week—*The Belle of Bow.* It's a comedy, but I don't think it's going to be very good. It's got the wrong people in it.'

'Who's that, then?'

'Donald Colgate. He's very good at brooding and smouldering and slapping women, but he can't do jokey stuff at all. He says the lines as if he doesn't understand why they're supposed to be funny. It's driving Mr Carleton mad. He's the director. Oh, and your friend is working on it, too. They're getting married.'

'Who is?'

'Mrs Calthrop and Mr Carleton.' As she spoke, Stratton went cold, the unexpectedness of it jolting him like an icy shower. 'Nobody's meant to know they're engaged, but of course everyone does, and the whole studio's been talking about them for weeks, because Mrs Calthrop isn't divorced from Mr Calthrop yet.' Monica talked on, about other people in the film's crew, but Stratton barely heard her. For Christ's sake, he told himself. Stop being ridiculous. What do you care about Diana Calthrop? It's not as if you'll ever see her again—and even if she wasn't going to marry this other chap, she'd hardly look at you, would she?

It was an enormous relief when, on reaching the allotment, Monica took off back home and left him to his thoughts and—despite what he'd been telling himself—his disappointment.

CHAPTER 33

James Carleton nodded at the row of slot machines on the promenade. 'That's how much we see of the outside world,' he said.

'What do you mean?' asked Diana.

Linking arms with her, he said, 'I mean, my darling, that film directors have a very narrow view of things. The studio isolates us and we don't see everyday life.'

'You're seeing it now. All this.' Diana waved a hand at the fountains and bandstand and the people dancing with the neon shining behind them in the inky twilight waters of the Thames.

'It's a show, my darling. The Festival of Britain is simply a vast advertisement for things we can't have because we're exporting them all.'

'But it's lovely all the same. And as far as *things* are concerned, we're luckier than most.'

'Well, I am, because you're going to marry me. Not sure it's such a fortunate arrangement from your point of view, having to put up with me for the rest of your life… But you're right about the things—you've done wonders with your new home. I'd no idea you had such a practical streak.'

'Neither did I.' Diana had spent every spare moment since she'd moved into her flat in redecorating; discovering, and revelling in, skills that she'd had absolutely no idea she possessed. Finding no wallpaper or paint to her liking in the shops, she'd taken to pestering the studio's technical department for advice and soon learnt how to mix up the colours she wanted and how to apply them. Once she'd persuaded the painters and carpenters that she was serious, they'd been very helpful, even lending her a brown overall which she wore over an old summer dress. Wearing sandals, her face, hands and bare legs flecked with paint, she'd spent whole evenings transforming the place into somewhere bright and welcoming. It was so much nicer than James's cramped rooms that they'd decided to make it their home after they were married.

'And you've got a good eye,' said James. 'You could be a designer if you were trained up a bit.'

'Do you really think so?'

'Yes, I do. Don't look so surprised. Do you remember when you said you weren't intelligent enough for me, and I said you were but you just didn't know it?'

Diana nodded.

'Well, this is the same sort of thing.'

'I suppose so,' said Diana. 'But when you're happy you feel as if you could do anything, don't you? And I've got lots more ideas from looking around today.'

'Darling...' James pulled her into his arms. 'At this rate, you're going to run out of house. I don't suppose they've got any vacancies in the Design Department right at the moment, but we could find out. I'd hate to lose you, but...'

'But you've got me at home.'

'That's true. And as long as you fetch my slippers and bring me drinks, I shan't mind. Well, well, well...'

'Well what?'

'Over there—your little friend from the Make-up Department.'

Following his gaze, Diana saw Monica and, following just behind—she blinked, but it was, it really was—Inspector Edward Stratton.

'Must be her father,' said James. 'They obviously haven't seen us, so let's—'

'No, please,' said Diana, delighted. 'I know him.'

'*Do* you? How?'

'Tell you later.' As she called out to Monica, Diana decided to tell James she'd met Stratton when her handbag had been pinched in the blackout. That was plausible enough—it must have happened to lots of people.

As they came towards her, she thought that, apart from a few grey hairs, Edward had hardly changed at all. The same impression of strength and calm, the broad shoulders and strong face, the broken nose and the wonderfully kind eyes... They really were the nicest eyes, she thought disloyally, of anyone she'd ever met. Realising that she was staring, she hastily stepped forward and made introductions. After a spot of handshaking and awkward remarks about it being unexpected and so on, no one seemed to know quite what to say until James started talking about the Dome of Discovery, which they all agreed was wonderful.

When they parted a few minutes later—Edward saying gruffly, 'Mustn't detain you'—James said, 'Another conquest, I see. Father as well as daughter. You obviously made quite an impression on him—and he on you, judging from the way you were looking at each other.'

'Don't be silly, darling.' Diana could feel that she was starting to blush, although, she told herself sharply, there was no reason for it. I shouldn't have called out to Monica, she thought. I should have let them go past us. 'In fact,' she added, hastily, 'I'm surprised he remembered me at all. We only met because—'

'I suppose you must have come across quite a few policemen during the war,' said James, matter-of-factly. 'Oh, don't look so alarmed—I'm not going to ask questions. I guessed you must have been a spy as soon as I met your friends, the Andersons.'

'What nonsense! Jock's a civil servant, and I certainly wasn't—'

James laughed. 'Oh, it's all right. But even if you weren't exactly a spy, I know you can't talk about it, whatever it was.

Woman of mystery…' He swung round to face her and put his hands on her shoulders. 'Just adds to the attraction, my darling.'

'Well,' said Diana defensively, disengaging herself, 'you've never said anything about *your* war, either.'

'I was a junior member of the Crown Film Unit. Propaganda—very unheroic and not the least bit hush-hush. All very dull, which yours evidently wasn't.'

'I—'

'Look, Diana, even before I met the Andersons, I knew that *something* must have happened to you, or you'd still be mouldering away in Hampshire, opening fêtes and giving out cups at gymkhanas.'

'I didn't—'

James put a finger on her lips. 'I don't want to know. It's the past. Over and done. All this'—removing his finger, he flung out his arms—'is the future. *Our* future. And you are so beautiful. Utterly radiant. Would you care to dance?'

'Why not?' At that moment, flooded with relief, everything seemed so exciting and momentous that, with a waltz striking up in the background, Diana felt as though she were in a musical.

'Come on, then.' James took her hand and led her into the dancing throng.

Stratton wrenched off his tie and flung it down on the bed. He couldn't ever remember feeling such a complete and utter idiot. Seeing Diana like that and not knowing what to say…what an ass she must have thought him. Mr Carleton, too—he'd caught the amused look on the man's face as he'd stammered and fidgeted and generally behaved like an imbecile.

He sat down on the bed, his head in his hands. Seeing Diana again, in his mind's eye, he recalled the sensation of breathlessness, as if he'd just been walloped in the solar plexus, the feeling that suddenly, nothing else existed in the world but her. She was even more beautiful than he remembered. All he could think of to say—Oh, God, he hadn't actually said it, had he?—was '*You.* It's *you.*' Everything seemed to go into slow motion, and the touch of her hand, cool and soft, had seemed to go on for ever as, dry-throated, he'd mumbled a few words.

She'd only called out to them to be friendly and had obviously begun to regret it when he couldn't manage to string two sentences together, and they'd stood there, awkwardly, until Carleton had said something about the exhibition. God knows what he'd said in reply—he couldn't remember. He couldn't even remember what the bloody man looked like. Young and fine-featured, damn him, and clearly intelligent and well-educated and witty and all the rest of it, otherwise he wouldn't be directing films, would he?

It was all too easy to imagine the conversation afterwards, the two of them laughing at his ineptitude—he'd not dared to look back—what a clumsy, slow-witted creature, what a clod, what a big lummox... Even his *own daughter* was embarrassed for him. She hadn't looked at him once, never mind spoken to him, the entire way home.

He wondered how Diana would have explained knowing him—'The war, darling... One ran into *all sorts* of odd people...' That was all he was to her—a curious memory of a strange time with no place in her world.

He lifted his head and looked around at the cheap furniture—the wardrobe and the bedstead, the shoddy bedside table with its barley-sugar legs, and the utility dressing table which didn't match any of the other bits—at the curtains, faded with washing and several inches too short for the window, and at the rag rug on the lino. This is where you belong, chum, he told himself, and don't you forget it.

Diana belonged—would always belong—with a man like Carleton, and he was a fool to waste his time mooning after a woman he could never hope to have.

'...And she keeps complaining that Mr Hotchkiss has shaved off her eyebrows—as if it's my fault!' said Anne.

'Never mind. It's nice to be outside.' Monica and Anne were leaning against the back wall of the department, enjoying the May sunshine after a hectic morning making up dancers as chorus girls for one of *The Belle of Bow*'s music-hall scenes.

'Yes, isn't it? Ooh, I forgot to tell you—I saw Raymond Benson this morning. He's gorgeous, isn't he?'

'Yes, very handsome,' said Monica, wearily. She was sick and tired of hearing about Raymond Benson. She could see that he *was* handsome, with his corn-coloured hair and insolent blue eyes—looks that had got him a score of parts playing wayward but ultimately decent young men who saved the day and won the heart of the girl whilst being terrifically modest and self-deprecating—but honestly...

'Shame we're so far away from D Stage.'

'Yes, isn't it?' Benson was working in a picture about Bonnie Prince Charlie. Every single woman in the studio, it seemed to Monica—as well as several of the men—was sneaking over there every chance they had to catch a glimpse of him prancing about in a kilt like something off a McVitie's biscuit tin.

'He's just my type,' said Anne dreamily.

Thinking that if she had to listen to any more she might not be able to stop herself screaming, Monica changed the subject. 'What about your boyfriend?' she asked. 'You said you were going to the Festival with him, and Kenneth's *real*.'

'So's Raymond.'

'You know what I mean. Did you go?'

'Yes. I did enjoy it, but there was so much of it—we kept getting lost. Have you been yet?'

'Yes, on Saturday. We had a family outing.' Seeing Anne's look of pity that she didn't have anyone else to go with, Monica said, quickly, 'It was wonderful, wasn't it? Pity they didn't have much in the way of fashions, but the crafts were really interesting—all those people making things—and the fabrics and furniture…'

'Those funny spiky legs?' Anne made a face. 'I bought a nice tea caddy for Mum, though, and a scoop. One of those red, white and blue ones. She was ever so pleased.'

'We bumped into Mr Carleton and Mrs Calthrop. My dad knows her—he met her during the war. It was a bit odd, really. Nobody quite knew what to say.'

'I'm surprised they even saw you. They never seem to have eyes for anybody but each other. Oh, sorry, Monica. But you know he's spoken for.'

Anne's constant references to her being keen on Mr Carleton were irritating, but Monica played along because it saved her from questioning. It was expected that she'd have a crush on someone, and her reticence on the subject had led to Anne choosing a candidate for her. Carleton, she knew, had been arrived at because he was often spoken of in the same breath as Mrs Calthrop, and Anne had misinterpreted her reactions—or rather, the person to whom she was reacting. But Dad had reacted to Mrs Calthrop, all right. Monica didn't think she'd ever seen him so stiff or tongue-tied—stammering, almost. She hadn't known what to say to him afterwards. Not that it had been a problem, exactly, because he'd hardly said a word for the rest of the day. She wondered if Mr Carleton had noticed—awful if he had, and even more awful if *she* had given herself away, somehow. The whole thing made her feel sick with shame—at least Dad, even if he was *Dad*, was feeling something entirely normal, whereas *she*...

Glancing at her wristwatch, Anne said, 'We've still got a few minutes left. I think I'll go for a walk in the direction of D Stage... You coming?'

Monica shook her head. 'You *are* stuck on Mr Carleton, aren't you?' said Anne. 'You can finish my cig if you like. Here...'

'Thanks, Anne. Don't be late, will you?'

'For your precious James?' Anne winked. 'I'll be back, never fear.'

Left alone, Monica slumped back against the wall and, turning her face up to the sun, closed her eyes. I must stop this, she thought. It's horrible. I'm horrible. And, after all, it had been a thoroughly enjoyable day, even with Uncle Reg talking nineteen to the dozen about scientific advances and the shape of things to come all the way round the Dome of Discovery. There'd been a funny moment when Uncle Donald, dragged along by Auntie Doris against his will and grumbling all the way, had tapped an 'Out of Order' sign on one of the exhibits and said that *that* was the shape of things to come. He and Uncle Reg were still arguing when they stopped to eat their sandwiches by the fountains, but then he'd cheered up a bit and taken some snaps of them standing in front of the Skylon. She and Dad had gone off by themselves after that, which was a lot more fun. He'd wanted to see the farming exhibition, which had been quite interesting—except the new battery cages for hens, which anyone could see were cruel—and then they'd had a ride on the Water Splash at the funfair and had a look round the Mississippi Steamboat that was moored on the promenade...

Hearing her name called, she opened her eyes. Mrs Calthrop

was waving to her as she crossed the lawn on the other side of the causeway. Self-conscious and aware of her heart beating like a tom-tom, she waved back, then stared after Mrs Calthrop until Anne's cigarette, which she'd completely forgotten she was holding, burnt her fingers.

1953

CHAPTER 36

Alone in the Make-up Department, Monica sat in front of the line of mirrors, sponging foundation over her face and rubbing it in, careful not to overdo it. She'd kept her promise and hadn't told anybody where she was going, even Anne. Actually, especially not Anne, because she knew that if she did she'd never, ever hear the last of it. They'd agreed to meet in the lane around the corner from the main gates to minimise the chance of anyone seeing—which, Monica thought, was pretty unlikely at seven o'clock in January. She'd told them at home that she was working late. She'd been promised a ride back, so at least she didn't have any worries on that score, and she could get out of the car a few streets away from Lansdowne Road...

On just about every other score, though, she felt more agitated than she could ever remember. Her hands, so deft when applying cosmetics to other people, were nervous and clumsy. Putting down the sponge, she picked up a pencil and began darkening her brows. Her elbow nudged something on the work surface and the pencil slipped, leaving a line down her cheek. Scrubbing at it, she decided it might be better to give up and just put on some lipstick—she didn't want to go out looking like a clown.

Brushing her hair, she wondered, for the thousandth time, if she were doing the right thing. Despite all her efforts to change, her feelings and inclinations were exactly the same as they'd ever been—more so, if anything. In desperation, she'd been on lots of dates with local lads, but each had proved more disastrous than the last, and only served to cement the fact that she simply wasn't attracted to men. The problem wasn't the lack of offers—rather the reverse, if anything—but after so many failures on her part to feel anything at all, she'd given up hoping that she'd wake up one morning and think differently about them. Her cousin Madeleine was engaged to be married now. So was Anne, and both of them were madly excited about it, so that all the chat, both at home and at work, was of very little else. Monica made a face at her reflection; Anne certainly would be talking about something else if she got wind of what's happening this evening…

I must do this, she told herself. I must try… After all, if she couldn't manage to fancy Raymond Benson, who was everybody's heart-throb, what hope was there for her?

Tilly was Raymond Benson's fourth film for Ashwood Studios and the first in which he'd been given top billing. Monica, now promoted from extras and occasional retouching to full make-up for supporting actors and actresses, was also working on the picture. It was the story of an aristocratic widow who, discovering that her wheelchair-bound son—Benson—had secretly wed a dancer, tried to prevent them from consummating their marriage. In the end, the dancer faked a drowning accident in order to demonstrate that her husband's inability to walk was all in his mind—which it proved to be when he leapt into the river and saved her. Originally, Mr Carleton had been the director. He'd had a great deal of time away from the studio in the past six months, and there was a rumour that he'd wanted to do a project of his own—a drama about life in the slums of Liverpool or somewhere—but the studio wouldn't let him. What was definitely not a rumour, but a horribly obvious reality, was that, despite the fact that he was now married to the person Monica still could not help thinking of as her ideal woman and the loveliest in the world, he was drinking very heavily indeed. This, and his disgust at having to work on yet another costume picture—*Tilly* was set in Edwardian times—had made him uncharacteristically savage, so that everyone on the set had been walking on eggs for weeks.

Carleton had been sacked a couple of months ago, after an incident on E Stage. As the film got further and further behind schedule, the atmosphere on the set had grown ever more tense and miserable. The final straw came when Carleton, enraged by what he saw as interference by the studio head Mr Vernon, had taken a swing at his assistant, Mr McPherson, causing him to stagger backwards into the makeup trolley, knocking it over and breaking his wrist in the process. Carleton had stormed out after that, leaving poor Mr McPherson on the floor, cradling his arm.

In the confusion that followed, nobody quite seemed to know what to do, but all the same she'd been astonished when Benson, who'd been lolling in his wheelchair nearby, had got up and begun to help her gather the bits and pieces scattered across the floor. She'd noticed him watching her a few times—at first, she'd thought she must have imagined it or that perhaps it was the way he looked at all women, but she kept catching him eyeing her. Not so much her face, but the rest of her, in an intense, speculative way that made her feel unpleasantly self-conscious.

She'd righted the trolley, pushed it into a dark corner to be out of the way and was just beginning to rearrange the things when he came up behind her. Depositing a handful of stuff on the top, he'd said, standing so close that she could feel his breath on the back of her neck, 'I've been watching you.'

Monica had frozen.

'Has anyone ever told you how attractive you are?'

She'd felt his hands on her shoulders, and he'd turned her round to face him. 'Don't worry, we can't be seen. I've been wanting to talk to you alone ever since we started this wretched picture.'

'Have you?'

'Don't sound so surprised. As I said, you're very attractive. I've been thinking I'd like to get to know you better.' He'd stared down, quite unashamedly, at her breasts.

'I...' Amazement that the film's heart-throb should be making a pass at her, and the fact he was uncomfortably close and she couldn't move because of the trolley behind her, had made her falter. 'I don't know.'

'Don't you like going out and having fun?'

'Well, yes, of course I do, but I don't really...'

'Don't really what?'

'It's just... I'm not very good at all that sort of thing.'

'That's only because you haven't met the right person.' She'd stared at him, hypnotised, as, locking his eyes on hers, he put up a hand and stroked her cheek. 'You think about it. I've been feeling very lonely on this picture.' He'd gazed pointedly over her shoulder, and Monica, turning her head, saw that he was looking in the direction of the actresses playing his mother and his wife, who were standing in the gloom beyond the arc lamps. 'Not exactly a bed of roses, if you know what I mean.'

'No,' said Monica. It was common knowledge that the three stars didn't get on well, which compounded the already strained atmosphere.

He'd patted her on the shoulder, then stepped back. 'Why don't you think about it, hmm?'

Relieved, she'd gabbled, 'All right, yes. I'll think about it.'

She had thought about it. In fact, she'd thought of little else for the next three weeks, during which Benson didn't come anywhere near her, so that she wondered if he'd forgotten about it or gone off the idea. Perhaps he hadn't liked her not saying yes immediately. He certainly seemed to assume that she'd find him irresistible—but that, she supposed, was because women did find him irresistible. And when he'd finally asked her to come out to dinner, she'd agreed.

In the end, what had persuaded her was thinking about *Tilly*. Of course, it was only a film, but all the same, if something as physically serious as paralysis could be shown to be all to do with the mind and therefore conquerable, surely something that was emotional might respond to the same treatment? Going out for the evening with Raymond Benson wasn't like jumping into a river to save someone from drowning, but in this situation it seemed, as an incentive, to be on a par with it. And he could have chosen *anybody*, couldn't he? But he hadn't. He'd chosen her, Monica Stratton, lowly make-up girl.

Fluffing up her hair, Monica put on her coat and gloves and set off down the causeway towards the main gate. Even at this late hour, there were lorries and things rumbling up and down, so she didn't hear anyone come up behind her and the shout of 'Monica!' somewhere near her ear almost made her jump out of her skin.

Turning, she saw that it was Mrs Carleton, standing under one of the roadside lamps and looking pale, but—if possible—more lovely than ever. She'd been working in the Design Department for the past year, which meant that Monica hadn't had to avoid her because she'd seen very little of her anyway. Now—especially after what had happened with Mr Carleton—she couldn't think of anything to say.

'I thought it must be you,' said Mrs Carleton. 'I recognised your coat.'

For a second, Monica experienced a sensation of mad happiness that she'd committed such a detail to memory—but then she realised that, working in the Design Department, Mrs Carleton would be bound to notice what people were wearing, even if it wasn't good quality or anything. After all, she noticed those sorts of things, didn't she? In that way, they were alike… Staring into the beautiful blue eyes, she was lost until Mrs Carleton, frowning slightly, said, 'Is there something wrong, Monica?'

'Oh, no, no… I'm sorry… Sorry about Mr Carleton, I mean.'

'Yes,' said Mrs Carleton in a matter-of-fact way. 'So am I. Are you going home now?'

'Yes.'

'Let's walk, then—it's freezing out here. I'm going home, too, but I've got to go back to Design first.'

'He was really good,' said Monica, after they'd walked in silence for a moment. 'Everyone thought so. And everyone liked him.' Percival Addington, who wasn't half so good as Carleton, had taken over the reins.

'I know,' said Mrs Carleton. 'But these things happen.' She sounded tired.

'It wasn't really his fault,' said Monica. 'The picture was behind schedule, but there were lots of other reasons—'

'No, Monica. It's very kind of you, but it isn't true and we both know it isn't. While we're being honest,' she smiled wistfully, 'I don't know how much longer I shall be working here myself. So I just wanted to say—in case I don't see you again—that it was nice meeting you, and do please give my regards to your father, won't you?'

'Yes. It was nice meeting you, too.' As she said this, they reached the turning for the Design Department.

'Goodbye, Monica,' said Mrs Carleton, 'and good luck.'

'Good luck to you, too,' said Monica, with more daring than she'd thought she possessed.

'Thanks.' Mrs Carleton walked off at a fast clip, and Monica stood watching until she merged with the darkness.

Monica supposed that Mrs Carleton must be leaving because of Mr Carleton, which seemed pretty rotten. She hadn't told Dad about what had been going on at Ashwood. Even though the incident at the Festival of Britain was almost two years ago, it was still, in her mind, excruciatingly vivid—the clumsy, fumbled handshake, the way his eyes had never left hers, the fact that his behaviour seemed to mirror, so exactly, the turmoil inside her… Just thinking about it made her squirm with embarrassment. But she ought to pass on Mrs Carleton's regards, really, if she could bring herself to do it. It would be so much easier, she thought, if Dad had met somebody else, but his heart wasn't in it, any more than hers was.

Still, there was time enough to worry about that. Now, she must put Mrs Carleton right out of her mind and concentrate on the evening ahead of her. Stomach churning with apprehension, she continued walking towards the main gate and Raymond Benson.

'That's the way to do it!' Inside the red-and-white-striped booth, Punch, with his glazed pink face, hooked nose curving down to meet jutting chin, battered Judy about the head with his cosh.

We should be laughing, thought Diana, shoving her hands deeper into the pockets of her coat in an attempt to keep warm. The bright weather promised for the end of April had failed to materialise, and the Brighton sky and sea were the matching dull grey of old saucepans. It was mid afternoon and, but for a solitary child running aimlessly about while her mother stood by and a couple of scruffy-looking donkeys with drooping heads, the beach was deserted.

In front of the booth, deckchairs were scattered about at odd angles, some upside down, giving the al fresco auditorium a dismal, abandoned air. Apart from the attendant, who was lying in one, apparently asleep despite the puppets' distorted shrieking, she and James were the only audience. It had been he who'd wanted to see the show, not her. He'd persuaded the professor, a lugubrious individual who'd been packing up his wares when they'd arrived, to perform for them, with a story about scouting for a Punch and Judy show for his next film. Judging from the racket and the vigorous jerking of the figures, the man was giving his all, but there was, in fact, no next film to cast. Although James had made light of her reaction when he'd told her, all that time ago, that he was born several drinks behind the rest of the world and was doomed to spend his life trying to catch up, Diana knew now that it was no more and no less than the truth. No matter how much he drank, he never could catch up, and his intake had increased to such a degree that he was not only bankrupt but unemployable.

Shivering on the damp deckchair, Diana recalled, as she often had in the last six months, the demeanour of the barman at the studio when she'd gone to fetch the brandy in that first week. She'd assumed that the man's comment about thinking the sobriety couldn't last was aimed at Anthony Renwick, but now she knew that wasn't wholly the case. After all, who would know better than a barman? It was certainly true that James had encouraged Renwick to drink because he needed to finish the film, but it was also because he was slipping off the waggon himself and wanted an excuse. She remembered, too, what Alex McPherson had said to her in the restaurant, about warning Mr Vernon. Now she understood that what he—and probably others, too—had warned Mr Vernon about was putting two drunks on the same picture, but she hadn't known that at the time. Or had she? Perhaps her subconscious had known it, but, being in love, she'd failed to acknowledge that anything could be wrong. And it was certainly true that the highly visible nature of Renwick's problem had masked James's, because he held his drink well, and it was only in the last few months that he'd started slurring words and lurching unsteadily into the furniture. This, and the covert nature of his drinking, and the fact that, apart from that terrible last week at Ashwood, he'd never become aggressive—and, she had to admit, her own tendency to deny that the problem existed—were the reasons why it had taken her so long to face up to the extent of it. Anyone who'd worked at the studio for any length of time had known but, because James was well liked, they'd covered up for him repeatedly. And none of them had warned her. But then, she thought resignedly, I wouldn't have listened even if they had.

Despite the initial appearances, a mocking chime in the back of her mind had been telling her for some time that this was history repeating itself. It was Guy, her first husband, and then Claude Ventriss, all over again. She'd been impetuous, rushing headlong into love, refusing to let her feet touch the ground and never stopping to reflect, and pain and shame had followed. How much, in the past year, had she hung onto the memory of her whirlwind romance with James, even as it had become—first slowly, and then with escalating speed—as destructive as a hurricane that raged about them both and would not set them free? Drying out had only resulted in shaking hands and hallucinations so bad that they'd led, at one stage, to a straightjacket. The doctors hadn't let her see him then, but she remembered all too well his terror of the huge cockroaches that crawled over his skin and the hideous crippled lobster that followed him around, dragging one giant claw along the floor.

As Punch gleefully hurled the baby out of the window and massacred Judy in a rain of blows, Diana felt as though she was in one of those hallucinations now. Beside her, James was rapt as a child, revelling in the anarchy of the performance.

He'd been the one who suggested coming to the coast. A spot of sea air to blow away the cobwebs, he'd said. They'd arrived the previous day and spent the evening wandering up and down the promenade, too cold and dispirited to talk. Besides, what was there to talk about any more? They couldn't even find refuge in a hotel bar, because James was in a 'drying-out' period, aided by some medicine that was supposed to make him sick if he so much as smelt alcohol. Diana found these times actually worse than when he was drinking—the wait for the inevitable fall off the waggon, hoping against hope and against experience, was agonising. She'd stayed because, in spite of everything, she still loved him—and even if she hadn't, the burning shame of having to admit another failure at marriage was too terrible to contemplate—but she was beginning to wonder if she actually had any choice in the matter.

She knew, now, that the drinking wasn't his fault. At first, she'd been angry—wasn't she, on her own, with her gift of love, enough to make him stop? *He* had thought she would be. He'd told her that, but it seemed, after all, that the urge to drink was stronger. Then she'd tried drinking with him. It had seemed easier than the torment of watching, coldly sober, while he destroyed himself. That had been a disaster—she'd lost her wonderful job in the studio's Design Department, and with it, their only income and the flat which had been her pride and joy. She'd tried to get other work, but every time she declared this intention, James, sodden in the armchair in their pokey, chilly new home, a blanket round his heaving shoulders, had groped for her hand and sobbed, 'Don't go, darling, don't leave me.' If she did go out, he'd manage to scrape together enough to buy more to drink, and, in the end, she'd given up and they'd settled into a dreary, never-ending game of hide-and-seek as she searched the place for hidden bottles and emptied their contents down the sink while James alternated between defiance and remorse.

She'd gradually lost touch with Lally and Jock and her other friends, so that they were now marooned, a wrecked island of two, afloat in a sea of alcohol. Lally and Jock had given her enough help already, and such pride as she had left would not allow her to call on them yet again.

How Evie would love this, she thought. She'd heard through the grapevine that Guy's mother finally had the grandson she'd always wanted—the one Diana hadn't been able to give her. If Evie could see her now, she'd think she'd got her come-uppance, all right.

The hangman was fixing the noose around Punch's neck. 'It's the end for you, Mr Punch. Say your prayers.'

Punch ducked his head and, cackling in gleeful self-satisfaction, sent the hangman flying with one swipe of his cudgel. 'That's the way to do it!'

Diana closed her eyes to block out the sight of the malevolent doll as it twirled and flailed in a triumphant dance. The small amount of money raised by the sale of Hambeyn Hall and what she'd managed to save from the allowance Guy had given her—and which had stopped when she remarried—was gone, much of it on 'cures' for James, and such inheritance as she had, that she'd thought might buy a flat for them, had been plunged, instead, into a disastrous film that had never, in the end, been completed. Why the hell, she thought, didn't I have the sense to hold onto it—or at least to keep some of it back? Now—she groaned at the thought—they were already weeks behind with the rent and the landlady was growing restive.

Diana clapped half-heartedly as the puppets took their bows. James did not join in, and when she turned to look at him she saw that he was sitting quite still with tears coursing down his cheeks.

'What is it, darling?'

He shook his head. What had started him crying? The sausages, the policeman, the crocodile? Lost in the tangle of her own thoughts, she hadn't noticed. The Punch professor, emerging from behind his booth, looked first mystified and then downright annoyed when James, noticing him, rose from his deckchair and walked hastily off down the beach. 'What's his game?' he asked Diana. 'He might have told me himself if he didn't like it. I've gone to all this trouble...'

'It's not that,' Diana assured him. 'He's always like this when he's working. When he gets an idea he needs to think about it immediately. Doesn't want to break his concentration. You've obviously given him an idea.'

'Oh.' The professor sniffed, but seemed to accept this. 'I suppose that's all right, then. Now,' his tone became wheedling, 'seeing as I did it special for you, shall we say—'

'Two shillings,' said Diana quickly, naming the smallest sum she felt would be acceptable. She'd thought that James's story would suffice but the man clearly expected payment for the show and she didn't feel she could refuse. She looked around for James, but he was heading down the beach towards the flight of steps that led up to the esplanade. The man stiffened, his doleful face becoming taut with angry disgust. She had no idea how much he usually got from holidaymakers, but he'd obviously hoped for a lot more from film people. He looked her up and down—the tightfisted bitch in the fur coat. He wasn't to know that nowadays the thing often did duty as a blanket as well as a garment.

'I'm sorry,' she said, 'I—' Unable to complete the explanation, she took her purse out of her handbag, scrabbled for the coins and pushed them into his hand saying, 'Here you are,' and walked away as fast as she could with her heels sinking into the pebbles.

She caught up with James at the bottom of the steps, grabbing hold of his arm and yanking on it to make him stop. She saw, as he turned to her, that his face was blurry and smudged with tears. 'What are you doing, James? I had to give him two shillings, and I'm not sure we've got enough money to get home without—'

'Diana!' He took her by the shoulders, crushing her to him in an embrace. 'I'm sorry. I'm so sorry. Please forgive me.'

As he drew her towards him, she became aware of a hard, flat shape bumping against her leg. Pushing him away from her, she said sharply, 'What's that in your pocket?'

'Nothing, darling. You're imagining it.'

'No, I'm not.'

She made a grab for it and this time he shoved her away, hard, so that he lost his balance and sat down with a bump on the bottom step. Swiftly, Diana bent down and before he could stop her yanked the half-bottle out of his coat. It was whisky, and the seal was unbroken, which explained why she hadn't smelt it on his breath. 'When did you get this?'

'This morning. When you were buying stamps.'

The postcard to Anthony Renwick, who was now in hospital, had been his idea. At the time, she'd been encouraged by the thoughtfulness of the gesture, but now she saw that it was merely a ruse to get her out of the way. It also meant that they had even less money than she'd thought.

'I'm sorry, Diana.' As he held out his hand for the bottle, she looked down at his face and saw the forlorn hope of the beggar. 'Please. I can't manage—'

'You'll have to bloody manage.' Stepping backwards, she turned and, holding the bottle above her head, elbow bent, was about to hurl it away from her as far and as hard as she could, when she heard a crunch of pebbles behind her and felt something tugging at the hem of her coat. Looking down, she saw that James was stretched at full length on the ground, dragging himself on one arm in a horrible parody of a parched man in a desert, blood trickling down his wrist from a cut on a sharp stone and soaking into the exposed cuff of his shirt. He wasn't looking at her: his eyes were fixed on the bottle.

'I'll walk into the sea,' he said quietly.

'It would certainly be quicker than drinking yourself to death,' said Diana, acidly. What was the point? If she threw the bottle and it shattered on the stones, there would only be another, and another, and another… 'Oh, for God's sake. Get up!' She went back to sit down on the step and broke the seal on the bottle. Averting her eyes from James, who was half-walking, half-crawling, to join her, she thrust the whisky at him. Not wanting to see the abject expression and the relief on his face as he took a greedy pull on the bottle, she stared straight in front of her at the indistinct line of the horizon.

'Bless you, darling.'

'James…' She couldn't bring herself to look at him.

'Wait.' James took another drink. She heard him set the bottle down carefully on the far side of the step so that she could not reach it and begin rooting in his pocket for cigarettes.

'I can't do this any more,' she finished.

James fumbled with the matchbox, opening it upside down so that the matches fell out, scattering around their feet. He scrabbled after them with trembling hands, dropping as many as he collected. She watched him with growing impatience and then, unable to bear it any longer, bent down to help. They grovelled about in silence until all the matches were restored to the box, then James, leaning his elbows on his knees to steady himself, managed to light two cigarettes.

'You should go,' he said, handing one over. Beneath the red blotches his face was a sickly greenish-white. 'Go home.'

'And leave you here to kill yourself? Anyway, what home? In case you've forgotten, we haven't paid the rent in over a month.'

'I know. I'm sorry.'

'Stop saying that!'

'It's all I can say.' James turned his head away, as if he couldn't bear to look at her either. 'I've dragged you down far enough, Diana. We both know it's hopeless. You said so yourself—that you couldn't do it any more. If it's any consolation, you can't be half as sick of me as I am of myself.'

Wearily, Diana got to her feet. 'It isn't.'

James didn't look up at her. His shoulders sagged, and she wanted to bend down and put her arms around him. This charming, intelligent, talented man who had such appetite for all that life had to offer… No, said a small, cold voice inside her head. She must recognise, as he did, that there was, quite simply, no more to be said or done. She stood for a moment, staring down at James's bowed head, and then, very slowly, began to walk up the steps to the esplanade.

'I love you,' he murmured. Diana turned, but he wasn't looking at her—the words were addressed to the sea.

As she reached the top, a torn newspaper borne on the light wind slithered round her ankles like a cat, so that she had to shake it off. Apart from a couple of spivs, jacket shoulders as wide as yokes, talking together, there was no one around. From one of the peeling shopfronts, their garish colours faded by sea-spray and long neglect, she could hear the rumble of distant, placid voices intoning numbers after the bingo caller, like responses in church.

Standing on the top step, she heard a retching sound from below and, turning, she looked down and saw James, still sitting where she'd left him, bent forwards from the waist. Her last sight of him was a heaving back and vomit splattering the cold, grey stones of the beach.

A battered chocolate box with grey ash scattered across the empty waxed paper casings; a bottle of powdery aspirins; a cup of cold tea, scummy white on the surface; an open pot of face cream; a plaster model of an Alsatian dog with its tail snapped off; a broken carriage clock, and a lot of dust: Iris Manning's mantelpiece. The rest of the room was no less depressing—dingy wallpaper, filthy windows, and shoddy, chipped furniture. It stank of stale cigarette smoke and unwashed clothing. Standing on the stained rug and trying not to breathe too deeply, Stratton stared down at the tangle of grimy blankets on the bed. On the off-chance, he knelt down to look beneath the sagging frame but found nothing except an enamel chamber pot lined with a foul-smelling crust of dried urine.

Stratton doubted if Iris had ever conducted any business in this room. As far as he knew, she'd always worked outside. There was nothing high-class about her: ten bob for a wank; fifteen for a plate; thirty for the lot. Stratton knew her from way back. They all did. She'd been living and working on their patch since she'd absconded from reform school in 1938 or thereabouts, and no matter how many times they'd taken her back, she'd always returned. Now she was missing and had been for five days, and there was nothing amongst her belongings to indicate why, or where, she'd gone. Her sister, who'd decided to look her up after a separation of five-odd years, had reported it.

Missing tarts were not exactly top of the station's list of priorities at any time but at the moment, with yet another spate of car thefts—there'd been a steep increase in the three years since petrol had come off ration—and Lamb's obsession with the preparations for the Coronation in June, they were very low indeed. Stratton himself had not taken the news of Iris's disappearance too seriously, his initial reaction being that she'd got behind with her rent and scarpered, but now he was beginning to wonder. If she had done a midnight flit, she'd surely have taken such clothes as she owned with her, but the presence of a battered valise on top of the wardrobe and several frocks inside it suggested otherwise. Bugger the Coronation, he thought: I should have got here sooner.

A loud thump and several shouts from the stairwell suggested that Policewoman Harris was not having an easy time with the house's other occupants. Stratton clattered downstairs and found a slovenly creature in a soiled dressing gown barring the way to the kitchen. 'You know your trouble,' she was shouting at Harris, 'you've never had it!' Seeing Stratton, she added, 'Why don't you have a bash at her, take that expression off her face?'

'That's enough, Bessie,' said Stratton mildly, recognising her as a tom who'd been hawking herself around Soho for nearly as long as Iris.

'It's not my turn,' whined Bessie. 'You done me last week and I paid the fine. And you have to nick me on the street or it don't count. I know the law.'

'We're not here to take you in,' said Stratton.

Bessie stuck her chin out aggressively. 'Well, what you poking around for, then?'

'Iris is missing, and we need to have a look round.'

Bessie, who didn't seem at all bothered by this news, sighed and moved away from the door. 'Oh, go on then.'

The kitchen was in an even dirtier state than Iris's bedroom. Stratton, shifting his feet on the sticky lino, tried not to recoil as he caught sight of mouse tracks in the congealed fat of a frying pan. He could tell by the stiffness of Policewoman Harris's back and shoulders as she looked in the cupboards that she was doing the same. Bessie pushed the remains of a meal to one side, and, perching on one end of the newspaper-covered table, began examining the soles of her bare feet. They were, Stratton noted, hard and yellow, with deep splits in the heels that made him think of cheese left in the air for too long.

'When did you last see Iris?' he asked her.

'I told *her*,' Bessie let go of her foot long enough to jerk a dismissive thumb at Policewoman Harris. ' 'Bout a week ago.'

'Where did you see her?'

'Here. She was on her way out.'

'Did she say where she was going?'

Bessie shrugged. 'I don't know, do I?'

'Do you think she was going to work?'

' 'Spose so.'

'Do you remember what she was wearing?'

'Well, she'd have had her coat on, but apart from that...' Bessie shook her head.

'Where did she go when she was working?'

'All over.'

'Didn't she have a regular patch?'

'Not any more. Got taken over, didn't it? She hangs round the cafés and pubs, mostly.'

'Which ones?'

'The Panda Café, mostly. And she goes into a lot of the pubs round here, but the Champion's her favourite.'

'Does Iris have a current man friend—someone who looks after her?'

Bessie shook her head. 'He's long gone—six months or more. Gave up on her and found himself something better, didn't he? She was always saying how skint she was. Even tried to borrow some money off me. I told her, I'm not that stupid.'

'You thought she wouldn't pay you back?'

'*Iris?* Not likely.' Clearly feeling that there was no more to be said on the subject, Bessie pulled a grip from her hair and began poking at the grime beneath her toenails. Averting his eyes, Stratton spotted an advert, torn from a magazine, tacked to the opposite wall: a drawing of a model draped in tulle and lounging on a sofa surrounded by eager suitors, accompanied by the legend 'Charm and Beauty Course—Change your life for just 50 guineas'. A clip round the ear and a bar of carbolic soap would be a better bet, thought Stratton. Feeling that they were on a hiding to nothing, he coughed a discreet enquiry to Policewoman Harris and, receiving a shake of the head in return, thanked Bessie for her trouble and left.

The elderly proprietor of the Panda Café had a ravaged look, as though he were in the grip of some ferocious and terminal illness. His cheeks had collapsed and his teeth—which to Stratton's surprise were clearly his own—seemed to have grown as his gums shrank so that his mouth was always slightly open, sticky white saliva clogging its corners.

His customers didn't look much better. Such rays of sunlight as had managed to penetrate the dirt and steam on the windows and the fug inside illuminated dandruff on shoulders, ingrained dirt on necks, and clumps of bristles on imperfectly shaved chins. In one corner, an old woman was muttering to herself from behind a copy of the *Daily Mail*. Peering across at the masthead, Stratton saw that the newspaper was over three months old.

The proprietor studied the photograph Stratton had produced. Swollen-eyed and truculent, Iris Manning glared back at him. 'I know her,' he confirmed, 'but I haven't seen her for a good bit.'

'How long, would you say?'

'Week, ten days… Something like that. She comes in quite a lot. I've had to speak to her about trying to pick up men in here.'

'Did you have any conversation with her the last time you saw her?'

'If I did I can't remember. Nothing out of the ordinary, at any rate. What's happened to her, then?'

'That,' said Stratton, 'is what we're trying to find out.'

They got the same story in the Champion, and the rest of the pubs yielded no further information, except for the fact that she'd been barred from both the Red Lion and the Dover Castle for drunken and abusive behaviour. The man on the desk at the Pontefract Hotel, a flyblown and seedy establishment that rented rooms by the hour, gazed at them with watery, disillusioned eyes and told them he hadn't seen Iris in a fortnight and didn't care if he never saw her again because she was nothing but trouble.

'You don't think she could have gone off with a customer for a few days, sir?'

They'd come in a full circle and were now standing once more at the top of the street where Iris Manning lived. Stratton stared down the row of soot-blackened terraced houses, their windowsills crusted with pigeon dung, towards Tottenham Court Road. A black cat which had been sniffing around a jumble of rusty dustbins on the pavement shot him a filthy look and slunk away to merge with the shadows in a nearby alley.

'She's not the type for that,' he said. 'Not nowadays, anyway. Strictly short-time. If she'd left a note in her room, I'd have seen it. Don't suppose you gleaned anything, did you?'

Policewoman Harris shook her head. 'The other girls were just as unhelpful as Bessie. Couldn't remember when they'd last seen her and didn't care. One of them said good riddance because Iris had borrowed ten bob off her last month and still hadn't paid it back.'

'Both parents are dead, according to the sister, and there aren't any other relatives,' said Stratton, 'so that's out. Let's get back to the station.'

As they arrived, Sergeant Ballard was escorting a slight, fair girl of about eighteen out of the door. 'Be right with you, sir,' he murmured as they passed. The girl detained him for a moment, talking earnestly, a look of anxious entreaty on her face, before he caught up with them. 'Any luck, sir?'

'Not a dicky bird. I don't suppose that she,' Stratton waved a hand in the direction of the departed girl, 'had any information, did she?'

'Not about Iris Manning, sir. She came in to report another missing girl. Brought this with her.' Ballard produced a small photograph of the head and shoulders of a woman who was both younger than Iris Manning, and, with her big almond-shaped eyes and full lips, considerably more attractive. 'Kathleen McKinnon. Gone missing, according to her chum. Brown hair and eyes, about five foot three.'

'Tom, is she?' asked Stratton. Ballard nodded. 'Can't say I recognise her,' said Stratton, and Harris's shake of the head told him that she didn't, either. 'Must be new.'

'She is, sir. Only been here a few weeks.'

'Well, she's obviously got a friend, which is more than you can say for poor Iris.'

'They often work together, sir. That's why she came in. I asked if she could be sure McKinnon hadn't gone off for a holiday or to visit relatives—got a kiddie up in Scotland, apparently, her mother looks after it—but she said no, they'd had an appointment with some chap who wanted to photograph them together, and she never turned up. That was three days ago, and she's not seen her since. Told me they usually meet up for a drink before they start, but she didn't appear, and she hadn't said anything about going away.'

'Let's just hope there's not a spate of them,' said Stratton gloomily. 'Lamb'll go spare.' With the Coronation procession passing so near their manor, the DCI was determined to eradicate all vestiges of crime and vice from the streets surrounding Piccadilly Circus, so that the huge influx of people expected could enjoy their day's outing without being propositioned or having their pockets picked. Stratton, who, like most of the station, viewed Piccadilly Circus as the centre of an Inferno-like series of concentric circles, each with a denser and more dangerous concentration of corruption, vice, and crime, had remarked after the pep-talk that he hoped it would keep fine for him.

'Wouldn't be the first time we've had someone killing tarts, sir,' said Ballard.

'That's true. Did you ask this…'

'Joan Carter, sir.'

'Did you ask her if she knew Iris?'

'Said she'd never heard of her. Sorry, sir.'

'And the chap with the camera?'

'Told her his name was Charlie, but she didn't have an address. They met him in the Red Lion, and they'd made an arrangement to see him there again. She said he was going to take them off somewhere to do the pictures.'

'Try asking in the pub. Perhaps McKinnon met him on her own.'

'Yes, sir. This is Miss Carter's address, and that's McKinnon's—round the corner from each other.'

Glancing at them, Stratton recognised the streets. More sagging rows of houses chopped up into dismal single rooms, with a pervasive atmosphere of damp, mould, and rot. If failure had a smell, Stratton thought, that was it: ambitions and desires unfulfilled and, in the case of these girls, lives spoiled and broken before they'd got properly started. All of them somebody's daughter… He thought of Monica—lively, happy, sensible—and shuddered inwardly. 'Come on,' he said to Policewoman Harris. 'Let's take a look.'

CHAPTER 39

They'd moved twice in the past few months, each time to cheaper and poorer accommodation, and this flat was… A refuge, anyway, thought Diana. A shabby, threadbare cocoon where she could hide away until she could think straight about what to do next. But not now. In order to save money, she'd walked from Victoria Station, over a mile, and she was exhausted, too tired even to scratch up a meal from whatever remained in the cupboard. All she wanted was to lie down. Dragging herself up the stairs, she didn't think she'd ever been so glad to be home.

There was a note pinned to the door. Diana's heart sank as she recognised her landlady's handwriting. *Dear Mrs Carleton, I have taken your belongings in place of the rent which you have not paid for seven weeks…*

Grimacing, she crumpled up the paper and pushed her key into the lock. She'd find the money somehow, and redeem their things, but, right at the moment, she just wanted to get inside, away from everything. She turned the key and jiggled it, but the door remained firmly closed. After a couple of minutes' desperate pushing and rattling, she gave up and, leaning against the wall, closed her eyes. This isn't how it's supposed to be, she thought. Random images from the past flickered behind her eyelids: the morning of her wedding to Guy, bright-faced with anticipation in the mirror while the maid dressed her hair; lying in Claude's arms on the mattress beneath the improvised shelter in his flat during an air-raid; her mother-in-law's venomous face; the despoiled desolation of her childhood home; running through Green Park with James. Shaking her head in a sort of hopeless wonder at her situation, she remembered James's words about walking into the sea. I could go down to the river now, she thought; it isn't far. What difference would it make?

Wearily, clutching the banister, she went back downstairs and out into the street. There was no point trying to talk Mrs Pritchard into letting her back in, and anyway, she couldn't face it. She walked down the road to the corner. It was twilight, and she stood, swaying slightly on her feet, just outside the spill of light from the open door of the pub. From inside she could hear laughter and the clink of glasses as the evening's business got under way. All down the street, people coming home from work were turning in to their front doors. Lights were being turned on and curtains drawn against the gloom. They'll soon be having supper, Diana thought, settling down for the evening. Hats and coats will be removed, slippers will replace shoes. The wireless and the paper. The children, the cat, the dog. Life carrying on.

Was that what she wanted, life to carry on? If you wanted something badly enough, you were supposed to get it, weren't you? Perhaps she hadn't wanted James to stop drinking badly enough. Perhaps he hadn't wanted it himself. Or perhaps it didn't work like that after all.

The river was to her left. Only a short walk... She'd be able to manage it. If she turned right instead, she would eventually, after several miles—provided she didn't get lost on the way—arrive at Lally and Jock's house. Overwhelmed by the thought of the distance, all the streets, squares, road-crossings, turnings off, the sheer effort of placing one foot in front of another, she took a few, faltering steps to her left. As she did so, a man emerged from the shadows by the wall of the pub, fumbling at his fly buttons, and grinned at her. For a moment, their eyes met. Then, with an impetus born of pure disgust, both with him and with herself, she turned right and began the long walk to Albemarle Street.

By the time she reached Piccadilly, Diana, though light-headed with tiredness, felt a new clarity of purpose. She'd decided not to die, hadn't she? Now, with the cold rationality of a chess player, she must calculate her next move. One step at a time. The first was to smarten herself up a bit. Bad enough to present herself on Lally's doorstep without warning, which, without even the tuppence needed for a telephone call, was what she'd have to do. She did, however, have one penny left, and that could be spent smartening herself up in the Ladies' at Piccadilly Circus. Clutching it, she marched down the stairs to the Underground.

The attendant, an elderly crone with a long nose and a flat chest, was chatting, mop in hand, to a couple of heavily made-up women, their conversation punctuated by the sound of dripping. Diana walked to the furthest basin and stared at herself in the mirror above it. The harsh electric light and white tiled walls gave her face a pallid, sickly look, and she must have been crying without being aware of it, because her eyes were pink-rimmed and there were the tracks of tears down her cheeks. Her hair, which she hadn't touched since her walk on the beach, was dishevelled. I look like a madwoman, she thought.

She was rummaging in her bag for a comb to repair the damage when a rasping Cockney voice said, 'Hello, dear.' Turning, she saw that the attendant, footsteps muffled by carpet slippers, had come over and was smiling encouragingly. 'New here, are you?'

'New?'

The two women eyed her from across the room. They didn't look half as friendly as the attendant, and it took her a moment to realise why. Her stomach contracted in fear, and she heard herself give a jittery little laugh as she turned back to the basin.

'You going to be sick?' asked the attendant, not so welcoming now. 'Cos if you are, you can go outside and do it.'

'No…' Diana found her comb and held it up. 'Just tidying my hair.'

'Been to a party, have you?' asked one of the women. The tone was menacing.

Feverishly, Diana began to smooth her hair. Both women were advancing towards her now. Unable to bolt, she carried on combing mechanically, not paying attention to what she was doing, staring into the mirror and seeing only the two hard slabs of their faces and the red gashes of their mouths, one on either side of her own.

'Somewhere nice, was it?'

'I haven't been to a party.'

The woman looked her up and down. 'Going to one, are you?'

'No…'

'You've torn your stocking,' said the other.

Had she? 'Oh… I didn't know.'

'I didn't know,' repeated the woman in mocking imitation. She had a smear of lipstick, like blood, on her top teeth.

'Nice handbag,' said the other. Diana shrank from her, clutching the straps tightly. The woman looked down at her shaking hands and said, 'You haven't told us where you're off to.'

'Nowhere,' said Diana, backing away. 'A friend…'

'Oh, a *friend*. Give you that, did he?' The woman took a quick step towards her and clamped a hand on her arm, gripping it so that Diana could feel the nails through her fur coat. 'You want to watch yourself,' she said.

Diana felt as though she might stop breathing at any moment. The room was beginning to spin. She looked round for the attendant, but the old woman had shuffled away into a corner and was doing something with a pail. 'Yes…' she heard herself say. 'Please, I'm sorry…'

'Bitch!' Diana felt a warm spray of spittle land on her face before the woman released her, shoving her backwards. She tottered for a moment before regaining her balance, then she grabbed her bag and fled, mocking laughter echoing behind her, back up to the surface.

She stopped at the top of the stairs to catch her breath. Everything around her was moving: traffic, neon signs, blurry bright, dancing in front of her eyes, and streams of people moving purposefully forward, rushing past her. Where were they all going?

She made her way down Piccadilly to Albemarle Street. Everyone seemed to be going in the opposite direction. It was as though she had become invisible—however much she tried to avoid the oncoming crowds, people kept knocking into her, pushing her from side to side so that she struggled to remain upright. Keep going, she told herself. Nearly there…nearly there. And then she was there, standing in front of the Andersons' front door.

All the windows were pitch dark. What would she do if they weren't at home? She hadn't thought of that. There were waiting rooms in railway stations…perhaps she could go there. Or ask a policeman? She had no idea, and without her address book, which must be amongst the belongings purloined by her landlady, she had no idea of anyone else's address or telephone number either. Heart thumping in her chest, she lifted the heavy brass knocker and brought it down sharply, twice. They must be there, they *must*…

After what seemed like an age, she heard footsteps in the hall and Mrs Robinson, looking more monumental than usual and very suspicious, opened the door a couple of inches. Her eyes widened on seeing Diana, and for a moment she did not speak, but stared, taking in her disordered appearance, almost bristling with disapproval. 'Good evening, Mrs *Carleton*.' The words were grudging and Diana's heart sank. She'd obviously heard about the divorce. People in the film community might be more accepting of—or at least, more used to—people divorcing, but Mrs Robinson, upright and cantilevered in her stiff black frock, was a true Victorian. She hadn't seemed to like Diana much before, but now…

For a second, Diana thought the door was going to be slammed in her face and involuntarily extended an arm to keep it open. 'Good evening, Mrs Robinson.'

'Mrs Anderson's not here at present,' said Mrs Robinson. 'She didn't say she was expecting any visitors.'

'I'm sorry,' said Diana humbly. 'She wasn't expecting me.' She added, as casually as she could, 'May I come in, do you think?'

Mrs Robinson looked her up and down once more, then pursed her lips, as if this request merited careful consideration. 'Well,' she said, after a long pause, 'I don't know when they'll be back.'

Abandoning the pretence, Diana said, 'Please, Mrs Robinson. I need to speak to her.'

There was no light in the housekeeper's eyes, no flicker of sympathy, but she stepped back to let Diana into the hall. 'Shall I take your coat?'

Suspecting that the fire wasn't, and wouldn't be, lit, Diana said, 'I think I'll keep it on, thank you.'

Once in the sitting room, Diana sank into an armchair and inspected her legs. The woman in the toilet had been right—one stocking was laddered badly. Mrs Robinson, who'd followed her, stood mute and unwelcoming in the middle of the room. Seeing that she was to be offered nothing, Diana said, 'Do you think I might have some brandy?'

Expressionless, but still managing to radiate hostility, Mrs Robinson stalked over to the drinks tray and poured a very small amount of brandy, scarcely more than a trickle, into a glass. Handing it to Diana, she left the room quickly, as if to remain might contaminate her in some indefinable way.

Tired almost beyond thought and profoundly relieved to be alone at last, Diana drained the glass, leant back in her chair, and closed her eyes. She imagined James's hand sliding up her arm, massaging the flesh as he had that day in Green Park. The feeling was so strong that she felt he was there, in the room, leaning over her, his breath warming her cheek. Then, as drowsiness overcame her, James's face seemed to melt and reform into that of Edward Stratton, eyes smiling and lips moving as though he were trying to tell her something, but she couldn't hear him... And then she slept.

'A *third* one?' said DCI Lamb. 'Are you *sure*?'

His superior's expression was George Formby at his most gormless and imbecilic, and for a second Stratton was tempted to say, 'No, I'm just larking about.' Aloud, he said, 'I'm afraid so, sir. Name's Mary Dwyer. Boyfriend reported it this morning. She promised to meet him three days ago but she didn't turn up and he hasn't seen her since.' He slid the photograph—head and shoulders, showing an angular face, handsome rather than beautiful, surrounded by a cloud of dark curls—across Lamb's desk, where it was given the briefest of glances before being flicked back to him.

'The first one's been missing quite a few days now, hasn't she?'

'Ten, sir.'

'And you've got nothing at all?'

'We're still making enquiries, sir.'

'And the second?'

'Nothing to go on yet, sir.'

Sighing, Lamb let him go with instructions to 'find out what's happened to these wretched women as soon as possible.'

As if he thought I was going to take Ballard and Harris on a coach outing to the seaside instead, thought Stratton irritably. Lamb was right about one thing, though—'Wretched' was what the three women were, all right—they were amongst the lowest and least successful of their kind. Dwyer and her boyfriend didn't even have a permanent address.

The next two days were spent traipsing round interviewing toms, from adolescent, gawkily provocative girls to aged whores, beneath a succession of hand-tinted pictures of Princess Elizabeth and Prince Philip in rooms that smelt of mice. When they weren't doing that, they were trudging round cheerless pubs with engraved mirrors and curly brass ornaments, showing photographs to staff and drinkers in the hope of jogging someone's memory. Such places had a regular clientele, but they also functioned as a sort of no-man's-land for a certain type who, impelled by randiness or curiosity, made a foray to pick up a tart, throwing off the shackles of respectability for a brief time before retreating in self-disgust to his daily life.

At the end of the second day, Stratton dispiritedly bade Ballard and Harris goodnight and went off home, reflecting that the whole thing had been a waste of time, and tomorrow didn't look as if it was going to be much better. *Tomorrow*. He'd completely forgotten. Pete was coming home, and Monica had reminded him, several times, that Doris was making a special dinner and he must be sure to be back in time. Much to Stratton's surprise, his son, despite his initial reservations about the army, had decided to stay on when he'd finished his national service. Stratton thought that, although Pete had never said as much, the boy had come to enjoy the uniformity of it all—the drilling, the rules, the ranks. He had avoided thinking too deeply about this, because it smacked too much of Reg. Not, of course, that Reg was a blood relation, whereas he himself, being in the police force… He couldn't quite put his finger on exactly *why* it should make him so uncomfortable, but it did. If only he found it easier to talk to Pete…but, if anything, the gap between them had widened. When something that smacked of introspection or emotion reared its head, they both took refuge in hearty good humour until the danger had passed off.

He suddenly wondered if Pete went with prostitutes. It would be nice to feel sure that the answer was no, absolutely not, but he didn't. There were always plenty of girls in garrison towns, and if his pals went along… Anyway, Stratton told himself, angry for speculating, it was a bloody sight better than promising the moon and stars to some innocent young girl when all you wanted was…but for all he knew, Pete had done that, too. It was yet another thing they'd never discussed, and that was *his* job, not Jenny's—even if she were here—and he'd failed.

He supposed that there had been prostitutes in the local towns when *he* was growing up, but he'd never encountered one until he started working in London. His first sexual experiments had been with the Ellens and Doras of neighbouring villages. There'd been no broken promises, no anguished wranglings, just good fun. Of course, there'd been plenty of gentlemen's daughters who went hunting and attended county balls, but they'd filled him with awe, not lust, and it wouldn't have occurred to him to raise his sights so high. In fact, he couldn't remember ever speaking to one of these lofty creatures. Here, the spectre of Diana, smiling in welcome as she had when they'd met at the Festival of Britain and he'd made a prize idiot of himself, flitted across his mind. Wincing, he pushed it away.

What he needed was a quiet pint, but he didn't get it. In the pub, Donald and some of the neighbours were engaged in a discussion about clubbing together to rent a television for the Coronation, and his opinion was immediately solicited as to where the viewing should take place. After suggesting the church hall, he withdrew to a table in the corner and left them to it. He'd be working, but, judging from what he'd seen of television through the windows of showrooms, he didn't think he'd be missing much: everything on the little screens looked to him as though it were taking place in a snowstorm. He regretted his lack of enthusiasm, but there it was—he wished the new queen the best of luck and all that, but he had other things on his mind: Pete's visit and the three missing women. If only they could make some progress…

Some hope, thought Stratton sourly, as he and Ballard sat in the detectives' office at West End Central the following morning, reviewing their progress—or rather, the lack of it.

'We'll need to widen the search, sir,' said Ballard. 'That's everything in Conway Street, Warren Street, Grafton Mews—'

A knock on the door produced Policewoman Harris with two cups of tea. 'There's a call, sir,' she said. 'Urgent. Cudlipp's putting it through.'

Stratton gestured at Ballard to pick up the telephone and went back to studying his list of informants. The obvious ones had proved useless, but perhaps—

'What number?' Something sharp in Ballard's tone made him look up. His sergeant's handsome face had turned rigid, a blank-eyed mask. He took the receiver away from his head and was staring at it as if it were about to disgorge a stream of poison. Stratton stared as, collecting himself with a visible effort, Ballard returned the telephone to his ear and said, 'Don't touch anything, sir. We'll be there right away.'

Putting the telephone down, Ballard stared at Stratton. The air between them was static with unspoken, and very bad, news. Stratton swallowed. 'What is it?'

'That was the new tenant of the ground-floor flat at number ten, Paradise Street.' The sergeant's voice was expressionless. 'Just moved in this morning. He's found a woman's body in the kitchen alcove.'

CHAPTER 42

Stratton's shoes echoed on the dusty boards of the kitchen floor. The small room was empty but for the range and the deckchair with its sling of knotted rope that he remembered from when they'd visited the Backhouses. Then, in the company of the table and chairs and other domestic paraphernalia, it had looked merely odd; now, on its own in the middle of the room, it was downright sinister. Stratton sniffed. There was a smell of decay—what one might expect, perhaps, from a dead mouse or rat under the floorboards —but, although unpleasant, it wasn't overwhelming. He could see the gap in the wall where the new ground-floor tenant, Mr Maynard—currently being interviewed by Ballard—had torn the paper away, revealing the ragged tops of rough wooden boards. Stratton remembered that these formed the door of the alcove cupboard where the Backhouses had stored baby Judy's things.

Don't jump ahead, he told himself. It must be coincidence. It has to be. In the ten minutes that had elapsed between the telephone call and their arrival at the house, he'd mentally repeated this over and over again, like a prayer, trying to hold at bay the panic, the dread of what he might find. Feeling as precarious as a man on a high wire with no safety net, he pulled the torch from his jacket pocket and switched it on. As he did so, he noticed, quite objectively, that his hands were trembling. Could this really be happening? Couldn't the man have made a mistake—seen something that merely looked like a body, a dummy or doll, perhaps, somebody playing an evil practical joke, or—

There was no mistake. The moment he pushed the torch through the aperture, the beam illuminated a knobbly backbone beneath grey, grimy skin, bisected by the strap of a brassiere. The body appeared to be seated on something and was leaning forward facing the back of the alcove so that the head was almost between the knees, dark hair flopping around it. Something thick and grey—a blanket, Stratton thought—had been looped through the bra strap. Following it with his torch beam, he saw that it was attached to something lumpy and wrapped in another grey blanket, and that this was part of a larger parcel—human-sized, in fact—which appeared to be fastened with a cord, and that behind it was a second one.

I cannot believe this is happening. Stratton blundered back into the hall and found Ballard talking to Mr Maynard who was sitting, ashen-faced, on the bottom step of the stairs. Leaving the unfortunate man in the care of Policewoman Harris, he led Ballard outside. 'Get down to the box. We'll need a photographer as well as the pathologist. I think there's three of them.'

'Think they're our girls, sir?'

'I don't know. Two of them are wrapped up and I can't see the other one's face. What did he,' Stratton jerked his head towards Maynard, 'have to say for himself?'

'Says he's only been here once before, sir, and that was yesterday, with the landlord. That's a Mr...' Ballard checked his notes, 'Morrison. Says they looked round together, and he agreed to take the flat, but apart from this morning, he's not been here on his own at all. In any case, Morrison told him the previous tenant had tried to sub-let the place without his knowledge and he wanted him to know he wouldn't stand for it.'

'And the previous tenant was...?'

'He didn't know, sir, so I sent Policewoman Harris next door to find out…' Ballard faltered.

Feeling that the world was disintegrating around him, Stratton said, 'And…'

'Still Mr Backhouse, sir,' said Ballard, apologetically. 'The lady told Harris Mrs Backhouse had gone up north a few months ago, to stay with her sister, and she'd not seen him for a few days so she thought he must have left. Said he'd told her he'd given his notice at work because he'd got the offer of a job up there.'

'Oh, Christ. I just hope…' Stratton didn't complete the sentence. He could see that Ballard knew only too well what he just hoped, because he was hoping the same. It didn't need spelling out. Just as well, he thought, because he didn't think he could bring himself to say it. 'Go down to the box and talk to Lamb. We've got to find the fucker.'

Ballard opened his mouth, and Stratton saw, from his expression, that he was about to offer a palliative lie, but then he seemed to decide against it and merely nodded. Speech temporarily defeating him, Stratton clapped the sergeant on the bicep. His stomach seemed to be filled with cold ash so that he felt hollow and sick. His legs felt unsteady and, if Maynard hadn't been sitting on the bottom step of the stairs, he'd have sat down on it himself. As it was, he leant against the adjacent wall. Policewoman Harris, who'd been carefully avoiding his eyes since the telephone call came, continued to do so, staring grimly down at the floor.

The kitchen was crowded with coppers but, beyond the brief acknowledging nod of greeting, nobody looked anyone else in the eye. The unexpressed sympathy, curdled by the beginnings of blame, made the atmosphere even more uncomfortable, but Stratton knew that he mustn't leave the room. He was meant to be in charge—to desert his post, even for a moment, would be taken for either cowardice or admission. The pathologist,

McNally, busied himself with his bag and gloves, and the rest of them watched in thickening silence as PC Canning removed the remains of the wallpaper from round the alcove and then pulled open the wooden door, stopping at each stage of the operation for the photographer to do his work. The man's bright lights seemed to illuminate the splintered kaleidoscope of hideous pictures inside Stratton's head: the baby's tiny, curled feet on the mortuary slab, Muriel's legs sliding out of the bundle they'd dragged from the washhouse, and worst of all, Davies's haggard face as he stared into infinity... He put a hand over his eyes to try and block them out, but it was useless.

'Sir?' Ballard was beside him, a hand on his arm. 'Can we move the body now?'

Stratton nodded dumbly then forced himself to watch as Canning and Ballard manhandled the corpse, arms and legs flopping, out of the narrow space and across the passage where, following McNally's instructions, they laid it on the floor of the now empty back room.

The face, despite its discolouration and bulging eyeballs, was recognisably that of Mary Dwyer. She looked pathetic—a human object used and then, just as callously, discarded. Her wrists tied together with a handkerchief, and dressed only in a brassiere, stockings and suspenders—the knickers were missing—she was a pitiful sight: jutting hipbones and ribs clearly visible, the skin flashing a hideous greenish-white in the harsh glare of the photographer's bulb. The only thing that wasn't greenish-white was the groove of the ligature, the brownish-red of raw liver, that circled her neck.

CHAPTER 43

Stratton swallowed, trying to work saliva into his mouth. Aware that everyone was watching for his reaction, he opened his mouth to ask a question, but McNally got there first. 'The rigor's passed, but she's not been there long. Forty-eight hours perhaps.' The gentle tone and the expression of sympathy on the man's face were far harder to take than the usual rebuke for wanting answers before a proper examination had been carried out at the mortuary. 'You know her?'

Stratton wondered how McNally had deduced this. 'Possibly…' Taking refuge in professional language, he added, 'There'll have to be a formal identification, of course.'

McNally nodded solemnly, a priest taking an unspoken confession. 'Of course.'

Stratton followed Dwyer's sheeted body as it was carried out to the ambulance on a stretcher. He stopped just inside the door. He could hear the crowd that was gathering in the street, but he didn't want to see them—the eager faces agog with excitement, reminding each other of the events of two and a half years earlier. 'Newspapers, too, sir,' said Ballard, behind him. 'They'll be here shortly.'

McNally, crouched inside the alcove, was running his gloved hands over the blanketed objects. Turning round to come back out he said with an apologetic grimace, 'Three's a crowd…The one at the back's standing on her head. That's assuming it's a woman, of course.'

Canning goggled at him. 'You mean she's upside down?'

' 'Fraid so.'

Canning's face contorted, and barging past the others he shoved open the back door and almost fell into the garden. They listened in silence as the sound of loud retching followed by liquid splattering told them that he was being violently sick.

'Sorry about that, sir.' Canning returned looking slightly sheepish and wiping his mouth with his handkerchief. 'Think I'll be fine now.'

'It's all right,' said Stratton, catching a faint, sour whiff of vomit as the big policeman edged past him. 'Ready to go again?'

Canning nodded. With Ballard's assistance, the second body was carried across the passage and laid on the floor of the back room. McNally, kneeling, began to loosen the knots that held the hideous parcel together. 'Must have been a Boy Scout,' he said grimly. Finally, a pair of legs was revealed, then some sort of flannelette garment bunched up between the thighs like a diaper, then the stomach, which was covered in rough-looking white patches, and the torso, small breasts beneath a grubby white cotton vest, one strap secured lopsidedly by a safety pin. Finally, the head emerged, covered entirely by a pillowslip which was secured around the neck by a tightly knotted stocking.

McNally looked up at Stratton, who nodded assent, and began removing the pillow case. As it was pulled upwards, Stratton saw that there was a piece of flowered material fixed across the mouth like a gag, some tendrils of brown hair trapped underneath on either side. When that was removed, Stratton could see that the blackened end of the tongue was sticking out from between the teeth.

'Think it's McKinnon, sir?' asked Ballard, beside him.

'Could be.' Stratton didn't turn to look at the sergeant. What had they done, he thought. What had *he* done?

The skin of the face looked dried, and the eyeballs were distended, the irises a dull brown. As McNally removed the stocking, Stratton saw the pressure marks on the neck. 'Is that from keeping the pillowslip in place?' he asked.

McNally shook his head. 'Too deep. Probably strangulation. I imagine that's why the…' he gestured at the wadded material between the woman's legs. 'Fluids.'

'Can you say how long she's been dead?'

Again, no rebuke for the question. The pathologist said thoughtfully, 'Not sure. She's in pretty good condition, all things considered—must be the dehydration. Not more than a week, I'd say. Ten days at the outside.'

'There's not much of a smell.'

'Decomposition hasn't really got going. The weather's not been that warm, and although that cupboard wasn't entirely airtight, with that wallpaper, and being wrapped…that would certainly have helped retard it.' McNally pointed at the face. 'Heading for partial mummification, I'd say. There's mould, though. From spores and such.' He pointed to the area below the vest. 'She's ready to move.'

The third body appeared, at first sight, to be fully clothed in a dress and cardigan. She was fatter than the others, and there was a towel wrapped around her head and another between her legs, visible where her skirt and slip had become disarranged. McNally peered down. 'This one's not wearing knickers either.'

Hearing this, Ballard murmured, 'Muriel Davies wasn't wearing any knickers, sir, remember?'

'Wasn't she?'

'No, sir.'

'We can't jump to conclusions, Ballard.'

The sergeant stared at him for a moment, eyes widening with irony, then said, 'No, sir.'

'For God's sake,' snapped Stratton, 'we don't know. But Backhouse is obviously out of control—judging by what we've found, it's only a matter of time before he does it again. I doubt he's bothered about being caught...'

'I shouldn't think he'd have left the place like this if he was, sir.'

'Exactly. He's got beyond that point—doesn't care any more. Still, if it makes him reckless, he should be easy to catch, which is something. As soon as McNally's finished here, we're going to take this fucking place apart. Brick by brick, if necessary. We'll need some men for the garden, too, so you'd better go back to the box—but not Arliss. I don't want him anywhere near the place. Then you better take Canning, and...how many men are out at the front?'

'Three, sir.' Ballard's neutral expression betrayed no reproach, but Stratton felt both guilty and, perversely, irritated by the man's sympathetic demeanour.

'I'm sure two can manage, so take one of them and start on that bloody washhouse and the toilet, and if you don't find anything there you'd better get cracking on the floorboards. Don't do anything else. We'll need to get the surveyors' department in for that—don't want the place falling down round our ears.'

'Right, sir.'

'And, Ballard...'

'Sir?'

'I'm sorry.'

'No need, sir.'

'Yes, there is,' snapped Stratton, goaded by Ballard's understanding tone. 'There's every bloody need. This is a fucking nightmare, and it's my fault.' He turned his back on the sergeant and fixed his eyes once more on the body on the floor.

'Shall we have a look at her now?' asked McNally. Again the voice was soft, hesitant.

Stratton nodded, gritting his teeth. For Christ's sake stop *humouring* me, he thought. Just get it *done*.

Again, the distended eyeballs, congealed and purple skin bleached in the glare and flash of the photographer's bulb, the black tongue protruding. White mould on the skin around the mouth and a stub of white stalactite, like a horn, sticking out of one nostril. Was it Iris Manning? He thought so. Unlike the others, he'd known her in life, but in this condition... We could have saved her, he thought. I should have. I should have saved all three of them.

'She may be pregnant,' said McNally, gently. The words seemed to hover somehow in the air of the dismal room, reverberating so that Stratton heard them not once, but several times over. Dragging his eyes from the ruined face, he saw that the pathologist was feeling the belly with the palms of his gloved hands, as delicately as if she'd been a living woman. 'There's something here, quite bulky. Could be something else, but...'

'How far gone, if she is?'

'*If* she is, I'd say four or five months.'

Stratton, well aware that it was normally impossible to extract such speculation from McNally or any other pathologist, suddenly wondered if he knew about Jenny. He hadn't conducted the post-mortem himself, but he would surely know the man who had, and perhaps... McNally's expression wasn't telling him one way or the other. The pathologist was staring at him with intense concentration, as if willing him to focus on the job. Grasping for some sort of logic, he said, 'Do you think either of the others might have been pregnant?'

'Won't be able to tell that until we get back to the mortuary.' Until they were cut up, Stratton thought. 'Won't know if this one's been interfered with yet, either. The pregnancy, I mean—if that's what it is.'

'Muriel Davies's pregnancy wasn't interfered with.'

'No,' McNally looked away. 'It wasn't.'

No one had said anything about Iris Manning being pregnant. Perhaps she hadn't told anyone. Perhaps Backhouse had offered to get rid of it for her, enticed her in...

A thump from outside made him turn his head in the direction of the back yard, and he saw that Ballard and the others were trooping back inside and down the passage to the front room. Nothing in the washhouse then, this time, but there was always the garden...

McNally was saying something. '...move her now?'

'Yes. You can take her away.'

As they stood back for the sheeted corpse to be removed, McNally said, 'Do I take it that you'd like me to stay?'

'I'm afraid so. Pulling up the boards shouldn't take long. Would you excuse me for a moment?'

Averting his eyes from the drying puddle of spew where Canning had voided the contents of his stomach, Stratton stared around the small back yard. It seemed even more untidy than it had been in 1950—but then, he thought, they'd only seen it by torchlight. The wrecked Anderson shelter was still there and the twisted chicken wire, the old tin cans, crumpled newspapers, broken bricks and odd tufts of grass sticking out of the dry mud, as well as a surprisingly vigorous mock orange and another bush that he didn't recognise. Seeing a small bone, gnawed white, that looked like the remains of a chop, Stratton wondered where the dog was. Had Backhouse taken it with him?

Unless it wasn't an animal bone, of course... Some human bones were small and a dog, knowing no different, would enjoy chewing one of those as well. Human remains could fertilise plants. They did in graveyards. Was he looking at a graveyard now? And if he was, had there been women buried here when they found Muriel and Judy Davies? For Christ's sake, he told himself, you were only looking for Muriel and Judy, not a lot of dead tarts. There was no reason then—*none whatsoever*—to think that anyone else had been killed. And certainly no reason to think that Norman Backhouse, with his fibrositis and his diarrhoea, his visits to the doctor and his old-womanish ways…No reason to think that Backhouse, the former police Reservist, the reformed man…No reason to think that Backhouse, who had a nice quiet wife and a nice quiet life—except that *he shared his nice quiet home with Christ-knows-how-many dead whores…*

If Davies was innocent, why had he confessed? Because he felt guilty about what had happened to his wife? Guilty that he hadn't protected her?

'Jesus Christ!' He smashed his fist against the wooden panels of the washhouse door. He, of all people, should have understood about the guilt. But it was Jenny's death, Jenny and their unborn child, that had made him pursue Davies with such certainty; resentment against a man who, it appeared, had had a pregnant wife and killed her, and who'd killed a baby, when he'd have given anything, anything at all—

'Yes.' That's what Davies had said when he'd shown him the clothing at West End Central. He'd reached forward and picked up the tie that was used to kill his child, and he'd said 'yes'. Then he'd wept. And Stratton had been *absolutely sure* that he'd got his man. 'Yes.' One word: it could mean everything or nothing.

And the stupid bastard had lied about practically everything else, hadn't he? No one, not even his mother, had believed a word he said…

'Sir?' Ballard stuck his head round the back door.

'Found anything?'

'Not yet, sir. Canning and Tillotson are getting started on the floorboards in the back room.'

'That was their bedroom, wasn't it?'

'Yes, sir… And there are a couple of things you ought to see.'

'Oh?'

'A length of rubber tubing and a bulldog clip. We found them by the fireplace in the front room. And there's this, sir.' Ballard took a small object wrapped in a handkerchief out of his pocket. When he laid it on the scabby, flaking paint of the windowsill, Stratton saw that it was a rusty tobacco tin: Old Holborn.

'It seems he took souvenirs, sir.'

'Sou— Oh, *Christ.*' The lid open, Stratton could see four separate clumps of short, coarse hair, which had been carefully teased out into ringlets so that they looked like nests for miniature birds. 'Pubic?'

'I think so, sir, yes.'

'Where did you find that thing?'

'Medicine cabinet in the kitchen. Behind the door, sir.'

'Anything else in there?'

'Lot of tablets, sir. Tonics and sedatives and God knows what else. Harris is making a list. And the other tenants are back—the ones who live on the top floor. Young coloured couple.'

'See if you can't get one of the neighbours to make them a cup of tea. What about the ones on the first floor?'

'It's the same chap, sir—Mr Gardiner. He's back in hospital, so I don't think—' Ballard was interrupted by a discreet cough from the direction of the back door, now blocked by the burly form of PC Canning, claw hammer dangling from one meaty hand. 'Found another one, sir.'

The floorboards from the centre of the room were stacked in front of the fireplace. Looking down, Stratton saw that one of the joists had been sawn away to make room for body number four, which was encased in a flannelette blanket, lashed at each end and covered with a dusting of earth. When the photographer had finished, Canning and Tillotson removed the body with an effort and stood back for McNally to do his work.

'Definitely a Boy Scout… Safety pins as well, this time. Perhaps he ran out of rope.'

Like the previous two, the head was wrapped, this time in what looked like part of a sheet. The body, which was considerably stockier and heavier than the others, was naked apart from stockings. It was covered on top by a nightgown, with what appeared to be a dress lying beneath. McNally lifted the nightgown, exposing the heavy breasts and belly. The skin was hard and mouldy like the outside of a cheddar cheese. As with the other two bodies, there was a garment of some sort stuffed between the legs. 'That first one…' said McNally, 'he must have been interrupted before he could do all this, so he just stuck her in the cupboard as she was. This one's a good bit older than the others,' he added. 'Both in terms of age and of how long she's been here.' Ballard and Stratton exchanged glances as he began unwrapping the material from the head. Suddenly, the reek of putrefaction hit Stratton like a blow to the face, making him gag.

'Damp air getting in somewhere,' said the pathologist in a matter-of-fact voice, as if giving a lecture. Forcing himself to turn his head, Stratton saw that while the right side of the woman's face was dry and covered with the same mould as her body, the left side was decomposing wetly so that the features appeared to have slipped and melted down the side of the cheek.

Fighting rising nausea, Stratton turned to look at Ballard who, although so pale in the face that he was almost translucent, seemed steady enough on his feet. He could feel the stink wrapping itself around him, clinging to his clothes like smoke. Better you smell of dead women than live ones, Jenny'd once said, in an unusual moment of black humour—except she wasn't there to care what he smelt of... Still, he'd better give himself a good scrub before— Oh, Christ. The bloody party. Pete. He'd never be able to get back in time—he'd have to telephone Doris later. Pete would understand.

'Cause of death?' he asked the pathologist.

'Not sure yet. There are some grooves here,' McNally pointed to the neck, 'but the condition of the skin...' He shook his head.

'Can you say how long?'

'At least a couple of months, I'd say.'

'The neighbour said Mrs Backhouse had been away for about three months, sir,' said Ballard quietly.

As they followed the draped and stretchered corpse outside to the ambulance, Stratton was aware of a low, expectant hum which stopped as Canning stepped backwards out of the front door with his end of the load. Following with Ballard, he stopped on the threshold and stared out at the crowd of mainly women and children who stood in a half circle around the ambulance, three and four deep. They were being kept at a distance by two policemen, helmeted and wearing overcoats, who were watching over the vehicle with the proprietorial air of shepherds guarding a flock.

Judging by the numbers, Stratton thought it was a fair bet that, as well as neighbours, the usual collection of ghouls were present, who'd thrill to carnage and catastrophe of any kind. In fact, Stratton often thought that given the speed with which they turned up in such situations, they must somehow be able to sense it. You could tell who they were by their gawping; they were avid and shameless. The other faces bore degrees of shocked or guilty fascination and some of the kids had a slightly distracted look, as if they couldn't concentrate wholly on what was unfolding because they had to be on the lookout in case their parents caught them at it. They needn't have worried: from what Stratton could see, most of the parents—the mothers, at least—were in the crowd as well. Some of them, he realised, must have been here when they'd come for Muriel Davies; but if anybody did recognise him, they were keeping it to themselves, which was a relief.

Still, you couldn't blame the neighbours for coming to see what was going on. I'd be out here, too, if I lived next door, he thought; I'd want to see what the next turn-up would be. And that, he thought, as a police van pulled up in front of the goods yard wall and men in overalls began unloading spades, sieves and stacks of wooden boxes, was anybody's guess.

Scanning the crowd once more, he spotted, towards the back, an anxious-looking coloured couple who must be the ones from the top flat. Several feet away, a slatternly woman whose hair was quilted by metal curlers stood talking to a couple of solid-looking men in fawn mackintoshes. Coarse-faced, they had a brazen look about them which, in Stratton's experience, meant one of two things. Either they sold stuff on commission or—far more likely in the circumstances—they were journalists. Well, they could whistle for it, because they weren't getting a peep out of him.

He looked past the crowd, down the short length of the street with its row of mean, bay-windowed front rooms surrounded by grimy brickwork. As the day started to draw in, a glum, grey pall seemed to shroud everything in view.

'Paradise Street,' said Ballard wryly. 'Evidently someone's idea of a joke.'

'Ha-bloody-ha.' Stratton was standing right beside the side pane of the smeary front window of number ten, and, as he spoke, he peered into it, almost expecting to see Backhouse's face, bespectacled and ghostly, hovering behind the net curtain.

To his left, he could hear the monotonous thrum of traffic and to his right, chugging and clanging from the railway tracks; the sounds of life continuing as normal. 'It's ordinary,' he said. 'Ordinary life in an ordinary street. I keep imagining him pottering around this house, brewing tea and taking bloody... *kaolin and morphine* for his diarrhoea, and all the time...'

'Do you think Mrs Backhouse knew, sir?'

'Back in nineteen fifty? She was very much under his thumb, so...' Stratton shook his head wearily. 'I just don't know. The whole thing is just...' Unable to think of a word that would accurately describe what it was, he illustrated it with a small, hopeless gesture.

'Inspector, if I might just...' Turning, he found himself confronting one of the journalists, who must have edged around the back of the crowd. Close to, he recognised the man as one who'd badgered him before, sidling up and offering to buy him a drink (or, as he put it, 'a gargle') on a number of occasions, always in the creepily confidential manner of a false friend. Now the voice was goading, aggressively cheerful. 'What about Davies now, Inspector? Still think he's guilty?' Revolted by the brutal breath and the predatory eyes, the man's whole air of gorging himself on misery, Stratton said, 'I've got nothing to say.'

'But surely, Inspector—'

'Piss off.' Stratton turned his back and, muttering, the man went to rejoin his colleague.

He shouldn't have said that—the man was bound to find some way of sticking the knife in... 'Stupid,' he said to Ballard. 'You should never lose your temper with them.'

'Quite understandable, sir, in the circumstances.'

'Yes, but he won't see it like that… It's all very well for them,' Stratton added, sourly. 'For them it's just the next sensation. Here and then gone, and they never have to worry about the consequences.'

Ballard was staring past him down the street. 'I think DCI Lamb is about to arrive, sir.'

Following the sergeant's gaze, Stratton saw the official car nosing its way round the corner. 'That's all we bloody need. I'd better go and meet him.'

He'd assumed that Lamb would insist on arriving with a great fanfare of horn-honking and was surprised when the car pulled up almost immediately, and his superior emerged from the back seat unaided. Stratton, who was bracing himself for the full performance from righteous anger to bravely borne resignation, taking in disappointment and endeavouring to rise above it and Christ knew what else in between, reflected that at last there was no convenient surface for the forefinger-jabbing that always accompanied a high-grade bollocking. Unless—Stratton winced—Lamb was going to use his chest and prod him backwards down the length of the cul-de-sac. I'll strangle him if he tries that, he thought savagely. I'll put my hands round his neck and shake him till his eyes pop out, and then I'll—

'How many?'

Stratton blinked. Lamb's voice was so quiet it barely reached him, and he looked not only defeated but stupefied. Watching him, Stratton's dismay and anger was transformed into the same intensity of amazement. It was as disconcerting as if a dummy had suddenly reached out a real, flesh-and-blood hand. 'Sir?'

'In the house—how many?'

'Four, sir, so far. I'm fairly certain that at least one of them is one of our missing girls. It's possible that the other two are there as well, but it's a bit hard to tell at the moment… We also think that the fourth body—we found her under the bedroom floor—might be Edna Backhouse. They're making a start on the garden now, sir. It's the usual drill—removing soil to a depth of two feet and sieving for evidence. I don't imagine they'll be able to finish today, but we'll station constables front and back overnight, and—'

'This is a fucking shambles.' Lamb shook his head in disbelief and Stratton, who had never heard his superior swear so harshly before, was as astonished by this as by finding himself entirely in sympathy with the man.

'Right.' Pulling himself together with visible effort, Lamb said, 'I suppose I'd better have a look'

'Yes, sir. This way.'

'Any reporters yet?'

'A couple, sir.'

'For God's sake don't speak to them. I'll have something sent out for tomorrow's papers. If they persist, tell them to contact the station.'

'Yes, sir. Thank you.'

Lamb was silent throughout the short tour, merely nodding at Stratton's explanations. Finally, as they stood outside the washhouse, watching the team of men dig and sift in the garden, he said, in a tone of baffled wonder, 'He was a special.'

Stratton, feeling it would be inappropriate to offer condolences of the anyone-can-make-a-mistake variety, and uncomfortable with the memory of enjoying a quiet gloat about Lamb being hauled over the coals after Backhouse's criminal record came out, settled for, 'Well, he was commended, sir.' He knew, even as he said it, that he should have kept his mouth shut, but Lamb didn't appear to have heard. Instead, he was staring at one of the diggers, who was gesturing from the far corner of the garden.

'Something here, sir. Could you take a look?'

The digger was pointing to the corner where the rickety wooden planks of the back fence met the brick wall of the goods yard, and Stratton, approaching, saw something dirty white sticking out of the earth. Squatting down beside it, he saw that beneath the soil and grime was the smooth, rounded end of what looked like a thigh bone. Judging by its fleshless condition, it had been there for some time and it was, he thought, too large to belong to a cat or dog.

'He must have been at it for quite some time, sir,' said the digger. 'This must have worked itself loose somehow or other, because he's been using it to prop up this end of the fence.'

'Those women in the lavatory at Piccadilly,' said Diana. 'They thought I was one of them. A tart.'

'Why on earth didn't you tell me what was happening, darling?' Lally was sitting on the end of the bed, looking worried. 'You were in such a dreadful state last night—a sort of faint. We didn't know what to think… And the last time we saw you, you seemed so *happy*. I know that was some time ago, but I had no idea. I thought you were just…well, busy.'

'I'm sorry, Lally. I didn't mean to cause…you know. But I couldn't tell you. You've been so kind to me. It wasn't fair to keep on running to you for help, and I thought it would be disloyal to James.' Diana lay back on the pillows. At some point the previous evening, Lally and Jock had returned and persuaded a reluctant Mrs Robinson to make up a bed for her. She'd been so exhausted that she scarcely remembered Lally leading her up the stairs and helping her into bed. Looking down, she saw that she was still wearing her underclothes. 'I didn't know what to do. I thought I could help him, but… He *told* me to leave him, Lally. I didn't want to—or maybe I did. I don't know any more. I'm just… just… It's all such a failure. Guy, James, everything. My whole life. I should never have got married again—or not so quickly, anyway.'

'I did wonder, when you told me you were going to marry him,' said Lally. 'But you seemed so in love and so *sure* and these things often do work, so...' She made a face. 'But you're not hopeless, and it isn't your fault. James's drinking wasn't your fault, and neither was the rest of it.' Lally's tone was sharp, and Diana was surprised to see that her face was white with tight-lipped anger. 'It's the way we were brought up. We weren't taught to think for ourselves. Beauty, compliancy, *complaisancy*... That's all that's ever been expected. No useful skills and precious little education—beyond what we've managed to scrape for ourselves, that is. What the hell *are* you supposed to do if you're a cross between a...a...brood mare and an ornament? Especially as half the men our generation of girls married—or were supposed to marry—were killed in the war, and all those big houses we were supposed to run have either been knocked down or sold off as boarding schools or something because nobody can afford to live in them any more.'

Taken aback by her friend's vehemence, Diana said, 'It's not that bad. And you seem to manage pretty well.'

Lally shot her a rueful look. 'Sorry. I suppose that was a bit about me. But not everything in the garden is roses, you know.'

'Better than no garden at all. I was thinking about those things—what you just said—when I was up at Hambeyn Hall... You've put it much better. We're dinosaurs, really, and it's hard to be any different, no matter how much you want to. You'd think, with the war, one would adapt one's thinking, but somehow one just goes back—behaves as if nothing had changed... Or perhaps that's just me. God knows... Anyway, thank you, darling, for letting me stay.'

'Don't be silly.'

'Mrs Robinson doesn't like me much, does she?'

Lally grimaced. 'I suppose she's another kind of dinosaur—a Victorian one. Divorced women not allowed across the threshold... She's been with Jock's family for about five hundred years. But don't worry, I'm sure we'll manage to get round her somehow. Now, you look absolutely shattered, and I forbid you to set foot out of bed until you've revived a bit. When you're better, Jock will take you to see your landlady and sort out the rent.'

'Are you sure? I don't know when I'll be able to repay you.'

'Don't you get any money from Guy? I don't mean to pay us back—you mustn't worry about that—but to live on.'

Diana shook her head. 'I was getting a small allowance, but it stopped when James and I married. We ploughed what was left of my money into James's projects, but none of them came to fruition, so… That's it, really.'

'What about James's family?'

'All dead. The close relatives, anyway. There are some others somewhere—abroad, I think, but I don't see why they should help me. In any case, I hate the idea of leeching off people. I need to find a job.'

'Well, what about the film studio?'

'I doubt they'd have me back.'

Lally frowned. 'You won't know until you try. I shan't open the curtains—you need to rest. You can have a bath later.'

'Thank you, Lally. I really am grateful.'

'Listen, darling…' Lally stood up. 'It may feel like the end of the world, but it isn't—not really. "If at first you don't succeed, try, try, try again," as Nanny used to say.'

'Mine used to say, "Those who ask don't get,"' said Diana, glumly. 'And she said, "You're so sharp you'll cut yourself." Or perhaps that was a different nanny. I had quite a procession of them. I was always told they wouldn't stay because I was such a naughty little girl. It was only years later that I realised they'd all fled because Pa used to take liberties.'

'My nanny was obviously a better philosopher than all of yours put together—and I'd have backed her against your Pa any day.' Lally adopted an outraged tone, chin up and hands on hips. 'None of your sauce, my man!' Bending to smooth the bedclothes, she added, 'I may have reconciled Mrs Robinson to your presence, but I certainly won't be able to change her mind about the decadent implications of sitting on beds. Now then,' she wagged her finger, 'good night, sweet repose, lie on your back, and not on your nose.'

I've fallen flat on my nose, Diana thought when she'd gone. How shall I ever recover? *Try, try again*... To succeed at what? She stared up at the smooth white emptiness of the ceiling. The same as my future, she thought with dread: nothing there.

Waking with a start as the front door slammed, Stratton realised that he must have fallen asleep in the armchair. Stiff-necked and befuddled, with a foul taste in his mouth, it was a few seconds before he remembered: Pete's dinner. Oh, hell. He'd meant to telephone Doris to apologise as soon as he got in, and he'd only sat down for a moment…

What time was it? Past eleven. The footsteps in the kitchen were heavier than Monica's, so it must be Pete. She must have come in already and gone upstairs to bed. Why hadn't she woken him? The sitting-room light was on, so she must have realised he was there.

He was just about to get up and go through to the kitchen when Pete appeared, larger and beefier than ever. He was still in uniform with a bottle in his hand and a loose co-ordination to his movements which—together with his general air of beery belligerence—suggested that he was, if not actually drunk, then certainly well on the way.

'Hello,' said Stratton, cautiously. 'Pete, I—'

'Hello, Dad. Want one?' Pete held up the bottle in one hand, and attempted to point to it with the other, but missed.

Stratton, realising that he did very much want one, and deciding that it couldn't make a bad situation worse, and might even help a bit, said evenly, 'Yes, thanks.'

Pete withdrew and, after some banging about, returned with a second bottle. Positioning himself once more in the doorway he lobbed it, underarm, at Stratton, who lunged forward and caught it just in time to field the bottle-opener that followed. 'Steady on, old chap!' Stratton placed both objects on the sideboard. 'Why don't you sit down? I'll fetch a glass.' Pete, he noted, hadn't bothered with one, and was swigging straight from the bottle.

He took a glass from the kitchen cupboard, then went into the scullery and splashed his face with water. Standing in front of the sink, wet hands resting on the wooden draining board either side of the porcelain rectangle, images crowded his mind: the bodies in the alcove, Davies's face, the baby lying on the slab, the squalid terror of the women's last moments… He shook his head violently and began to count to ten. Deal with the situation in hand. Pete was clearly in a dangerous mood. He must have been to the pub after leaving Doris's, Stratton thought. All the guilt that formed the undertow of every thought he'd had about his son since Jenny died seemed to wrench itself upwards like a shipwreck breaking through to the surface: his preference for Monica; not loving Pete enough or even, in truth, liking him all that much; his utter failure to communicate with the lad…

At least, he thought, he could go back in there and apologise properly for not being home—wait until they were both settled so that the words could be given—and, he hoped, received—with the weight and importance that was due. Taking a deep breath, he picked up his glass and returned to the sitting room.

'Thought you weren't coming back.' Pete was slumped in 'his' armchair, legs outstretched, and Stratton noticed that he'd almost finished his beer. Concealing a flash of irritation—you're not in the bloody NAAFI now—he sat down opposite his son.

'Well,' he said, 'as you can see, I'm here.'

Pete nodded as if confirming this fact and then, peering down at his feet as if from a very great height, bent forward so suddenly that he almost fell on the hearthrug and began unlacing his boots with a series of savage jerks. This done, he heeled them off, punted them in the direction of the empty fireplace and looked up at his father expectantly.

'I'm sorry,' said Stratton. 'I got held up at work. New case.'

Pete waved a dismissive hand. ' 'S'all right, Dad.'

'No, it isn't. But it was unavoidable and, as I said, I'm very sorry that I wasn't there. Did you have a nice time?'

'Uncle Reg bored us all stiff with a lot of guff about the Coronation, but the food wasn't bad.'

This would ordinarily, given the trouble that Doris must have gone to, have deserved a rebuke, but Stratton felt that this was neither the time nor the place. 'Went down to the Swan after,' Pete continued. 'Some pals from school… One of them's working in an abattoir, out Woodford way. Kept going on about how they kill the cows. Wouldn't get off it. Even worse than listening to Uncle Reg.'

'You should have asked him if he can't get us a bit of meat off ration.'

Ignoring this feeble attempt at levity, Pete said, 'So, this case that kept you, this *unavoidable* case… What was it, then?'

'You don't want to hear about that.'

'Yes, I do,' said Pete aggressively. 'I want to hear *all* about it. Got to be more interesting than anything else I've heard this evening.' Widening his eyes so that his face became a horrible parody of an eager child's, he added, 'Go on, Dad. Give us a bedtime story.'

'All right, then…' Stratton, thinking that actually enunciating the whole wretched business might help him clarify things a bit—and that, given the state of Pete, he'd be talking mainly to himself anyway—said, 'Well, it started a few years ago, when—'

'Hold on.' Pete was pawing at his top pocket. 'Lemme get a fag going.'

Not wishing to witness the owlish fumbling with matches that was bound to ensue from this, Stratton lit two of his own and passed one across. 'There you are.'

Pete sucked in the smoke hungrily, then leant back and shut his eyes. 'Go on, then, Dad. Once upon a time…'

Stratton began to talk. He spoke for some time, trying as best he could to relate the events in chronological order and as objectively as possible. All the while, at the back of his mind, he was conscious that he was looking for things to salvage from the mess in order to reassure himself…of what, he wasn't entirely sure. The possibility that Davies might, after all, be guilty, that he'd done his job to the best of his ability, that…he didn't know. A leaden numbness had settled on him, burying all his previous reactions beneath its weight. 'So,' he finished, 'that's why I wasn't there tonight.'

Pete's eyes remained closed and, for a moment, Stratton thought that he must have fallen asleep. He lit another cigarette and sat staring into the empty grate. Why had Pete asked him about it all, anyway? He was about to suggest going to bed when Pete opened his eyes. 'Looks like you hanged the wrong man, then.'

'Well, the investigation's barely started, but—'

'But you hanged an innocent man.'

'We don't actually know that he was—'

'Don't you?' Pete leant forward. 'Don't you, Dad? After all, two stranglers in one house—taking coincidence a bit far, wouldn't you say?'

'Yes, I would, but—'

'But what, Dad?'

'But it's not that simple.' Aware of how feeble that sounded, and aware, too, that Pete was staring at him with an intensity of scorn he'd only ever seen him direct at Reg, he struggled for something to say that might redeem him in his son's eyes. What? *I'm not perfect?* Pete was only too well aware of that, and, in any case, he was of a generation who, given the events of the last sixty years, had every right to condemn both parents and grandparents. It was bad enough having colleagues at work solicitously monitoring his failure, without attacks from his own family as well. 'We all make mistakes, I'm afraid.'

'As *mistakes* go, Dad,' said Pete with heavy sarcasm, 'I'd say this one rather takes the biscuit.' This was said in a derisive parody of an upper-class accent—the voice, Stratton imagined, that he used for mocking officers behind their backs. Before he could reply, Pete continued, switching back to his normal voice, 'When you felt so sure that Davies was guilty, was that because of Mum?'

Stratton stiffened. This was almost the first time his son had mentioned Jenny in his hearing since she'd died. There was an almost demonic shrewdness in his eyes. He'd meant the question to strike home, and it had. In as calm a voice as he could manage, Stratton said, 'One tries to keep one's emotions out of these things, but I suppose that might have had a bearing on it. With that sort of crime—a mother and child—it's hard not to think of your own family. And usually, with a case like that, it is the husband who's responsible.'

There was a moment's silence—Pete was tipsy enough for it to slow his reactions—before his son said quietly, 'Yes. Isn't it just?'

Stratton took a deep breath, biting back his instinctive reaction—you're drunk and you don't know what the hell you're talking about. There was no ducking this. Useless to pretend he hadn't understood, because he could see from Pete's expression that his own face had already betrayed him. In any case, he told himself, Pete doesn't know Jenny was pregnant. He's angry, and he's lashing out: don't rise to it.

'I do feel guilty about your mother,' he said evenly. 'I should have been there to protect her. Not a day goes by when I don't think about that...and when I don't miss her. I loved her very much. You do know that, don't you?'

'Oh, yes,' said Pete. 'I know that. But perhaps,' he leant forward, gripping the arms of the chair, and Stratton saw a flash of malicious triumph in his eyes, 'if you'd been thinking a bit less about that and a bit more about a few other things that are under your nose...' He stopped, jerking backwards as if tugged by an invisible thread, a flush of guilty confusion flooding his face, cockiness evaporating so that he seemed like a small boy conscious of blurting out more than he'd meant to say.

'What do you mean, *under my nose*?'

'It's nothing.' The tone was sullen, defensive. 'Doesn't matter.'

'It obviously does, or you wouldn't have said it.'

'It's none of your business.'

Pete was looking furtive now, seeking a way out. Sensing that he was about to get up, Stratton rose and took a step towards him. 'If it's happening in this house, then it is my business. Tell me.'

Shrinking back in his chair, Pete stared up at him, wide-eyed, shocked into sobriety by fear. Stratton placed his hands on the arms of Pete's chair and glared at him. 'Just bloody tell me!' he roared.

'All right.' Pete reared back even further, holding up his hands in a gesture of surrender. 'But stop shouting. Sit down, for God's sake.'

Stratton, backing off, complied. 'I'm sitting down. Now, what's going on?'

With a visible effort, Pete gathered himself together. 'It's Monica.'

'What about her?'

Now he'd made the decision to speak, Stratton saw Pete's former bravado returning in leaps and bounds. 'You really have no idea, have you? Well, let me enlighten you.' The officer-mocking tone was there, and then, in the next second, gone. The look in his son's eyes was a challenge, brutal and direct. 'She's pregnant.'

CHAPTER 47

Dressed in borrowed finery and bejewelled at wrists and neck, Diana fiddled with her fork and wished she felt like eating. She'd already had two glasses of wine on top of quite a lot of champagne and she knew she ought to attempt to soak it up with food, but she was far too jittery to be able to do more than toy with what was on her plate. Lally and Jock had taken her to Ciro's in an attempt to cheer her up, and she was trying her best to *be* cheered up, but it wasn't working. All the shining silver and glassware sparkling in the light cast by the rows of chandeliers, the dazzling white napery, the bright music and the alcohol could not dispel her heavy, dull despair, and knowing that she was worrying Lally and boring Jock didn't help.

Jock's manner had been brusque the previous day when they'd driven over to pay her landlady the arrears on the rent. The wild hope she'd had of finding James waiting for her on the steps outside had crystallised into an almost-certainty on the journey, so that finding that he wasn't there plunged her more deeply into gloom even than before. Jock had insisted that she stay in the car while he sorted things out, and, hating herself for her passivity, she'd waited miserably until he returned with a new key to the second-floor flat.

Jock hadn't been able to disguise his disgust as they walked into the cheerless sitting room. 'It's not normally as bad as this,' Diana said defensively. 'She's packed away all our things.' They'd been stacked in the hall in suitcases and wooden boxes.

'Is this everything?' Jock had asked incredulously, surveying the small pile. 'Or has she taken some away? She told me she hadn't, but…'

'I think so,' said Diana. 'I'll check later.' She knew she wouldn't have to check—one or the other of them had already pawned all the larger or more expensive items.

'Well,' said Jock awkwardly, 'if there's nothing else, I'd better be going.'

'Yes… Thank you, Jock. For everything.'

'Oh, that's all right. No need to make a fuss.'

When he'd gone, Diana opened the first suitcase and, finding that it contained her clothes, began unpacking in a mechanical fashion. The second suitcase contained what was left of James's wardrobe. She was about to lift out a pile of shirts and underclothes when it occurred to her that it was pointless to go through the charade of hanging them up or folding them away in drawers if he wasn't coming back.

He must come back, she thought. Surely, he would. He couldn't leave her like this, so alone. Then with agonising clarity came the image of him as she'd last seen him, grovelling at her feet on the beach, the poached eyes staring past her to the bottle she'd been holding in her hand. He's not coming back, she thought. He's not capable of it. She closed the suitcase, snapped the locks, and pushed it into the hall cupboard, closing the door.

The books and ornaments—those that were left—would keep until tomorrow. She went into the kitchen where she found a tin of soup and a bottle of sherry with half an inch left that must, somehow, have escaped James's notice. She placed them side by side on the draining board and got as far as putting a saucepan on the stove before realising that she had neither the energy, nor the desire, to cook or eat even this simple meal.

Wandering into the bedroom, she glanced at herself in the mirror over the mantelpiece. The face that looked back from behind the light coating of dust was dazed and cloudy. Turning away, she kicked off her shoes and lay down on the bed with all her clothes on, including her fur coat, which she hadn't felt warm enough to remove. As she closed her eyes, she thought detachedly, I ought to be afraid, but I'm not. I'm too tired, even for that. It seemed to her that somewhere, somehow, she had lost the instinct for self-preservation. Had she ever thought that her life would, at some point, turn out right, and she would be happy? Or had she always known this would happen? She couldn't remember.

She'd remained in bed, getting up sometime in the middle of the night to undress to her underclothes, for over twenty-four hours, until a sharp tapping on the door compelled her to rise. Pulling back the curtain, she saw that it was dark outside and the streets were lit. Dressing hastily, she found Jock and Lally, dressed in evening clothes, waiting on the landing.

'Surprise, darling!' Lally's voice seemed excruciatingly bright. It's started already, thought Diana bleakly: the pity. 'We're taking you out to dinner, darling. I thought you needed a bit of a cheer-up. I've brought you some things to wear,' she indicated a suitcase held by Jock, who looked markedly less enthusiastic, 'so you can't use that as an excuse, and there's jewellery and things in there.' She pushed a dressing case into Diana's arms. 'Aren't you going to let us in?'

Diana blinked at her, bleary-eyed. 'I don't think… I mean, I'm not…'

'We know you're not, darling,' said Lally, 'and that's why you need some fun. Now, come on…' She advanced towards the sitting room and, looking round at its dusty anonymity, said, 'Heavens, this is all very…*bijou*, isn't it?'

'I think,' said Diana, 'that "small" is the word you're looking for. And "dismal".'

'Nonsense. Once you've got your things sorted out it'll be

fine. Smaller places are so much easier than great barns like ours, anyway. You can make it really modern.'

She meant well, but the vehement optimism was more than Diana could bear. 'I haven't anything to offer you,' she said ungraciously.

'Doesn't matter, darling. Why don't I come and chat to you while you get ready? Jock can wait here.'

Jock was standing in the middle of the room, a look of detached politeness on his face. Clearly, thought Diana, all this was Lally's idea, and she had a strong suspicion that Jock had tried to talk her out of it. 'It's very kind of you,' she said, 'but I really don't feel… As you can see, there's an awful lot to do here, and I don't suppose I'd be terribly good company, so…' But Lally had overridden all her protests and borne her into the bedroom to change and dress her hair, and now, an hour and a half hour later, they were all three sitting in sumptuous surroundings like strangers in a railway carriage who have started a conversation out of politeness and exhausted all subjects of mutual interest. Jock wore an expression of thin-lipped endurance, and Lally, who was facing the door, had begun discreetly searching the room for anyone they might know who could be persuaded to come over and enliven things. Laughter and chatter rippled the air all around them, and Diana felt lonelier and more hopeless than ever. 'I'm sorry,' she said, when Jock excused himself, 'but honestly, everything just feels like a dream at the moment. Everything since the war, really… No, since I went back to Hampshire. None of it seems real—as if I'd…I don't know… *died* or something, somewhere along the line. Or part of me has.'

'I know, darling.' Lally reached across the table and patted Diana's hand. 'But things will get better.'

'Will they?'

'Of course they will!'

Diana sighed. 'I shouldn't have come out,' she said. 'This is all so kind of you, but I feel like the ghost at the feast.'

'There'll be dancing soon,' said Lally. 'That's bound to cheer you up. Do you know, I'm sure I spotted Phyllis Garton-Smith just now. You remember, she was at Bletchley Park during the war—of course, you told me you'd seen her when you went there with F-J. Well, she's engaged to the strangest man—his family are something to do with shipping, but apparently he didn't want any part of it, so he went off and became an explorer.'

About halfway through this speech, the focus of Lally's gaze had switched to somewhere past Diana's left shoulder. When she stopped talking—clearly too distracted by whatever she'd seen to keep up the flow of chatter—Diana turned to see what had caught her friend's eye and, almost immediately, caught her breath. Lounging long-limbed and elegant in the doorway, louche in immaculate evening dress and, nine years on, more absurdly handsome than ever, was Claude Ventriss.

'Diana...' Lally's voice was low, warning. '*Diana...*'

Diana caught her breath. Claude was scanning the room. She couldn't work out from his expression whether or not he was looking for someone in particular. The arrogant tilt of his lazy, half-closed eyes suggested that every woman in the room was available to him and he was just deciding which one to snap his fingers at... Presumptuous as ever. Smiling involuntarily, Diana shook her head.

'Diana...' said Lally, again. 'For God's sake! Stop staring at him.'

Claude's gaze swept past Diana and, for a second, she thought he hadn't noticed her. Just as she was wondering if this was genuine or deliberate, his face seemed to break open in recognition, and his glowing, velvet-brown eyes looked directly into hers.

CHAPTER 48

Unable to sleep, Monica leant over and fumbled for her bedside lamp. Turning it on, she saw from her alarm clock that it was quarter past three in the morning. All her nights had been like this recently—lying awake, her thoughts going fruitlessly round in circles, the imagined outcomes growing worse each time. At first, it hadn't been too bad, because she'd been able to tell herself it would be all right in the morning, or, if not then, during the day, or the following morning—that her period would come, must come, soon. Now, such wishful thinking was impossible.

It wasn't as if she'd *wanted* to have intercourse with Raymond. They'd seen each other a lot over the past months, always travelling miles from the studio to spend evenings at little, faraway places because—or so he'd told her—he didn't like being recognised by fans. He never had been, although he'd made plenty of nervous jokes about it. She'd thought, then, that it was just the inconvenience of people asking for autographs or gushing over him when he wanted to be alone with her. She was so taken up in playing the part of his girlfriend that she'd never even considered that there might be another reason.

The really idiotic thing was that she could see it would be a whole lot worse if she'd been in love with him. She'd found that she quite enjoyed his company—it didn't matter that he talked mostly about himself, because it was interesting, and he had lots of funny stories to tell about the plays and films he'd done. He'd had an off-screen romance with Patricia Regal, who was one of her favourite stars, and she'd wanted to know so much about it that he'd teased her for being jealous. Which she was, of course just not in the way he'd thought…

When he'd suggested that they spend a night together somewhere, she'd agreed. Not immediately, of course, but when she considered the matter, she'd come to regard it in the same heroic, desperate light as Tilly's action in the film, when she'd pretended to be drowning in order to show her husband that he wasn't really crippled at all. It would be like a cure for her, because if she could bring herself to do *that*, then perhaps there would be a normal future for her, after all. Following a couple of days' consideration, she'd come to regard it as a perfectly sensible—in fact, an almost scientific—course of action.

They'd only done it three times, and she must have made the right noises, or done *something* right, anyway, because he'd seemed very pleased afterwards. The odd thing was, it hadn't been as bad as she'd feared—more uncomfortable than anything. She'd kept her eyes tight shut all the time so as not to have to look at him, but he had been gentle, especially the first time. He'd probably had heaps of practice because he wasn't at all awkward about it, and he hadn't seemed to mind her shyness one bit. When he'd told her that intelligent, sophisticated women didn't believe in saving themselves for marriage, because it was vulgar to use virginity as a bargaining chip, she'd seen his point immediately, because women ought to be equal with men.

Except that it was obviously more for men than for women—she really didn't see how they could get any fun out of it—and men didn't have babies, did they? He'd said he'd take care of that side of things—and obviously thought he had done so, because he'd been appalled and furious when she'd told him. That was when he'd told her he was married.

She wondered, pointlessly, which of the acts had conceived the baby. Not that it mattered. She wasn't going to have it, was she? She'd argued when Raymond insisted, but, thinking about it—and she'd thought of practically nothing else since she'd missed her period—she didn't have much choice in the matter. She hated the idea of an abortion, but, as Raymond said, the baby was hardly there yet, just a collection of cells, a nub of a thing, and—although she hadn't admitted it to him—she certainly didn't feel any connection with it. Sometimes, when she was busy at work, she'd manage to forget about it for minutes together and then, suddenly remembering, she'd be struck by the sheer unbelievability of her situation. Now, she was struck by the feebleness of her arguments. She couldn't have a baby—of course she couldn't. As if to underline this, there was a faint noise from behind her head. Dad. He sees this sort of thing all the time at work, she thought: abandoned infants, runaways, tearaways, girls cast out, prostitutes, married women who'd tried to pass off a cuckoo in the nest with disastrous consequences… She'd heard the tales often enough. Not that he'd ever preached morality at her, but sometimes, when she asked him how his day had been, the stories had come out, the pathetic, sordid lives, the single, impetuous acts that led down the road to ruin… Clearly, he pitied them, but he would think her no better. Why should he? After all, they hadn't had her advantages or her luck.

No. It was out of the question. She was going to do as Raymond told her. He'd seemed to know all about that, too, fixing it up. He's done it before, she thought. There'd been another—maybe several other—stupid girls like her, easily wooed, easily used, and just as easily discarded. But she'd lied to him, too, hadn't she? Or not told the truth, anyway. And if it was a question of using people, didn't that make her as bad as he was? Worse, in fact, because his desire was natural, and hers was not. And why had she told *Pete*, of all people?

What a stupid question. She got up and lit a cigarette, breaking her self-imposed rule about not smoking in her bedroom. Pete had taunted her, as he always did, goaded her until she'd got so blazingly angry she'd heard herself blurting it out. She'd seen horror replace the malice in his eyes, and he hadn't said much at all after that—except for agreeing not to tell Dad. Now she'd just have to trust him… After all, he'd promised, hadn't he?

The television, encased in a wooden cabinet and crowned with a doily and a china shepherdess, had pride of place in the stuffy, cluttered front room of number eight Paradise Street. 'We're the only one in the street,' said Mrs Anson proudly. She was a sensible, bulky woman whose frock and cretonne overall hid all but the very top of a monstrous chasm of cleavage. 'We've had quite a few of the neighbours in to watch. Mrs Backhouse used to come every Thursday. She'd get her book from the library and then she'd come in to see the children's programmes. That's what she liked—*Andy Fundy* was her favourite, and *Prudence Kitten*. I think…' Mrs Anson leant forward conspiratorially, lowering her voice, 'she'd have liked kiddies herself, but they were never blessed. Still,' she added, 'that's probably just as well, isn't it?'

'So you saw quite a lot of her?' asked Stratton.

'A fair bit, yes, up until she went away a few months ago.'

'Did she tell you she was going?'

Mrs Anson thought for a moment, then said, 'No, it was Mr Backhouse who told me. To be honest, I was a bit surprised she didn't pop in to say goodbye. Of course *now*, with all those bodies…' Eyes widening, she added, 'She wasn't in there, was she?'

'We don't know yet,' said Stratton. 'We're still making inquiries.' They hadn't heard anything from McNally, but a telephone call to Edna Backhouse's relatives in Sheffield had revealed that the family hadn't seen hide nor hair of her for at least six months, although they had had a card from Backhouse saying he was writing on Edna's behalf because she had rheumatism in her fingers. As it seemed increasingly likely that the poor woman *was* their fourth body, her brother was coming down to see if he could identify her. 'So,' he continued, 'she said nothing about going away the last time you saw her?'

Mrs Anson shook her head. 'She was on her way to the laundry, I remember that. Just passing the time of day. I thought she seemed quite cheerful—more than usual, in fact.'

'How do you mean?'

'Well, she was always a nervy sort, and the last few months she'd got a lot worse. Said the darkies upstairs were getting on her nerves. They seem nice enough to me—always very friendly, and you never hear any noise—but she was quite frightened of them. Mr Backhouse told me she was terrified of him going out and leaving her alone in the house with them.'

'I see.' Stratton hadn't actually 'seen' anything all morning, and feared he wasn't doing a very good job of hiding this fact from Ballard. Pete had gone straight up to bed after the previous night's revelation, refusing to discuss it any further. Unable to sleep, his son's words in all their vicious triumph echoing over and over again in his head, he'd woken late to find that Monica had already left for the day so he'd not been able to find out whether or not they were true.

In the absence of any definite information, the torrent of speculation that had been flowing through his mind for the last twelve hours continued to torment him, fuelling his sense of frustration and helplessness. Why had Monica chosen to confide in her brother and not him? Or why not Doris or Madeleine, or even *Lilian*? Unless, of course, they knew and were deliberately keeping it from him... And who was the father? Was he going to marry her? Or was he—God forbid—married already?

Visions of a cravatted Lothario from the film studio, all suede shoes and glib sophistication, seducing his innocent child with false promises, goaded him to an inward, impotent fury, all the worse for being inexpressible. Monica had never really talked about any boyfriends apart from that chap a couple of years ago. If only Jenny were here now, none of this would have happened. He'd assumed that she—or Doris or even Lilian—must have explained the facts of life to Monica, but he'd never asked. But he shouldn't have *needed* to ask about a thing like that—it was women's business, not his.

Pete's behaviour the previous night was troubling, too. The circumstances of the war had made his fathering a passive, rather than an active affair, removing his power to shape his children's lives. But it was no good casting around for excuses. The brutal fact was that he'd failed both his children. And they weren't the only ones: Muriel, little Judy, Davies himself, and all those poor women, who'd still be alive if he'd got the right man…

'Sir?' Ballard's anxious tone cut across his thoughts, and he wrenched himself back to the present. Mrs Anson was looking at him askance, and, realising he was glaring at her, he hastily adjusted his features to an expression of professional concern.

'I said, he told me he'd had letters from her,' repeated Mrs Anson.

'Mr Backhouse said that?' asked Stratton.

'That's right. He said she was getting along well now she wasn't being bothered by the negroes. I told him I was surprised they'd taken the upstairs flat in the first place, after what happened—who'd want to live in a place like that?—but I suppose they don't get a lot of choice, poor things, all those notices you see saying they won't let rooms to coloured people.… Mr Backhouse didn't like them, either. Said he was going to write to the council to see if he could get them put out. Said they'd been pestering him to use the garden and it wasn't part of the tenancy agreement. I thought it was just prejudice, but now we know why, don't we? Mind you, he was always on about that garden. Poor Muriel told me she'd asked if she could put the baby out there to get a bit of air, and he'd said it was against the regulations.'

'Did you see the dog out there much?'

'Not often. I suppose it must have done its business there sometimes, although he did take it for walks. Twice a day, more often than not. Whatever's in that garden,' she added, narrowing her eyes, 'he didn't want it disturbed. And I'll tell you something else, too—several times I've seen him going about with Jeyes Fluid, sprinkling it in the hall. He told my husband it was because of the blacks and their dirty habits. We thought that was a bit strange at the time—I mean, you can see they're not dirty from the way they're both turned out—but of course *now, well...*'

'When was the last time you saw Mr Backhouse?'

'Four days ago. I know that, because Mr Anson always goes to the British Legion on a Monday, and I remember telling him about it when he came back. Mr Backhouse had had a van come for his furniture, and when I saw that I asked him if he was leaving, and he told me he was going to live in Sheffield with Edna. Said he'd got a job up there. I saw a suitcase in the hall, so I thought that must be his clothes.'

'Did you go into the house when you spoke to him?'

'No, we were just outside.'

'Do you remember what he was wearing?'

'Let me think...' Mrs Anson's forehead crenulated in a frown. 'Well, he had his overcoat on, and his hat... I remember that because it made me think he must be leaving at once, but when I asked him he was a bit foggy about it. You know, vague... but he must have been going somewhere, otherwise he wouldn't have had the coat on.'

'What colour was it?'

'Dark blue. A double-breasted one with a belt. And the hat was a trilby, dark brown. He'd got a tie on, so I suppose he must have been wearing a suit. Suit trousers, anyway. Grey, I think.'

'And this van—was it from a removal company, do you know?'

'No, it was the second-hand place, Lorrimer's. I don't suppose they paid much. I wouldn't have given you tuppence for any of it. That mattress! Absolutely filthy, it was—and crawling,

I shouldn't be surprised. Probably blamed those poor darkies for that, as well. Mrs Backhouse always did her best to keep things nice…' She paused for a moment, hitching up her bosom for emphasis, then said, 'I'm surprised at him. He seemed such an *educated* man. A cut above most people round here. Used to give people advice, you know.'

'What sort of advice?'

'Well, if they needed help with anything—a legal matter, or something like that. With him having been in the police during the war—not that he ever let you forget it. He was always telling people, anybody new… And about the St John's Ambulance. Had the certificates up on the wall, all framed. Just goes to show you can't judge by appearances. And,' she added shrewdly, 'he fooled you lot, didn't he?' Before Stratton could say anything, she nodded sagely. 'Yes, he did. And now we've got all sorts coming here gawping, newspaper men poking their noses where they're not wanted. My husband went out this morning and got this to read about Queen Mary's funeral, and look what's there, right next to it on the front page!' She brandished a copy of the *Daily Mail* and Stratton saw the headline, *FOUR WOMEN DIE IN MURDER HOUSE* and, in smaller type underneath, *Police Dig in Garden*, illustrated by a photograph. Mrs Anson stabbed at it with a chunky finger. 'You know how they got that picture, don't you? Mr Pyle upstairs. He's been renting his back room out to the photographers from the papers. He had two pounds off them yesterday, and he told me they'll be coming back later for more. I don't think it's right, making money out of those poor women like that, and I'm certainly not reading *this*,' here, she gave the paper a little shake, like a terrier with a rat, 'thank you very much.'

Stratton and Ballard interviewed Backhouse's upstairs neighbours, Mr and Mrs McAndrew, who, as Mrs Anson suspected, had only taken the flat because they couldn't get anything else and were now embarking, in horrified bewilderment, on what was very likely to be a fruitless search for a different place to live. They confirmed the business about the Jeyes Fluid but had little else to add.

'Poor sods,' said Stratton, when they'd left the house and were out of earshot of the clutch of reporters stationed outside who were watching the procession of men ferrying out boxes of debris from the garden. 'Imagine coming to a country where you stand out like a sore thumb and the reception's as cold as the bloody weather.'

'It seems to me,' said Ballard thoughtfully, 'that you're always reading stuff in the papers about whether there ought to be a colour bar, but from the way they get treated, there might as well be one already. As far as I can see, they're no dirtier or worse behaved than anyone else.'

Policewoman Harris was waiting for them in the corridor outside the Middlesex Hospital mortuary. 'Positive identification of Mary Dwyer by Mr Fleet,' she said briskly. 'He was the man friend who reported her as missing—and Iris Manning's been identified by her sister, Mrs Cartwright. DI Grove's taken their statements, and DS Porter's gone to fetch Joan Carter to see if the other one is Kathleen McKinnon. Mr Foulds—that's Mrs Backhouse's brother—is due here this afternoon.' Still she wouldn't look him in the eye.

'That's some progress, anyway,' said Stratton, writing notes. 'And I've got a spot of information that might help with the description of Backhouse, if you wouldn't mind relaying it to the station...' He passed on what Mrs Anson had said about the clothing and they went to find McNally, who was in his office dictating a letter to his secretary, Miss Lynn. 'Do have a seat. This is for the lab at New Scotland Yard,' he explained. 'Blood samples and stomach contents and so on. There's also the matter of the pubic hair. Our initial analysis tells us it's from four different women, so we're sending samples from each of the bodies so that the lab can try to match…I take it they're aware of the urgency.'

'I imagine my superior's had a word with them,' said Stratton, adding wryly, 'And if he hasn't, they'll have read all about it in the papers. What can you tell us?'

'Well,' McNally pushed his spectacles up his nose, 'from the tests we've been able to do here, I can tell you that spermatozoa were present in the vaginas of the three women in the cupboard, but not in the one under the floorboards. None at all in the swabs taken from the rectum…' Pulling a sheaf of typewritten notes towards him, he continued, 'The body under the floorboards is of a well-nourished woman, height five feet, three and a half inches, between fifty and sixty years old, death caused by asphyxia due to obstruction of the air passages… No pregnancies—ovaries quite atrophic, in fact, so I don't suppose that was ever on the cards. Certainly no sign of any disease that could have caused her death.'

'How long?'

'Twelve to fifteen weeks.'

Stratton made a note. 'What about the others?'

'Well, asphyxia was the cause of death in every case. Number one—that's the first one we removed—she's now been identified as…'

'Mary Dwyer,' supplied Stratton.

'Yes… Twenty years old, I gather. Never been pregnant. She was the only one who wasn't covered up, and she didn't have a diaper, either. Number two—not identified yet—was between twenty-five and twenty-seven years of age and had had at least one pregnancy at some stage, but not at the time of death. She'd been dead for between seven and eight days. Number three—'

'Iris Manning.'

'Yes. Thirty-two years old—I'd estimated slightly older, but that was the sort of life she'd led, I'm afraid. Approximately six months pregnant—a male foetus, not interfered with in any way that I can see—' Stratton, who was staring intently at the floor at this point, heard Ballard catch his breath. 'Dead for around three weeks.'

'Do you think they were put into that alcove immediately after death?'

McNally considered this for a moment and then said, 'I can't say "yes", because I don't know, but I can see nothing to indicate any other sequence of behaviour. Now, about the findings from the garden… What we do know for certain is that there are two of them, and they're both women, but at this point I'm afraid we know precious little else. I've enlisted the help of a colleague from the department of anatomy and our professor of dental surgery—he's getting rather excited about an unusual type of crown… Perhaps you'd like to come and have a look?'

In one of the mortuary's side rooms, two partial skeletons, one with a skull, were being painstakingly assembled on slabs side by side, with other bones scattered randomly on a third slab, and all of it surrounded by wooden boxes full of bits and pieces from the garden at Paradise Street. An intense young man with a pale face and a forelock of black hair who Stratton thought looked more like a poet—or a certain type of artist's idea of a poet, anyway—than a doctor, was standing between them, weighing what looked like a kneecap in one slender hand. Higgs was behind him, scrabbling around in one of the boxes.

'Dr Gilpin—Inspector Stratton—DS Ballard.'

Gilpin put down the patella and held out his hand. 'Pleased to meet you. I'm sure you know Higgs, Dr McNally's extremely capable assistant. He's quite something—better at anatomy than most of my students.'

Higgs grinned. 'Learnt it in the war, Dr Gilpin. Always doing these sorts of jigsaws, we was—only the pieces mostly had flesh on 'em.' Seemingly embarrassed by his outburst, he ducked his head and applied himself once more to the contents of the box.

'Miss Lynn's been getting to work with her coloured pencils,' said McNally, gesturing at two diagrams pinned to the wall, one showing two skeletons with various bones shaded in different colours, and the other showing the areas of the garden divided into squares. The hard blocks of red, blue, green, and yellow made them look like a grotesque version of a children's board game.

'That's pretty well everything. All the bones are coded to show which part of the garden they came from. Those,' McNally added, pointing at the small piles on the third slab, 'are animal bones. That garden seems to have been quite a rubbish dump.'

'It was a fair old mess. Probably Backhouse's dog. The neighbour said it didn't go in the garden much, but all the same I was a bit surprised it hadn't dug up those bodies before. If it had smelt them, I mean.'

McNally looked thoughtfully at the boxes. 'I should think with all the other stuff in the garden, there was plenty to keep it occupied without digging them up... And perhaps Backhouse didn't let it out there for long enough to have a really good crack at them.'

'I suppose so. Can you tell me anything else about them?'

'Well,' said McNally, 'this one here was on the tall side for a woman—five feet eight or nine inches, and we think she was about twenty years old. The other was five feet two. She was older—twenty-eight or -nine. We do have her skull, but there's been some attempt to burn it. There was part of a dustbin recovered with evidence of burning, so that might have been used for the purpose. We've sent it to the police lab. We have this'—McNally gestured towards a makeshift table on which lay a mass of brittle-looking dun brown hair, one side of it held with a rusting metal kirby grip—'and these,' he pointed at some fragments of rotted cloth which lay beside the hair, 'which appear to be portions of clothing. We'll be sending them along for analysis as well. There were a number of small bones—fingers—mixed up in it.'

Stratton applied himself to the diagrams, rubbing his eyes. Hot with tiredness, they felt as if they were cooking in their sockets. 'Just a moment,' he said, looking at his notebook. 'I'd like to make sure I've got it all clear... The first body from the alcove—we'll call her Body One. She...' he glanced at the page, 'has been identified as Mary Dwyer. She's twenty years old, never been pregnant, she'd been dead around forty-eight hours when she was found and there were traces of spermatozoa inside her.'

'That's right,' said McNally.

'Body Two,' Stratton continued, 'who may or may not be Kathleen McKinnon, has been dead for between seven and eight days. She was between twenty-five and twenty-seven years old, and has been pregnant, but not when she was killed. You found spermatozoa there, too.' McNally nodding in confirmation, Stratton moved on. 'Body Three, identified as Iris Manning. Dead for around three weeks, six months pregnant, thirty-two years old, body contained traces of spermatozoa...fine so far?'

'Yes.'

'Body Four, found under the floorboards, a woman between fifty and sixty years old, who might be Edna Backhouse. No pregnancies, no spermatozoa... And all of the deaths were caused by asphyxia. Is that correct?'

'Yes, that's right.'

'Good. Now, the two from the garden...have you any idea of how long they've been dead?'

'Impossible to say. We don't know how the soft tissues were lost—the mechanism, if you see what I mean. Unless, of course, you can establish who they are and when they went missing and there's collateral evidence and so on. The lab might be able to help with that, because there were some pieces of newspaper in amongst the debris. Quite a lot from Area Three, where the skull was found.'

'I don't suppose you've any idea of the cause of death, have you?' asked Stratton.

McNally shook his head. 'As I said, you'd need collateral evidence for that. Speaking of which, there's the matter of the four pubic hair samples in the tobacco tin. I imagine,' he said, carefully, 'that it's already occurred to you that one of them might have been taken from Mrs Davies.'

Stratton nodded. 'What about spermatozoa? In Mrs Davies's case, I mean?'

McNally shook his head regretfully. 'I've been reading through the notes. We—I—didn't check for that. I realise now that it was an oversight, but the...complexion, shall we say, of that case, at the time...'

'I understand,' said Stratton. 'We weren't looking for anything like that either.'

McNally nodded. 'When I received the telephone call, I...'

He tailed off, shaking his head, and they stared wide-eyed at each other, united in recognition of the catastrophic extent of the whole business, bound together by an invisible and inescapable cat's cradle of assumptions made and things left undone. Keep a lid on it, thought Stratton. He could just imagine what Lamb would say if he started talking about exhumation orders on Muriel Davies, who, together with her child, was buried in Kensal Rise Cemetery.

'I understand,' he said. 'The facts at the time...'

'Yes,' said McNally. Perhaps it was just because he was tired, emotional, and susceptible, but the word seemed to Stratton to echo around the tiled room, bouncing off the harsh, tiled surfaces, and for a second, the pathologist's spare, ascetic features transmogrified into the docile, bewildered ones of Davies. 'Yes,' McNally repeated. 'Yes.' A single word, that could mean both everything, and nothing at all.

Diana woke at eight. For a moment she wasn't sure where she was. Cautiously, she levered herself into a sitting position, resting against the headboard. Her brain seemed to arrive in this upright position some seconds later than her body, and when it did, a large lump of dry, hard pain in the core of her head made her wince. God, how much had she had to drink? It was an effort even to blink. Mercifully, the curtains were pulled shut, but she could see, in the half-light, that she was in the bedroom at her flat, and that there was an evening dress—not her own—draped across the stool in front of the dressing table and that her fur coat lay curled on the floor in the corner like a sleeping animal. Thirsty and confused, she wondered where James had got to, and then her warm, vague impression of whispers and fumbles and giggles resolved itself into an actual, cold memory—it had not been James at all, but Claude. He'd been here… But, judging from the dent in the pillow beside her, and—but for the distant roar of buses passing the end of the street—the silence, he was gone.

What had she done? Looking down at herself, she realised that she was naked. Where were the rest of her clothes? Dragging her body across the bed, she peered down and saw that her stockings and underclothes were lying in forlorn heaps on the rug, discarded in the progress towards the bed. Disorientated and nauseous, she dimly remembered Claude peeling them off her, his gloating face—an excited boy unwrapping a longed-for birthday present—next to hers, his hot breath on her face... Dredging her memory, she came up with fragments: dancing with Claude at Ciro's; him sitting down with them and ordering champagne, and then more champagne; Claude talking about the Mau Mau Uprising and Jock barely civil; feeling tipsy and reckless, not really listening to them, tapping her feet in time to the music; seeing, as though through a veil, disappointment on Lally's face and the cold disapproval on Jock's...She wasn't sure how it had been decided that Claude should accompany her home. Lally and Jock had left before they had, and Diana remembered protesting against their offer of a lift on the grounds that it would take them right out of their way. The recollection of Jock's curt 'Good night' made her face burn with shame. How he must despise her.

It's all right for him, Diana thought angrily. He's a *man*. She'd known that Claude was manipulating her and hated herself for being manipulated, but she'd let it happen because she couldn't bear the thought of going home alone to the dreary flat. After Lally and Jock had left, they'd danced some more, drunk some more, and Claude had hailed a taxi and asked Diana for the address. She'd talked about F-J then. He already knew, of course, but he hadn't seemed to care. When she said, 'He cared about you,' Claude had said, 'Yes, and a bloody nuisance it was, too—surely you weren't jealous, darling?' and laughed it off. She'd tried to impress on him how awful it was, but he'd dismissed it—'Life goes on'—and kissed her. She should have pushed him away then, got out of the taxi, but she hadn't.

Where was he staying? she wondered. He hadn't said, only that he was going back to Kenya. He'd fit in beautifully with all those bored, promiscuous expatriates, she thought sourly. If the Mau Mau didn't get him, an irate husband almost certainly would. She remembered sitting on the sofa with him and him producing a bottle of champagne like a conjuror—they'd drunk it out of tea cups because she hadn't been able to find any glasses—and then banging her leg on the door frame as he'd carried her across the threshold of the bedroom…and then, once undressed, only numbness as he'd entered her.

Had it been like that with James? She tried to remember the last time they'd been intimate, but couldn't. She supposed she ought to feel guilty, but she didn't. She didn't feel anything except sick. Gingerly, she got up, dragging the counterpane off the bed and wrapping it around herself. As she crossed to the window, her bare foot struck something hard and she looked down to see an empty champagne bottle rolling across the floor. Pulling aside the curtain, she peered out of the window, but a blast of morning sunlight hit her, making her draw back. It didn't matter—who, or what, was she looking for? Claude would have left hours ago.

Turning, she saw on the small table beside the bed a piece of paper with a short message. *Didn't want to wake you, darling. Until next time x*, she read.

As if I was just there for the taking, she thought, as angry with herself for being so as she was with him for assuming it. She screwed the note into a ball and was about to go and drop it into the wastepaper basket beside the dressing table when she caught sight of another piece of paper, folded into four—Claude must have left that, as well.

It was a five pound note.

Having returned to the station and sifted through what seemed to be a small avalanche of statements taken by Canning and Arliss from the Paradise Street neighbours, Stratton was desperate for a few minutes on his own. DI Grove had telephoned to confirm that the other victims were Kathleen McKinnon and Edna Backhouse, the winnowing of the garden was now, by late afternoon, completed, and there was a large pile of reports about sightings of Backhouse on his desk—Colwyn Bay, Kettering, Berwick-on-Tweed and God Only Knew Where Else. Stratton shovelled up handfuls of them and put them aside. He needed to clear his head. With all that was in there jostling for space, he felt as if he might simply explode into pieces if he had to deal with any more people. Staying in the office meant constant interruption, and the lavatory was out of the question—Arliss, who was having one of his periodic bouts of flatulence, was bound to come in and poison the air. The answer, he thought, was a walk round the block. Nothing too peculiar about that, and he'd look in at the tobacconist's while he was at it.

He set off at a brisk pace and, striding past the end of Cork Street, suddenly thought of what Higgs had said about learning anatomy from doing human jigsaws. This, in turn, made him think of a conversation he'd had with the man sometime towards the end of the war, when he'd asked him whether a former mortuary assistant might have been a bit too keen on corpses... Anyone who'd been in civil defence or the police in London at that time would have seen, and handled, their fair share, and that included Backhouse. Had he learned to like it then? Stratton thought of the bodies he'd seen: tattered, shattered, and crushed, caked with plaster dust and grime. How anyone could have found them in any way sexually arousing—unless they were stark raving mad—was completely beyond him. Perhaps Backhouse *was* mad. In any case, thought Stratton grimly, he did seem—quite literally—to be at home with the dead. Dead women, anyway.

There'd been no spermatozoa inside Edna Backhouse, though. Stratton wondered about Muriel Davies. Presumably, nothing would be detectable after such a long time, or McNally would have mentioned the possibility.

It seemed pretty stupid to foul your own doorstep in that way, but then Backhouse had killed in his own home, and one of his victims had been his own wife. And Davies was the ideal scapegoat—like so many of the liars Stratton had encountered, he was no good at recognising when he was being lied *to*, and being a dullard made him all the more vulnerable.

If you were attracted to dead women, perhaps you couldn't get it up for living ones? That would explain the lack of children—except that McNally had said there was something wrong with Edna Backhouse's ovaries, hadn't he? Perhaps he'd killed her because she knew—or had discovered—something about Muriel and Judy. Or perhaps just to get her out of the way so he could have his murderous way with a few tarts in the comfort of his own home...

He passed a newspaper seller whose board read: *MURDER HOUSE GIRL NAMED*. Presumably the rest would make the late edition or tomorrow morning's. Nothing like a good murder, Stratton thought bitterly, and this one had it all: sex, a rising body count, a national alert for the missing killer, and all topped off with a massive police cock-up—*his* cock-up. He watched as a few discarded sheets, clawed from the pavement by a sudden gust of wind, fluttered away down the street.

As for where Backhouse actually was…The description had been in the newspapers twenty-four hours now, but not one of the dozens of reports that had come in so far was any use at all.

'I thought I might find you out here, sir.' Ballard, having apparently materialised out of thin air, was standing beside him.

'Just needed a breath of air.'

'Yes, sir. I thought you might like to see this.' He gave Stratton a copy of the *Daily Mail*, folded to show a photograph of Muriel Davies, captioned *Found Strangled With Her Baby*. 'Have a look at the fourth paragraph.'

'"It has been established that the tragedy has no link with the murder of 19-year-old Muriel Davies and her 14-month-old daughter Judy who were found strangled at the same address in 1950." No, it bloody hasn't been established. Where did that come from?'

'DCI Lamb, sir. Trying to discourage speculation.'

Stratton sighed. 'Closing the stable door after the horse has gone, more like it.'

'That's what I thought, sir, although it might keep them off our backs—for the moment, at least. I've just had a word with DS Porter. He's been talking to the British Road Services.' Noting Stratton's blank look, he added, 'Backhouse's former employers, sir. Apparently, he gave his notice a month ago, and they've not seen him since. His records show that he was working as a clerk at the Ultra Radio Works before that, during the war—after he'd resigned as a special. I did a spot of checking, and it appears that one of the employees there, May Drinkwater—29-year-old spinster—was reported missing in nineteen forty-four. Of course,' Ballard ducked his head as if ashamed at his efficiency, 'it's possible that it had nothing to do with Backhouse—might have been a flying bomb or something—but she's described as being the same height as the shorter skeleton, and she had brown hair, so…'

'So we ought to look into it,' finished Stratton. 'Well done, Ballard. At least one of us is on the ball.'

'Thank you, sir. And we've got this photograph...' he palmed it from his pocket and handed it to Stratton, 'from Mrs Backhouse's brother, to send to the papers. Obviously, it'll have to be doctored to show the overcoat.'

Stratton stared at the domed, bald head, the glasses, the prissy mouth and the weak, sloping shoulders. 'Doesn't look like a monster, does he?'

Ballard shook his head. 'No, sir. But they never do.'

When Stratton eventually arrived home and opened the front door, he caught a glimpse of Monica in the sitting room, reading—or anyway looking at—a magazine. She called out a greeting but as she made no move to get up he went into the kitchen to make himself a cup of tea. He couldn't face her just yet—his mouth was dry and foul, and the way he was feeling, having brooded on the matter all the way home in the bus, he feared he would start bellowing accusations at her and not be able to stop. Pete was gone, back to his unit, and except for the rustle of pages the house was silent, but the very air seemed to be poised and ominous, waiting for something to erupt. It must not be him, thought Stratton. He must remain calm.

He stared down at the plate of food that had been left out for him—ham and lettuce, with two slices of beetroot bleeding over the leaves. Eating was out of the question; his stomach had contracted into a tight ball of anger. Hands trembling, he picked up the kettle and then, almost immediately, set it back down on the gas ring with a clatter. At this rate, he'd end up breaking something. He went down the passage into the scullery and cupped his hands beneath the tap, gulping some water and splashing his face.

Slowly and carefully, he retraced his steps and went into the sitting room. Monica—who, thought Stratton, certainly didn't *look* pregnant, although she seemed tired and very pale—put her magazine down and, for a long, dangling moment, during which time seemed to hover rather than pass, they stared at each other. Then she said quietly, 'Pete's told you, hasn't he?'

The feeble hope that Stratton had been nursing at the back of his mind that Pete was, for some reason of his own, lying to make trouble, crumbled. His last illusions about having control over his daughter fell sharply away, leaving him with the vertiginous sensation of standing on the very edge of a precipice. He sat down on the sofa. Swallowing, he said, 'It's true, is it?'

'Yes. It's true.'

The air seemed to tighten around him and, for a moment, he felt as though he were suffocating. 'You're certain about it, are you?'

Monica nodded miserably.

'How far...?'

'Two months. Well, two and a bit.'

'How did it happen?' God, what a stupid thing to say. 'I mean...'

'It's all right, Dad. I know what you mean.'

'It isn't bloody all right!' Stratton checked himself with an effort, biting back a torrent of stuff about you're my daughter and how dare you and I should never have let you go to work at that studio. He knew that, however much he felt all this, it was both pompous and pointless to come out with any of it. Closing his eyes for a brief moment in order to try and contain his feelings, he opened them again to find that Monica, her face set and white, was gazing at him with something a lot like fear in her eyes.

'I'm sorry, Dad.'

'It's a bit late for "sorry",' Stratton snapped. 'You'd better tell me,' he continued, 'what the hell has been going on.'

'He's an actor,' said Monica. 'I met him at the studio. I was working on his picture. He started talking to me, and invited me out, and things just...' Mouth wobbling and eyes blurred with tears, Monica blinked and gulped, trying to get the words out. 'Just...sort of...he just...'

'He's married, isn't he?' asked Stratton grimly.

Monica nodded miserably. 'Last year. He didn't tell me before.'

'Why didn't you know? Surely, with him being in the public eye, that sort of thing is common knowledge.'

'Not with people like him. With male stars—the younger ones—the studio tends to keep quiet about that sort of thing because the fans don't like it. Oh, Dad, I don't know what to do.'

'I do,' said Stratton viciously. 'He wants horsewhipping.' Monica had fallen for the oldest trick in the book, one he'd seen dozens, perhaps hundreds, of times in the course of his work, but had never for one second imagined would be played on his own daughter. 'Who is he? What's his name?'

Shoulders heaving, face collapsed and soggy, Monica said, 'Dad, you *can't*. He said...he told me...' the next words came out in a wet rush, 'he'd pay for me to go to a clinic where it's safe...'

'An abortion,' said Stratton, flatly. 'That's what he wants, isn't it?'

'He said it would be for the best. He got so angry, Dad. He said I was trying to trap him, and if I told anyone he'd deny he'd had anything to do with it, and no one would believe me because we'd kept the whole thing secret, but it wasn't like that, Dad, it really wasn't... I didn't know what to say.' Monica stared at him, stupefied. 'He was like a different person.' Monica pulled her handkerchief from her sleeve and buried her face in it, shoulders heaving.

'I'll bet he was.' And if I ever get hold of him, thought Stratton, I'm going to tear his head off his shoulders and piss down the hole. Trying to contain his mounting fury he said again, through clenched teeth, 'Who is he?'

Monica, face still hidden by her handkerchief, shook her head. 'No...Dad...please...'

'He's got to face up to his responsibilities.'

'He can't, Dad. He's *married*. He said he'd never leave his wife, and he thought I knew that it was just a...a sort of...game. But that wasn't what he said, not at the start.'

'I'm damn sure it wasn't. *Bastard!*' Unable to stop himself, Stratton thumped his fist into his palm. He couldn't remember the last time he'd wanted—ached—to hit someone so much. Jumping up, he began pacing up and down the room as Monica sobbed. 'Tell me his name.'

'If I do...' Monica paused, gulping and snuffling, 'you won't...do anything, will you?'

'What, thump him? No, I won't—much as I'd like to. But something's got to be done. As I said, he needs to face up to his responsibilities. He obviously thinks he can just shell out money to get rid of his mistakes and go sailing on regardless. Abortions aren't just illegal, Monica, they're dangerous. They can mess you up for life.'

'But he says it'll be safe—and that if I don't he won't have anything to do with me or acknowledge the baby or anything.'

'We'll see about that,' said Stratton, grimly. 'If he's the father, then he needs to contribute to the child's upkeep, and that's all there is to it. Now, who is he?'

'His name's Raymond Benson.'

'And he's a film actor.'

'Yes. He's not one of the biggest stars, though—at least, not yet.'

'How old?'

'Twenty-eight, I think. I *am* sorry, Dad,' Monica wailed. 'I truly am. I've let you down. And Mum.'

Stratton stopped pacing and stood over his daughter who, hunched in an armchair, seemed very young and very small. 'Yes, well...'

Monica gazed up at him with enormous, wet eyes. 'It was an accident,' she whispered. 'I didn't mean it to happen. I wish Mum was here.'

'So do I,' said Stratton, fervently. 'So do I.' Stiffly, he reached over and patted her on the back. 'I'm sure you didn't mean it to happen, love.'

This reassurance produced more choking sobs and, without quite knowing how, Stratton found that he was standing with his arms around her and his chin grazing the top of her head. 'It's all right, love, it's all right,' he repeated, stroking her back. 'Look,' he said after some minutes of this, 'why don't you go up to bed? We can't do anything about it tonight.'

Monica disentangled herself and picked up her handbag, saying meekly, 'Yes, Dad.'

'Have you told anyone about it, apart from Pete?'

'Only Ray.'

'Who's— Oh, yes, of course. Well, it might be an idea to keep quiet about it for the time being. Until I've spoken to this man. I presume he's on the telephone, is he?'

'Yes.'

'Do you know his number?'

'Yes. He gave it to me when his wife was away once, on tour. She's an actress.'

Stratton held up his hand. He didn't think he could bear to hear any of the details, however marginal. 'What is it?'

Monica dug around in her bag and scribbled it on the corner of a piece of paper on which was printed some sort of schedule, including the name of Raymond Benson. 'Don't you need this?'

'No. The picture's finished.'

'He was in it, was he?'

Monica nodded.

'Will he be in the next picture you're working on?'

'No, but he'll be at the studio, on a different stage. He's under contract. You won't do anything to him, will you?'

'I've said so, haven't I?'

'Thanks, Dad.' Monica sniffed. The small sounds coming from her seemed to intensify the silence around them, and for a moment Stratton's thoughts boomed so loudly that he wondered if they hadn't somehow escaped from his head to reverberate round the room. Suddenly awkward, they avoided each other's eyes as they said their goodnights.

Stratton sank onto the sofa. God, he wanted to punch Benson into the middle of next week. Knock his handsome white teeth—

he didn't know what the man looked like but he was in films so handsome white teeth seemed a fair bet—right down his lying throat. He felt so helpless. It was all right when they were little, if they hurt their knees or fell out of a tree or something, because you could always kiss it better. But *this*… If Jenny was here, he thought, this wouldn't have happened. Or perhaps if he'd got married again after she'd died and Monica had had more of a woman's influence… Grief had made him selfish, and he'd assumed that because he didn't want another wife, they wouldn't want, or need, a stepmother. Maybe Doris and Lilian had been right, trying to push widows at him. In the last year, he had tried to take an interest in a couple of them. He'd even taken one out to supper, at a Lyons Corner House. It was a perfectly pleasant evening; she was sweet and mercifully unaffected, but when he got home he found himself wondering why he'd done it. With no desire to repeat the experience, he'd written her an awkward letter, using pressure of work to cancel the tentative arrangement they'd made for the following week.

Throwing back his head and closing his eyes, he wondered if it were possible to pinpoint the exact moment when things had started to go wrong. At present, it felt as though his entire life had been a sequence of catastrophes leading up to this one, but surely that couldn't actually be the case? There must have been a specific time. Why hadn't he known? Why wasn't there a siren or a warning bell or something? Why was everything in his life—Monica, Davies, Backhouse—spinning out of control?

Even if he murdered this Benson bloke, it wouldn't do any good. Monica would still be pregnant. The thought of an abortion made him remember Davies's story about Backhouse volunteering to get rid of Muriel's baby, and a vision of the man's bald, sweating pate as he bent over Monica's prone body and fumbled between her legs with grimy-nailed fingers made him wide-eyed and sick with horror. Clapping a hand over his mouth, he ran into the scullery and leant over the basin. Arms braced and head lowered like a bull about to charge, he remained there until the danger was over.

Seeing the empty beer bottles from the previous evening standing on the draining board, Stratton decided something stronger was needed. Remembering that there was some Scotch in the sideboard in the sitting room, he retraced his steps and poured himself a bloody big slug of the stuff. Then, shrugging off his jacket, and jerking his tie loose in a single, swift movement, he sat down once more.

He could go and see Benson and try to persuade him to look after his child, but beyond extorting the necessary conscience-money, there was fuck all he could do. Benson had obviously never had any intention of leaving his wife. For all he or Monica knew, they might be starting a family as well. If only he'd never agreed to Monica working at that bloody studio. He took a gulp of his drink. If only he'd been a better father, husband, copper—a better *person*…

He thought about Reg in…1940, it must have been…discovering the extent of his son's criminal activities and going berserk. He'd sat silently for hours at their kitchen table and then burst into fury at Stratton, calling him an interfering shit and accusing him of having cooked the whole thing up to, as he put it, 'make him look bad'. Stratton understood, now, how his brother-in-law had been feeling, although, as far as he himself was concerned, it was less to do with other people's opinions than with one's estimation of oneself. What Reg, with his unearned worldliness, would have to say about Monica's current situation, he couldn't bear to think.

Later, in the bathroom, he caught sight of himself in the mirror. Christ, he looked one step away from the madhouse. Perhaps he was going off his rocker, too. The pillow, usually comfortable, felt like a sack of potatoes under his head as he lay wet-eyed, staring hopelessly into the thick darkness of the curtained room.

CHAPTER 53

Monica sat hunched over on her bed, clutching her favourite cushion, found in a bric-a-brac shop and carefully washed and mended, to her stomach. It was definitely 'friendly'—she'd thought so the minute she'd spotted it—but it wasn't doing her any good now.

What on earth was she going to do? She didn't want a baby. Now Dad had found out—and she'd known, somehow, just as soon as he'd looked at her, that Pete had broken his promise—there was no chance of her being able to go to the place that Raymond had suggested and have it taken away… Lying to Dad had been horrible, pretending that she had normal feelings for Raymond, and all the time knowing that the truth was a hundred, thousand times worse. Saying the words out loud, and seeing the expression on Dad's face—his disappointment and fury—had made her feel sick. Oh, God… Why, *why*, had she allowed Pete to goad her into telling him? She should have known he couldn't be trusted.

Dad had called Raymond a bastard. The word had been reverberating in her head ever since he'd said it. This child really would be a bastard. It wouldn't be long before her belly started to swell and then everyone would know, and she'd have to leave her job. It would be like all the cautionary tales she'd heard—the knowing looks, the pointed remarks, the questions about who the father was, the shame for her family, and then having to give birth in one of those places where they humiliated you and made you scrub floors because no decent, proper hospital would take you…

The baby, she supposed, would have to be adopted. That would mean handing it over to strangers who might or might not love it, and that it would grow up knowing—supposing it were told—that its mother had rejected it, and it would hate her. But she couldn't keep it, could she? Here, a memory surfaced of a girl from school who'd vanished for several months and whose mother's 'late baby' had been greeted with nods and winks and tuts. She had no mother, so it would have to be Aunt Doris who pretended, supposing that she'd even consent to such a thing, and why should she? Everyone said babies were sweet and lovely and all the rest of it—she'd never thought so, particularly, although perhaps it was different if it was *your* baby—but they certainly seemed to involve a lot of looking after, and Aunt Doris had enough on her plate already.

Or would they expect her to look after it herself? After all, it was her responsibility. If that were the case, she'd never be able to go back to work, never do any of the things she'd dreamt of doing. And it wouldn't always be a baby. It would grow up, resenting her for its illegitimacy, for the taint and shame that she'd inflicted upon it. And as for her own life—that would be over before it had begun.

CHAPTER 54

Wrapped in the counterpane, Diana sat on the floor beside the dressing table, her face buried in the thick fisherman's sweater James had worn for filming outside in the winter. The curtains were still drawn, and she had no idea how long she'd been there, listlessly picking through the contents of her handbag, looking for...what? She didn't know. Just something, anything, to hold on to, to reassure, to comfort—but there was no comfort to be had from the stubs and scrapings of cosmetics, the balled-up handkerchiefs, the tickets from pawn shops for items she'd never be able to redeem, or the pitifully thin purse. Behind her, Claude's five pound note lay on the bedside table, an accusation in black and white, evidence of her weakness, her lack of judgement, her pathetic betrayal both of James and of herself. She hadn't wanted to touch it, but she knew that eventually self-disgust would be swallowed up by necessity, and the knowledge made her hate herself all the more.

Scrabbling once more in her handbag, she fished out a tattered piece of thick writing paper, folded into four: F-J's last letter. *You are the natural prey of an unscrupulous man (as I was)...* Never more so than now. Diana shook her head in weary self-recrimination and scanned the rest. *You might contact Edward Stratton...he is a good man.* 'How can I?' she muttered, letting the paper fall to the floor. Every time she'd thought of him since that awkward meeting by the river at the Festival of Britain, she'd squirmed inwardly at her gushy, girlish behaviour. He'd been so diffident—obviously horribly embarrassed by the whole thing. The past should remain in the past, she thought, remembering the look on his face in the café all those years ago as he'd tried to warn her about Claude. 'He'll destroy you, Diana.' Well, she'd proved fairly well capable of doing that all by herself, hadn't she?

Even if she did contact him, what was there to say? 'Oh, dear, I've made the same mistake all over again, please rescue me?' How pathetic! Besides, he had his own life, and, doubtless, his own troubles, and neither was anything to do with hers... And just the thought of doing anything was exhausting. In any case, it wasn't a matter of working out what to do next, because there didn't seem to be any 'next'. At least, she couldn't summon up either the energy, or the inclination, to work out what it might be.

She was woken, several hours later, by a loud, insistent pounding at the front door of the flat. Disorientated for a moment, she stared wildly around the room, and then remembered. Perhaps it was James! He'd come back. She scrambled off the bed. Everything was going to be all right—she'd *make* it all right, she'd do *anything* to make up for Claude, for— Catching sight of the empty champagne bottle, she kicked it under the bed. Dragging on her dressing gown, she glanced into the mirror, hastily patting her hair. She looked a fright, but it would have to do. Dabbing the last of her perfume behind her ears, she rushed across the sitting room to open the front door.

'Darling, I—'

'Expecting someone, were you?' Her landlady, diminutive and belligerent, was on the landing. With her pinched, beaky face and pecking head movements, Mrs Pritchard had always reminded Diana of a hen left behind in the rush for scraps, but she didn't look like that now. 'I can see it wasn't me.' Bristling, she pushed Diana back inside the flat and closed the front door firmly behind them both. 'Where's your husband?'

'He...' Wordless in her disappointment, Diana stared numbly at the small form that seemed almost to pulsate with righteous anger.

Mrs Pritchard eyed her shrewdly. 'Gone off and left you, has he? If he was ever your husband in the first place.'

'Of course he was!'

'No "of course" about it, if you ask me. One man coming round to pay your rent, and from what I've heard there was a different one here last night, sneaking out at six o'clock this morning. I don't know what you think you're doing, but you're not doing it under my roof. I want you out of here now.'

'But—'

'I've had complaints—noise and I don't know what else—and this isn't the first time. I told that man who paid your rent I wasn't happy about it. I was willing to give you a second chance, but now...'

Jock didn't mention any of that to me, thought Diana, wondering if the 'second chance' had been given in exchange for extra money. 'Please,' she said, 'I haven't got anywhere to go.'

'You should have thought of that before. There's plenty of people want rooms, you know. Decent people who'd pay double what you do for a place like this, and they wouldn't keep me waiting, neither. People who don't want the likes of you under the same roof.'

'But you can't just—'

'Oh, can't I just? You watch me!'

'But,' said Diana, desperately, 'what about my things?'

'You can come back for those. I want you out, and that's that.'

'But—'

'Listen, *Mrs* Carleton. My husband's waiting downstairs. You can pack a suitcase and leave quietly now, or I'll call him up here and he can throw you out. It's up to you.'

Diana had seen Mr Pritchard on a few occasions when she'd gone down to her landlady's flat to pay the rent. A bull-necked hulk of a man who breathed through his mouth, he was a silent, glowering presence in her kitchen. She fled to her bedroom, and with shaking hands dressed herself and packed as much as she could into a single suitcase. Mrs Pritchard followed her and began to inspect the room, sniffing and tutting, running her hands over her precious fixtures and fittings as though checking for contamination. With no fight left in her to counter the accusations or stand up for her rights—whatever they might be—all Diana wanted was to get away.

Closing her case, she turned to pick up the five pounds that Claude had left beside the bed, but the little table was bare and so was the floor around it. Perplexed, she rifled her purse, but it wasn't there, either, or anywhere in her handbag. Mrs Pritchard, now standing in the doorway, was glaring at her like a gorgon, arms folded in outrage.

'There was five pounds on that table,' said Diana. 'What have you done with it?'

'Accusing me of stealing now, are you?'

'It was *there*,' said Diana, pointing. 'Now it's gone.'

Mrs Pritchard shook her head. 'You're a fine one, you are, calling me a thief. Well, I'm not going to stand here and be insulted by the likes of you...'

'Mrs Pritchard, that money belongs to me!'

'Yes, and we all know how you earned it, don't we? On your back!'

'So you did see the money—'

'I never saw any money. I know your game, and I've had enough of it.' The landlady took a couple of paces back and, turning towards the still open door of the flat, bellowed, 'Arthur! Come up here!'

'Please,' said Diana. 'Wait...'

'Wait, nothing!' Eyes glittering with malice, Mrs Pritchard advanced on Diana. 'Now you'll get what's coming to you, all right. You won't look so fine when he's finished with you, my lady.'

Scarcely able to believe her ears—surely the woman couldn't threaten her like that?—Diana ran to the window. Struggling to open it, she said, 'You can't do this. I'll call a policeman.'

'And I'll tell him you're nothing but a common prostitute. You're the one who's been stealing—what about my rent? What about that?'

Shock rapidly giving way to anger, Diana shouted, 'You've got a lot more than your rent in your pocket. You've just taken it!' She tugged desperately, breaking two nails, but the sash refused to budge. Heavy footfalls in the next room made her redouble her efforts, but the window remained obstinately shut.

'What's going on?' Arthur Pritchard's huge frame filled the doorway of the bedroom.

'Calling me a thief, now, she is.'

'A thief, is it?' Pritchard advanced on Diana, catching hold of her arm.

'Take your hands off me!' Diana clawed at him, but his grip was vice-like.

'That's enough of that!' He slapped her across the face so hard that, if he hadn't had hold of her, she'd have fallen onto the bed. She clutched her cheek. Her right eye, hot and stinging, felt as if it were about to explode. Shoving her back against the wall and breathing beerily into her face so that she thought for a moment that she might be sick, he said, 'One more word…'

'Please,' said Diana, through clenched teeth. 'Let go of me.'

He leered at her, nose so close to her own that all she could see was a greasy landscape of pores. 'Out you go,' he said, and jerked hard on her arm so that she cried out in pain.

Pausing only to scoop up her suitcase in his free hand, he dragged her out of the flat to the top of the stairwell. 'Now,' he said, 'get out before I throw you out.' Flinging her suitcase down the stairs with one hand, he pushed her after it so hard that she'd have fallen if her flailing hands hadn't found the banister.

Her case had burst open on impact. As she scrabbled about on the landing, trembling with humiliation and fear as she shoved her clothes back inside and struggled with the locks, her handbag, thrown from the top of the stairs by Mrs Pritchard, with a cackle of 'Good riddance!' narrowly missed her head. Watched by the triumphant pair who stood side by side, arms folded, at the top of the stairs, she picked up her things and fled.

It was dusk. Diana dropped the suitcase on the path and sat down on the bench, watching the lights reflected in the sluggish, oily water of the Thames and wondering exactly where she was and how long she'd been walking. She wasn't even sure what she'd put in the suitcase, other than James's sweater.

Her arm still ached where Mr Pritchard had grabbed her, and so did her face, but a glance in her pocket mirror had told her that she didn't have a black eye. Something to be grateful for, she supposed. She hadn't gone to find a policeman—what was the point? Even though she was in the right about the five pounds, it would be her word against theirs, and Claude *had* spent the night with her. He'd left her the money, yes, but she hadn't offered herself to him for it… It would, she thought, be impossible to explain. How terrible to think that one wouldn't be believed. There must be people who go through their whole lives with everybody thinking the worst of them. She'd never really considered it before, merely assumed that some sections of society must be less honest than, say, her own. Now, for the first time, she saw how appallingly unjust this was.

But it was her own stupid fault, wasn't it? Going off with Claude like that… After all the resolutions she'd made…

After leaving the Pritchards, she'd simply walked, with no idea of where she was going. Not to Lally and Jock, that was certain—they must hate her too, and with good reason. Dazed, she stared at the lights across the river until they seemed to blur into a flaring, squirming network of tubes, obliterating everything but themselves. Where was James? Was he out there somewhere, walking aimlessly in the neon maze of central London? James's welcoming words to her at Ashwood came into her mind: *Welcome to the place where nothing is real*... Diana stretched out her legs, trying to ease her aching feet. At least her fur coat would stop her getting too cold.

An hour later, chilly and faint with hunger, Diana hauled herself to her feet and went in search of a café. The coins she'd found in her purse would be enough for a cup of tea, at least—and perhaps, if she were lucky, they might stretch to bread and margarine. If only she could get fed and warm, she might be able to form a plan.

After wandering through some backstreets, she came upon an all-night place, lights shining through the steamed-up windows. Peering in, she saw from the rows of caps, mufflers and dirt-stiffened jackets that most of the customers were workmen. A solitary woman sat in the corner near the door, dabbing at her face with a grubby shred of powder puff, a limp hat perched forlornly on her head and a mangy glass-eyed fox wreathing her neck. The moment Diana pushed open the door, the painted, rocking-horse eyes locked onto her with an aggressive warning stare. Diana patted her suitcase. 'I'm not after your business,' she murmured. 'Just passing through.'

The woman relaxed, modifying her expression to mild curiosity. She wasn't the only one—Diana was aware of half a dozen pairs of eyes following her as she selected an empty table and sat down, fixing her gaze on the prices chalked on the blackboard behind the counter. It was better than she'd thought—she had enough for tea and a fruit pie. She ordered and sat waiting, inhaling the fug of cigarette smoke mixed with grease fires from the kitchen, marvelling at her degradation. This was a world away from the previous night at Ciro's, but that no longer seemed real. Realising that she'd left Lally's dress and jewellery at the flat, she was wondering how on earth she could rescue them when a workman with a nose like a prize strawberry put a newspaper down on her table. 'Here, miss. Have that, if you like. I'm done with it, anyhow.'

'Thank you.'

It was a copy of the *Telegraph*. Surprised, she looked after him, but he was gone. Perhaps someone had given it to him, she thought. Or perhaps...but who was she to judge? *She* didn't look as if she ought to be here, did she? At least, she hoped she didn't, but after that run-in with the two women at Piccadilly Circus, she couldn't be sure about anything. Looking down at the paper, she thought, there'll be jobs advertised. Situations Vacant—that was what she needed. Of course! Why hadn't she thought of it before? She didn't need Jock or Lally—she could do it herself. Surely someone at Ashwood would give her a reference, and then... Feverishly, she began leafing through the pages then stopped, abruptly, arrested by the sight of James's face smiling up at her in smudgy black and white. Instinctively, she smiled back, and then, a second later, she saw the heading: *Obituaries*.

CHAPTER 56

The light penetrated her eyelids. Dazed and blinking, she gasped, 'Please…don't—' Black spots danced in front of her in the gloom, and as her eyes adjusted she could see a solid bulk in front of her—an overcoat, trouser legs. 'Wake up, miss.'

The voice was brisk and official. Looking up, Diana realised she was facing a policeman's torch. 'I…I wasn't asleep. At least, I don't think I was.'

Shining the beam away from her face, the policeman asked, in a softer tone, 'Do you know where you are?'

Shaking her head, Diana put her hand down and felt the cold, hard wood of a bench beneath her palm. How had she got here? She remembered sitting in the café in shocked disbelief, reading James's obituary again and again, about his achievements, his contribution—no mention of the drinking, of course—and how he'd died after being hit by a car, leaving a wife but no issue. *She* was his wife—why hadn't anyone told her? Perhaps they hadn't known where she was…if he'd become separated from his belongings and there was no address…

'I was in a café,' she said. 'And then…'

'Yes, miss?'

'I'm not sure. I was walking. I got lost.'

'You can't stay here, miss.'

'I haven't anywhere to go.'

'You've got to go somewhere, miss.'

Diana shook her head: 'He's dead. That's why he didn't come back.'

'Who's that, miss?'

'James… My husband. He's dead.'

'I'm sorry about that. When did it happen?'

'I've only just found out.' Diana held up the newspaper. 'It's in here. It says he was hit by a car.'

'In there, is it?'

He's humouring me, Diana thought. He thinks I'm mad. 'It's there,' she said, holding up the paper and tapping James's picture. 'That's him.'

'James Carleton, film director,' the policeman read. 'That's your husband, is it?'

'Was my husband,' said Diana.

'I see.' He didn't believe her.

'He *was*.'

'Of course he was,' said the policeman, soothingly. Bending down, he took her by the arm. 'Now, why don't you come along with me, and we'll find you a bed for the night.'

Diana allowed herself to be raised to her feet. 'My suitcase…'

'I've got it, don't worry.'

Walking was painful—she must have developed blisters—but she hobbled along as best she could.

Waking before dawn, the first thing Diana was aware of was the smell: body odour, stale linen, and carbolic. Then the sensation of something itchy next to her cheek: a blanket. She sniffed it and hastily drew her head away: the rough wool was impregnated with dirt. She wasn't alone. Somebody was snoring to her left, and from her right there came a series of yelps, muffled and puppyish. Turning on the narrow bed, she felt something soft and silky twist around her waist: my slip, she thought, and reached beneath the blanket—there seemed to be no sheet—to pull it down around the tops of her legs. The next thing she was aware of was the string tied around her neck. Fingering it in the darkness, she found a metal disc. Recalling an efficient, hospital matron's voice saying, 'Fifty-five!' she thought, this is my number. She'd been sitting in the café, hadn't she, looking at the paper, and then James was dead, and now…now she didn't seem to have a name any more, only a number. I ought to be crying, she thought. Why aren't I crying?

Vaguely, she remembered entering the hostel, the exchange between the woman in the wire-caged cubbyhole in the lobby and the policeman. She'd wondered why the woman, upright and stiff in a suit that looked like a uniform, was in the cage. To protect her? If so, it must be from the people here. A sudden lurch of fear jerked her into a sitting position, and she stared wildly into the unpredictable darkness. As her eyes adjusted, rows of grey humps appeared down the length of the room. In the gloom, they seemed petrified, as though an earthquake had encrusted them with dust or ash and converted them into concrete. The nearest bed was barely three feet away. She couldn't see the woman's face, but a wrist and hand, knuckle joints exploded by arthritis, protruded from the blanket.

She'd seen the policeman's eyebrows telegraph his disbelief to the woman in the cage when she'd given her name as Mrs Carleton, but she was too tired to make a fuss. She'd explained that she'd spent the last of her money in the café, but the policeman must have made it all right because her suitcase was taken from her and she was escorted upstairs to the dormitory. His face as she'd thanked him had said it all: she was now, officially, an object of pity.

...I have examined these and I found entwined in the roots of the philadelphus plant (from Area 3) a cervical vertebra and pieces of skull. There was also a mass of decaying fabric through which the roots were growing freely. From the debris labelled 'Area 3' there were found numerous pieces of burnt newspaper which appear to have been cut into strips before burning. Pieces of root similar to the philadelphus root were adhering to this paper. A date '9th July 1943' was found on one of the pieces.

In the material labelled 'Areas 2, 3, 6, 8, 9' there was found a quantity of rotted cloth. This cloth consists of 7 types of material which can be associated to form the remains of a black artificial silk crêpe dress, a black (?dark-navy) coat, and possibly a navy-blue skirt. The total quantity of clothing recovered represents a moderately extensive area of clothing...

Wondering what the hell 'moderately extensive' was supposed to mean, Stratton pushed the Metropolitan Police Laboratory report away from him and lit a cigarette. The lab had obviously been working round the clock, because there was an enormous pile of notes to be sifted. Stratton, who'd managed no more than a couple of hours' fitful sleep, stared at them blearily, trying to keep his mind on the job. Images from the nightmare that had woken him, shaking and dripping sweat, at half past five, kept recurring in his mind: Monica and Jenny prone on the dusty floor of Paradise Street; Backhouse, scarlet penis bursting out of his fly like some demonic jack-in-the-box as he pulled his tie over his head and snapped it taut between his fists; himself, held back by some invisible power, struggling lead-legged, unable to reach them...

Subdued at breakfast, Monica had avoided looking directly at him. The atmosphere was solemn, as if there had been a death in the house, and his daughter's face was pale, the skin under her eyes the translucent blue of sleeplessness. He'd wondered if he'd shouted out in his dream, and if so, whether she'd heard him. They didn't speak much over their tea and toast. Monica had given him her bacon, and he'd wondered if this was the onset of the morning sickness he remembered Jenny suffering but said nothing. Watching her, his helpless feeling had returned, and when he rose to leave, he'd rubbed her back and said, 'Chirp up, chicken,' just as he used to when she was small and something had upset her.

'You will keep your promise, won't you, Dad?'

'Yes, love. Just remember—least said, soonest mended. For the time being, anyway.' Except, he'd thought as he closed the gate, this couldn't be mended at all. Catching sight of the bloody man's name on an Odeon film poster from the top deck of the bus, jeering at him in bright red from beneath Phyllis Calvert and Stewart Granger, he'd had to fight the urge to tear down the stairs and rip the thing out of its frame.

At least, he thought, Lamb wasn't breathing down his neck. The discoveries at Paradise Street had knocked the wind out of his sails to the extent that he now listened passively when Stratton brought him up to date with the revolting litany of their findings. There'd been a couple of routine exhortations to 'get on with it, for God's sake', but his heart wasn't in it. Despite the statement he'd issued about the two cases having nothing to do with each other, Stratton knew he didn't believe it.

Pulling another section of the lab report towards him, he began to read: *I have examined samples of blood taken from all four women and found that samples 1, 2 and 3*—the women in the alcove, thought Stratton—*all contain carbon monoxide. The sample of blood (2)*—that was Kathleen McKinnon—*also contained alcohol. The amount found was 0.240%. This figure is equivalent to the consumption of 8 pints of beer or 13 fluid ounces of spirits. This figure, however, cannot be entirely relied on owing to the decomposition of the blood.*

Stratton whistled. Decomposition or not, the woman must have been blotto, or well on the way to it, when she died. Still, if it meant she hadn't realised what was happening to her, he supposed it was a blessing. *A small quantity of alcohol was found in the stomach contents of (2), and traces of alcohol in the stomach contents of (3)*. That was Iris Manning. Stratton scanned the rest of the page. No traces of drugs found in any of them… An area of seminal staining found on the top of the left stocking from (1)—that was Dwyer—information about laundry marks found on the linen, and at the bottom, a very long list of the contents of the bottles found in the medicine cabinet, which included sleeping pills and phenobarbitone.

Hearing an alarmingly viscid throat-clearing behind him, Stratton turned to see the bulky form of DI Grove. 'Been to see the furniture bloke, Lorrimer. Says Backhouse told him he was going up to Northampton to look for a job, and his wife was staying there with her sister.'

'He seems to have as much trouble with the truth as Davies,' said Stratton tiredly. 'Judging from this lot,' he gestured at the pile of statements taken from the Paradise Street residents, 'everyone got a different story. Two of them said Birmingham—that was for a woman's operation, apparently—and the rest thought it was Sheffield.'

Perching his substantial bottom on the corner of the desk, Grove gave a sympathetic grimace. 'Well, Lorrimer gave him twelve pounds for the furniture. Said he wanted fifteen, but most of the stuff was no good. According to him, the last time he saw

Mrs Backhouse—February sometime, he reckons she was in a terrible state of nerves and terrified of her husband.'

Stratton sighed. 'Isn't hindsight a wonderful thing? Mind you, we thought she seemed pretty well under his thumb back then.'

'Yes, well...' Grove adjusted his backside, sweeping several papers to the floor in the process. 'The bad news is that he's been talking to the press.' Holding up his arm, he extended his thumb and fingers to frame an invisible headline. '"Did She Know?"'

'Well, she certainly didn't know about the women in the alcove, because she was under the floorboards by the time they got in there.'

'Not about them, about the Davieses. They won't say that, of course, because of Lamb putting the mockers on it, but that's what they'll imply. "Mrs Backhouse was terrified by her guilty knowledge. Eventually her killer realised that her nerves were at breaking-point and decided that he must silence her forever." Or something like that.' Seeing Stratton's expression, Grove added, 'Still, at least the inquest tomorrow should be pretty straightforward.'

'Yes, except for the fact that we can't actually find the fucker.'

'Well, he can't stay hidden forever. We've had a lot more sightings. Likeliest was in Bognor but it didn't come to anything. You know they even stopped a theatre performance last night—someone thought they'd spotted him in the audience. Bloke turned out to be nothing like.'

'What was the play, sir?' Ballard was listening from the other end of the room where he'd been in conference with DS Porter.

'*Macbeth*, believe it or not. Sir Donald Wolfit.'

'Blimey,' said Ballard. 'He must have been cheesed off.'

'I don't know about that,' said Grove. 'Think of the publicity—murderer unmasked at *Macbeth*... You all right, Stratton?'

'Not so's you'd notice, no.' Mention of the theatre had brought Raymond Bloody Benson sharply to mind. He wasn't looking forward to that conversation *at all*. He put his hand in his pocket and fingered the paper on which Monica had written the phone number, touching it gingerly as though it might suddenly burst into flames.

Getting to his feet with a grunt, Grove laid a heavy hand on his shoulder. 'I can imagine…' he said, gruffly. 'But if it's any consolation, Lamb'll be feeling a lot worse.'

'It isn't,' said Stratton shortly.

'Oh, by the way, Backhouse seems to have forged his wife's signature to cash in her savings. We had a communication from the…' Grove flicked through his notebook, 'Yorkshire Penny Bank. Ten pounds, fifteen shillings and tuppence, it was. Right, I'd better get cracking—check we've got all our witnesses for tomorrow.'

'Thanks, Grove. It's…' Temporarily lost for words, Stratton said, 'I know you've got enough on your plate. I appreciate it.'

Two pinkish spots appeared on Grove's putty-coloured cheeks. 'This sort of thing…' He turned to stare out of the window for a moment, and then, tight-lipped beneath the drooping moustache, said, 'We're all in it together.' Taking his pipe from his pocket and jamming it between his teeth, he left the room.

Ballard came up to the desk, a sheaf of paper in his hand. 'We've got the name of May Drinkwater's dentist, and he's sending all her bumpf over to the Middlesex Dental Surgery Department for comparison. And Professor Anderson—he's the man in charge—says the crowns are made of some sort of alloy they use in Central Europe. DS Porter's looking into it.'

Stratton raised his eyebrows. 'Central Europe's a big place. Who was it reported May Drinkwater as missing?'

'Her brother, sir. He gave us the name of the dentist.'

'Did he give a description of what she was wearing?'

'Yes, sir.' Ballard leafed through his notebook. 'A dark-coloured dress and coat.'

'Looks like you might have hit the nail on the head.' Stratton handed over the lab report. 'We've got fabric samples from both and some buttons—partially burnt, apparently at the same time as the skull.'

'Fingers crossed, sir.'

'You bet. Oh, and there's a scrap of newspaper with a date which might help with identifying the other one—ninth of July, nineteen forty-three.'

'I'll look in the records, sir, although what with the bombing…'

'I know. Just do your best.'

'Yes, sir. And there's something else. A woman came in this morning—DS Porter spoke to her, sir. A Mrs Jean Halliday. She said she was in a café in Marylebone last week and she had a conversation with a man she now thinks must have been Backhouse—'

'Hold on. Last week's not much use.'

'Not as far as locating him goes, no, which is why Porter didn't think to tell you immediately. But what's interesting is that she told DS Porter they'd got talking, and he started asking her about her health… Well, turns out she's pregnant. Married, but she wasn't very happy about it because she's got four already and Backhouse—if that's who this chap was—said he could help her. Told her he used to be a doctor but he'd been struck off because he did a favour for a friend and got found out. He said that if she'd go round to his house, he knew a way to get rid of the baby. She said she wanted to think about it, so they arranged to meet the following day at the same café, but she got cold feet so she didn't turn up.'

'Did the man say *where* he lived?' asked Stratton.

Ballard shook his head. 'Just told her he lived nearby. And Euston's not far from Marylebone, sir. Oh, and he asked if her husband knew about the pregnancy, and when she said she hadn't told him, the bloke said there was no need to say anything because he could have it all sorted out in no time, and no one would be any the wiser.'

'It certainly sounds like him,' said Stratton. 'Did she give a description?'

'She did.' Ballard found the right piece of paper and read, 'Medium height, bald head, thick glasses, grey-striped suit—'

'No coat?'

'Not according to this. But she said she'd read a description in the paper and thought it sounded like the same man, and when Porter showed her a photograph, she told him it was spot on.'

'Well, if it was him, he certainly didn't lose any time lining up his next victim after Mary Dwyer.'

'That's what I thought, sir. He's out of control—can't help himself and doesn't care about getting caught.'

'It certainly sounds as if Mrs Halliday had a very lucky escape. And now he's left Paradise Street, he's presumably not got anywhere to take anyone... But if you're right—and you might well be—that he no longer cares about getting caught, that makes him even *more* dangerous. Christ! We'll just have to hope that—' Stratton stopped as Arliss's head appeared round the door, an expression of malevolent relish lighting up his normally morose features. 'A Mrs Davies at the desk, sir. John Davies's mother. Says she'd like a word, sir.'

Stratton, exchanging glances with Ballard, saw only compassion in the sergeant's eyes. Heart sinking still further, he rose and followed the constable down the corridor.

Diana headed towards Green Park—to the spot where James had proposed to her. Now, her single objective was to be close to him, and she could think of no other way to achieve it.

The obituary hadn't mentioned where he'd died, only how. Had he returned to London, she wondered and, if so, how had he managed it with so little money? Light-headed with hunger—the hostel had not provided breakfast beyond a cup of nauseatingly strong tea—she stumbled along as fast as the painful rubbing of the raw flesh on her heels would allow, her suitcase banging against her legs, impelled by the idea of being near him.

Reawakened at half past five by a clanging fire-bell and a rough hand yanking the blanket from her body, she'd seen, as though in a dream, the grey shapes rise off their beds, scramble into their clothes, and make for the door. Dazed, she'd followed them, barely able to remain on her feet in the middle of the elbowing, clattering descent down two flights of stairs to the basement washhouse. The room she'd found herself in was a wet version of hell, reeking of carbolic soap with dirty water everywhere, coursing in rivulets down the concrete walls and sluicing in soapy rivers across the floor to drain away down gulleys cut into the stone. The air was thick with shrieks and swearing, punctuated with flushing lavatories, as sixty women jostled each other for the use of three taps and fought over hanging space on the clothesline strung above their heads. Now, making her way from Victoria—where, it turned out, the hostel was situated—towards Hyde Park Corner, revoltingly detailed images detached themselves from the memory of the violent steamy blur: a single, pendulous dug with the thick, pocked surface of orange-peel; mottled legs disfigured by bulging knots of varicose veins; a discarded sanitary towel floating in a scummy puddle…

Just twenty minutes later, upstairs in the anteroom, those same women had sat waiting for the doors to open at seven o'clock, silent and withdrawn from one another, adjusting their dresses and pinning on the few pitiful ornaments they still possessed, the vestiges of self-respect that would enable them to face the world. She'd seen their sidelong, envious looks at her fur coat and been careful to keep her mouth shut for fear of exciting their scorn. Perhaps she needn't have worried—their lack of curiosity had suggested that, if she was there, she must be one of them.

Was she? She neither knew nor cared. All she wanted was to be with James. Wincing, she quickened her pace.

It was over two years since she'd last been in the park and, with the trees in leaf and mist still rising from the grass, it looked different to what she remembered. After five minutes' walking, she stopped, blinking up into the weak spring sunlight. She was sure she was near the place where James had proposed—or rather, where James had told her she was going to marry him—and she'd definitely chosen the same entrance, but she wanted to be sure. After turning round several times, she made for a clump of trees whose shapes she thought she remembered, but felt no sense of his presence. She stopped and removed her gloves, staring down at her engagement ring that sparkled next to the thin gold wedding band.

There's no such thing as too much champagne… James's voice echoed in her ear and, in a warm rush, the liquid heat of desire coursed through her body, just as it had when he'd touched her arm. Dizzy now, she could feel his lips on hers, his breath on her face, and then—she spun round—they'd run across the grass... Oh, God...

Her legs seemed to have turned to water, and she leant against a tree trunk and closed her eyes. When she opened them, she knew he was gone. There's no point in being here, she thought. He's nowhere. He's dead. She buried her face in her hands and wept.

When she straightened up, she noticed that there was a man standing on the path looking in her direction. Seen through a blur of tears, he looked as if he'd just risen out of the mist, middle-aged and ordinary in his tweed overcoat and trilby hat, the sunlight glinting off his glasses so that she couldn't see the eyes behind them. Turning her back on him so that she was facing the tree, she blew her nose and, taking her compact from her handbag, began to repair her face. Returning the cosmetics to their place and pulling on her gloves, she turned round once more and saw that he was still there. He seemed, although she wasn't sure about this because of the sun, to be staring at her. Discomfited by the blank spaces that were his eyes, and wondering what she ought to do next, she began walking in the direction of the railings. Out of the corner of her right eye, she saw him hesitate and then, as if he'd reached a decision, square his shoulders and begin walking towards her. Thinking that he might be lost, she stopped. He approached her and, removing his hat to reveal a domed, bald pate, he blinked several times, as if uncertain, and made a curious sucking motion with his mouth. 'Good morning,' he said, in a husky, confidential tone, 'I wonder if I might be of any assistance?'

CHAPTER 59

Stratton thought afterwards that it would have been easier if Mrs Davies had cursed and spat at him. The elderly lady's quiet dignity had filled him with shame. 'When I visited my son in prison before his trial,' she said, 'and I asked him what happened, he told me it was Backhouse. "He knows all about it, he's got medical books." That's what John said. "Get Mr Backhouse, he's the only one who can help me." When I asked him why he made all those statements, he said it was because Mr Backhouse told him that things would be fine if he confessed. Then he said only one of the statements was true, and that was the one where he said Backhouse had done it. When I asked him why he signed the confession, he said that when you told him Judy was dead he had nothing to live for. Until then, I didn't know what to believe, but when he said that, I knew he was telling the truth. He told you that, Mr Stratton, but you didn't believe him.'

'No,' said Stratton, 'I didn't. But he did have a reputation as a liar, Mrs Davies. You said so yourself.' Stratton forbore to point out that she'd also said, in a statement made to DI Grove, that her son had a terrible temper.

'Yes, I did. But I knew when he was telling the truth.'

Stratton doubted the veracity of this, but wouldn't have dreamt of challenging it. Death, especially in these sorts of circumstances, tended to simplify people into much better—or much worse—versions of themselves, and this black-and-white-ing process extended to their relationships with others. Bonds, especially intuitive links, such as Davies's mother was now claiming, became ever stronger as the dead person was dismantled and remade by those left behind. But if it comforted them, where was the harm?

'Do you still think he's guilty, Mr Stratton?'

Stratton hesitated. 'I don't know,' he said, finally. 'We need to complete our investigation before we can come to any conclusions.'

Mrs Davies held Stratton's gaze until he could bear it no longer and lowered his eyes. 'When John's appeal failed,' she said in a steady voice, 'I asked him again. I told him it couldn't make any difference now—it was for my own peace of mind and because I wanted him to make *his* peace with God. He looked me straight in the eye and said, "Mam, I didn't do it. Backhouse done it."'

Stratton had a fleeting image of Mrs Davies on the morning of the execution, flanked by relatives in a neat sitting room, all of them watching as the minute hand of the clock on the mantel inched nearer and nearer to the hour. He could imagine her clutching her son's photograph, waiting for the second when the present of his life tipped over into the past, gathering herself for the invisible but all-too-well-imagined snapping of the neck as the trap was released and the bag-headed, pinioned thing that had been her boy plummeted downwards…

I want to tell Mam what I done, but I can't do it… Stratton remembered Davies's words to him in the car on the way back from the committal. Could he have been referring to something other than the murders? It didn't seem very likely. If he *was* guilty, then clearly he hadn't been able to face confessing it to his mother. But it was a very odd thing to say if he wasn't.

'What I came to tell you,' Mrs Davies continued, 'is that I'm writing to my Member of Parliament to ask about an inquiry.

I've also written to the Home Secretary. I thought I ought to tell you because John said you were a gentleman. He liked you, Mr Stratton.'

This was said sincerely, without a trace of irony. Humbled, Stratton, said, 'Thank you.'

'Well…' Mrs Davies rose and stood, straight-backed and self-contained. 'I'm sure you're very busy.'

Stratton said goodbye to Mrs Davies at the station door. As she began to descend the steps, an impulse he was unable to resist made him put a restraining hand on her arm. She looked down at it and then up at his face, frowning slightly. Removing his hand, he said, 'I am sorry. Very sorry.' He didn't—couldn't—elaborate further, but Mrs Davies appeared not to require this. With a single, emphatic nod that made her tight grey curls bounce, she turned and left.

Leaving West End Central that evening, Stratton felt as furtive and mortified as a man coming out of a knocking shop and onto a street where he might easily meet someone he knows. Logic told him that Davies's death wasn't solely his fault. The man had done a great deal to hang himself, Backhouse had lied, and everyone, including the judge, had considered Davies to be guilty. He wondered if Mrs Davies had, initially at least, thought so too. If that were so, he thought, then by now she'd almost certainly convinced herself she'd always been sure of his innocence. He couldn't blame her for that—in the circumstances, he'd probably have done the same. But then what about what Davies had said in the car…

He'd turned this over and over in his mind during the bus journey home, but reached no conclusions. The house was unlit, and, turning on the kitchen light, he saw that there was a note lying on the table. Assuming that it must be instructions for heating up whatever was in the saucepan on the stove, he went through to the scullery and poured himself a glass of beer. Staring out of the window into the dark garden, he tried to rehearse what to say to Raymond Benson. At least, he thought, separated by a telephone line, he wouldn't be able to clobber the bloody man, no matter how strong the urge. Imagining him, sleekly handsome and languid in a velvet smoking jacket, he clenched his fists, but he knew that, however much he wanted to break the man's neck, he'd promised Monica—and, he repeated to himself, violence wouldn't change, or solve, anything. It'd make me feel a whole lot better, though, he thought grimly.

First things first. Supposing that he ought to try and eat something at least, he took his beer back to the kitchen and picked up the note. *Dad, I am sorry I have betrayed your trust and let you down, and Mum. I am going to see a friend who can help. Please don't worry about me. Love, Monica x*

Stratton felt sick. What friend? What help? The vision of his beloved daughter being mauled by some seedy struck-off doctor in a back room, or worse—appallingly, horrifyingly worse—encountering Backhouse, was so strong that he felt as if he'd been punched in the stomach. Backhouse bending over her, panting and sweating with lust, as he pawed at her knickers and... *Stop it!* Hands palm-down on the table and elbows locked, he took several deep breaths. He must not panic. He must find her before...before... No! He must not think about that. Monica wouldn't allow herself to be drawn into a conversation with a strange man and certainly not someone like Backhouse—but then Monica, at present, wasn't her normal, sensible self. She was upset and desperate and he had no idea what she might do. He *had* to find her.

Where to start? His mind raced. Monica had said that she'd only told Pete, but perhaps she had talked to Madeleine as well. They'd always been close, just as Jenny had with Doris. Except, said a voice in the back of his mind, Jenny hadn't told Doris that she was pregnant, had she? Telling himself that Monica wasn't Jenny, and that the circumstances were entirely different, he strode into the hall and picked up the telephone.

'Doris? It's Ted. Is Monica with you?'

'Hello, love. We haven't seen her today… Are you all right? You sound a bit—'

'Is Madeleine there?

'Yes.' Doris sounded surprised. 'She's in the kitchen. But what—'

'Can I speak to her?'

'Yes, of course.'

There was a pause as Doris handed the receiver to her daughter. 'Hello, Uncle Ted. What is it?'

'Have you seen Monica today?'

'No. Not since the night before last…Is there something wrong, Uncle Ted?'

'Did she say anything to you?'

'Say anything? No, we just…you know. Just normal things. Why?'

'If she telephones, can you let me know?'

'Of course, but… Is she all right?'

'I'm not sure. Do you know if she's got any particular friends at work?'

'Well, she's mentioned someone called Anne who works with her doing the make-up, but nothing…I mean, just about funny things that happen, not anything important.'

'Did she mention a surname?'

'Not that I remember. She told me about Mrs Calthrop, as well—she said you knew her before, from the war—but that was ages ago. She's not talked about her recently…I can't think of anyone else.'

'Did she mention Raymond Benson?'

'The film actor? No. I'd remember *that*, Uncle Ted. He's dreamy.'

'I don't doubt it,' said Stratton, grimly. 'Could I have another word with your mum?'

There was another pause, as the telephone was handed back to Doris. 'What's going on, Ted?'

'I'm not sure… Look, Doris, Monica's in trouble, and I don't know where she's gone. She's left a note, but…I'm worried she's done something stupid.'

'Stupid? What—'

'She's pregnant.'

'Pregnant?' Doris's voice was sharp. 'Do you know anything about this, Madeleine?' There was some muttering and then Doris's voice again. 'She says she doesn't. Are you sure?'

'It's what she told me.'

'Well, it's the first we've heard of it. Is there anything we can do, Ted?'

'No…just stay by the telephone in case she rings. I need to find her. Is there anyone local she might have gone to—a friend, I mean? Madeleine might know…'

Madeleine came back on the line. 'I can't think of anyone, Uncle Ted. I mean, there's girls from school, but she's never really had a special friend—if she'd told anyone, it would be me.'

His niece sounded both shocked and hurt, and Stratton didn't blame her. 'All right. But if she does telephone, you will tell me, won't you?'

'Of course I will! I hope she hasn't…I mean, I hope she's all right.'

'So do I,' said Stratton. Putting the receiver down, he rubbed his face. 'Christ, so do I.' Returning to the kitchen, he picked up Monica's note once more, and read it again, trying to make it yield some clue as to where she had gone. *Dad, I am sorry I have betrayed your trust…* But, he thought, it hadn't been a matter of trusting her; it had simply never occurred to him that anything of this sort might happen. Monica hadn't betrayed his trust—what she *had* done was to show up, with vile clarity, his utter negligence as a father: *he* was the one who had betrayed *her*.

Stratton fished Benson's telephone number out of his pocket and rubbed it with his thumb for a moment, staring fixedly at the thing as though expecting its owner to appear before him like a pantomime genie. Then, white-knuckled, he yanked the receiver from its cradle and, jabbing his finger into the relevant holes, began to dial the number.

'Hadley Green 521—'

'Mr Benson?' Cutting off the rich, silky tones, Stratton almost spat the words with the effort of keeping his own voice level.

'Yes. Who is this, please?'

'This is Detective Inspector Stratton. Monica Stratton's father.'

'I *see*...'

Stratton took a deep breath, taking in, with the air, the effortless superiority and poise of the man's tone. 'I should bloody well hope you *do* see. I'd like to kick your arse from here to Land's End.'

'Steady on, old chap.'

Old chap? Stratton took another deep breath. 'Much as I'd like to do that,' he said, every muscle in his body taut with the strain of maintaining any degree of calm at all, 'I'm not going to, because I promised my daughter I wouldn't. The reason I'm telephoning is because Monica has disappeared.'

'She's not with you?'

'Obviously not, or I wouldn't be asking.'

'Well, she's not *here*.' Benson managed to sound as if this was the most ridiculous idea he'd ever heard in his life.

'She left a note saying that she was going to see a friend who could help her, and I want to know if you have any idea who that is.'

'No, I can't say I—'

'So you didn't give her an address, or—'

'I have offered,' said Benson carefully, 'to…make reparations, as it were.'

'*Reparations?* You mean you've offered to pay for Monica to have an illegal operation which may very well ruin her health for life. I need to know where she's gone.'

'I think that's somewhat of an exaggeration, don't you? There are perfectly good clinics where every care is taken to do a competent job.'

'Monica,' said Stratton through gritted teeth, 'is not a piece of machinery. She is *my* daughter, and she has feelings, and I'm very concerned that she's done something stupid. Did you, or didn't you, give her the name of an abortionist?'

'No, I did not.'

'Did anybody?'

'I have absolutely no idea.'

'What about people at the studio? Friends? Anyone she's mentioned?'

'Well, she's pally with another make-up girl, Anne, but I don't know any more than that. You'd have to ask the studio, unless Monica's left an address book or something like that…'

Cursing himself for not having thought of this and feeling that there was nothing to be gained by prolonging the conversation, Stratton rang off, but not before leaving Benson in any doubt that they'd be discussing the matter further and face to face and assuring him that if anything happened to Monica then he would hold him personally responsible.

Stratton stood on the threshold of his daughter's bedroom. It wasn't territory into which he usually ventured—certainly not by himself, anyway—and he felt uncomfortable. He had a clear memory of himself in 1940, when the children were evacuated, coming in here and purloining a tiny pink scarf Monica had made for one of her dolls. Remembering the embarrassment he'd felt at this sentimentality, even though no one had seen him do it, he found himself wondering what had happened to the little scrap of knitting. If Jenny had found it in one of his pockets, she'd never mentioned it...

The dolls were gone now. Sketches—portraits, flowers, and fruit—from the evening classes she'd attended were pinned up on the walls, and there was a Jean Plaidy novel and a film magazine on top of the small bedside cabinet, a dish of hairpins and a bottle of scent on the mantelpiece, and a chiffon scarf draped over one edge of the mirror. Stratton glanced at the neatly made bed with its shiny pink eiderdown; the idea of his daughter lying in it and thinking about that bloody man, as she must surely have done, revolted him, and he turned away. Looking around the room trying to avoid the bed with his eyes—almost impossible, as it took up nearly half the available space—he couldn't see anything that looked like an address book. As far as he knew, Monica had never kept a diary. He stared at her chest of drawers. He really did not want to search through all her underclothes and whatever else she might have in there, but... Perhaps he ought to ring Doris? For Christ's sake, he told himself, this is no time for pussyfooting around. Just get on with it.

Gingerly, as if the action might detonate a bomb, Stratton opened the top drawer. Finding only the usual array of underwear and stockings, he slammed it closed as if that would shut the image of Benson fingering these garments, and the corresponding regions of their wearer, out of his mind. Finding nothing of note in the next drawer, he opened the bottom one. Beneath a folded cardigan, he found a bundle of letters. Perhaps they would help... Recognising his own handwriting, and Jenny's, and seeing the faded ink, he realised that Monica must have kept them from the war years, when they'd written to her and Pete in Suffolk. Blinking, he stuffed them back into place and stood up, staring round the room with scalded eyes.

He looked in the wardrobe, which seemed to contain the right amount of clothing. Monica's suitcase was sitting at the bottom, which was something to be grateful for at least. Finding that the bedside cabinet held nothing but a pair of gloves and a drawstring bag containing sanitary towels and a belt, Stratton turned his attention to the two small bookshelves. Perhaps the assorted Georgette Heyers, Daphne du Mauriers and A. J. Cronins would yield something. There were a few exercise books, too, kept from school, and an elderly jigsaw which, judging from the picture on the box, was of a deer in a woodland glade. He began with the books, flicking through the pages and shaking them before dropping them on the bed. Nothing there, and nothing hidden behind them, either. The exercise books were similarly barren, but when he opened the jigsaw box, he saw, beneath the jumble of cardboard, the corners of two letters. Scrabbling for them and sending half the pieces flying in the process, he saw that he was holding two notes in the same unfamiliar hand. Both were signed *With all my love, dearest one, R.B.* Scanning them quickly, Stratton saw that they were, underneath all the flummery and flowery language (Benson seemed to have been reading the same sorts of books as Monica), assignations, and, for his purposes, quite useless.

Stratton stuffed them back in the box and stood shaking his head and staring down at the cardboard fragments of bark and leaves scattered around his feet. He hadn't found a single clue to where she might have gone.

A call to Ashwood Studio, in Stratton's official capacity, yielded the information that Anne the-make-up girl, whose surname turned out to be Browne, lived in Clapham but wasn't on the telephone, and that the last known address for Diana Calthrop, now Carleton, was in Pimlico, but there was no telephone there, either.

Recollecting that Ballard lived somewhere in, or anyway near, Clapham, Stratton picked up the telephone once more and asked the operator to put him through. If the sergeant was surprised to hear his voice, he didn't show it, and when Stratton, as succinctly as he could, explained the situation, Ballard responded with commendably impersonal efficiency and agreed to go round to Tremlett Gardens and question the girl at once.

'Shall I telephone you at home, sir?' he asked.

'No… I'll telephone you later on—or leave a message at the station. I'm going out. There's someone else I need to follow up who might know where the hell Monica is.'

'Yes, sir. And, sir… Good luck.'

'Thanks, Ballard. Believe me, I appreciate this.'

By nine o'clock, Stratton was in Pimlico standing outside the address he'd been given for Diana and wondering if the man he'd spoken to at the film studio had made a mistake. The tall, thin house in the middle of a semi-derelict terrace looked as if it was being held upright by the buildings on either side. Clearly divided into flats, it didn't look like anywhere that Diana might visit, let alone inhabit. But then, he thought, as he walked up the four steps to the front door, 'his' Diana existed only in memory. She won't be the person I used to know, he told himself, or the one I met for those few excruciating moments at the Festival of Britain, any more than she'll remain the woman she is now. Everyone changes… Here, a sudden vision of Monica as a little girl made his eyes burn. Childhood was only an imagined cocoon of safety, he told himself. Look at poor little Judy Davies…

In answer to his knock, an elderly woman who smelt faintly of mildew put her head round the door and eyed him up and down with an irritable pecking movement like a parrot adjusting its plumage. Must be the landlady, thought Stratton. Large or small—and this one appeared to be pocket-sized—they tended to be of a kind.

'I've come to see Mrs Carleton,' he said.

The landlady let out a short yipping noise. 'Not here. You another one of her *gentlemen?*' She made the word sound like the worst of insults.

'I'm a policeman,' said Stratton, sharply, producing his warrant card. 'DI Stratton, CID, and I'd like to talk to her.'

The landlady's head, still the only visible part of her, twisted to one side in a way that didn't look possible, never mind comfortable. 'Police now, is it? Well you won't find her here. I gave her notice.'

'Do you know where she went?

'Didn't ask. I won't have that sort here.'

'What sort?'

'Well, she *said* she was married, but the husband—if that's what he was—disappeared a few weeks back, and then some other man came and paid all the rent they owed, and then she started having *visitors*, if you know what I mean. For all I know, she might have gone to live with one of those. She never had no money, or if she did I never got the smell of it. Now, if that's all…'

'Yes. Thank you.'

CHAPTER 62

Monica sat well back, not wanting to put her arms on the sticky surface of the café table. She didn't much want to touch anything in the place, including the tea she'd ordered. She knew she was just putting off the moment, but she couldn't face it, not quite yet.

The only other customer was an elderly, toothless man who, after sucking noisily at a forkful of mince to extract the flavour, removed the resulting pulp from his mouth with his thumb and forefinger and laid it on the side of his plate. It was only when he looked up from his gummy exertions that Monica realised she must have been staring and looked down at her lap, hoping the revulsion hadn't shown too much on her face.

She had to go through with it. The more she'd thought about it, the more obvious it was. People like her shouldn't have children because they were abnormal and would pass on their defects. Everyone knew that: it was how you ended up with cripples and kids with awful diseases who died young. Imbeciles, too. It would be as bad as if someone with venereal disease had a child. Auntie Doris had explained about that when one of their neighbours' sons turned out to be mentally defective: the mother had told her that her husband had caught something when he was serving overseas and passed it on to her so that she, in turn, had given it to the baby.

She'd never be able to explain any of that to Dad, of course. He might, in time, come to terms with what she'd done even though it was against the law and dangerous, but never with the other thing. That was why she hadn't asked Raymond about the special clinic. Dad, she was positive, would talk to him; and it was much better that Raymond knew nothing of her plans. Dad was a dab hand at getting information out of people, and Raymond, she felt sure, would be no exception.

Instead, she'd confessed to Anne. She hadn't wanted to, but a whispered confidence about an actress who'd found herself in trouble had persuaded her that her friend did know something of such matters, and there was nowhere else to turn. Initially, Anne had thought she was joking, and it had taken most of the day to convince her, but she'd managed it without revealing that Raymond was the father, inventing a local boy instead. Now, she had a name and address in her pocket, along with every bit of the money she'd managed to save since she started working. All she needed to do was to walk round the corner and knock on the door…

CHAPTER 63

Stratton was so completely revolted by the old woman and her insinuations that Diana had turned into some sort of prostitute that it was only after striding down the road in disgust that he stopped to consider what she'd actually said. *No money, or if she did I never got the smell of it.* The Carletons must have been badly off, and something had evidently happened to him. Had he deserted her? If she'd had any money, she'd have paid the rent herself, he was sure of it. Perhaps she'd had to borrow from a friend, and that was what had planted the idea about men and visitors in the old besom's mind. Surely, with no money, she'd have gone to stay with friends or relatives…in which case, she'd be impossible to find, at least at short notice. That was the obvious thing to do if one were thrown out with nowhere to go. But just in case, he'd try the women's hostel near Victoria Station. He couldn't believe he'd actually find her there—but then, he reasoned, he'd never have believed she'd have ended up in such ramshackle lodgings, either. It just went to show…what did it go to show? That one ought to expect the worst in any situation? No, he told himself firmly. Monica will be fine. I *shall* find her, and everything *will* be all right, somehow.

At least he was doing something. After the hostel, he'd go to West End Central and see if there was any message from Ballard about the girl in Clapham. Bound to set the cat amongst the pigeons, turning up when it wasn't his shift, but he could always make out it was something to do with the Backhouse case. As long as Lamb didn't get wind of it and start asking awkward questions...Walking fast in the direction of Victoria, keeping his eyes peeled for a passing taxi, he found himself wondering what his own father would have done in such a situation. He imagined the taciturn old farmer towering over the culprit, a shotgun jammed in his ribs until an early wedding was agreed upon. Except his father had had only sons—himself and two older brothers—and Benson was already married. He could just hear the wretched man bleating about his reputation... But film stars got divorced all the time, didn't they? In Hollywood, anyway. They weren't the same as normal people. But Benson might have children as well—they weren't to blame, and neither was his wife.

Eventually, he managed to flag down a taxi which took him to Victoria Station. Unsure of his bearings, he asked an elderly beggar whose face looked as though it had been under a harrow where to find the women's hostel.

'Down there, guv, on the right. Spare any change?'

Stratton gave him the price of a cup of tea and hurried off. The hostel was a squat, two-storey brick dwelling standing alone in the middle of a vast bombsite. In the windowless lobby, Stratton identified himself to a hard-faced woman of military bearing who sat, formidably, behind a wire grille. Unshaded, the single electric bulb gave her face a greenish cast, as if she were beginning to decompose, and behind her head, a series of metal rings hung like bizarre decorations, from lengths of coarse string. Halfway up a flight of stairs on the right, a stooped woman with an iron caliper on one leg pushed a mop backwards and forwards, punctuating their conversation with clanging noises whenever her metal support came into contact with the pail.

'Carleton?' The woman in the cage ran her finger down a list of names in a ledger. 'Yes, last night. Policeman brought her in.'

'Do you know where from?'

The woman drummed her fingers on the ledger for a moment, trying to remember. 'Oh, yes. Fur coat. Not our usual type at all. Quite confused—in fact, PC Eliot thought she might have lost her memory. Told me she'd showed him a picture of a man in the paper and said he was her husband and he'd died, and she'd only found out when she'd read about it. We weren't even sure that Carleton was her real name. Well,' she added, defensively, 'it doesn't sound very likely, does it?'

'Maybe not, but it is her name. Where did PC Eliot find her, do you know?'

'One of the squares near the station. That's his beat—he often brings women in here. He said she didn't seem to know *where* she was.'

'I see. And she hasn't come back?'

The woman shook her head. 'Mind you, if she's still…' she tapped her temple, 'we'll probably get her back. Is she wanted for something?'

'Only information. We think she may know about a missing person.'

After telling the woman to contact West End Central if Diana did return, Stratton returned to Victoria Station and telephoned to Ballard from a public box. When the sergeant's wife, an ex-policewoman remembered by Stratton with affection, reported that he had not yet returned, he put another tuppence in the slot and telephoned Doris.

'I'm sorry, Ted. She's not been in touch.'

'Oh, Christ… Sorry, Doris, I didn't mean to—'

'Listen, Ted—Don's just come in. He wants to know if there's anything he can do to help.'

'It's very kind of him, but I can't think of anything at the moment… That girl Madeleine mentioned, I've managed to run her down and my sergeant's gone round to talk to her, but beyond that, I really don't know what to do, I'm just so…' Words failing him, Stratton started on another tack. 'I'm trying to find the other person Madeleine mentioned—I don't think it can be her, but it's worth a go, and now I'm here…'

'Where are you?'

'Victoria Station. Look, I'd better go.'

'Ted, please... I know it sounds stupid, but try not to worry. Monica's always been a sensible girl. I'm sure she won't do anything...you know...'

Doris clearly didn't know what to say, either, and Stratton couldn't blame her. Hopelessly, he scanned the faces of the people who passed him, the echoing noise of their heels quickly swallowed up by a cacophony of steam engines, whistles, and porters trundling luggage trolleys. A needle in a haystack, a pebble on a beach... Why would Monica be in a bloody station, for God's sake? He'd go round to the local police and see if PC Eliot could shed any light on Diana's possible whereabouts. As he'd told Doris, he didn't really think it likely that Diana could be the 'friend' but, in the absence of any information from Ballard, he had to do *something* useful. Anything was better than going home and doing nothing.

Diana felt as though she were in a dream. The man in the park had appeared out of the mist like an omen—as if, somehow, James had sent him to her. Unprepossessing and shabby, certainly, and rather odd, but he sounded respectable enough—and he was *there*, wasn't he? Besides, what else did she have to do?

He'd offered to buy her a cup of tea, and they'd walked back towards Victoria Station, with him carrying her suitcase. He'd told her, in a husky whisper for which he'd apologised, explaining that his vocal cords had been damaged by gas in the Great War, that his name was Davies. 'I'm just passing the time,' he said. 'Since my wife died, I've had a lot of time on my hands. I'm waiting for my unemployment cards to come through, then I'll look for a job.'

'I'm sorry,' said Diana. 'It must be lonely.'

'Yes. But she'd had a long illness. I looked after her, you see—that's why I wasn't working. It was a mercy, really—terrible suffering, so hard to watch...'

'It must have been dreadful for you.'

'It was. She was one in a million...' Reaching into his overcoat pocket, he pulled out a pair of earrings and offered them to her. 'Would you like these?' They were cheap, screw-on things of the sort one might buy in Woolworth's, with a large blue stone set in a circle of smaller white ones.

Taken aback, Diana said, 'It's very kind of you, but I couldn't possibly... Did they belong to your wife?'

'Yes. I've been carrying them about. I often carry something of hers, to keep her near me. Are you married?'

'Yes. Or rather...' And she'd found herself telling him all about James and what had happened.

'Very regrettable. I suppose, with him being in the pictures, it's the sort of thing...oh, dear.' He shook his head several times, then said, 'How are you off for money? I could give you a pound.'

'No, really,' said Diana. 'I couldn't.'

'Well, how are you going to manage?'

'I need to find out about James. I suppose I ought to go to the police.'

'Police?'

'Well, to find out what's happened about the body and so on.'

'Yes...' murmured Mr Davies, vaguely, and then, with some pride, 'I could have helped your husband, you know.'

'Helped him?'

'Oh, yes. I used to be a doctor, you see. Before the war. That's why I could look after Edna—my wife—because I know about health matters. Anyone else, of course, and she'd have had to go to hospital, but I know what to do.'

'Were you really a doctor'?' She must have sounded more sceptical than she intended, because he said seriously, 'Oh yes. I trained as a doctor, but I was struck off the Medical Register for helping a friend.'

'Helping?'

He gave her a knowing look. 'I'm sure I don't have to tell you what it was for.'

They'd had tea in a café round the corner from the hostel where she'd spent the night, which was full of workmen having breakfast and indulging in cheerfully crude banter with its slovenly proprietress. 'Not really the type of person I'm used to associating with,' murmured Mr Davies, as they took the last available table. 'Or yourself, I should imagine.'

'You've been very kind,' said Diana, when she'd drunk her tea, 'but really, I mustn't take up any more of your time.'

Mr Davies looked flustered. 'Where are you going?'

'Well, the police. I—'

'Police?' he said, sharply.

'About James. I was hoping they could tell me where—'

'Oh, there's no need to do that yet. They won't be able to find out anything about your husband until all the tests have been done.'

'What tests?'

'Well,' he said, professorially, 'when somebody dies, and it's not expected, they have to do all sorts of tests...on the body, you see.'

'But he was hit by a car. That's what killed him.'

'All the same, they have to take extra care. Medical negligence, you know—very serious. They're not allowed to give out information to anyone until it's all been done.'

'Not even to the next of kin?'

Mr Davies shook his head. 'Those are the rules. It's very strict. When I was in the police—'

'Police? You said you were a doctor.'

'Oh, no...' Mr Davies chuckled. 'This was later, during the war. We did a lot of that sort of thing with bodies that were found. It was always very thorough.' He gazed into the middle distance for a moment, caught up in some memory of his own, then said, 'So there's no hurry. Why don't you have something to eat?'

With no breakfast and very little to eat on the previous day, Diana's stomach had been rumbling ever since they'd entered the place, and, after only a token demurral, she agreed. While she ate, Mr Davies told her stories about his time in the police, about criminals he'd caught and people he'd followed—even, apparently, in his free time—and the commendations he'd been given on two occasions. She was conscious, as he spoke, that there was a lack of focus about his conversation, its clarity and direction coming and going like a faulty wireless signal. Every so often, he would stop and look round the room as if searching for something. 'They wanted me to stay on,' he finished, 'but I couldn't because of my health. I was in a car accident myself, you know, before the war. That was why I had to stop training as a doctor. It was a pretty bad injury. Caused a lot of problems for me later on.'

'But you said you'd been struck off the medical register.'

'Yes,' he said, vaguely. 'Struck off... That's right.'

'So...' Diana gave it up and concentrated on her food. Why did it matter what this strange, creepy little man said? He'd bought her a meal, hadn't he? The least she could do in return was to listen politely until she could, reasonably and without giving offence, leave. She wasn't entirely sure that she believed all the business about the police not releasing any information to anyone before the post-mortem was completed—why shouldn't they be allowed to tell her where his body was, for heaven's sake? Anyway, she'd soon find out for herself whether it was true.

Now, he was pushing an item cut from a newspaper across the table. 'I was a witness in that case,' he said. 'For the prosecution. Three, four years ago. Perhaps you remember?' Diana read the headline: *BODIES ON HIS HANDS*.

'I don't think so,' said Diana. 'What happened?' She put out a hand to take the scrap of paper, but Mr Davies jerked it away from her in the manner of someone teasing a dog and tucked it back into his jacket pocket.

'It was all a long time ago,' he said. 'Mind you, it was quite a thing at the time. Yes...' He glanced round the café, repeating, 'quite a thing...' and then, with startling suddenness, reached out and took hold of her hand, so that she dropped her fork on the plate with a clatter.

Odd, Diana thought. He looks the type to have clammy hands, but his touch was warm and dry—not unpleasant, in fact, save for the fact that she didn't want him holding her hand in the first place. 'I've got other things,' he said in an urgent tone. 'Clothes and shoes. Jewellery… All a bit old-fashioned, I suppose, but good quality. You could have it. And you could come and stay with me. I'd have to lock the doors because I wouldn't want the coloureds upstairs to know I had a lady living with me… Dirty lot, always making a noise, and I'm afraid,' here, he lowered his whispery voice so that it became almost inaudible, and Diana had to lean forward to hear him, 'there's the matter of sharing a lavatory. I've written to the council to try and get them out. Edna—my wife—was terrified of them. But you could come…'

'It's very kind of you,' said Diana, gently withdrawing her hand, 'but I couldn't possibly impose. I'll go back to the hostel.'

Mr Davies contemplated her, his head on one side, making the strange movement with his mouth that she'd noticed when she'd first seen him. He really is creepy, she thought, with an inward shudder. 'They won't miss you, you know.'

'Miss me? What do you mean?'

'If you don't go back. It won't matter.'

'I know that, but—'

'I'm going to Birmingham soon. You could come with me.'

'Really, I don't think… I mean…'

'We could live together.'

Diana stared at him, asking herself, with a sort of miserable wonder, why on earth she was having this ridiculous conversation. It was, she supposed, just another measure of how out of kilter her life had become.

'I've got a job. They're putting me in charge of a firm of long-distance lorry drivers.'

'I thought you were waiting for your cards.'

'Oh…' He gave her a tight smile. 'That's just a formality. They've been wanting me to work for them for a long time. With my sort of expertise, you know…'

'I'm sure you'll be wonderful,' said Diana. 'Now I really must—'

He caught her wrist as she began to stand up, making her sit back down with a bump. 'Where are you going? I told you, the police won't be able to help.'

'Yes, you said. Please let go of me.'

'Oh…' Mr Davies looked down at his hand as if it had taken on a life of its own and removed it from Diana's arm.

'Thank you very much,' she said pleasantly, rising again, 'Now, I really must go.' In the last few minutes, something had seemed to click in her brain and she felt a new impetus: survival. A host of possibilities raced through her mind. If she pawned some of the clothes in her suitcase, she'd be able to get enough money for another night at the hostel and a meal, and then she'd leave the case at Victoria Station and find a library so that she could read the papers and see if there was any more about James. That would help her when she went to the police, and she could have a look for a job at the same time. She'd find out the address of the assistance board or whatever it was called—the librarian was bound to know—and surely they'd be able to help her when she explained her situation.

'Why don't we meet again this evening?' said Mr Davies. 'We could have a meal. There's a nice place down there,' he waved a hand in the direction of the station. 'Much better than this.'

With no intention of showing up, Diana agreed in order to be able to leave without more fuss, and they fixed on eight o'clock at a café nearby.

Dismayed at the small amount given her by the dismissive pawnshop owner in exchange for her silk blouses and dressing gown, and exhausted after her poor night's sleep, Diana dropped off over the newspapers in the library. The surprisingly kindly librarian let her be—'I thought you looked all in, dear'—and she awoke over an hour later, her face streaked with tears. The librarian had been very helpful about the assistance board, but when Diana got there she discovered that she could not be seen without an appointment, and the soonest she could speak to anyone was in two days' time.

Hungry once more, and realising that the pawnshop money would not, after all, cover a meal as well as the night's lodging, Diana resigned herself to another dose of Mr Davies's company. Although, she said to herself, if he thinks he's getting anything else out of me than a dining companion, he's got another think coming… And she could go to the police station first thing in the morning.

CHAPTER 65

Monica stared at the flaking paint of the front door of number three. Tregarth Row was a narrow, poorly lit alley with slippery cobblestones and four or five meagre houses huddled abjectly together, as if for warmth.

It had taken all her courage to get this far. Now she had to steel herself to knock on the door. You have to do this, she told herself. You have no choice.

She turned and looked back towards the main road. No one must see her going in… Not that anyone would know who she was, but if they lived nearby, they would surely guess why she was there. And the longer she stood outside, the greater her risk of being seen.

Resolved, and closing her mind as best she could to all thoughts of what was going to happen to her, she raised her hand and rapped on the door.

For a moment, there was no sound. Perhaps Mrs Lisle wasn't there. Perhaps she'd moved away, or died…or been arrested. Perhaps the police were waiting and it was a trap and she, too, would be arrested, and Dad would—

Hearing footsteps—only one set—from within, Monica told herself not to be stupid. It was bound to be unpleasant, but then it would be over. It occurred to her then, as she listened to the bolts being slid back, that she had no idea of what the procedure was.

The door opened a fraction, and a woman with a beetroot complexion surrounded by tight rolls of greasy hair stuck her head through the gap and eyed Monica suspiciously. 'Yes?'

'Are you Mrs Lisle?'

'Who wants to know?'

Taken aback by the woman's aggression but determined to stand her ground, Monica said, 'I do.'

'Why's that, then?'

'I understand that you might be able to…help me.'

'Help you?'

'Yes. I'm in trouble. I've got some money, and—'

In a flash the door opened and before Monica could think or act, Mrs Lisle had bundled her inside and shut the door. Under the gas in the hallway, she could see that the woman's face wasn't beetroot-coloured at all, but a fairly normal sort of dull pink and that her clothes and apron looked quite clean.

'Sorry, dear,' she said briskly, ushering Monica into a small back room which was empty but for a chair and a ratty-looking chaise longue with stuffing hanging out of the bottom, 'but I can't have you telling my business to all and sundry. Now then…' Her face softened. 'Been a silly girl, have you?'

'Yes,' said Monica. 'I'm afraid I have.'

'Well,' said Mrs Lisle, quite kindly, 'you're not the first, and I daresay you won't be the last. Got the money, have you?'

Monica nodded.

'You sit down there, then,' said Mrs Lisle, pointing to the chaise longue. 'Take off your knickers and make yourself comfy. Don't you worry, I always have a good old boil up first so it's all clean.'

Left alone, Monica did as instructed. She lay down gingerly on the lumpy, saggy cushions and stared up at the ceiling wondering how many women and girls had done the same thing before her. She must find something to concentrate on while it was happening. Unlike the spotless linoleum on the floor—a good sign, she thought, like Mrs Lisle's clean apron—the ceiling offered any number of possibilities. There were the brown clouds of damp stains in various shapes, an area by the door that was leopard-flecked with mould spores, and a cluster of frilly-edged mushrooms in one of the corners. Monica chose a damp patch that looked like a dog's face, or a shadow puppet of one, anyway, with a long nose and pricked ears. It looked like a friendly dog, with its mouth slightly open as though it were panting and smiling at the same time. She could imagine that it was real, an ally, guarding her… Keep looking at it, she told herself. Whatever happens, no matter how much it hurts, just keep looking.

'You're in luck, Inspector,' said the desk sergeant at Victoria Station. 'He's just brought someone in. If you wouldn't mind waiting...'

After about five minutes, the desk sergeant reappeared, tailed by a middle-aged man who appeared to be the size and consistency of a barn door. 'Well, sir,' he said, when Stratton had explained the situation—although without mentioning his personal involvement—'I don't rightly know where she might have gone. I know she didn't have any money to speak of, and she didn't seem quite right in herself, if you know what I mean... She was all-in last night, so I don't think she could have got very far, even with a bit of a sleep, although I don't suppose you get much in a hostel. I'd say your best bet might be one of the cafés round here. I could show you the likely ones. Do you want to stop for a cup of tea first? I hope you don't mind my saying, sir, but you look as if you could do with it.'

Understanding that Eliot's offer was made out of kindness, rather than the—perfectly understandable—desire to keep the weight off his feet for a few more minutes, Stratton declined, and the two of them went out into the night.

'There's Handy's Café, just down there next to the boot repairer. The New Scala Café's in the next street, and then there's Rossi's Café down by the scrap metal yard and the Croxley Tea Room.' PC Eliot paused to grin, then added, 'That makes it sound a lot more respectable than it is, by the way.'

'Right you are,' said Stratton.

As they made their way towards Handy's, PC Eliot said, 'Your Mrs Carleton seemed a cut above the usual type we take off the street, sir. Quite a long way above, in fact. Nicely spoken, good clothes... Was it some sort of breakdown?'

'I'm not sure,' said Stratton, truthfully. 'I was given her name in connection with the disappearance of this young woman'—also true, as far as it went—'but if she is in some sort of trouble, perhaps we can get in touch with her family.'

'I had the impression,' said Eliot, slowly, 'that she didn't have anyone. And she said she'd just read about her husband's death in the newspaper.'

'Well,' said Stratton, 'we'll get to the bottom of it somehow.' Distancing himself from the whole business by treating it as though it were an official inquiry made it easier somehow and, for the first time since he'd read Monica's note, he felt as if he had room in his mind to think. He certainly wouldn't get anywhere if he kept letting his feelings get in the way. If, he wondered, he hadn't kept thinking about Jenny and the baby, would he have come to a different conclusion about Davies? Preconceived ideas meant that you were looking for evidence to support your theory, which was exactly what he—and everyone else—had done. However much he might want to excuse himself, that was what it came down to in the end.

There was only one person in Handy's Café, a grim-faced elderly woman who was scanning the flyblown menu in her hand as though it were a casualty list. When the proprietor, who looked scarcely more cheerful, shook his head at Stratton's description of Diana, they left. The New Scala and Rossi's were both closed for the night, but a glance through the steamed-up window of the Croxley Tea Room—festoons of dusty artificial ivy nailed across faded bamboo-patterned wallpaper—showed that it was packed.

'Do you see her, sir?' asked Eliot, at Stratton's elbow.

'Not sure...' There were three women with their backs to him, two of whom were wearing fur coats, but the condensation and fug of smoke made it hard to tell. 'Let's go in.'

As the two men entered, rows of docile, tired faces turned in their direction. At the sight of Eliot's uniform, the murmur of conversation ceased, and a dozen loaded forks and slices of bread seemed to hang in the air, arrested in their progress towards partially open mouths. Stratton's eye took in bright, lipstick-smeared gashes, yellow teeth, glimpses of liver-coloured tongues, and then, as if led by an invisible pointer, came to rest on a bald, domed pate in the very centre of the crowded room.

He stopped in his tracks, staring in disbelief. Everything seemed to have slowed down, so that the next few moments had an unreal, almost dreamlike quality. The owner of the pate, who was still staring down at the table, was slight and wearing a tweed overcoat. His thumb and forefinger were curled around the handle of a cup of tea, the little finger stretched out in an exaggerated show of gentility as he began to lift it to his mouth. As he did so, he raised his head, and Stratton found himself looking straight into the eyes, blinking rapidly behind their pebble glasses, of Norman Backhouse.

'Two birds with one stone you might say, sir.' PC Eliot looked jubilant. Stratton couldn't blame him. 'Extraordinary that none of them had recognised him when he's had his face all over the papers.'

'Well, he'd changed his clothes—the description we put out had him wearing a blue overcoat, so I suppose he must have swapped it somewhere along the way. And perhaps the people in the café hadn't read the papers.' Stratton knew, as he said the last bit, that it was ridiculous. It was far more likely that several of the patrons of the Croxley Tea Room—and wherever else Backhouse had been—had seen someone who looked vaguely familiar, but, not knowing why he was familiar, had dismissed it with no more thought. But it was, by a very long chalk, the strangest arrest that he'd ever made. Eliot's gasp of recognition, the loaded, expectant silence in the café as he spoke the words, the look on Backhouse's face—something, to Stratton's astonishment, that was almost like relief—then hearing Eliot say, 'Mrs Carleton?' and then a woman's voice, small and clear, like something dropped into a void: 'Inspector Stratton?'

When he'd turned and seen Diana sitting on the other side of the table, he'd thought for a second that he must be having a hallucination and had stood, blinking and openmouthed, until a discreet cough from Eliot recalled him to his senses. Then, turning from Diana to Backhouse in confusion, seeing that they were together but unable to make any connection between them in his mind because it seemed so unlikely—so *wrong*—he'd stood silent and appalled, and it was left to Eliot to hustle Backhouse out of the place and onto the pavement. 'We'll need a statement,' he'd told Diana abruptly, hiding a welter of feeling behind his official self. 'So if you would accompany us…?'

The journey to West End Central had been extraordinary, too. In the car (PC Eliot had taken Diana in a separate vehicle) Backhouse had started rabbiting on about his health as though Stratton were a doctor or something—fibrositis and enteritis and hospital and a nervous breakdown caused by persecution from the coloured tenants at Paradise Street—and he'd listened, incredulous, his mind reeling. Clearly, Backhouse wanted—perhaps even expected—his sympathy, or at least his understanding. But what the hell had Diana, of all people, been doing with him?

'Where did you meet Mrs Carleton?' he asked, cutting across Backhouse's whispered, carefully enunciated confidences about his diarrhoea and how he'd left his medicine in his suitcase at the Rowton House at King's Cross.

Backhouse swallowed. 'In the park. Green Park. We were just having a cup of tea together. I'm afraid, Inspector, that she wanted me to…' He cleared his throat. 'Well, she was making suggestions. She wanted me to go away with her…'

Sensing Stratton's outrage, Backhouse fell silent for a moment and then, as if unable to help himself, continued, 'Of course, I told her I wasn't interested in anything of that sort—'

'If I were you,' Stratton said, 'I'd keep my mouth shut until we get to the station. Otherwise…' He jerked the wrist that was cuffed to Backhouse's. 'Understand?'

Backhouse pushed his lips into an 'o' and moistened them with the tip of his tongue. 'Yes,' he whispered. 'Yes, of course.'

Stratton stared fixedly ahead. There'd be hours of this to come—unctuous, self-serving hypocrisy—but he was buggered if he was going to listen to it now, especially if it involved lies about Diana. Just occupying the same space as the snivelling little sod was nauseating enough. Ballard must have left a message by now, he thought. Surely the girl Anne must know something...

'There's something, Inspector, it's about my wife...'

Stratton clenched his free fist. 'I've warned you, Backhouse. No more until you're at the station.'

'But I'd like you to know, Inspector.' Backhouse blinked at him. He seemed to know that there wasn't anything Stratton could do to him in the car, no matter how much he wanted to. Stratton saw the driver's shoulders stiffening, and every single sinew of his own body seemed to throb with the desire to throttle the man. 'She was suffering so much, and I couldn't bear to see it... I didn't want to be separated from her, Inspector. That's why I put her under the floorboards in the bedroom, to keep her with me... I wanted her to be near me, you see.'

He thinks he's showing me what a loving husband he was, thought Stratton, revolted. Wound now to breaking point, he snapped. 'If you're so keen to talk, *Norman*,' he said, 'tell me this. When did you fuck them? Was it before or after you murdered them? Prefer a cold fuck, do you, *Norman*? A tart without a pulse? Why don't you tell me about that?'

The rest of the journey took place in silence. Backhouse having been removed to the cells at West End Central—'I'll deal with him later,' Stratton had growled at the officer in charge, 'just get him out of my sight before I do something I'll regret'—the desk sergeant appeared with a message. 'From Sergeant Ballard, sir. Came in half an hour ago. We knew you were on your way, so... He said you'd know what it was about, sir.'

Informant unwilling but eventually persuaded to talk, Stratton read. *Following lead Camden Town. Have alerted station there. Will call back soonest.* That was something, at least, he thought. Firmly suppressing any speculation about what might be happening to Monica if Ballard—or the local constabulary—had failed to get there in time, he made arrangements for Backhouse's suitcase to be retrieved from the doss house in King's Cross and transferred to the police laboratory. There is nothing I can do for Monica, he told himself. Ballard was a good man—the best—and could be trusted to look after his daughter and handle things at the Camden Town station with discretion. All he could do was wait for news of Monica and for Diana to arrive. Telling the desk sergeant to let him know immediately if Ballard telephoned again, he went to the office, which proved to be full of jubilant coppers waiting to slap him on the back. There was even a message of congratulation from DCI Lamb.

Excusing himself as soon as he decently could, he made for the lavatory which, thank God, was empty. Finding coherent thought impossible, he settled for pacing up and down in front of the row of basins, trying to blot out the hideous carousel of images—Monica, Backhouse, Davies, cupboards full of corpses, soil planted with bones and teeth, stains of decomposition on clothing and bedding, and the filthy deckchair with its canvas of knotted rope—that went round and round inside his head.

Diana, dishevelled and exhausted, was slumped over a cup of tea in the interview room. She was thinner, Stratton thought, as he sat down opposite her, and, under the harsh light of the single bare bulb, her expression seemed somehow harder and more vulnerable at the same time, the cheekbones sharply angular and the enormous eyes bruised with tiredness. 'PC Eliot explained everything to me,' she said, before he could speak. 'He said you probably saved my life.'

'I think that's putting it a bit strongly,' said Stratton, embarrassed. 'I'm sure,' he added, 'you wouldn't have placed yourself in that sort of danger.' As he spoke, he realised that he wasn't sure of any such thing—Diana had put herself in danger before, with Ventriss, hadn't she? And she'd seemed so helpless, so bloody *passive*, when he'd warned her about the man, unwilling or unable—perhaps both—to protect herself. Remembering his visit to her former landlady and his feeling of outrage at the woman's implication that Diana was some sort of whore, he thought, surely she couldn't have sunk so low? People did change, but not *that* much... Still, there was clearly a lot more to it than met the eye.

'Those women,' said Diana, as if she'd guessed what he was thinking, 'the ones he killed, they were prostitutes, weren't they?'

Unable to look at her, Stratton said, 'Most of them. One was his wife. That man,' he said, in a lighter tone, 'makes Claude Ventriss look like an angel of mercy.' He felt, rather than saw, Diana's head jerk back as though she'd been slapped in the face, and wished he hadn't spoken. It wasn't fair, and certainly not chivalrous, to remind her of what he knew. Ashamed, he busied himself patting his pockets for his cigarettes. When he raised his eyes to hers again she was sitting upright, and—despite the dereliction of hair and make-up—was once more recognisable as the well-bred, expensive product of deportment lessons and finishing school that he'd first met thirteen years earlier.

'PC Eliot said you wanted to see me,' she said coldly. 'Why was that?'

'It's about Monica,' said Stratton. Now that she was here, in front of him, the whole thing seemed absurd, but he felt that some sort of explanation, however lame, was in order. 'My daughter. I know you both worked at Ashwood—she mentioned you. She's in some trouble, and I thought you might know...'

Diana was shaking her head. 'I haven't seen Monica since I stopped working at the studio. Didn't...' She stopped, the veneer cracking. 'I mean... Oh, dear. I suppose PC Eliot must have told you what happened.'

'Yes. Your husband.' Stratton tried momentarily to think of something adequately comforting to say, failed, and settled for, 'I'm very sorry, Mrs Carleton. If there's anything—'

'Diana, please. We're a bit past Mrs Carleton now, aren't we? What's happened to Monica?'

'She's pregnant. The man's married; and she...well, she's run off, and I'm worried she might have done something stupid. I had an idea she might have...well, she mentioned you on a number of occasions, and I thought—'

Two hard blotches of colour had appeared on Diana's pale cheeks. 'You thought that I might have helped her arrange a backstreet abortion without your knowledge? I can well imagine what you must think of me, Inspector Stratton, but I can assure you I have done nothing of the sort.'

'Please...' Stratton's face felt as though it were on fire. 'I'm very worried about her, and I just... I didn't know what to think. My sergeant's gone to see if he can find her—she seems to have gone to see someone in Camden Town—and I'd be there myself, but it seemed like a bit of a long shot and... Well, I'm sorry. I'll find someone to take your statement, and then you're free to—'

'No, please!' Diana cried out, and Stratton stared at her, disconcerted by the sudden change of tone. He felt a sudden bond with her—both wretched, both unhappy in their different ways, both uncertain of the future. 'Please,' she said, 'I'm the one who should be sorry, not you. It was a perfectly fair question, and I shouldn't have reared up like that. You must be out of your mind with worry. Why don't you stay here? Unless you've got other things to do, of course—but you could take my statement about that man. Mr...'

'Backhouse.'

'Backhouse? He told me his name was Davies.'

'Did he, indeed?' said Stratton, grimly.

'Yes. If I tell you about him, it might help to take your mind off things, at least until your sergeant's got—'

A rap on the door heralded the desk sergeant. 'Call for you, sir—Sergeant Ballard. Will you take it in the office?'

'Sorry I've been so long, sir, but it was like pulling teeth. That girl was—'

'What's happened?'

'Well, I managed to prise the information out of her eventually, and I told the Camden lot—they were at the place by the time I arrived, and they'd talked to the woman. Turned out Monica had been there, but she'd changed her mind. The woman didn't know where she'd gone—said she went out of the room, and by the time she came back Monica had disappeared.

I persuaded them to let her off with a warning, but they'll be keeping an eye on her from now on. They've no idea it was a…a personal matter…so there's no need to worry on that score. Do you think Monica might have gone home, sir?'

'I'll telephone my sister-in-law—she lives down the road from us, so somebody can keep an eye out. Where are you?'

'Camden Town Police Station.'

'You'd better get along home, then. Rather a lot's been happening—we've got Backhouse.'

'That *is* good news, sir. How—'

'Tell you tomorrow. It was a fluke, really, but still…'

'Ted? We've been frantic trying to get hold of you—she's here. Walked in about twenty minutes ago.'

'Thank God for that. Is she all right?'

'I don't know about that. She's exhausted, poor thing, but she's safe, and that's what matters.'

'Yes…My sergeant tracked down that Anne girl Madeleine mentioned and found out where she was going. Where is she now?'

'I put her to bed on the couch, and Madeleine's getting her some hot milk.'

'Can I talk to her?'

There was a moment's hesitation, and Stratton could hear the sigh of his sister-in-law's breath coming down the line. Then she said, 'I don't think that's a good idea, Ted. She's upset enough as it is.'

'I don't want to upset her, just to tell her…' Stratton ground to a halt, a lump the size of a boulder in his throat. There was a whole mountain of things that needed saying, and he had no idea where, or how, to start. There didn't even seem to be words for most of it. 'Give her my love,' he said, finally. 'Tell her to get some sleep, and I'll see her tomorrow evening. And tell her that everything's going to be all right, and I'm glad she's home.'

Stratton replaced the receiver and sat back in his chair, weak with relief. He wanted to be with Monica now, to hug her and make her laugh and see her roll her eyes and say, in exasperated fondness, 'Oh, *Da-ad*!' and feel the unspoken bond between them like a tug on a wire that encircled his heart. At that moment, he felt an actual pain in his chest, although whether it was from emotion, release of tension, or merely slight indigestion, he couldn't have said. He was going to be a grandfather. No good—that wasn't, yet, comprehensible. He'd have to wait a bit for it to sink in—but, right at the moment, all that mattered was that his precious daughter was out of harm's way. He sat, smiling foolishly into space, for several minutes, before the memory of Davies's words, *When I knew my daughter was dead I had nothing to live for,* snapped him out of it as if cold water had been hurled in his face.

As he made his way back to the interview room, it occurred to him that he hadn't said thank you to Ballard. No matter. Such things were better done face to face—and if that didn't merit standing the man a drink, he didn't know what did. And perhaps he could help Diana, too… Straightening his back and thrusting out his chest, he pushed open the door.

'Forgive me.' Diana indicated the cigarette in her hand. 'I took one from your packet. I hope you don't mind.'

'Not at all. I'll join you.' Grinning, Stratton sat down and lit one for himself.

Seeing his expression, Diana said 'Monica… It's good news, is it? You've found her?'

'Not me, my sergeant. She's safe.'

'So she didn't…'

'She changed her mind. She's back home—that is, she's at my sister-in-law's.'

'She told me about your poor wife. It must have been terrible for you.' Diana gazed at him, eyes luminous with sympathy, and shook her head. 'It's… Well, one doesn't know what to say, really.'

'Yes…' Stratton didn't know what to say, either—he never had and knew he never would. It was yet another thing for which no words were adequate. Not wishing to pursue it, he produced his notebook and pencil and said, 'Well, let's get on with your statement, shall we?'

For a moment, Diana looked bewildered by his change of tack, then said, 'Yes, yes, of course. But really, I don't know how much help I can be.'

'You've been a lot of help already,' said Stratton. 'I found Backhouse when I was looking for you. There has,' he added gently, 'been a nationwide hunt for him, you know.'

'I'm afraid I didn't. I haven't been reading the papers recently—at least, apart from the obituaries.'

'I understand. Look...*Diana*...' Her answering smile told him that using her Christian name was not only acceptable but desirable and, reassured, he continued, 'When we're finished, do you have anywhere to go? Eliot said you spent last night in a women's hostel at Victoria.'

'That's right.'

Stratton made a sympathetic grimace. 'Not very nice, I shouldn't have thought. There must be somebody you can stay with,' he said. 'Someone who can help. If you give me a name, I'm sure we can arrange—'

'I don't think I can face going back there,' said Diana in a small voice.

'I'm not surprised. So, who should we telephone?'

'It's difficult. Lally—Mrs Anderson—she's an old friend, but we've rather fallen out. My fault, of course—she and her husband have been very kind to me, and I'm afraid I've rather thrown it in their faces...'

Diana recounted the events of their night at Ciro's. When she reached the part about meeting Claude Ventriss, Stratton felt a jolt of sheer rage shoot through him. 'He spent the night at my flat,' she said, miserably. 'He'd gone when I woke up. He'd left me,' she added, in a hard, self-mocking voice, 'a five pound note, but my landlady took it...Tell me, is that the going rate?'

Stratton stared at her, aghast. 'Diana...But your husband... I don't understand.'

'James and I had already parted company,' said Diana. 'Thank you for not saying "I told you so".'

'I'd never... I mean, it's not my business.'

'I suppose not. But whatever you're thinking about me, you're right.'

Stratton began to deny this, but she cut him off. 'I can see it in your face. I don't blame you.'

'We all make mistakes,' said Stratton helplessly. 'I do. Everyone does.'

'Well, it's fairly put the kibosh on my friendship with Lally.'

'I'm sure that's not the case,' said Stratton. 'Does she live nearby?'

'Albemarle Street. But I couldn't bear—'

'Why don't you let me speak to her? I'm sure she'll understand. I imagine that they will have read about your husband in the papers.'

Diana sighed. 'I suppose I've got nothing to lose…'

'Good. Now, let's have that statement, shall we?'

'Can I ask you something before we start?'

'Fire away.'

'It was something he said—Backhouse, I mean. When I told him I'd only found out from the papers about James, I said I was going to go to the police to find out what had happened to him—to his body—and he said they wouldn't tell me anything before they'd done medical tests on him.'

'That's nonsense. It was an accident, wasn't it?'

Diana stared at him, surprised. 'How do you know?'

'PC Eliot told me. He was quite worried about you.'

'Oh, I see… He was very kind to me, although he must have thought I was mad or something. And,' she added, ruefully, 'I suppose he was right to think that.' With a painful little laugh, she continued, 'I don't think I know who I am any more. Perhaps I never did know… Anyway—' Pulling herself together with a shake that seemed to Stratton to signal the end of the subject, she said, 'James was run over.'

'And you read this in yesterday's paper, did, you?' Diana nodded. 'Do you know where it happened?'

'It didn't say. But the last time I saw him was in Brighton.'

'The seaside?' Stratton was surprised. 'Was he making a film there?'

'No. He hadn't had any work for a while. He…Well, he drank, you see. I didn't realise at first, but then it got worse—

so bad that no one would employ him. We'd gone to Brighton because he thought, with a change of scene, that things might be better.'

'But they weren't?'

Diana shook her head. 'It was somewhere he'd been happy—he'd had holidays there as a child—but it didn't work. I told him I couldn't go on as we were, and he told me to leave him, to…to save myself, I suppose he meant. Then he said he loved me, and…well, that was it, really.'

'But he loved the bottle more,' said Stratton, as gently as he could.

'Yes,' said Diana sadly. 'That's what it boiled down to, in the end. It was like a disease,' she added, defensively. 'He couldn't help it.'

Stratton wasn't at all sure about this, but he didn't challenge it. Instead, he stood up and went to the door. 'I'll ask someone to find out where he is,' he said. 'Far from not telling you anything, the police will be trying to locate you. Backhouse—for obvious reasons—didn't want you going anywhere near us.'

The woman's a magnet for unsuitable men, Stratton thought, impatient with Diana for her recklessness and almost morbid inertia in the face of certain trouble and impatient with himself for his attraction to her. Not that he was any more suitable than either Ventriss or Carleton, but he, at least, would neither treat her like a prostitute nor succumb to alcoholism. That's probably, he thought sourly, why she'd never even look at me. She wouldn't anyway, he told himself. *He* wasn't a glamorous spy or a film director, was he? But if she could not, or would not, fit into the life that society prescribed for her, then why not? That was the only way he'd ever stand a chance. And, even tired and unkempt, she was still the loveliest thing he'd ever seen… But she'd made herself a victim, hadn't she? She was no different to poor, pathetic John Davies.

It struck him then, so forcefully that he stopped in the middle of the corridor, that whatever she might say, she still had her sense of herself and her courage. Look at the way she'd stood up to him over Monica! She'd made him feel about an inch high. In any case, who was he to judge her? It wasn't her fault he'd stuck her up on a pedestal. She was just another poor devil of a human being doing her limited best—and she'd just lost her husband, for Christ's sake. He was being a bloody fool.

Jock Anderson's handshake was perfunctory. Stratton had spoken to him after taking Diana's statement and, while he didn't sound exactly enthusiastic, he'd agreed, after listening to a summary of events, to collect her from West End Central. Now, standing at the station door, he said, 'We read about Carleton's death. My wife has been trying to contact Mrs Carleton. We went to the place where she was living, but we were told she'd left.'

'She was wandering about,' said Stratton. 'She's still in a stage of shock.'

Anderson nodded curtly. 'We'll manage.'

'I realise that,' said Stratton, curt in his turn. 'If there is anything I can do, I'd be more than happy—'

'That's very kind of you, but I can't imagine…' Anderson allowed the rest of the sentence to hang in the air, leaving Stratton with no doubt that he'd overstepped the mark. He watched as Anderson greeted Diana, who was sitting on a bench in the lobby, huddled inside her fur coat. He raised his hand in a valedictory gesture as they passed, intending to leave it at that, but Diana broke away from Anderson, and, standing before him, held out her hand. 'Thank you,' she said, her voice cracking. 'I don't know what I'd have done…Edward…thank you so much.'

Surprised that she'd remembered his name, Stratton took a step back.

'Aren't you going to shake hands with me?' she asked.

'Yes. Yes, of course…'

Retaining his hand in both of hers, Diana said, 'Colonel Forbes-James… I don't know if you know, but he died.'

Confused, Stratton shook his head.

'He left me a letter. He said if I was ever in trouble, I should contact you. He said you would help me...that you are a good man.'

His throat seeming to have sealed itself up in astonishment, Stratton merely nodded, staring at her. The liquid eyes, soft pink lips and blonde hair appeared to float before him in a sort of nimbus. Catching his breath, he said, 'Diana...if there's anything I can do, anything at all, please...I'd be delighted...' He stopped, realising he must sound like a fool.

'Thank you, Edward.'

Releasing his hand, she turned away and went to Anderson, heels clicking across the stone floor. As she walked through the door and away down the steps, Stratton felt as though he were watching her pass through a veil and into another world.

CHAPTER 70

'She was choking. I tried to help her, but it wasn't any good. Her face was blue. I couldn't bear to see her like that… I had to tie a stocking round her neck and put her to sleep.'

As though Edna Backhouse were an animal, Stratton thought in disgust. He watched Backhouse flick a speck of dust from his lapel with a fastidious movement of his thumb and finger and fought the urge to lunge across the table and swat his hand down. He could see, from the tight set of Ballard's jaw as he bent over his notebook, that he was experiencing something similar.

'You didn't think of calling an ambulance?'

'It was too late for that, Inspector. I could see that. She was convulsing—that's the medical term, of course. I saw the empty bottle afterwards. Phenobarbitone. The doctor had given them to me because I couldn't sleep from all the trouble with the coloureds upstairs, but I'd only taken two, so she must have had the rest. An overdose—'

'There were no drugs found in your wife's body, Mr Backhouse.'

'Well, she'd taken them. I acted out of mercy, Inspector.'

Pull the other one, thought Stratton, it's got bells on. 'And what did you do after that?' he asked.

'I left her in bed for...' Backhouse paused to consider. 'Two days, I think, or three, because I didn't know what to do. Such a shock.' Here, his eyes widened and his mouth trembled slightly.

What does he expect, thought Stratton. Sympathy? Narrowing his own eyes to show that none was forthcoming, he said, 'Go on.'

'It must have been then that I remembered the loose floorboards. I knew there was a space underneath so I took them up. I put her in a blanket and I tried to carry her over there, but she was too heavy, and with my fibrositis...' Backhouse paused, shaking his head and then ducking it as if remembering a trial bravely borne.

'Never mind your fibrositis,' said Stratton. 'Get on with it.'

'Well, in the end I had to half-carry and half-drag her, and I put her in there and covered her with some earth. I felt,' he added sententiously, 'that it was the best way to lay her to rest.'

Stratton glanced at Ballard, and saw that the sergeant was looking as if he might be sick. If you're determined to keep playing it that way, Sunny Jim, he thought, let's just see how you explain the tarts, shall we?

'We have identified the three bodies found in the alcove at your former home as Iris Manning, Kathleen McKinnon, and Mary Dwyer,' he said. 'Can you tell us about them?'

Backhouse frowned and took off his spectacles, rubbing his forehead and pinching the top of his nose, giving the impression of one valiantly trying to solve a problem that was not of his making. 'I'll help you if I can, Inspector,' he said. 'It's hard to keep it straight in my mind.'

'Let *me* help *you*,' said Stratton. 'You killed those women and you're going to tell us how you did it. So, the first one, Miss Manning?'

Backhouse repeated the head-rubbing, nose-pinching, you-know-I'm-trying-to-help-you act. 'If you say that they were in my flat,' he said, 'then I suppose I must have had something to do with it.' Resting his arms on the table, he frowned thoughtfully. Then, seeing that this was making no impression on his stony-faced audience, he said, 'I believe...yes, that's it. I met her in a café by the station. She must have come up to me... I think she asked me for a cigarette and then started a conversation. She mentioned that she had nowhere to live. It was some story about a friend who'd let her down—I can't remember the details.' Backhouse ran his tongue over his lips. 'I'm not sure... I must have mentioned that I was thinking of moving, because she asked if she could see my flat. She wanted to come that evening and have a look—that was her suggestion. I said that would be all right...' Backhouse tailed off and his eyes darted furtively round the room as if seeking something.

'And then...?' prompted Stratton.

'Well, she came along. We had a cup of tea together... That's right. A little cup of tea.' He indicated the littleness of the tea with his hand, accompanying it with a small, tight smile. 'She said she'd like to take the flat. I said that was up to the landlord, he'd have to give his permission. She asked me if she could stay for a few days until it was sorted out. She indicated—said to me—that we could have sexual intercourse if I put in a good word for her about the flat. Well...' Backhouse leant forward, an expression of theatrically outraged horror on his face. 'I told her that sort of thing didn't interest me. She got into quite a temper when she saw there was nothing doing and said I was accusing her of things, all sorts of stuff. I told her she was talking a lot of nonsense and asked her to leave, but she wouldn't. I got hold of her arm and tried to lead her out of the kitchen, but she started struggling and then....then...' Backhouse's voice had sunk to a whisper. After swallowing several times and fingering his collar, he continued, 'It seemed that she was on the floor at one point... I don't know—there was something...it's in the back of my mind. A picture, but I'm not sure... Perhaps it'll come back to me. If it does,' he added, ingratiatingly, 'I shall tell you straight away.'

'Iris Manning was six months pregnant,' said Stratton. 'Did you know that?'

Backhouse made the odd sucking movement with his mouth that Stratton remembered from before. 'That is unfortunate. *Most* regrettable.' It was obvious to Stratton that what was regrettable to Backhouse was the fact that Manning was unmarried, not that he'd murdered both her and her unborn child.

'Did you offer your services as an abortionist?'

Backhouse blinked at him, his mouth silently framing words as if trying them out, then shook his head sadly and whispered, 'Oh, no... As I told you, Inspector, I don't know about that sort of thing.'

Stratton contented himself with raising his eyebrows in disbelief. 'We'll come back to that in due course,' he said. 'Tell us about Kathleen McKinnon.'

Backhouse looked puzzled. 'Kathleen McKinnon,' repeated Stratton, glancing down at his notebook. 'Five feet three inches in height, brown hair, brown eyes, full lips... Quite a looker—when she was alive, that is. Before she became the second body in your alcove. Didn't you know her name?'

'I don't think...' Backhouse shook his head. 'No. She didn't introduce herself.'

Give me strength, thought Stratton, closing his eyes momentarily. Anyone would think they were talking about a fucking garden party. 'That was her name,' he said. 'Kathleen McKinnon.'

'She came up to me in the street,' said Backhouse. 'I'd gone to get some fish and chips for my dog and cat...' He must have seen the look of puzzlement cross Stratton's face, because he said, 'A tabby cat. I was very fond of her.' Remembering the animal he'd seen in the garden the night they'd found Muriel and the baby, Stratton nodded for him to continue.

'I was on my way home when the woman—McKinnon, you said—came up and propositioned me. I could see,' he added, reprovingly, 'that she was drunk. I don't like that sort of thing.' He paused, looking from Stratton to Ballard as if expecting agreement that they didn't like that sort of thing, either.

'I was annoyed, Inspector. I'm well known in the area and I didn't want a scene. She wanted a pound for me to take her round the corner. I told her I wasn't interested, and she began threatening me.' The upright citizen act all over again, thought Stratton, wearily. 'She followed me home, shouting at the top of her voice, and the whole thing was most unpleasant. She forced her way into the house and started fighting. I remember she picked up a frying pan and tried to hit me with it, so I got hold of her… There was quite a struggle, and she kept shouting that she'd get the police down to me. I must have pushed her at some point, because there's an impression in my mind that she fell onto the deckchair. There was a piece of rope—I suppose it must have been on the chair, but I'm not sure… I'm finding this very difficult, Inspector.' He paused; this time, Stratton thought, in search of sympathy. He stared, trying to keep his face impassive as Backhouse polished his glasses and fussed with his handkerchief. The precise fastidiousness of the man's movements enraged him.

'How did you kill her?'

Backhouse opened his mouth and put his hand up to his throat as if trying to force sound from it. 'I don't remember,' he whispered. 'I must have gone haywire. The next thing I remember, she was lying on the chair with the rope round her neck. I must have put her in the alcove, because then I made a cup of tea for myself and fed the animals.'

'Did you gas the women before you killed them?'

'Gas?' Backhouse looked perplexed.

'Their blood samples contained carbon monoxide,' said Stratton. 'All three of them.'

'Well, if…Yes, I suppose I must have. It's not clear in my mind.'

'You're telling us you don't remember, are you?'

'Yes. I'm not sure. If it comes back to me…'

'Poor Mr Backhouse,' said Ballard, when they stopped for lunch. 'Just think, all those dirty women throwing themselves at him.'

'Most regrettable,' mimicked Stratton. 'And him so virtuous. Course, he couldn't say that about a respectable woman like his wife, so it had to be a mercy killing...but, do you know, I think he believes it.'

Ballard looked surprised. 'Really, sir?'

'Well...' Stratton picked up his sandwich, which was beginning to curl at the edges, inspected it closely, then, disheartened, returned it to the plate. 'In a way, I do. He wants to be on our side, doesn't he? Former police reservist, pillar of the local community and all that. That's how he sees himself. He doesn't want to remember how he gassed and strangled those women because he doesn't want to lose his self-respect. Oh, I don't know. I'm not a trick cyclist, but that's how it seems to me... It's the way he talks about it, as if it doesn't have anything to do with him... What was it, "an impression that she was in the deckchair", or something like that?'

'Yes.' Ballard consulted his notebook. 'And when he was talking about Manning he said, "It seemed that she was on the floor." As if he were watching it happen.'

'And he didn't admit to gassing them. Or ravishing them.'

'Hardly that, sir. I mean, if they were toms, they probably agreed to it. The sex bit, anyway.'

'That's true. We'll leave the gassing for later, once he's been remanded. I've got a fair idea his account of killing Dwyer is going to be more of the same—all her fault.'

'I wonder why he killed his wife,' said Ballard. 'I mean, if she knew about Muriel Davies, why wait so long? Unless she'd found out, somehow, and was threatening to tell us.'

'Or perhaps he just wanted her out of the way. I don't think she'd have come to us even if she had suspected. Too much under his thumb.'

'She can't have had much of a life, poor woman. Remember the neighbour? She made it sound as if watching *Andy Pandy* was the high spot of her week.'

'That neighbour told us she was scared of the black tenants, didn't she? Perhaps she'd got so fed up she told Backhouse she was going back up north to wherever it was—she'd already done it once, remember, before the war. Maybe he thought that if she was with her family she might start talking about what she suspected.'

'Or perhaps she'd taken to digging in the garden.'

'You know, I still don't understand about that bloody dog... God, you can just imagine it, can't you? Nice cosy scene, him feeding his pets with fish and chips and a dead tart still warm in the cupboard not three feet away.'

'I've been trying not to, sir.' Ballard pushed his plate from him. But for a single bite, his sandwich was untouched.

'Not hungry?'

Ballard shook his head, then shuddered. 'He makes me feel sick. Have you noticed, sir, that when it's something he doesn't mind talking about his voice is quite normal, but when you ask him a question he doesn't want to answer he goes all whispery?'

'Yes...' Stratton considered this. 'You're right. So much for the old war wound. I suppose he must have done the same when he was in court, only we never cottoned onto it.'

'Can't remember, sir. I remember him bursting into tears though, straight after.'

'Relief, I suppose. He'd got away with it, hadn't he?'

'I was thinking about that, sir. About six months ago, I was down at Pentonville—one of those safe-breakers, I think it was—and one of the warders I spoke to had been in the cell with Davies when they told him the appeal had failed. They'd been playing cards, and this bloke said that he just stared at the governor for a minute and then sat down to get on with the game. Said he wondered afterwards if Davies understood what the governor was telling him. Made me wonder how much he'd understood at all. That's not to say,' he added hastily, 'that he didn't do it, of course, but—'

'But it's not very likely, is it? That'll depend on what Backhouse has to tell us. I thought I'd leave it till last. I'd say that when he learns how much we know, he might be more likely to confess. I get the impression that he's not going to tell us anything he doesn't have to—all that stuff about wanting to help but not being able to remember. He isn't stupid…'

The words 'unlike Davies' hovered, unspoken, in the air between them, until Ballard said, 'Still fancies himself with the medical stuff, doesn't he, sir?'

'When it suits him. He's strangely unforthcoming on the matter of backstreet abortions… Look, changing the subject for a moment, I still haven't thanked you properly for what you did last night.'

'It's nothing, sir.' The tips of the sergeant's ears had gone faintly pink. 'I hope Monica's recovered.' Apart from a brief exchange that morning, when Stratton explained that Monica was safely home, they hadn't had time to discuss it. Lamb had insisted that Stratton speak to the press, which he hated. There were policemen who'd speak to the newspapers at any opportunity, but he'd never been one of them. It was too much like showing off, and, in any case, journalists were better kept at arm's length. Besides which, they seemed to regard it as a foregone conclusion that Davies was innocent and had asked a lot of questions that he was in no position to answer. He'd hardly covered himself in glory, but Lamb was so relieved that Backhouse had been caught that Stratton reckoned he'd have forgiven him if he'd recited 'Humpty Dumpty'.

'She's fine,' said Stratton. 'I hope that…' he stalled, realising that he had no idea what former Policewoman Gaines's Christian name was, 'your wife—'

'Pauline, sir.'

'Pauline wasn't too put out.'

'She understood, sir. If it had been Katy…'

Seeking to display some degree of knowledge about—and therefore interest in—Ballard's family, Stratton said, 'Walking now, is she?'

Ballard grinned. 'Walking, talking, the lot. She's three, sir.'

'Yes, of course, she would be. I wasn't thinking.'

'Actually, we've got another on the way. Only a few months, now.'

'Congratulations. Another reason for me to buy you a drink when all this is over.'

As Stratton had suspected, it was more self-justification over Mary Dwyer—this time, her clothes had become caught around her neck in the struggle. After that, they got onto the two skeletons in the garden. Backhouse confirmed that the women had been killed sometime in forty-three or forty-four while Edna was staying with her family in Sheffield. His account of the first, whom he remembered as being called Else Kircher or Kirchner, an Austrian—which explained the foreign fillings in the teeth—was markedly similar to his stories about the other prostitutes. The second—who turned out, as Ballard had suspected, to be May Drinkwater—obviously caused him more of a problem because, not being a whore, he couldn't claim that she'd thrown herself at him. Instead, he recounted a story about luring her to the house on the pretext of treating her catarrh and getting her to inhale a mixture of Friar's Balsam and gas.

'I may have had intercourse at that time, but I'm not sure,' he finished, frowning. 'Or it might have been the other one. I can't remember...'

How very convenient, thought Stratton. Hard on the heels of this came the thought that it was entirely possible that a man like Backhouse might *not* remember—at least, not clearly. His desires gratified, he'd dispose of the bodies and go on to the next... It occurred to him then, that for all Backhouse's greater intelligence, he had just as little thought for the consequences of his actions as had Davies. 'Were there others during that period?' he asked.

'Others?' came the whisper.

'Other women you killed at that time?'

Backhouse looked momentarily thoughtful, then said, 'I don't think so. That is, I can't remember. If you say I did, then...'

In other words, thought Stratton, produce the evidence. 'We found your souvenirs,' he said. 'A tobacco tin with four samples of pubic hair. Now, assuming you didn't go around asking *living* women to help you with your collection'—Backhouse looked outraged at this idea—'then you must have taken them from *dead* women. Women you'd killed. A little something to remember them by, was it?' Stratton deliberately kept his tone conversational as if asking a perfectly reasonable question. 'Those tender moments when you put a stocking round their necks *and strangled them and fucked them while you were doing it?*'

The eyes glittered for a moment behind the glasses, and then Backhouse put his head into his hands. His shoulders heaved, and a snorting noise told Stratton that he was crying. 'There's something,' he spluttered, 'but I can't get it. It's forming a picture and then my head hurts and it gets all jumbled up again. It doesn't get clear, but there's something...'

'I'll say there is,' said Stratton, ignoring the tears. 'There's Muriel Davies.'

Backhouse sat up straight. Staring at Stratton, eyes wet and blurry behind the glasses, he seemed suddenly soft-bodied as if, boneless, he'd assumed the shape of his chair.

'Muriel?'

'Yes,' snapped Stratton. 'Muriel. Muriel Davies. Don't tell me you've forgotten *her*. And for God's sake, speak up.'

Backhouse cleared his throat. 'There is something in my mind,' he said, hesitantly, 'about Mrs Davies, but I can't quite remember...'

'If he tells us he can't remember once more,' said Stratton, 'I'm going to knock his block off.'

'I know what you mean, sir.' The report having arrived from the police lab, they'd adjourned and were sitting in the office.

'The ones in the garden, fair enough,' said Stratton. 'It was a while ago. But he bloody well *does* remember about Muriel Davies. In fact, Mrs Carleton said that he was about to show her an old newspaper cutting about a court case he'd been involved in, but then he changed his mind. Was it with his clothes when he came in?'

'They're checking them now, sir. I'll find out.'

'He told her he'd been a witness. And he told her that his name was Davies, too.' Mentioning Diana, Stratton was aware of concentrating on negative things like not turning red or spilling his tea.

'She was the one with him when you found him, wasn't she?' Ballard, who didn't seem to have noticed anything amiss, spoke in a neutral tone.

'That's right.' Stratton did not enlarge on this. His feelings were too confused to enunciate, and besides, as far as Diana was concerned, he didn't want to make himself feel even more of a fool than he did already. 'You know,' he said, partly to change the subject and partly because he was genuinely puzzled, 'I don't see how he could have gassed those women. May Drinkwater, fair enough—he said he'd got some sort of device, didn't he? Presumably he put it over her nose and she let him because she thought it was going to help with the catarrh. But with the others, how did he persuade them? If he'd just left the tap open, he'd have been overcome himself, wouldn't he?'

'Perhaps if he'd opened a window…'

'But then the gas would have been dispelled. And surely they'd have smelt a rat if he'd suddenly stuck his head out of the window—unless he'd made some excuse, I suppose. But it's a bit odd.'

'Perhaps he persuaded them as some sort of game. We found tubing in the flat, remember, sir?'

'Well, he certainly didn't tie them up—there weren't any marks.'

'Mary Dwyer had her wrists tied in front of her with a handkerchief—*that* could have been part of a game—and McKinnon must have been pretty drunk, judging by the lab reports, so perhaps she didn't realise what was happening to her.'

'And Iris Manning was pregnant,' concluded Stratton. 'Backhouse denied offering to help her get rid of the baby, but if he had, he might have said the gas was to knock her out while he did it. That makes sense.'

'He might have done that to Muriel Davies too, sir.'

'It's possible. We didn't find anything like that device he mentioned, but he could easily have thrown it away.'

Stratton pondered this for a moment before Ballard spoke again. 'Last night, sir, when you telephoned, you said you were going to follow someone up… Did you find them, sir?' The sergeant's gaze was so penetrating that, for a horrible moment, Stratton thought the man must be clairvoyant and connected this to his earlier comments about Diana's statement.

'No,' he said. 'I had an idea they'd be somewhere near Victoria, but…' He shrugged, hoping it looked realistically offhand. 'Anyway, turns out it didn't matter.'

Ballard looked at him carefully, a bit too much like a man who realised he'd been warned off for Stratton's liking, but all he said was, 'True enough, sir,' then bent his head to the pile of paper in front of him. 'There's a whole list of stuff from the suitcase we fetched from the Rowton House at King's Cross, sir. Ration books—his wife's as well—identity card, ticket for the doss house, seven nights' accommodation... That's interesting. When Canning went to fetch the case they told him that he'd only stayed for one.'

'Probably wandering about trying to pick up women,' said Stratton. 'What else?'

'Rent book for Paradise Street, marriage certificate, three pawn tickets, St John's Ambulance badge, two first-aid certificates, gloves, scarf, handkerchief—all the usual men's clothes, and there's women's stuff here, too. Nightdress, petticoat, necklace, lipstick...

'Mrs Carleton said he'd offered her some clothes. Said they'd belonged to his wife.'

'Charming. There's a whole list of medicines, too.'

'There would be.'

Ballard leafed through the pages. 'Lab report's right at the end, sir. Blimey...'

'What is it?'

' "I have examined package no. 4,' read Ballard 'and found on the trousers an area of seminal staining containing spermatozoa on the inside of the right fly opening near the bottom... spot of seminal staining on the lining of the left pocket... On the front flap of the shirt there are extensive areas of staining, semen containing spermatozoa was identified... On the vest there was an area of old staining with semen, the other vest shows comparatively extensive areas of staining... On another pair of trousers... On the plimsolls there were found some spots and smears of seminal staining..." '

'All right,' said Stratton, utterly revolted. 'I've got the picture. Is there anything else?'

' "Awaiting the clothes worn by Backhouse on arrest..." '

'They'll probably be covered in wank-stains as well.'

'...and the comparisons with the samples found in the women show that it's possible they could be from the same source.'

'Anything on the pubic hair?'

'It's a bit inconclusive, sir. It says here, "It should be pointed out that while it is possible to say that two samples of hair are dissimilar, it is not possible to say that a sample of normal hair must have come from the same source, since the range of structural and colour variations of human hair is limited, and there are millions of people having hair within this range of variation."'

Stratton sighed. 'Tell us something we don't know. Any similarities then?'

Ballard frowned. 'It says that one of them might be from Mrs Backhouse, but there are no matches with the women in the alcove. So if two of the samples turn out to be from the women in the garden—assuming the stuff they picked out of the earth isn't too far gone to test—that still leaves one unaccounted for...'

'Muriel Davies.'

'That's what I was thinking, sir. Are we going after an exhumation order?'

'Let's see what Backhouse says about her first. Then I'll talk to Lamb.'

When they returned to the interview room, Backhouse had straightened up and looked at them with something like defiance on his face. Stratton knew immediately that they'd missed their chance.

'Muriel Davies,' he said, firmly. 'Tell me.'

There were no ticks of the mouth now, no fussing with his glasses, no blinking. Backhouse looked him squarely in the eye and said in a clear voice, 'If you can prove it, Inspector, I'll admit it.'

Two days later, shivering in the chilly dawn air amongst Kensal Rise cemetery's thickets of marble and stone, surrounded on all sides by crosses and angels sprouting at awkward angles from the earth, Stratton and Ballard stood beside McNally and another, older, pathologist, Dr Tindall—who was to perform the second post-mortem—and watched the men digging.

It was five a.m., but despite the closed cemetery gates and the barricades and constables outside, there were dozens of reporters and photographers with stepladders lining the road. At least—apart from the odd curious early riser—the public weren't there, thought Stratton, wondering, not for the first time, why on earth people came to gawp at this sort of thing. The idea of being part of something, perhaps, in the sense of bearing witness, or hoping, misguidedly, for a glimpse of the killer—although they must, having followed the case in the papers, already know what he looked like.

Stratton saw that the newest graves were blanketed with bunches of flowers. The older ones had only a single bunch, wilting and apologetic, and the oldest of all had ivy and ragged grass. There hadn't been anything in front of the plain stone slab that marked Muriel and Judy's grave, now removed: too painful, perhaps, for the family to visit. Or maybe, like him, they didn't see the point. He'd never visited the plot where Jenny's ashes were scattered and nor, as far as he knew, had Monica or Pete. It was just a place: Jenny wasn't there.

The coffin being raised, the earth was brushed away to reveal the brass plaque. The original undertaker, McLeavy, stepped forward and nodded. 'That's the one.' The dark boards—elm, Stratton guessed—looked in good condition, with the lid only slightly warped. 'We'll need to raise the lid a little,' said Tindall. 'For the release of gases.'

The diggers unscrewed the lid and pushed it to one side. There was no smell, at least not from where he was standing, and Stratton could see nothing but darkness within. There was a short, solemn pause, as though an invisible vicar had requested a silent commemoration, and then Tindall nodded, satisfied. The lid was screwed back into place, the coffin lifted up, and the cortège, led with sombre authority by McLeavy, moved off in a hail of clicking camera shutters to the waiting van.

At the mortuary, Higgs removed the coffin lid, revealing stalactites of white mould hanging down from the inside. The same white mould covered the shroud, through which the outlines of the two bodies—Muriel and the baby, Judy, who lay on her stomach—were clearly visible. Stratton, who'd placed his handkerchief over his nose in readiness, was surprised at how little they added to the usual mortuary smell of decay and disinfectant. Nevertheless, he was aware of a heaviness in the air, as though a thick cloth had been pulled around him, close and stifling. He stared down at the runnels in the concrete floor until a sudden, vivid memory of the country abattoir where his father had occasionally taken him as a boy when they were delivering stock, with its sluiced tides of blood and offal, jabbed him, making him blink and jerk his head up again.

He withdrew a little as Higgs and the other assistants began to remove the bodies from the coffin. Ballard, who'd done likewise, murmured, 'Are you all right, sir?'

'Not really,' muttered Stratton, grimly. 'It was bad enough the first time. But I'll manage.'

'Of course, sir.' From this simple exchange Stratton knew that the sergeant was remembering it, too—the horror of seeing the baby's little clothes taken off, one by one, and the toy duck, just like the one he'd said his daughter had to have in her cot or she couldn't sleep, and then sitting up late in the office afterwards, when he'd told the sergeant about Jenny being pregnant when she died and how determined they'd been to see Davies swing… He shuffled further away, towards the door.

Ballard followed. 'Do you suppose he ever thinks of them, sir?' he asked quietly. 'Backhouse, I mean.'

Stratton shook his head. 'Or about Davies, either. I'd like to think they all bloody haunt him, but I doubt it—I mean, you'd need to have a conscience, wouldn't you? Christ, I hope this works.'

Hearing Tindall's voice, 'Very well preserved,' they turned back to see him bending over the dun-coloured shape on the slab. 'A sample of the outer shroud, if you would, Mr Higgs… thank you.' They kept their distance, and Stratton glanced into the coffin, now empty save a bed of sawdust, stained brown, then watched as Tindall, bald head shining waxily beneath the electric bulb, lifted Judy, who was clad in her own separate shroud, away from her mother. The little bundle lay in his arms as he held her secure against his white rubber apron, carrying her across the room and gently laying her down.

The shroud being now removed from Muriel, Stratton could see that her face was, incredibly, almost recognisable. He nodded when Tindall looked to him for confirmation, then focused his attention on the rough line of McNally's sutures down the stomach that disappeared into the dark mound of pubic hair. The organs detached from Muriel the first time would have been crammed back inside her, he knew, like so many parcels in a bag of skin and bones… These were things one shouldn't have to think about, never mind *see*. She—*it*—is here because of me, he thought. I must watch, and I must not be sick. It occurred to him then that Jenny would have looked like this now, had she been buried and not cremated. The doctors of death had performed a post-mortem on her, laying claim to her flesh by cutting, removing, replacing, and stitching, with others standing by, watching while she lay there, wounded, naked, and forlorn…

At the time she'd died, he hadn't thought about those things. The heavy pall of grief had dulled him, blunting his mind, so that the post-mortem had been simply another fact, a stage in the process, not something actively imagined.

Swallowing hard, he felt Ballard's hand, gentle, on his arm. 'Sir?'

'I'm all right,' he said through clenched teeth, and moved away, keeping his eyes fixed on the corpse.

Muriel's skin was a dirty white, but there were two areas of pink on her thighs where the child had lain. 'Cherry pink,' said Tindall. 'We'll need specimens for carbon-monoxide analysis. McNally, if you would…'

'Of course,' said McNally, adding defensively, 'It would have been evident the first time. I'd say that patch of colouring's more likely to be post-mortem pink, but by all means…'

'Best be on the safe side,' said Tindall, a slight edge to his voice.

'Is it likely to show up now?' asked Stratton, mildly.

'Pretty unlikely, I'd say,' said McNally.

'Must do the thing properly,' said Tindall, in a manner which suggested it might not have been done properly before. Privately, Stratton doubted this—McNally was experienced and, from what he'd seen, painstaking and careful about his work. Besides which, even his untrained eye could see that the pink colour was slowly beginning to fade. 'Let's have a look at the pubic hair, shall we?' continued Tindall, briskly. 'Doesn't look like anything's been cut. We'll need a sample of that, too, for the lab, so if you would… Now, let's begin, shall we?' He held out a gloved hand. 'Scalpel, please, Mr Higgs.'

CHAPTER 73

Stratton sat in the office, trying to ignore the thump and ping of a dozen typewriters from across the corridor. He was looking through the list of samples sent to the police laboratory—*Jar labelled 15, both lungs of woman, Jar labelled 16, vagina and labia of woman, Jar labelled 17, sample of sawdust from coffin*—and trying to get his thoughts into some sort of order, when a telephone call came through from Dr Sutherland at Pentonville Prison where Backhouse, like Davies before him, had been remanded in custody.

'I've interviewed him twice,' said Sutherland. 'He was physically exhausted when he arrived and underweight. He was complaining of fibrositis in his back and shoulder, but it proved pretty mild on examination… I've taken a medical history, and barring the incidents during the war, which I believe you know about—loss of voice and so on—he seems to have spent his life taking refuge in minor ailments, fibrositis, diarrhoea, sleep disturbance, and so forth. Quite the hypochondriac, in fact, always in and out of the doctor's surgery.'

'Yes, the first thing he did when I arrested him was to tell me about his health,' said Stratton.

'Well, I can certainly give you some more information if that would help. I believe you're going to interview him again, about Muriel Davies.'

'That's right…' With the receiver wedged uncomfortably between his chin and his ear, Stratton flicked through his old notes to find the details of their conversation about Davies. Coming to something heavily underlined, he said, 'When we spoke about Davies, you were under the impression that he was telling the truth about killing his wife and child. Is that still your opinion?'

There was silence—no radiating of quiet strength or square-jawed film-actor stuff this time, thought Stratton—just the hesitation of a confused human being.

'It *was* my opinion, yes…'

'And now?' persisted Stratton.

'It's difficult to say. I've been looking at my notes, and I certainly was confident of it at the time. Backhouse hasn't said or indicated to me that he killed Mrs Davies. The only time he spoke of it was when I was taking his medical history—and he told me he'd given evidence at Davies's trial and he'd been very much upset by it. Treated for chronic diarrhoea and insomnia afterwards, according to my notes. He was distressed that Davies had said he was an abortionist. Said Davies had mistaken his St John's Ambulance first-aid manuals for medical textbooks and jumped to the wrong conclusion. I have to say that did give me pause—judging from what I wrote down at the time, I wouldn't have said that Davies possessed the mental agility to make such a leap. He was a liar, certainly, and imaginative, but it was more in the realm of storytelling than putting two and two together to make five, if you see what I mean.'

'I think so,' said Stratton. 'What did Backhouse say about the other women?'

'Told me the wife was a mercy killing, and he showed some signs of emotion while talking about her, but I had the impression that it was more to impress me than from genuine feeling. He was very anxious to tell me how happy they'd been together. As far as the others were concerned, he tried to tell me that the women had died accidentally and then he said…wait a minute… Ah, here we are: "I must have done them, the police said I did." Distancing himself… Yes, again, "If I did it, I must have dismissed it from my mind afterwards." '

'Very convenient,' said Stratton drily.

'In my experience, it's not uncommon in people accused of murder. There's also the lack of remorse—but then one can hardly regret things that one can't remember… That's a protective mechanism of the mind, of course. He's not going to remember something that might incriminate him. When I asked him about the evidence of the semen in the women he said, "It must have happened at the time of strangulation." I asked him if he meant he'd had sexual intercourse with them, and he said he thought it *had* happened, but he wasn't clear about it. He didn't say anything about gassing them. When I asked him, he said he didn't remember anything like that.'

'Well, it's a bit more than I got, I suppose… Do you have any idea *why* he did any of it?'

'It's always hard to say when these abnormal impulses begin. There doesn't seem to be any history of sadism—torturing animals and so forth, and—'

'Talking of animals, did he mention any pets?'

'Yes, a dog and a cat. Seemed very fond of them…Wait a minute—the cat died a few years back and the dog was getting very old and blind so he took it to the vet and had it put to sleep before he left his flat. Got quite emotional telling me about it. Anyway, as far as his sexual history is concerned, nothing much seems to have happened—at least not out of the ordinary—until an incident when he was sixteen or seventeen. He used to go to a local place—that was in Halifax—he described as being "frequented by girls of loose morals"—what one might call a "Lovers' Lane", I suppose, judging from what he said. There was an occasion when he was there with a couple of male friends and was unable to have intercourse with one of these girls. He was teased about it afterwards—by the boys as well as the girls, apparently. They called him "Norman No-Dick".'

'And you think that might…?'

'It's possible. Hatred of women, and so on. Of course, thousands of men might have had an experience like that in boyhood, but it wouldn't affect their subsequent behaviour in such a way. He was very damning about anything to do with sex—masturbation, prostitutes, et cetera. Tendency to moralise… Oh, yes, and there was an incident around the same time where a local girl became pregnant out of wedlock and he told me she'd thought a lot of herself before but…here we are: "That took her down a peg or two, she couldn't hold her head up after that, with everybody talking…" He seemed to take a good deal of pleasure in remembering that. And he said his sisters—four of them and one brother—were always bossing him about and he didn't like it… Afraid of his father, told me he had a violent temper, very critical, bullied him…He said he'd had recourse to prostitutes while he was in the forces…difficulty with intercourse during the first two or three years of marriage. Said they'd stopped having sexual relations by mutual consent about two and a half to three years ago—'

'Around the time of Davies's trial.'

'Yes, I suppose that would be right. Both disappointed in not having children. He's physically quite normal in terms of his development. He spoke about all this quite freely—unlike his discussion of the murders. However, I ought to point out that what he says seems to depend on who he's talking to. I was told this morning that he's been quite happy to talk about the case with the other prisoners. In fact, one of the warders overheard him boasting that he'd…where is it? Oh, yes, that he'd "done twelve of them". Those are his words, of course.'

'Twelve?' echoed Stratton.

'I shouldn't read too much into that. Probably just an attempt to impress. He's very conscious of his status—how other people view him. The other possibility, of course, is that he's beginning to form the idea of a defence of insanity. So, the more the merrier, as they say—or madder, in this case. If that's what he's doing, it's possible that he may confess to the murder of Muriel Davies in order to bolster it, although none of the staff or—so far as I'm aware—the other prisoners, have heard him mention her or the baby.'

'So you *don't* think he killed them?' asked Stratton, rumpling his hair in frustration.

'As I said, it's hard to tell. The confession—if he makes one—may be entirely genuine.'

Stratton sighed. He knew it wasn't worth asking for anything more definite, because he wasn't going to get it. 'Do you think he's insane?'

'No, I don't. The psychologist appointed by the defence may, of course, have other ideas, but in my opinion, he's sane. Highly abnormal, certainly, but not suffering from mental disease.

'I suppose that's something to be grateful for,' Stratton told Ballard at the end of the day, when they were comparing notes.

'Yes, sir…' Glancing at his wristwatch, the sergeant added. 'If you don't mind my saying, you look as though you could do with a drink.'

'I don't mind at all,' said Stratton, gratefully. 'But I'm buying. Come on.'

By unspoken consent, they headed for the Three Crowns, known to be favoured by policemen and therefore not too popular with villains, and found a quiet corner.

'We ought to get results with that lot,' said Ballard, once they were settled with their pints. 'All those samples…'

'Ballard?'

'Would you mind if we talked about something else?'

'Of course, sir. Anything in particular?'

Stratton shook his head. 'Just anything that isn't *this.*'

'There's always football, sir. *We*,' Ballard grinned, 'are doing rather well at the moment.'

Stratton pulled a face. 'Perhaps not such a good choice of subject.' Ballard had a lot more reason to be cheerful than Stratton, whose team, Tottenham Hotspur, had not been enjoying nearly so much success. 'Why do you support Arsenal, anyway?' he asked. 'You live in Putney.'

'I grew up near there—the Holloway Road, up towards Archway. My dad used to take me to matches when I was a nipper. Haven't been for a while, though,' he said wistfully. 'Being so far away doesn't help.'

'I had an idea you came from south of the river.'

'Heavens, no. That's the missus. I'd have preferred to stay north—doesn't feel like proper London, somehow, being across the river—but Pauline likes it, being close to her family. My father-in-law's a Chelsea supporter, always giving me stick... What about you, sir? You grew up in Devon.'

Stratton, detecting a faint undertone of accusation—the suspicion that he might have done the unthinkable and turned his back on a boyhood, and therefore formative, allegiance—said hastily, 'I wasn't really interested as a kid. The local team wasn't up to much, and I didn't play beyond the odd kick around. Other things to do in the country, I suppose, and my dad had us all helping on the farm as soon as we could walk. When I was courting Jenny, her dad invited me along to White Hart Lane—I think it was his way of showing his approval—and I enjoyed it, so,' he shrugged, 'I carried on going.'

Going home afterwards on the bus, aware of the three pints he'd drunk but not unpleasantly so (he'd emptied his bladder before leaving the Three Crowns), Stratton thought what a relief it was to talk about something normal. Ordinarily, he avoided the hearty confidences of pub intimacy, but this was different. He'd never given any thought to Ballard's domestic setup—any more, he supposed, than Ballard thought about his. It was nice to have a small glimpse of the other side of the sergeant's life, he thought. It made him think of when his own children were small, before the war. Kicking a ball in the garden with Pete, Monica proudly showing him her drawings and the doll's clothes she'd made out of scraps, great big-loopy stitches... Now that the sheer relief of knowing she was safe had worn off a bit, he wondered how they were going to manage when the baby came. She'd have to stop work, of course, as soon as the pregnancy started to show. What was she going to tell them at the studio? The truth was bound to cause all sorts of speculation, and he doubted if the girl Anne could be relied on to keep her mouth shut for long... He'd bet that, in a place like Ashwood, gossip about anyone, no matter how low down the pecking order, was valuable currency. And Raymond Benson, of course, was pretty high up the pecking order... What would he do if it came out? Deny it, probably, but whether he'd be believed or not was another matter.

He spent the rest of the journey with his mind tangled in pointless hypotheses and suppositions, so that by the time he stepped off the bus in Tottenham High Road, the gentle glow cast by the chat and the pints had worn off completely, and the suffocating feeling of worry combined with failure had returned in spades. At least Monica will be home now, he thought. She'd spent the last couple of nights at Doris's, but she'd be back tonight, and they could have a talk about the future.

Passing the hedge two doors down from his house, he was jerked out of his gloomy thoughts by a man's voice bellowing in anger. He couldn't make out the words, but somebody, somewhere, was having a hell of a row. He stopped and looked around but couldn't immediately pinpoint the noise. The only thing that looked in any way unusual was a strange car, a Jowett Jupiter sports model by the look of it, parked beneath a street lamp on the other side of the road. Only three families in the street possessed vehicles—there was a Morris Minor, a Wolseley four-door saloon, and an elderly Baby Austin, none of them nearly as new or as smart as this one. Someone's wealthy relative, perhaps, come to visit? Stratton shrugged and carried on walking.

It was only when, seconds later, he got to his own front gate that a shrill scream, followed by a thud, removed in one horrible, visceral second any uncertainty about its origins.

CHAPTER 74

'Monica!' Stratton jabbed the key into the lock and turned it, but the door would not open. He walloped it with the flat of his hand and it yielded, but only a small fraction, as though somebody, or bodies, were bracing themselves against the other side. 'Monica!'

Stepping back, Stratton dropped his shoulder and charged. There was a moment's resistance, and then the door flew open. Caught off balance, he toppled forward into the hall, catching himself painfully on the bottom of the banister.

'Dad!'

Pushing himself upright, he saw Monica cowering in the doorway of the kitchen, a livid red mark on one side of her face. Turning round, he saw a man scramble up from the floor of the corridor and make for the back door. 'Oh no you don't!' Stratton charged after him, grabbed him, and shoved him face-first against the wall.

Grunting in pain, the man made a single convulsive effort to break away from his grip and then stood, still and limp, where he was. Monica appeared at his side. 'Let go of him, Dad. Please. Don't hurt him.'

'I should have guessed,' spat Stratton, manhandling him round so that they were facing each other. *'Raymond Benson.'* He'd be handsome, all right—a real Romeo, in fact—if he wasn't about to shit himself. Grabbing him by the lapels and yanking him forwards, Stratton said, 'Well? What have you got to say for yourself? You've obviously hit my daughter—don't bother denying it. That mark didn't get there by itself. What else have you done to her, you bastard?'

'Dad.' Stratton turned his head to see Monica by the stairs, pale with fright. 'Please, you won't—'

'Don't worry,' he said grimly. 'I won't harm a hair on his pretty head, much as I'd like to. You go upstairs and bathe your face.' Turning back to Benson, he said, 'You and me are going to have a little chat.'

'Dad...'

This time Stratton didn't turn round. 'Upstairs, Monica. Now!'

When she'd gone, Stratton let go of Benson. 'Are you going to talk to me,' he asked in a low voice, 'or are you going to try and make a run for it again?'

'Talk,' spluttered Benson, looking as if his legs might give way at any minute.

'I thought so.' Stratton walked him into the sitting room and pointed to an armchair. 'Sit.'

Benson sat down with a bump, his eyes round with fright. 'Now,' said Stratton, standing directly in front of him. 'What's going on?'

'I wanted to see Monica. I was worried.' The rounded, silky tones were gone now, replaced by a reedy tenor.

'Like hell you were. You were shouting at her—I could hear you halfway up the street.'

'I'm afraid I...' Benson swallowed. 'I might have lost my temper a bit.'

'I see. You were worried about her, and you lost your temper. And you hit her. What else did you do?'

'Nothing. I swear... I didn't touch her.'

'But you came to see if she'd got rid of your baby, didn't you?'

'Well...'

'Disappointed, were you? Tried to persuade her but she wouldn't listen? That's what the argument was about, wasn't it?'

Benson didn't answer, but his face said it all for him. Stratton could see the man's mind racing, the speech being prepared. 'I do appreciate your feelings,' he said at last. 'I also appreciate that I must take my share of the blame in this...this matter... I thought if I could speak to Monica, we might be able to work out a solution that—'

'—that meant you could waltz off to your next conquest and forget all about it!'

Benson swallowed, his Adam's apple bobbing convulsively. 'I really don't see what else I can do,' he said, helplessly. 'These things do happen—'

'Not in this house they don't.'

'And I do have my reputation to think of.'

'Shame you didn't think of it before you took your trousers off,' said Stratton, acidly. 'My daughter's reputation doesn't matter, I suppose.'

'I didn't say that, Mr Stratton. All I meant was that, unlike myself, Monica is not the subject of public scrutiny.'

'I should have thought that public scrutiny, as you call it, was a very good reason to face up to the consequences of—'

Stratton was cut off by a scream from above. Whirling round, he dashed out of the room and up the stairs. On the half-landing he was stopped in his tracks by the sight of Monica, standing at the top of the stairs outside the bathroom. In the weak light afforded by the bulb on the landing he saw that not only had she removed her stockings but that there was a thick, dark trickle of what could only be blood flowing down the inside of one leg towards her ankle. For a moment, he stared at her stupidly, not realising what it meant.

'Daddy, the baby...it's the *baby*...'

'Baby, yes...yes...' Mind racing, he looked wildly about him as if a solution might pop out of the walls.

'Help me...' Monica bent double, clutching her stomach.

'Look,' said Stratton, as calmly as he could. 'Just... Here...' He leapt up the last few stairs and put an arm round her, steering her into the bathroom and lowering her onto the toilet. 'Keep as still as you can... Use this.' Grabbing two towels from the rail, he pushed them into her lap.

'Daddy...' Monica stared at him, eyes wide and bewildered. 'The baby,' she repeated, as if he hadn't understood.

'I know. Just stay put. I'm going downstairs to telephone Aunt Doris—she'll know what to do.'

He closed the door and charged back down the stairs. Benson was standing in the doorway of the sitting room. 'What's happened?'

'Monica—she's losing the baby.'

As he turned to pick up the telephone, Stratton caught, out of the corner of his eye, a flash of unmistakable relief cross Benson's features. Without thinking or even realizing what he was doing, he pivoted on the balls of his feet—a move learnt in his boxing days, now unconsciously and perfectly replicated—and punched him: a single knockout blow to the jaw.

'No evidence of carbon monoxide,' said McNally. 'As I mentioned, I'm pretty sure I'd have picked it up the first time round if there had been.' The calmly professional tone didn't quite mask the pathologist's relief. Not that Stratton blamed him—the tension between him and Tindall had been obvious during the post-mortem, and it would definitely have been one-up to Tindall if any traces had been found.

Tucking the telephone beneath his chin, Stratton scribbled a note. 'Anything on the pubic hair?'

'Well…it's a bit complicated, this. One of the samples in the tin could have come from Mrs Davies but not just prior to death.'

'I don't understand.'

'The problem is the ends of the hairs. Without going into too much technical detail, if the hairs in the tin *do* come from Muriel Davies, then they must have been cut at least six months before she died, and I don't suppose that the lady went around giving out samples of her pubic hair, so… I'm afraid it doesn't help much.'

Stratton grimaced. 'That would have gone a bloody long way to establishing that Backhouse killed her.'

'It does mean that there's at least one sample unaccounted for. I'm sorry it's not better news, Inspector. But surely it doesn't rule out Backhouse as Muriel Davies's killer? There were four samples in the tin and—assuming that he's responsible for everyone we found on the premises—he killed six, so that means he didn't always take souvenirs, or you'd have found the other two samples as well.'

That's all I need, thought Stratton, replacing the receiver. For Christ's sake… Why couldn't anything—even pubic hair—be simple? His eyes felt prickly, as though they had sand in them, and he rubbed them with the heels of his hands, but it made no difference.

It had been a long night, made longer by the fact that, when it was over, he'd felt far too tense to sleep. Monica, now tucked up in bed after the ministrations of Doris and their doctor, had lost the baby. When questioned, she'd told them that, far from not touching her, Benson had slapped her so hard that she'd fallen across the back of a chair, and then he'd picked her up and punched her, this time in the stomach. The doctor, whose raised eyebrows had signalled disbelief at this story, changed his tune abruptly when, on examining Monica, he found the emerging bruises that confirmed it. Fortunately for Benson—and, probably, in retrospect, himself—the actor, who'd dropped like a sack of potatoes when Stratton punched him, had been brought round with a wet sponge and frog-marched, groggy and whimpering, out to his fancy car before the doctor arrived. Don, who had come round with Doris, had assisted in the process, and stood by while Stratton delivered his parting shot in a flat, menacing tone. 'Don't even think of making a complaint, chum. And if you ever come near my daughter again, I'll kill you.'

They'd left him muttering to himself and inspecting his face in the rear-view mirror, and five minutes later, hearing a car start, they'd pulled back the sitting-room curtains to see him driving slowly away.

'Let's hope you haven't damaged him for life,' said Don.

'Don't know how they'd tell,' Stratton had replied. 'Unless it was his face. Shame it won't be his balls.'

Don had produced some Scotch, and they'd sat on either side of the fireplace, drinking it while the doctor and Doris were upstairs with Monica. His brother-in-law, as always, had been a godsend, but the fact that it reminded him of sitting helpless, in the same place, while Jenny had given birth to both children upstairs, didn't help. At least, he thought, there were no yells of pain. About halfway through, Doris, emerging from the bedroom to boil water for some mysterious medical reason that neither man was inclined to question, had reported that although Monica had lost the baby, the doctor thought there would be no lasting damage. When she'd gone, Stratton and Don had exchanged glances, and he'd known that his brother-in-law was thinking the same as he was; that, aside from the way it had come about, it was, in the long run—Monica's future health being assured—for the best...

They hadn't talked about it, just sat in silence for a while, and then Don had made a remark about something he'd seen in the newspaper to do with nuclear artillery testing in Nevada. Both men had fallen on it with gratitude and a relish that Stratton knew neither of them felt, but at least the topic was far enough away from the immediate circumstances to render it a subject for emotionally neutral conversation.

The doctor had given Monica a sedative, and she'd been fast asleep when he'd looked in on her after everyone had gone. As he'd stood in the doorway, watching her soft face and swirl of dark hair on the pillow, he'd experienced an uprush of love and anxiety so great that it took his breath away, and it was all he could do not to weep. Not daring to disturb her, he'd contented himself with blowing her a kiss and murmuring, 'Sleep tight,' before retreating in a torrent of confused and confusing feelings to his own bedroom.

When he looked up again, Ballard was at his shoulder. 'You all right, sir?'

'Fine.' Stratton didn't think he could bring himself to mention the events of the previous evening without hitting something and besides, it was no part of the sergeant's job to act as his nursemaid—he'd done quite enough of that already. Briskly, he told Ballard about the pathologist's findings, or lack of them, from Muriel Davies, and then the pair of them set off in silence for Pentonville.

CHAPTER 76

'I believe I wanted to help Mrs Davies,' said Backhouse. Now washed, shaved, and decked out in prison clothes, he looked a lot better than he had at the station, and—thank God—there was a lot less of the outraged-eye-and-indignant-nostril routine, too. Behind him, a warder stood impassively, like a statue, arms folded. 'It was after the business when he went off with that friend of Muriel's—'

'Do you mean Shirley Morgan?' asked Stratton.

'I think that was the name, yes. After that, Muriel told my wife that she was going to leave her husband. We talked about it and agreed that if the Davieses did separate, we'd see if we could adopt little Judy. My wife mentioned this to Muriel, but she said that Davies's mother would look after her, which we were quite sorry about, especially my wife, because she was very fond of the child, you see.'

Backhouse paused, looking very much the worthy and concerned citizen. Stratton indicated, with a curt nod in Ballard's direction, that it was all being taken down, and said, 'And then...?'

'Some time after that, Muriel came to me, very upset, and told me Davies had been knocking her about, and she couldn't bear it any more. She said she was going to make an end of it.'

'Meaning?'

'I took it to mean,' Backhouse's voice was hushed—this time, thought Stratton, for effect—'that she was planning to commit suicide.'

'Go on.'

'Well, it must have been shortly after that when I went upstairs and found her lying in front of the fireplace in their kitchen. She'd taken the quilt from the bed and was making an attempt to gas herself. When I saw her, I knew I had to move quickly.' This was said as one modestly recounting a heroic act. 'I turned off the tap—she'd attached a piece of tubing to it, and the end was near her head—and opened the window.'

'Have you any idea how long the gas had been on?'

Backhouse shook his head. 'She'd done it before I got there. There was a lot of gas in the room—that's why I opened the window. She came round after that, and I made her a cup of tea. She asked me not to tell anyone about it, and I said I wouldn't.'

'Was there anyone else in the house at the time?'

'Well, my wife was downstairs.'

'What about Davies?'

'He wasn't there.'

'The workmen?'

'I'm not sure... They weren't there when I went downstairs. My head was thumping from the effect of the gas, you see, and I wanted some air. I didn't say anything to my wife about it... I was very worried about Muriel—it was playing on my mind—so I went upstairs again the following day to see if she was all right. As far as I remember it was about lunchtime when I went up, after my wife had gone out... Muriel told me she still intended to do away with herself. She begged me to help her—in fact, she said she would do anything if I would help her.' Backhouse gave a meaningful nod.

'What did you understand by that?' asked Stratton.

'That she...she would let me be...intimate with her. She brought the quilt in and put it down in front of the fireplace and lay on it. As far as I can remember, she was fully dressed...' Backhouse tailed off, as if in a reverie, and when he spoke again his voice was almost inaudible. 'I got down on my knees then, but wasn't capable of having intercourse because of the fibrositis in my back… I couldn't do it. She begged me…'

'Begged you for what?'

'To help her… As far as I can make out, I must have turned on the gas tap and put the tubing close to her face. When she became unconscious I turned it off again. I was going to try to have intercourse with her then—'

'You weren't affected by the gas?'

Backhouse blinked, looking confused, then shook his head. 'The gas wasn't on for very long, not much over a minute.'

'Did you hit her? Punch her?'

Backhouse shook his head. 'No… I'm sure there was nothing like that.'

'But she became unconscious in that time?'

'Yes, that's right… I couldn't have intercourse because I couldn't bend over her. I think that's when I strangled her.'

'What with?'

'A stocking, I think. I found one in the room. I'm not certain about it, but I think that's what I did. I left her where she was and went downstairs. I think my wife was there then, but I didn't say anything about it.'

More holes than a Dutch cheese, thought Stratton. Still, it was a confession, and probably as good as they were going to get. 'What happened after that?'

'Davies came home about six o'clock in the evening, I think. Anyway, I remember it was dark when I heard him come in. I went into the passage and told him what had happened—that his wife had committed suicide by gassing herself. He was very upset'—You don't say, thought Stratton—'so I went upstairs with him. He picked her up and carried her into the bedroom and put her down on the bed.'

'Was the stocking still round her neck when he did that?'

'No… I think I took it off before I went downstairs… I must have thrown it into the fireplace—I think there was a fire in the grate.'

'A *fire*?' asked Stratton, incredulous. 'And you'd turned on the gas?'

'I'm not sure... The fire might have been the day before.'

'But there was even more gas then.'

'That's why I opened the window. I was worried about an explosion. Yes, it must have been the day before.'

Stratton raised his eyebrows. 'So Davies didn't know that his wife had been strangled.'

'No.'

'What happened then?'

'I made Davies a cup of tea to calm him down. I told him—I said it was likely—that he'd be suspected of having done it himself—'

'Gassed Muriel himself?'

'Yes, because of the rows and fights they'd been having. He agreed with me—he said he'd bring the van he'd been driving and take the body away somewhere. I went downstairs after that... I had the impression that he'd taken his wife in the van.'

'This was on the Tuesday, was it, the seventh of November?'

'I think it was.'

'And you didn't check to see if the body was still there?'

'No, I thought... I'm not sure what I thought. A few days later—the Friday, it must have been—he told us he was going to Bristol, and he left. He'd sold the furniture, and they came for that afterwards.'

'What about the baby?'

'I don't recollect seeing the baby again. I remember Davies saying to me that he'd fed her, but I can't remember when that was. Sometime that week, it must have been... Davies came back the following week, but he didn't stay long. That's when we had the conversation about the money—I told him he should be careful with it. We left the house together, because I was going to the doctor, and we got on the number seven bus. I remember, because I paid his fare... I got off at the doctor's, and he stayed on because he was going to Paddington.'

'Why was that?'

'He told me he was going back to Wales.'

'Did you kill the baby?'

Backhouse's mouth twisted round to the side, and he closed his eyes for a moment before answering in a whisper. 'No.'

'Did you see the baby again after you killed Mrs Davies?'

'No. I didn't see her. I didn't know what happened to the body—'

'Whose body?'

'Muriel. Mrs Davies. I didn't know what happened until the police came and found them both in the washhouse.'

'Are you prepared to sign a statement saying all that?'

'Yes.'

CHAPTER 77

Monica lay quite still, eyes closed, for a long time. Although she still felt groggy and strange, she was definitely awake. The house was quiet. Perhaps Auntie Doris had gone… She'd definitely been there when the doctor came, holding her hand and wiping her face with a wet flannel.

Raymond had been *so* angry. When he'd arrived, she'd thought it was Dad and rushed to the door to find him on the step. When she'd told him how she hadn't gone through with the operation, he'd just exploded. He'd asked her why she hadn't come to him to fix something up, and when she'd tried to explain about Dad, and how it was Pete who'd told him and not her, he'd got even more furious. 'He threatened me!' he kept shouting. 'He dared to threaten me!'

She'd thought, for a moment, that he was going to kill her. She remembered, in a blur, him coming towards her, knowing what he was about to do but being too late to stop him, the blow and the fall, being unable to save or protect herself, her gestures as feeble as if they'd been made underwater. Then her relief when Dad had come home, and her fear that he would kill Raymond or hurt him badly, and get into trouble because of her; and then she'd gone upstairs and the pain had started. Like a cramp at first, doubling her up, and then the feeling that her insides were separating, that something was giving way, and seeing the blood…

She didn't remember much about the doctor's visit—hushed voices, probing hands, something soft being slid beneath her bottom, and Doris leaning over her, brushing the hair off her forehead …

She gazed up at her favourite damp patch that was the shape of a smile and thought about the dog's head on the ceiling of Mrs Lisle's back room. Lying and looking up at it she'd thought that she would be attended to immediately, but as the minutes passed and she lay listening to footfalls from upstairs and Mrs Lisle still did not come, she began to experience an odd sensation. It was as if her mind or her spirit, or possibly both, had become divorced from her body so that she was looking down at herself from above. Quite coldly and dispassionately, she'd considered what might happen if she were to die as a result of Mrs Lisle's ministrations. Strangely, she'd found that she didn't mind much for herself. In fact, she'd reasoned that dying in such a manner would guarantee that her family never discovered what was—or had been—wrong with her. Then she'd thought of Dad. Dad who'd already lost Mum, and who didn't deserve to lose her as well, no matter how unsatisfactory a daughter she was.

It was this that impelled her, robot-like, to stand up, pull on her knickers, fasten her stockings, put on her coat, and leave. Moving like a sleepwalker, she'd gone down the passage, opened the door, and walked away into the night.

It occurred to her now that during all that time she hadn't thought once about the baby. But Raymond had seen to that himself, hadn't he? So things had turned out for the best after all. Even if the baby had managed not to inherit whatever it was that was wrong with her—being one of 'Nature's Mistakes' Anne had called it—it would still have been Raymond's child, and Raymond was…

Monica shook her head. She was too tired and confused for her emotions to be anything but a vague jumble. Grief, she certainly felt, like she had when Mum died, but for what she wasn't sure. The baby, she supposed. That must be it. The baby. But there was relief as well, and the absolute, certain knowledge that, whatever happened, she was never going to have anything to do with a man ever again.

Monica turned over and was about to drift back to sleep when out of the corner of her eye she saw a little card on her bedside table. Reaching out for it, she read, *Have a good rest. See you later. Love, Dad x*

He will forgive me, she thought. And Pete will never dare say another word after this… She was safe. Just as long as they never found out what she was really like, everything would be all right… And that was up to her—to make sure they didn't. Kissing the card, she propped it up against the lamp and then positioned her head on the pillow so that—assuming she didn't turn over in her sleep—it would be the first thing she'd see when she woke.

'Doesn't sound very likely,' said McNally. 'The recovery Backhouse is alleging the first time Mrs Davies tried to gas herself doesn't sound possible, especially given that *he* was affected after so short a time...'

'The thumping head, you mean,' said Stratton.

'Yes. And as for the second time, the actual administration of the gas, he must have got quite near the outlet himself... And there's the business about the fire, well...' Stratton could imagine the pathologist, who was on the other end of the phone, shaking his head.

'I thought so.'

'I assume it's not germane, is it?'

'Not as far as the trial's concerned, no—DCI Lamb's just told us they've decided to proceed with the murder of Edna Backhouse.'

'Well, you shouldn't have any problems there.'

'That's true,' said Stratton. 'Thanks, anyway.'

'If he's so keen on "the more the merrier",' Stratton asked Ballard when he came into the office several minutes later, 'why hasn't he confessed to the baby?'

'Well, sir, whatever's going on in his mind, I don't think it's as straightforward as all that. He's justified all the others, hasn't he? The prostitutes were making the running, being aggressive and starting fights and so on, and Muriel and Mrs Backhouse and the woman from the factory were mercy killings.'

'Except that someone punched Muriel in the face.'

'That might have been Davies—I mean, if they'd quarrelled earlier on. But if it was Backhouse, he's not going to admit it because it won't fit his story. And how on earth could he justify strangling a *baby*?'

'Because it was in the way?' said Stratton. 'Making a noise and attracting attention?'

'Yes, but there's no way to say that without putting himself in a bad light.'

'People have killed babies for less. We've come across it a few times.'

'Parents,' said Ballard. 'End of their tether and whatnot. It's not the same—and anyway, it's no sort of defence'.

'No, you're right. It isn't. If he did, I don't believe that Edna Backhouse knew about it. And Davies had bought a teddy bear for the baby, hadn't he? He showed it to his aunt and uncle in Wales. We thought at the time he wasn't bright enough to do that to put them off the scent.'

'And the duck, sir. Remember? With the body…tucked into the clothes. I remember it because my Katy had one just like it.'

'You mean that it might have been her favourite toy and only a parent would have known that.'

'Yes, sir.'

'But perhaps it was just there—in the cot or wherever she was, and got caught up in the things when Backhouse bundled her up, if he was doing it quickly—but then again, he claimed not to know anything about how the bodies got into the washhouse.'

'That's true, sir. I suppose it was because it made an impression on me—it just made me wonder about it.'

Stratton leant forward across the desk. 'But what do you really *think*?'

Ballard looked genuinely helpless for a moment, then said, "I honestly don't know, sir.'

'Me neither.' Stratton shook his head, remembering his son's scorn, his own pathetic attempts to justify himself, and Pete's voice, dripping with sarcasm: *As mistakes go, Dad, I'd say this one rather takes the biscuit…* If only Davies could be proved guilty, he thought, that would go some way to redeeming him in Pete's eyes—although nothing, he knew, could make up for Jenny's death. But wishing wouldn't make it so… And what one thought about the logic of the thing didn't, and couldn't, square with what he instinctively felt, which was that Davies had been innocent all along. 'Mind you,' he added, 'I suppose Davies taking the body—or bodies—off in his van would explain why no one spotted them with all those workmen about… But then why bring them back, especially if he'd planned to scatter the bits about, like the torso murder—remember those cuttings we found in the flat?'

If Ballard thought he was clutching at straws, he didn't show it. 'Backhouse could have planted them, sir. He's pretty keen on newspaper cuttings himself—he had quite a few in his suitcase about Davies, and there was that one he almost showed Mrs Carleton. That was about the Davies case, too.'

'Was it?'

'Arliss gave me a message from the lab—it got sent there by mistake. I asked him to bring us some tea, by the way.'

'Well done… Coming back to what we were saying before, I should have thought taking an adult's body downstairs and out the front door would have caused a bit of a racket, and if Davies had done it at night that would be all the more reason for the Backhouses to hear…'

'Here you are, sir.' Arliss shuffled in with two cups of tea, most of which seemed to have ended up in the saucers.

Hastily shoving all his papers aside as the elderly constable's unsteady hand pushed the china onto the desk, Stratton thought that Arliss's retirement, due in a few months, couldn't come a moment too soon. With ill-health in the form of tremors being added to his habitual incompetence, he'd become a one-man liability in the last year, regardless of how simple the task.

'Thanks, Arliss.' Stratton turned back to Ballard. 'The Backhouses said they heard him bring Muriel's body down to the washhouse, didn't they? He said he thought Davies was moving furniture… Of course, if the last statement's true, that means he was lying before, so… But somebody must have heard something, for Christ's sake, and—' Stratton, suddenly aware that Arliss was still standing somewhere over to his right, stopped and looked at him. The constable seemed suddenly alert—or rather his usual expression of morose vacancy altered sufficiently for him to look grotesque and slightly shifty at the same time.

'Was there something else?' Stratton asked pointedly.

Arliss sucked his teeth and shook his head, as if contemplating a piece of exceptionally shoddy workmanship. 'I can't see why you're bothering about all this, sir.'

'What?'

'All this about Davies and his missus and baby.'

'Well,' said Stratton with withering sarcasm—not that anyone as dim as Arliss could be expected to recognise it as such—'let me enlighten you. In the first place—'

'I know Davies did it, sir.'

Oh, for Christ's sake, thought Stratton, irritably. What next? Maybe the station charlady would come and favour them with the benefit of her opinion. 'What are you talking about?'

'He told me.'

'*Told you?* When?'

'When he was here.'

'Yes,' said Stratton, exasperated, 'obviously when he was *here*. But when, exactly?'

'It was the morning after he come in, sir. I remember it was early because I'd just had my tea, and I was on duty downstairs, keeping observation. We got talking because I was outside the cell. I told him I could understand him killing his wife'—Stratton could well believe this; Arliss had been blaming *his* wife, or, more accurately, her cooking, for the fact that he'd been locked in mortal combat with his bowels for years, with the results of which his colleagues were all too well aware— 'but I couldn't understand an innocent kiddie. He said it was because the crying got on his nerves and he couldn't put up with it, so he'd strangled her. Those were his words, sir—I remember it clear as day.'

'Why the hell didn't you say anything?'

'Well…' Arliss stared at him with an air of absorbed mystification, like a chimpanzee meddling with the workings of a watch, then said, 'you'd got the confession off him, hadn't you, sir? I never thought there was any need… Anyway, I say it's all a waste of time. He done it, all right. He told me himself.'

'Who in their right mind,' asked Stratton, after the constable had taken himself off, leaving him and Ballard staring at each other, 'would make a confession to *Arliss*?'

With a carefully neutral expression and tone, Ballard replied, 'A man like Davies would, sir.'

'I suppose so. Maybe he recognised a kindred spirit. I mean, they can't have been that far apart mentally.'

Ballard looked reproachful. 'Arliss was once seen to read a newspaper, sir. Or rather, he was caught turning over the pages and moving his lips at the same time, so—'

'Point taken. You know what I mean. Actually, I suppose I can see how it might have happened. For all his faults, Arliss has a good way with prisoners, especially the younger ones, and he's not threatening.'

'Do you believe it, sir?'

'Arliss obviously does, and he certainly isn't sophisticated enough to have tricked Davies into saying it, or anything like that. Perhaps he was the one person that Davies felt comfortable enough with for him to tell the truth. Or…' Stratton and Ballard stared at each other for a long, uncomfortable moment, 'we'd put the idea into his mind that it was necessary for him to confess it.'

'You've got to admit, though, sir, that it has a ring of truth about it. Davies must have been in a terrible state of stress at the time, and…' Ballard broke off, shaking his head in confusion, and fiddled with a paperclip.

'And,' Stratton finished for him, 'we just don't know.'

Ballard looked up. 'No, sir. And I know it's not much comfort, but I don't believe anyone else does, either—except Backhouse, that is, and he's not going to tell us, is he?'

THREE MONTHS LATER

CHAPTER 79

Stratton stood on the pavement in Albemarle Street, looking up at the Andersons' house, which was impressively large: five floors and a basement, and it obviously went back a good way, too. Diana had telephoned the station the previous day, asking to see him. She'd not said much, just invited him to come and see her—for tea, he supposed, as it was half past five.

He was wearing a clean shirt, which at least went some way to make up for his baggy suit and the shaving cut on his chin. As surreptitiously as he could, he shone the toes of his shoes, in turn, on the calves of his trousers, before mounting the three steps to the door and raising the enormous brass knocker.

He'd been surprised when the telephone call came. After all, he reasoned, the last time he'd seen Diana, she'd been at her lowest and most vulnerable, and it was only human not to want to be reminded of that. *He* certainly didn't like being reminded of himself at his weakest points—and, in the last few months, what with the inquiry into the Davies case and Backhouse's trial, there'd been nothing but reminders. He couldn't pretend that he hadn't been relieved when the inquiry had ruled that Davies was, after all, guilty of both murders, and exonerated the police.

However, judging by the furore this had caused in the press, the thing wasn't going to go away any time soon, even though Backhouse had been found guilty. There being no appeal, he'd been hanged the previous week, but instead of making Stratton feel better, it had only served to give him nightmares about the things left undone and questions unasked.

At least, Stratton thought, Monica was all right, back at Ashwood and apparently quite happy in her work. Benson, she'd told him, had gone to America. He was in two minds about this, pleased that the man was separated from his daughter by God knew how many thousands of miles, but also feeling that work in Hollywood constituted a reward for bad behaviour. As he'd said to Don, he'd have preferred it if Benson's enforced separation from Monica had been caused by, say, a fatal step in front of a bus, but, as Don had remarked, one couldn't have everything…

The door was answered by a large woman with a pair of vast bosoms that looked, in their casing of stiff grey cloth, like some sort of defensive fortification. Once it became clear that Stratton, who hadn't given his official title, wasn't there to repair the drains or sell a vacuum cleaner but had been invited by Diana—about which she clearly hadn't been told—she seemed unsure of quite what to do with him. She was on the point of making him wait outside when an attractive blonde woman appeared and, introducing herself as Mrs Anderson, whisked him into what he imagined must be known as the drawing room. Dark and high-ceilinged, with plenty of fancy cornicing and whatnot, it was full of the sort of furniture which was never bought but handed down from generation to generation.

Mrs Anderson offered him a seat and a glass of sherry. He'd have preferred a cup of tea but didn't like to say anything, so he accepted. Mind you, he thought, sipping it, it was a lot less sweet and consequently much nicer than any sherry he'd had before—clearly the real stuff. While not betraying any hint of snobbery, his hostess spoke to him—'Diana's told us so much about you… I'm sure she'll be down in a minute… Don't mind Mrs Robinson…' and so forth—with an odd mixture of friendliness and impersonality. Although she was obviously trying to put him at ease, Stratton couldn't help wondering if this was how she would have spoken to an old family retainer if they'd happened to meet in unusual circumstances. All in all, he felt pretty uncomfortable, so it was quite a relief when, a few minutes later, the sound of a distant telephone bell was followed by the appearance of Mrs Robinson to say that Lady Melling was on the line.

Mrs Anderson excused herself and left, and Mrs Robinson stayed long enough to give him a look that stopped just short of telegraphing the fact that she'd be counting the spoons before following suit. Left alone, Stratton stood up and went to examine the line of silver-mounted photographs on the mantelpiece. The one in the middle showed a stately country pile; Mrs or perhaps Mr Anderson's childhood home. Stratton picked it up, weighing the frame in his hand. Diana, he thought, would have grown up in a similar place. This was 'the other half' all right. The sheer, unassailable *poshness* of the whole thing... The long line of noble sperm stretching back through history and culminating around the eleventh century with Sir Somebody de Something who'd been rewarded for his services to the king—and not for roasting oxen or shovelling shit, either.

He was glaring down at the photograph when he heard a discreet cough behind him, and turning, he saw Diana standing about two feet away. 'Sorry,' he said, 'I didn't hear you.'

'That's all right.' Her smile was hesitant, but she looked far healthier than when he'd last seen her, glowing and fresh as if newly minted and wearing a smart grey suit that showed off her elegant legs. 'Hideous, isn't it?'

Confused—surely she couldn't mean what she was wearing?—it took him a second to realise that he was still holding the photograph. 'It's certainly very big. And old, of course,' he added, feeling stupid.

'Fourteenth century, I think—originally, anyway. Until it got smothered. Some Victorian ancestor of Lally's obviously told the architect to lay it on with a trowel.'

'Yes...' Unable to think of anything to say, Stratton stared at the photograph in silence until Diana took it, very gently, out of his hands and repositioned it on the mantelpiece with the others.

'You know,' she said when she turned round, 'that's the past. That house'—she indicated the photograph—'it's a white elephant. Like the one I grew up in. That's...well, it's a ruin, really. Once the army'd finished with it...' She shrugged. 'I managed to sell it in the end, but it didn't fetch much.'

'But don't you...I mean, aren't you sorry? I mean... Well, you must have felt an attachment...' Stratton tailed off, embarrassed.

'Not really,' said Diana, moving briskly towards the drinks table. 'It's just a place. I wasn't very happy there.' Picking up the decanter, she said, 'More sherry?'

Stratton was surprised, when he looked at his glass, to find that it was empty. 'Thank you, if it's not too much trouble.' God, what a ridiculous thing to say...What the hell was the matter with him?

Diana refilled his glass and, pouring a glass for herself, held it up. 'Cheers!'

'Er...cheers!' Stratton touched his glass to hers, carefully. There was a moment's silence as they both sipped and then, as Diana didn't seem about to speak, he said, 'What... I mean, why did you want to see me?' God, she was staring at him—it was the wrong tone, too abrupt... 'I mean, I'm delighted to see you, and you look...you look...much better, and... If there's anything I can do...'

'You've been very helpful,' said Diana. Two hard spots of colour had come into her cheeks and, speaking very fast, she continued, 'I don't know what I'd have done if you hadn't.... I mean, that man... I've been staying here, and Lally and Jock have been very kind. I've been doing some decorating for them as payment for bed and board.'

'Have you?' Stratton couldn't for the life of him imagine her up a ladder, wielding a paintbrush.

'Surprised?' Diana grinned.

'Yes, frankly.'

'I like doing things like that—and I'm quite good at them, believe it or not. I only discovered I could do that sort of thing quite recently. After I married James, actually—I wanted to get our flat decorated and I couldn't find anyone to do it, so I decided I'd set to and do it myself.' Stratton was relieved that she said this quite neutrally—imparting information rather than painfully reliving a memory of happier times. But then, he thought, she'd hardly do that in front of me, would she?

'I didn't think,' Diana continued, 'that I'd be able to get another job like the one I had before, so I've been taking a course in shorthand. We had to do an examination, to test our speeds.'

'Did you pass?'

'Yes! Believe it or not, I'd never taken an examination before. I haven't had much in the way of...well, formal education, I suppose you'd call it, and I was terribly nervous, but I practised like anything, and it all went swimmingly.'

'Well, congratulations,' said Stratton, raising his glass once more.

'They're taking me back at Ashwood,' said Diana. 'The Design Department, so I shan't need the shorthand after all, but I'm glad I did it because you never know about the future... I'm starting on Monday. Oh, I'm sorry, I meant to ask—how's Monica?'

'Fine,' said Stratton. 'She lost the baby, but she's fully recovered. I'm sure you'll bump into her at the studio.'

'Oh, good. I mean, about seeing Monica again, not about... But as long as she's not hurt, physically... It's always so... I mean, I've been in that situation—losing a baby.' Diana looked down at her feet. 'Several times, in fact. It was pretty horrible, but,' looking up, she gave him an encouraging smile, 'one does get over these things, you know.'

'I'm sorry,' said Stratton, surprised by this intimacy and hoping he wasn't blushing. 'It can't have been easy for you. Any of it, I mean.'

Diana acknowledged this with a nod, then, after a second, carried on in a normal voice. 'Well, there has been one piece a luck. An aunt of James's died several weeks ago. He'd never spoken of her—in fact, I didn't even know she existed—so they obviously weren't close, but she left him some money. Her death was sudden—a heart attack—so I suppose she hadn't got round to changing her will… Anyway, it comes to me. It's enough for a small house or a flat somewhere. Lally's going to help me look. Oh, dear. You're looking at me as if I'm mad, and I don't blame you, but—'

'No,' Stratton protested. 'I wasn't. I'm sorry if that's how it seemed. I just…' He stopped, swallowed hard, and feeling that there was nothing, at this point, to lose, ploughed on. 'I just like looking at you.'

'Oh…' Diana gave a little laugh and turned away slightly. The redness of her cheeks seemed to have intensified. She took another sip of her sherry—quite a large one this time—and said, 'I wanted to tell you. I suppose I want you to know that I'm not completely useless. I don't really expect you to understand or anything, but I just…' Shaking her head, she looked miserably down at her glass.

'I've never thought you were useless.' said Stratton, bewildered. 'Just…different, that's all.'

'That's it, isn't it? Different.'

'Well, you are. I mean, we are. Oh, dear, I'm not doing very well, am I?'

'Neither am I. It's just, when I saw you again, I was so glad, and… Well, I was glad, that's all. And,' she continued fiercely, 'I want to stand on my own two feet, and I wanted you to know that.' Her eyes blazed for a moment, as if she thought he was about to contradict her or laugh at her.

'I understand,' said Stratton, staring at her. Suddenly, the room, and all it implied, seemed to fall away and Diana herself was all he could see. 'Perhaps,' he said cautiously, 'if you can find a free evening in your new schedule, you might like to come out to dinner. Nowhere fancy, I'm afraid, but I'd like to hear how you're doing.'

Diana's eyes widened, and Stratton took an involuntary step backwards. Was she going to raise her chin and coldly ask him to leave? Scream? Slap his face?

She didn't do any of those things. Instead, she smiled, a wide, genuine smile. 'Yes,' she said. 'I'd like that. I'd like that… very much. Thank you, Edward.'

A NOTE ON HISTORICAL BACKGROUND

Part of the storyline of this book is based on a pair of true cases: that of Timothy John Evans, who was hanged in 1950 for the murder of his fourteen-month-old daughter, Geraldine, and that of John Reginald Halliday Christie, who was hanged in 1953 for the murder of his wife, Ethel. Both resided at the same address, 10 Rillington Place, Notting Hill Gate, London W11. Although names and places have been changed and there has been some tinkering with dates, I have stuck as closely as possible to the known facts in both cases in the writing of this book. However, it should be noted that I have treated them as a novelist, rather than as a historian. Some of the characters are, of course, based on real people, but others are entirely made up and have no resemblance to anyone either living or dead.

I first heard of these cases in the mid-seventies, from my mother. At the time, I was attending a school situated close to the street that had been Rillington Place (the area immediately surrounding it has now been redeveloped and the roads renamed). I cannot now remember how the subject came up, but my mother, a doctor, had studied the medical aspects of the cases when she trained at St Andrew's and she told me what had happened. It was the story rather than the forensic details that drew my attention, and I remember feeling desperately sorry for Timothy Evans and his family.

Many years later, considering the cases as potential material for a novel, I began to wonder about the feelings of the detectives in the Evans case. In 1950, when Evans was hanged, everybody was sure that justice had been done—there seemed no doubt at all that he had killed not only his daughter, but also his wife,

Beryl. What must those policeman have felt when, in 1953, six bodies, two of them skeletons, were discovered at the same property, in Christie's flat and in the garden of which he had sole use?

When it emerged that Evans's conviction had been, in large part, secured on the evidence of a serial killer, doubt was cast on the fairness of his trial. With a growing number of people feeling that two stranglers of women living in the same house was too great a coincidence, there were demands for an inquiry. On 6 July, a fortnight after Christie was sentenced, the then Home Secretary, Sir David Maxwell-Fyfe, announced to the House of Commons that he had instructed Sir John Scott-Henderson QC to hold an inquiry which would determine whether a miscarriage of justice had occurred in the case of Evans. Scott-Henderson interviewed not only Christie (who was hanged on 15 July), but also twenty witnesses who had been involved in one, or both, of the investigations. In his report, he concluded that Evans was guilty of both murders and that Christie's confession to the murder of Beryl Evans was not reliable. He wrote: *I am satisfied that Christie gradually came to the conclusion that it would be helpful in his defence if he confessed to the murder of Mrs Evans.*

As Scott-Henderson had accepted, apparently without question, not only Christie's confessions relating to the other murders but also the evidence he had given at Evans's trial, many people felt that the report was flawed and the controversy over the case continued. Besides numerous articles in newspapers and magazines, several books were written on the subject. The most famous of these is *10 Rillington Place* by Ludovic Kennedy (1961), which began with an open letter to R. A. Butler (known as Rab), who was Home Secretary at the time, requesting an urgent review of the case. In this letter, he quoted a statement from the Rt. Hon. James Chuter Ede, the Home Secretary who had sanctioned Evans's execution, saying that he felt a mistake had been made.

A second inquiry, chaired by the High Court judge Sir Daniel Brabin, was held at the end of 1965. This was a longer and altogether more thorough investigation than the Scott-Henderson inquiry, which had been criticised, by Kennedy and others, for its haste and lack of proper analysis. The Brabin report included information about an apparently spontaneous confession by Evans that he'd killed the baby because 'he had to strangle it as he could not put up with the crying'. This was made to Sergeant Trevallian of the uniformed branch while the Welshman was in custody at Notting Hill police station in 1949. It is on this that I based Davies's confession to PC Arliss, although, unlike Arliss, Sergeant Trevallian mentioned the confession to a senior officer immediately but was told that 'they knew all about it as Evans had made a statement'.

Neither of the reports reached the conclusion that the police in the Evans case had acted improperly. After examining the evidence, Brabin made the following statement about the murders of Beryl and Geraldine Evans:

> *. . . it would now be impossible for me to come to a conclusion in respect of the guilt of Evans beyond reasonable doubt.*
>
> *The warrant under which I was appointed to hold this Inquiry does not call only for a conclusion reached with that degree of certainty, for I am called upon to report such conclusions as I may find it possible to form. If the evidence permits me to come to a conclusion on the balance of probability, I must do so.*
>
> *I have come to the conclusion that it is more probable than not that Evans killed Beryl Evans. I have come to the conclusion that it is more probable than not that Evans did not kill Geraldine.*

As Evans had been tried only for the murder of his daughter—the one crime, incidentally, to which Christie never confessed—the then Home Secretary Roy Jenkins recommended a posthumous pardon for Evans, which was granted in October 1966.

Although Evans had been declared not guilty of the crime of which he was convicted, there was still the matter of Brabin's refusal to accept Christie's confession to the murder of Beryl and his decision that Evans was responsible for her death. Leading pathologist Professor Keith Simpson, who had assisted with the exhumation of Beryl Evans, agreed. In his book *Forty Years of Murder* (1978), he stated: *the Brabin Report upheld the coincidence [of there being two stranglers of women living in the same house], and it never seemed to me very far-fetched. Coincidences are far more common in life than in fiction.* Books by Rupert Furneaux (published in 1961) and John Eddowes (1994) also argued the case for Evans's guilt. However, the version of events that has become generally accepted is Ludovic Kennedy's. His book, *10 Rillington Place*, was made into a film of the same name in 1970. Directed by Richard Fleischer and starring Richard Attenborough, Judy Geeson, Pat Heywood and John Hurt, it gives a vivid and persuasive account of Evans's innocence and wrongful conviction.

A pardon does not formally erase a conviction, and in 2003 Evans's family applied to the Criminal Cases Review Commission for his conviction to be reexamined. The Commission decided that, although there was what it termed a 'real possibility' that the Court of Appeal would not uphold the conviction, it would not refer the case. The Commission's report stated that the free pardon, with its attendant publicity, was sufficient to establish Evans's innocence in the eyes of the public and that the formal quashing of the conviction would bring no tangible benefit to his family and was not in the public interest. An ex gratia payment was, however, made to the family by way of compensation for the miscarriage of justice.

In the months I spent researching this book, I read everything about both cases that I could lay my hands on, including the files of the Metropolitan Police, the records of the Director of Public Prosecutions, the trial transcripts and correspondence, and the Prison Commission and Home Office files, all of which may be found in the National Archives. What do I think happened? The honest answer is that I just don't know. The forensic evidence, such as it is, doesn't point conclusively to either man. There is also the fact that, in the words of the Brabin report, *One fact which is*

not in dispute and which has hampered all efforts to find the truth is that both Evans and Christie were liars. They lied about each other, they lied about themselves.

As Professor Simpson says, coincidences *are* far more common in life than in fiction. It seems to me to be pretty unlikely that Evans killed his wife and child, but it isn't actually impossible. My heart doesn't believe it, but in the course of writing this book, my head has told me time and again that one cannot entirely discount the possibility that that is, in fact, what happened. There are many things unaccounted for, such as the dog, the timing, and why, if Beryl Evans's body was in the tiny washhouse for several days, while the workmen were constantly in and out, they did not notice it. There is also the fact that baby Geraldine, unattended for two days in a very small house, wasn't heard to cry—even, apparently, by Ethel Christie, who was used to listening out for her on the occasions when Beryl left her by herself. All these are mysteries that cannot now be unravelled.

It is, however, an extraordinary story, and it's certainly true that controversy surrounding the Evans case and a number of others from the same period contributed to the abolition of capital punishment in Britain. That, I believe, can only be a good thing.

ACKNOWLEDGEMENTS

I am very grateful to Tim Donnelly, Claire Foster, Stephanie Glencross, Jane Gregory, Liz Hatherell, William Howells of Ceredigion Libraries, Trudy Howson, Maya Jacobs, Jemma McDonagh, Claire Morris, Lucy Ramsey, Manda Scott, June and William Wilson, Jane Wood, Sue and Alan Young, the staff at the National Archives and Florence Mabel Basset Hound for their enthusiasm, advice and support during the writing of this book.